T_H_E S PACE BETWEEN

Antipodes Series Book 2

ANTIPODES SERIES BOOK 2

THE SPACE BETWEEN

T.S. SIMONS

4 Horsemen
Publications, Inc.

4 Horsemen
Publications, Inc.

4 Horsemen Publications, Inc.
1497 Main St. Suite 169
Dunedin, FL 34698
4horsemenpublications.com
info@4horsemenpublications.com

Typeset by Autumn Skye
Cover Design by Jen Kotick

Library of Congress Control Number: 2021951159

Audio ISBN: 978-1-64450-372-0
EBOOK ISBN: 978-1-64450-373-7
Print ISBN: 978-1-64450-374-4
Hardcover ISBN-13: 978-1-64450-955-5

For my family - thank you for believing in me

What would YOU sacrifice for family?

CAM IS CONTENT WITH his new life on Lewis, happily married and working as an active member of the community. As life settles into a kind of mundanity, Cam learns a shocking truth: someone he loves may still be alive. Compelled to embark on a monumental journey, he discovers the true value of family and loyalty in a bleak and challenging world.

The Space Between is the second novel in the Antipodes series. This series asks, "If we had the opportunity to start over, would we? Or is our society destined to make the same mistakes?"

Melbourne

Kerguelen Islands

August Island
Auckland Island
Bellcamp Island

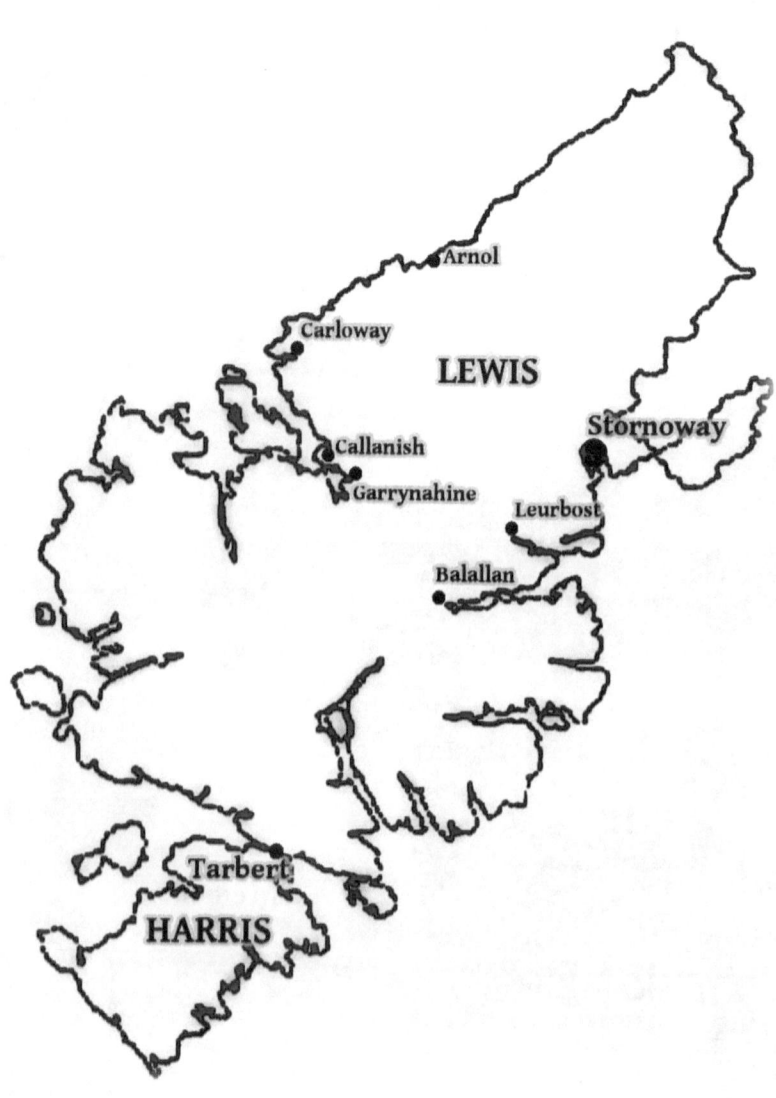

Arnol

Carloway

LEWIS

Callanish

Garrynahine

Stornoway

Leurbost

Balallan

Tarbert

HARRIS

CONTENTS

Acknowledgements: xiii

Chapter 1.................................... 1
Chapter 2................................... 22
Chapter 3................................... 30
Chapter 4................................... 39
Chapter 5................................... 50
Chapter 6................................... 57
Chapter 7................................... 62
Chapter 8................................... 66
Chapter 9................................... 75
Chapter 10.................................. 92
Chapter 11.................................. 98
Chapter 12................................. 109
Chapter 13................................. 121
Chapter 14................................. 125
Chapter 15................................. 132
Chapter 16................................. 147
Chapter 17................................. 156
Chapter 18................................. 167
Chapter 19................................. 185
Chapter 20................................. 198

Chapter 21. 218
Chapter 22. 224
Chapter 23. 230
Chapter 24. 241
Chapter 25. 262
Chapter 26. 268
Chapter 27. 280
Chapter 28. 289
Chapter 29. 294
Chapter 30. 298
Chapter 31. 307
Chapter 32. 312
Chapter 33. 324
Chapter 34. 340
Chapter 35. 348
Chapter 36. 360
Chapter 37. 368
Chapter 38. 377
Chapter 39. 385
Chapter 40. 394
Chapter 41. 399
Chapter 42. 403
Chapter 43. 406
Chapter 44. 411
Chapter 45. 421

Book Club Questions 423
Author Bio 425

ACKNOWLEDGEMENTS:

READING IS ONE OF the most joyous pleasures in life, and books provide us with a window into so many diverse and colorful worlds. They allow us to think, "what if....?" and a million possibilities present themselves.

In particular, my thanks to Caitlin Baile for the medical proofreading.

THANK YOU to everyone who reads, buys, or recommends one of my books. All authors put a lot of time and effort into writing them, and it is quite surreal knowing that people enjoy this world I created.

If you enjoyed this book, it would mean a great deal to me if you could spare a few minutes to leave a quick review on GoodReads, Amazon, BookBub, or any other platform.

GoodReads:
www.goodreads.com/author/show/20861749.T_S_Simons

Amazon:
www.amazon.com/T-S-Simons/e/B08MT6YYDL

Bookbub:
www.bookbub.com/profile/t-s-simons

CHAPTER 1

"NOT LONG NOW." FRASER'S smug grin was blatantly clear from his tone. I could sense it, even as I focused on the dirt-laden shovel I was heaving. "Excited?"

"Absolutely shitting myself," I confessed, glancing up, momentarily blinded by the haze of the orange sun setting behind him, blurred from the dome's transparent fabric. "But I would never tell *her* that." It seemed ludicrous that I would be the one fearful in this situation. I didn't want to admit that it was the massive leap into the cavern of the unknown that kept me awake at night. Curiosity got the better of me, and, pausing in my work, I looked across at him and asked, "What's it like? Being a father?"

"All I can say is that it is quite a ride." Fraser, now with two daughters of his own, toddler Niamh and newborn Iona, was in an excellent position to make an assessment.

"My friend, your life will never be the same."

"Ugh. Please don't say ride." I grimaced. Vivid technicolor flashbacks of the horrendous journeys I had taken through the antipodean portal between August

Island off the southern coast of New Zealand and Lewis in the Scottish Outer Hebrides flashed before my eyes, temporarily disabling me from my work. The third and final journey from Bellcamp Island to Newgrange, Ireland on the equinox a year ago had been even more traumatic, especially the mid-point. Each time I had not only thought I was going to die, but I had fervently *wished* for death. Death was decidedly preferable to … *that*. I shuddered again.

I was lucky. Until the last few years, I had lived in a comparatively safe time of human history, a time where medicines were readily available, and disease didn't wipe out complete villages in the space of a week. Despite the waterborne protozoa that had obliterated nearly the entire human population in the comparatively short period of a year, I had never actually been near death. But swirling through the vortex, feeling my limbs being stripped of their muscles, sinew, and tendon, knowing I was being torn apart, I had *wished* to be dead.

The first time I had traveled had been a genuine accident, and that had been the most harrowing—not knowing what had happened and wondering if it would go on forever. The second time had been a deliberate attempt to find my first wife, Freyja, and the last time to return to Laetitia. Gorgeous, sweet Laetitia, who was now very pregnant with our first child. She looked much like a ripe cherry, glowing and fit to burst, but cheerful despite her size and obvious discomfort.

"Any hot tips on parenting?" I asked Fraser, only half-heartedly. I wasn't sure that I wanted to know. But I also didn't want to dwell on the antipodal passage any more than entirely necessary.

2

Fraser's face instantly lit up with such glee that it startled me. Sitting back on his heels, he rubbed his hands together joyously. I had opened Pandora's box. Just as I was about to blurt, "I was only joking," he began his jubilant monologue.

"Get used to no sleep. Some kids don't sleep through the night for *years*, so start practicing now by setting your alarm every hour, getting up and walking around, then trying to get back to sleep just in time for the next alarm to go off. Sunset is the witching hour. They scream and cry, and you will get nothing done, so don't even plan it. Get used to everything smelling like baby. Little Iona's smell permeates *everything*: clothes, furniture, even my hair. I think it is a biological thing, so you don't forget them and accidentally leave them somewhere. Before Niamh, I never knew that babies had a scent, but seriously man, they do. *Everything* smells like them."

After a pause, he continued. "Ooh. You will never again be able to speak to your partner without being interrupted. Speaking in broken sentences and inter-preting each other's facial expressions is key here. I think this might be practice for when they are older, and you want to talk about something that you don't want them to understand, so learn secret code now. Don't even bother cleaning anything because the minute you do, they will vomit everywhere. Ever heard the expression heli-spew? Number threes?"

Reacting to my nonplussed face, he cackled and taunted, "Well, get used to it, buddy. This is your new normal."

Seeing my bewildered expression, Fraser's face softened somewhat as he smiled. "Man, when I was where you are now, expecting my first, I was absolutely shitting my shorts. I had no idea what to expect. But the truth is, you can never really prepare for it. You just ... well, you just adapt. Despite the challenges, the sleepless nights, and the turmoil, they are the most amazing, magical creatures. You don't think you could love them more. Then they do something, something tiny like smile at you with their enormous eyes fixated on you, and your heart dissolves into a pile of mush. You would defend them with your life armed with nothing more than a toothbrush. Like if a bear came to attack your child, you know without question that you would fight it off bare-handed just to protect them."

I had seen this side of Fraser when he was around his daughters. Soft, nurturing, gentle. Different from his usually outgoing and somewhat forceful personality.

I would hate to be the boyfriend of one of his daughters, I thought with a snort. When he was near his children, Fraser morphed into something else. *A father*, I realized. Self-doubt crept into the dark recesses of my mind. *Will I be a good father? What is a good father, anyway?* My parents had been loving, firm, yet always supportive. As a child, I had thought of them as very harsh, making us do chores and helping with household maintenance.

Until my mid-teens, I thought I had it tough compared to my friends who seemed to cruise through life, gifted with everything they wanted and a lot of free time in which to get into trouble. Mum, with the control of a well-seasoned regimental sergeant major, controlled our time with jobs and wouldn't let us even watch TV until we had done our allocated chores for the weekend. Mum was the boss. Dad, being a shift worker, often worked weekends. But it was Mum who didn't allow slacking off until the work was done. Once we had finished, she would tell us, "Your time is your own." All of us had a list, and no matter how much we whinged or complained we were sick or tired, Mum ensured we finished it. It wasn't until I lived on August that I realized what my parents had instilled in us was a strong work ethic, something taught over a long period. They had treated us as equal members of the family, and therefore needed to understand the enjoyable things but also the responsibilities. We knew we needed to maintain things or do basic jobs like emptying bins, vacuuming, walking the dog, or mowing lawns. Bills needed to be paid and came as a priority over recreational spending. They included us in plans for saving for big holidays or a new car. As a family unit, we chose what we would cut out, things like take away meals and trips to the cinema to save for our family projects. Sorcha and I valued our free time as we felt we had *earned* it. Both she and I had held down part-time jobs while studying, something few of my friends were able to do. My parents had taught me the value of prioritizing. I knew that if I tackled a task, I had to do it well and complete it. Mum's mantra was, "Do it well; Do it once." It had taken me a very long time to work out what she meant, but now I always worked with this in mind.

Laetitia had grown up with no such role models, yet bizarrely she too had a strong work ethic. Hers, unlike mine, arose from being the primary caregiver for her alcoholic mother. Likely she had done far more than I ever did, but I guiltily suspected that I had complained about my allocated chores far more. Memories of faking illness or doing a crappy job by

5

rushing it made me ashamed. Pleading that I was too sick to walk the dog crossed my mind. Mum, resolute, demanding that it be done regardless, and on one embarrassingly memorable occasion even handing me a sick bag to take with me, just in case. A pang for my parents wrenched my heart for the millionth time. I fervently wished they were here to welcome their grandchild and help guide us on this parenting journey. If only I could thank them for teaching me so many useful things that had stood me in good stead here. I had life skills—thanks to them. All those weekends spent helping Mum and Dad maintain the house and later building the cottage on our holiday block of land meant I had learned skills without even realizing it.

Lae was quite unperturbed with the concept of impending motherhood, despite having no siblings of her own. We were close to Fraser and Isla, so perhaps she had learned what to do by watching Isla and the other mothers here? Or maybe it was just innate knowledge in a woman? Parenthood was such an abstract concept for a man. Your partner gets fatter and fatter then ... boom! Baby. She has months to get used to the idea, infinitesimal movements, tiny kicks, an indicator of the change to come.

When I asked her, curious, what it felt like, she described it as the flutter of a butterfly inside her belly or a quick jerk on a fishing line. One second it was there, the next ... gone, making her question whether she really felt it at all. For a man, it went from a theoretical concept to a noisy, messy reality within minutes. Sure, I got to feel the occasional kick or squirm with a strategically placed hand on her bulging stomach, but it wasn't quite the same. For men, it was a life-changing moment—quiet life, to crying baby all in the space of minutes.

Finishing my work in silence, I thought, as I did now and then, of my childhood—my sister. Sorcha, her own tragedies still so recent in the death of her fiancé when I had left, hadn't lived to become a parent or an aunt. All because she had asthma, and I didn't. The luck of the draw, that one. Why does one child inherit an illness and the other doesn't? Despite looking alike, both tall and muscular, inherited from our father, she was red-haired, inherited from our mother, while I was dark-haired, like Dad. But it was Sorcha who had inherited Dad's asthma, whereas I had not.

Watching Fraser pulling potatoes in the garden bed next to my own, I realized that my mother would have had the most terrible case of granny-lust, that condition when an older woman desperately wants to become a grandparent. No one would have been permitted to hold *her* grandchild while my mother still had functional arms. I smiled, thinking of my mother. The long red plait down her back, swishing as she weeded her garden or bustled around the kitchen. I had the sudden image of my mother smiling down at a baby she cradled in her arms, wrapped in a blanket. A memory. *Whose baby was it?* Wracking my brain, I couldn't place the image. It just hadn't seemed important at the time. Another one of her friends or colleagues had given birth. I hadn't really paid any attention. Now I would have given my right arm to see her smiling down fondly at her own grandchild, *my* child. Spoiling him or her in a way that you can't with your own children. Allegedly.

Ten months ago, I returned to Lewis after traveling through the portal on Bellcamp Island off the coast of New Zealand to Newgrange, Ireland. The Newgrange residents had a productive and friendly reciprocal relationship with their antipodal neighbors and had welcomed me wholeheartedly. They used the portal mainly to share cargo, but people braved the journey as well.

Initially happy to rest, eat and socialize, they had wanted to know everything about August Island, and Lewis, Scotland, the two communities I had lived in. Although I was only there for three days, I would find myself continually retelling the stories of my adventures, the hot springs with the Celtic symbols on August where I first came through. The welcoming community in Scotland centered near the standing stones of Callanish. A few of the Irish had been to Callanish on holidays. Geographically, it just wasn't that far—at least not by Australian standards. Like most Irish, they were friendly, outgoing, and loved to chat.

On my final evening, they had summoned me to the home of Kevin O'Sullivan to recount my tales. A studious-looking man in his early thirties, he was graying at the temples of his dark hair, making him appear older than he was. Despite his unassuming manner, it was clear from the respect shown to him by the other residents that he was a leader of sorts. Not officially. None of the communities I had visited had a democratically elected leader, but he had that aura of a natural leader. People followed his instruction, listening when he spoke, looking up to him, and seeking his guidance. He was a born leader, whether he realized it or not.

Settled in his cozy study, Kevin had listened intently to my tale. But he had not interrupted or acted surprised. Respectful and pleasant, I knew from my conversations with Blake on Bellcamp that nothing I told him *was* a surprise. They knew about antipodal points, what the journey was like, the feeling of discovering another community of survivors at the opposite end of the world. My fantastical tale of traveling across the globe on the days of the solstices, approximately twenty thousand kilometers in the space of minutes, was one they knew themselves, and for some of them, from personal experience.

When I reached my conclusion, he leaned back in his chair and surveyed me thoughtfully. Waiting for what he would say, I watched him. His face was calm and betrayed no thought or emotion. I couldn't tell what he was thinking, and I found this fascinating. Everyone who knew me had said that everything I thought showed on my face the second I was thinking it. It meant I was a shocking liar, but it had taken me years to work this out. Mum had laughed hysterically the day I had finally realized that she had always been able to tell when I was lying to her.

Finally, Kevin had spoken.

"We had wondered if there were other portals like Newgrange." He waved his arm toward the enormous ancient complex, the community being several kilometers to the east. "We speculated we were the only ones. But now..." He paused. "How fantastic to think there is a *network* of such passages. That our ancestors knew of this and used it to travel to places that must have appeared unreal to them. You said that there were Pict markings in the cave on your island, August, you called it?"

Nodding, I replied, "There were. Two large menhirs, upright stones, you know, both with spirals and triquetra, very similar to the ones here at Newgrange. I had been *here,* before. Many years ago. My mother is, was," I corrected, "a teacher, and she loved ancient Celtic sites, especially stone circles. We came to Newgrange on one of our trips back to visit family. I must admit, I didn't appreciate it at the time."

Kevin smiled. "I, too, have been to Callanish. The strange thing is, there are no markings at Callanish."

"You are right. There aren't. But Callanish was buried for centuries under the peat. I wondered..." I stopped, not wanting to appear foolish. I wasn't a historian or an archaeologist.

Kevin's sparkling blue eyes, bright and receptive over his dark beard, graying ever so slightly around his chin, encouraged me to continue.

"Well, I just wondered. If the sites were always a point of travel, generations of people must have known. The Picts, the Celts, the Norse, Romans even. How did Callanish become lost for so many centuries?"

"Newgrange is Neolithic," Kevin said thoughtfully, scratching his beard. "Before 3200BCE, it is thought. Older than the pyramids of Egypt by 600 years and older than Stonehenge by nearly a thousand years. Historians estimate it took a team of 300 men over 30 years to build. But did you know that the menhirs, the standing stone circle that surrounds Newgrange, are much newer? Bronze Age, it is believed. Answering your question, many generations knew that this was a special place because they built it in stages. The carvings are probably Neolithic. We often attribute them to the Celts, but in reality, they are far older."

Seeing the quizzical look on my face around the different periods of history, he explained. "In the 19th century, the three-age system was developed: Stone Age, Bronze Age, and Iron Age based on the tools and artifacts that were discovered from each period. It wasn't long before other archaeologists added further classifications. One of them described the Stone Age as further broken up into Paleolithic, Mesolithic, and Neolithic periods. Historians use the terms somewhat interchangeably."

Contemplating this aloud, I asked, "So if Newgrange is Neolithic, which I assume is at the end of the Stone Age, and the monoliths are Bronze Age, then the markings are Neolithic, not Celtic then?"

Kevin nodded, not interrupting, but standing and reaching for a well-worn volume on his bookcase, flipping pages as I contemplated this.

"So, was there a long gap between the Neolithic period and the Bronze Age?"

"Well, no. The periods overlapped, as the development of tools was slightly different in each region."

"But what you are saying is that for several thousand years, people knew this place was special."

Kevin nodded but said nothing, recognizing my statement for what it was, musing aloud. Not a question.

"The Callanish stones are Neolithic too?"

"That's right, but several hundred years after Newgrange. Archaeologists think around 3000BCE, so fairly close to the Bronze Age period. There was evidence of Bronze Age activity at Callanish, so we know they were still in active use then."

"I wonder when they stopped being used then? As portals, I mean."

"That is an excellent question, and one we don't really have answers to. When Newgrange was redis-covered in 1699, there were Roman coins there, some dating to the first century BCE, so it appears it was still being used as a portal until then. Callanish, and specifically the chambered tomb where you came through, appears to have fallen into disuse..." Kevin referred to the volume on his lap, "around 800 BCE and wasn't rediscovered until the mid-1800s when the peat was removed. Now, there are two key sets of questions—why did the Bronze Age people stop using them? Then, after they were rediscovered, when were they deactivated, by whom and why?"

"I have no idea. Did you say Newgrange was lost too?"

"It was. It was lost for nearly 1500 years."

That was puzzling. I sat in silence, taking this in. Why were *both* sites abandoned?

"Archaeologist?" I asked as I pondered this question. Kevin's immense knowledge was no passing hobby.

The generous smile widened, the intelligent eyes alert beneath his dark brows.

"Historian. But yes, British history and archaeology were my particular areas of expertise. For the first few years here, I was fairly useless. I'm sure people couldn't work out why on earth the teams choosing survivors had chosen a university lecturer and one with a Ph.D. in Pictish history at that. I wasn't of much use with building, farming, or fishing, although I knew a little about making cider. But in time, I am hopeful that I may have been somewhat useful."

"I imagine so." I grinned at Kevin. It was apparent that he was more than a little beneficial to the community, both here and on Bellcamp. "Returning to the point though, why did ancient people let these amazing portals fall into disrepair?"

Kevin replied calmly, "I can see two fairly logical answers to this. First, people died either at the other end, or in transit, and they considered the passages too dangerous. As the islands our communities connect to are both off the coast of New Zealand and were uninhabited, I wouldn't have thought the threat of invasion was the cause. The second possibility, and the one I suspect was the case, is knowing that it took a large magnetic charge to reactivate the portals, it is possible that they were *de*magnetized with a powerful lightning strike. If the portals lost their magic, that could also explain why they were abandoned. People would have thought their Gods had abandoned them, so they, in turn, would have abandoned the sacred sites after a time. It just seems unlikely that both of the sites were deactivated, both Callanish and Newgrange, I mean."

"But didn't you say they abandoned the stones at Callanish 900 years before Newgrange?"

"Hmm, that is true. Two lightning strikes in 900 years are certainly possible. Likely even. You need to remember that until you arrived, we thought Newgrange was the only portal in existence. To learn that there is another at Callanish, well, that changes the game somewhat..."

Following his train of thought, I continued, "If Callanish was struck by lightning, and the portal deactivated, that could explain why the site was abandoned. But Newgrange remained a revered site until much later. But if it too was struck by lightning or was in some other way deactivated, that would explain why it was also abandoned. You know, there are more out there, antipodean portals, I mean."

Kevin looked ecstatic at this. "Really? More? That's ... amazing!"

"I haven't seen them all myself, but I know of a search party from Lewis who found more. An active one in the Kerguelen Islands that links to central Canada. A suspected one on Gibraltar. And another active one in Mauritania on the west coast of Africa that linked to New Caledonia in the South Pacific."

"That is phenomenal!" Kevin gushed. "More portals! What do you mean by suspected, though?"

I shrugged, trying to remember what Heidi had said. "By the time the Scots team arrived in Gibraltar, the people had all gone, but they thought they hadn't been dead for long. As in, they could see that it *had* been a protected community, but that the dome had failed or been breached, and the community had abandoned the site. I'm not one hundred percent sure. I heard about it secondhand."

"Did all the communities have an ancient site as ground zero then?"

"I'm not sure, but I don't think so. They all had a portal, and some at least were on top of large deposits of magnetic lodestone. In Mauritania, they called it the Adrar Plateau I think he said. While most of the site was arid desert plain, it also included steep rocky plateaus. One of the party from Scotland allegedly described it as 'like a scene from Star Wars.'"

"You would think Africa, and a dry part of Africa, would be a strange place to set up a domed community, wouldn't you? Though I recall seeing journal articles about stone circles in The Gambia once," Kevin mused.

I agreed. "I thought it was odd too. But if it houses an antipodal point, and it evidently does, then it makes sense, doesn't it?"

"It does. Also, if it were arid, then the water wouldn't be infected. As long as they had an original uncontaminated water supply, then the residents could still grow crops and survive. Where did you say it linked to?"

"New Caledonia. I don't recall exactly where. When the Lewis team stopped in Africa, they met French-speaking people who had traveled from New Caledonia. Most of them spoke some English, and one of the Scots had some basic French, although it was a little rusty. They made themselves known, though. They were certain they got the story straight. I have been to New Caledonia. There was a lot of rugged rainforest there, and it is fairly sparsely populated outside of the capital, Noumea. It isn't all idyllic tropical beaches."

Kevin nodded. We sat quietly for a while, thinking of those other communities. *Are they so different from ours? A group of strangers, working together, growing crops, and raising children. Trying to survive.*

"Did you see the carvings in the caves on Bellcamp, then?" Kevin's question pulled me from my trance.

Shaking my head, I said, "I hadn't thought to look. Or ask. I was focused on just surviving another passage and praying it would be my last."

"That's a shame. I would be interested in knowing if the markings were the same as the ones on August. If there are more portals, I wonder if they all have markings."

The disappointment must have shown on my face as Kevin laughed. "It's fine. Really. You know, you are likely the first person to step foot through *four* antipodal doorways. That is a fairly special achievement."

I groaned audibly. "I have to say, special is not the word I would use. Nor doorway. That word does not adequately reflect the absolute torture that those hellmouths generate."

Kevin laughed easily. "If they are so bad, and don't get me wrong, I hear they are, I have to ask: What made you do it so many times?"

Pausing, I tried to think of a logical answer. The first journey from August to Callanish had been unplanned, a true accident that had occurred fundamentally out of grief. The return had resulted from loyalty. To find Freyja. This last journey, from Bellcamp to Newgrange, was to return to my life on Lewis, to Laetitia. Silently, I prayed she wanted me.

Looking for a simple way to sum up the complexities of my travel, it stumped me.

"Love," I finally responded.

Kevin nodded knowingly. "From what I hear, no amount of wanderlust is enough to want to do *that* twice."

"Agreed. But I am surprised. You know so much about the history of these places, you haven't been through yourself?"

"I want to. Really, I do. But I can't, not yet. My children are so young. They lost their mother two years ago, just after we had discovered the passage. Lynda was a historian, too, with a special interest in Egyptian history and mythology. Since she passed, I have missed having someone to talk to about this stuff. How thrilled she would have been to know that there were more antipodean portals."

For the first time, I saw the loss etched in Kevin's face.

"I'm sorry." I hadn't meant to cause him pain.

He looked directly at me. "I want to go, and I will, soon. My youngest, Arden, has only just turned two. I can't leave her for three months. Not yet. These temples have been here for over 5000 years. I figure I can wait another year or two. It isn't like we are going anywhere."

"Why do you think the symbol on most of the ancient sites is a spiral?" Kevin broke into my maudlin thoughts, and I looked up at him. "You said they were on the markers in the cave at your original community in August. Four menhirs are marking the passage at Bellcamp and also here around the circumference of the mound at Newgrange. Some inside, too. There aren't at Callanish, but it is widely accepted by historians that the site was plundered for its rock over many thousands of years. Carved stone often turns up in churches. Think about it. What symbol would you use to warn other people that this was a special place, a sacred place, but also one that was a portal? You have made the journey several times. How would you describe the travel itself? The feeling I mean."

"Spinning," I replied, recalling the motion so vividly from three days before that I could barely get the word out. "It was a spinning sucking vortex between two points."

"Exactly. If you were a verbal storytelling community with limited ability to write, and you wanted to place a simple warning to others—beware! This is a portal! What symbol would you use?"

Nodding, I followed his logic. "There were spirals carved into the rock menhirs on August."

"Do you think that other ancient sites that also have that symbol carved into them could also have been portals? Perhaps they haven't been reactivated yet, but there couldn't be a clearer sign of where to look."

"I think you are onto something!" I exclaimed, energized by his excitement despite my exhaustion. "Now my brain is struggling to remember all the places where I have seen that Celtic spiral carved in stone."

"Not just the spiral, but the double spiral too." Kevin was getting enthusiastic now. "See here." He pointed to a black-and-white photo in the book he was still holding. "I have read reams of literature since we found the portal here, but this is the first time I have had *proof* of other antipodal sites. The double spiral is found at many gravesites and has been linked by scholars to the sun but to the idea of death and rebirth. But what if it wasn't? You said yourself that you spin one way, then when you reach the center, you slow, and spin in the opposite direction."

"Exactly. The Coriolis effect. It feels like … being caught in a cyclone. It spins in the opposite direction, depending on the hemisphere you are in."

"But that is exactly what the double spiral would represent, would it not? We find the double spiral on the curbstones at Newgrange. It is also common in New Zealand Maori culture; it makes up a significant part of their facial and body tattooing. But it is more than that."

Kevin was positively reverberating with his new theory.

"A carved spiral is found on a Hohokam petroglyph found in the Saguaro National Monument in

Arizona. There was a prominent, spiral pattern on Danish shields and ornaments dated back to 3000 BC. Prehistoric petroglyphs in Colombia are covered with both clockwise and counterclockwise spirals. Ancient Greece. Egypt. They all use the spiral symbol, particularly on artifacts found close to ancient temple sites. What if the use of a spiral in these ancient cultures means exactly the same thing? Warning! Portal."

"We could be dealing with hundreds of portals. More."

"Exactly. What if some portals haven't even been reactivated yet? What could that mean for the continued survival of our species? I can think of a few potential sites, and they are spread out too. Temple Wood at Kilmartin Glen on the west coast of Scotland, south of Oban. The passage graves at Clava Cairns, up in the highlands near Inverness. There are many sites on the Shetlands and Orkney Islands in Scotland, and hundreds here in Ireland. Even the Channel Islands of Guernsey and Jersey have Neolithic stone circles and passage graves. The problem is, so many of them have been removed from their original locations and positions over the years."

"I know the Clava Cairns," I exclaimed. "I have been there several times. I don't know the others. That entire site at Clava has an extraordinary feel to it."

"It does. Clava and Temple Wood don't have spirals, but the older ring and cup marks, common to hundreds of ancient sites across the UK, Ireland, and even continental Europe. With limited tools with which to carve the stone, deer antlers, for instance, they may have chosen a simpler symbol. Historians have long thought it was a symbol reflecting the Celtic cyclic nature of life—birth, death, rebirth. Others believe it represents labyrinths. Labyrinths are common in ancient myths and appear in ancient Egyptian, Celtic, and Greece myths, but remember that these weren't translated from verbal storytelling to written text for centuries afterward. They associated labyrinths with the dead and one's journey through the afterlife. In that view, nothing and no one ever dies; all things merely change and become something else. The seemingly linear path one travels between birth and death does not begin at birth or end with death; everything that dies comes back in some renewed form or continues eternally. Generations of historians and archaeologists have believed they raised the cairns at Clava to commemorate those who had passed on to the next phase of existence on their eternal journey. But I ask you, what if it wasn't a metaphysical journey, but a *physical* one—to another place across the earth? All these years, we have thought it was symbolic, based on lore and legend. But it may have been a warning sign—watch out! This is a place where people disappear and get sucked into the spinning tunnel—a labyrinth—but not a metaphorical one. Ancient people may well have believed the journey was based on people's moral standing. A good and just person would survive and possibly return. A bad person might not. Once the portals were demagnetized, especially if it was by accident, the temples became a place of mystery, but no longer one of veneration or worship. This could explain why so many of them were lost over time, buried under the landscape. No longer recognized for the magical places they once were."

My head was spinning with this concept, but I had to agree. It was a fascinating one—antipodal points marked by ancient stone circles and spiral carvings.

I yawned widely, forcing Kevin to apologize for keeping me for so long.

"I am sorry," I said regretfully. "I am quite exhausted."

Kevin stood and shook my hand profusely as I prepared to leave. He was an interesting man, and one I wished I could spend more time with. Excusing myself, I staggered off, found my bed, and slept like the dead.

CHAPTER 2

IT WASN'T UNTIL THE following day when Eoghan and I had been battling the blustering wind of the Irish Sea, replaying the conversation in my head, that I realized that Kevin referred to the portals as temples. *They were temples,* I recognized with a jolt. All of them. The stones at Callanish, the caves, and the passage tomb at Newgrange. I had always thought of them as ancient sites, historical places of interest, but the actuality was that for thousands of years, they had been centers of worship and reverence. Sacred, holy places that people had used for special occasions for millennia, no different from cathedrals, synagogues, or mosques. Yet relatively recently, it seemed, some of them had been deliberately deactivated. Perhaps Blake was right. Perhaps it was just to control them and prevent accidental travel. What could that knowledge do in the wrong hands? The alternative was that they had been naturally decommissioned thousands of years before. If that were the case, it seemed highly unlikely that all the sites around the world were naturally deactivated. Otherwise, how would we have even discovered them? Despite the agony that those portals had caused me personally, I was eminently grateful for their existence. If nothing else, we had formed linkages to other people, other communities like our own. We had a shared experience, and when the time came to leave our little bubbles of safety, we had other people to rebuild with.

Despite being an excellent sailor, Eoghan was a man of few words, which suited me as I pondered my return to Lewis. He had taken me in a small skiff down the River Boyne to Drogheda, where we left the sanctuary of the dome and changed to a slightly larger, unattractive but sturdy fishing vessel. The community used it semi-regularly and had stocked it with fresh water and canned food. Once it had been painted red and white; now it was faded to a dull gray, the paint flaking off. But it provided an enclosed cabin for piloting the vessel, windows at 180 degrees, and a lot of protection from the weather and potential infection.

Days passed as I watched the islands of Islay, Mull, Rum, Uist, and Skye drift past. Once spectacular and green, now they were dead and devoid of color. The voyage to the Hebrides, a rocking and vomit-inducing journey, had made me wish longingly on more than one occasion that I had gone back to August and traveled through the portal there. When it rained, which it regularly did in this part of the world, we dropped anchor and waited it out, making for a painfully slow journey. Closing my eyes, I prayed for the rocking to stop. But deep down, I knew that this was far better than returning to the desolation of August.

On the ninth day, we arrived in the port town of Tarbert on the southern part of the island, Harris.

Eoghan dropped me at the dock and left me with a warm handshake, a bicycle, and my backpack, which besides my clothes and sleeping bag, contained two bottles of cider. I was so eminently grateful to be on solid land. The cider was a gift from Kevin. One of his early vintages, it had been cellared and was now ready to drink. Eoghan had enough food and was now refueling for the return journey, keen to be on his way, hampered by rain and storms. Thanking him warmly, I bid him farewell as I spent nearly half an hour wobbling around like a newborn foal, trying to get my land legs back. Recognizing that I was at the opposite end of the island from the community, I set out on a decent mountain bike that one of the Newgrangians had kindly gifted me.

Spending time in the Alpine area of Victoria as a teenager, I knew a bike with decent suspension when I rode one. Over this rugged terrain, I was grateful for it. As a teen, when traveling to visit Mum's sister, we caught the car ferry from Skye to Tarbert. The ferry had only taken a few hours, and we had driven our hire car from Tarbert to Aunt Ang's house in less than two hours. Thus, I had stupidly forgotten that riding a bicycle, no matter how good the suspension, on roads subjected to wild storms that had not been used nor maintained for the past few years, was not the same as being a passenger in a modern car. Cursing Eoghan for the millionth time for not dropping me closer, I hit a massive pothole as I rounded a bend in the A859, and my front wheel wobbled precariously, my heavy backpack threatening to topple me and smash the cider on the road. I held on, but only just, my heart pounding from the scare.

Making camp that night near Aird a' Mhulaidh, I watched the darkening sky. A storm was brewing, forcing me to waste precious riding time searching for a croft or barn in which to sleep. I passed several, and they were all ruined—stone walls but no roof, offering little protection from the rain. With no living trees or plants, and foliage that had once covered the hillsides shrunken and dried out, the rocks stood out even more prominently now. Distinct grays lay against the browns of the dead earth. With no buildings in sight, I started looking for protection behind a cluster of rocks. I didn't want to be outside with no protection when the rain hit. With no remaining plant life, it wasn't hard to find a small alcove that would contain me, although I had to wriggle in on my belly, feet first, as there was inadequate room to turn around. But once inside, there was room to sit upright, although not stand. Seated, or even outstretched, my head was inside the granite cave by a few feet and protected by the protruding natural rock ledge that prevented me from getting wet. Halfway up a steep hillside, it was also reasonably likely that any rain would run downhill and not into my hidey-hole. The relative dryness of the tiny cave supported this theory. Regardless, I estimated I could use my pack to block most of the entrance. I would hate to cop a face full of wind and infected rain with it.

Exhausted but realizing that I wouldn't sleep well if I was hungry, I dug out the can of beans I had in my pack. If I farted all night, there was no one here to smell it.

Outside the geodesic dome, there was no point in wasting the gas burner I had taken in Invercargill with Hugh. Keeping a close eye on the storm front, I gathered largish rocks to form a ring, filling it with dry twigs, and dug a few wedges of peat with a sharp rock. A precious match taken from the camping store lit the dried foliage. It was strange, smelling peat smoke again after all this time. Peat smoke gives off a distinct scent, one immediately familiar, even when you haven't smelled it for years. I coughed and spluttered initially as the damp wood caught, then watched the smoke as it billowed up into the night, higher and higher, thicker at the base, then thinner as it disappeared. Peat burned hot and for an extended period, so it was used by Scots and the Irish for many generations.

After dinner, mesmerized by the flame flickering in different colors and patterns, I grew sleepy. Pulling my body as far into the cave as I could fit, I remembered to use my pack as a windbreak, and it didn't take me long to drift off to sleep, the wild wind raging outside. The noise echoed through the rocks and kept me awake for much of the night. Sometimes it sounded like children crying, other times like the roaring of water. Dreaming fitfully, I could see Freyja screaming and desperately reaching out to me as it sucked her away, and me, unable to save her.

I woke at dawn, but the storm continued to rage. Blustering winds pierced the cave opening at irregular intervals, forcing me to pull my jacket closed and scoot back as far as I could in the limited space available. Rain had flooded the fire through the night. Even though I knew the dangers of peat fires reigniting, especially when there was an oxygen source, there was little chance this one would. Gazing at the sky, I acknowledged it was pointless for me to leave. Even between showers, I wouldn't get far caught out in the open. Frustrated to be so close to the community yet unable to move, I sat in the cave watching out over the valley, waiting for the storm to pass. It didn't, and my thoughts tortured me. *Is this a sign? Will I not be welcomed back? I have been gone for nearly four months. What if Lae has moved on?* I had left her with no assurance that I would return. There was no promise or commitment between us. Slowly eating what little food I had to pass the time and trying to save the limited water I had left in my water bottle, I fervently wished I had thought to bring a book as my thoughts continued to torment me. The books I had taken in New Zealand I had left with Callie on Bellcamp, not wanting to take much in my backpack, which accompanied me through the passage.

Finally, I cracked open one bottle from Kevin. At least I wouldn't need to carry it anymore. As I drank my way through the bottle of what turned out to be a crisp and flavorsome cider and watched the storm rage over the valley and the ocean beyond, my thoughts drifted, flitting between places and things.

It is funny what you think of when alone, in nature, with absolutely nothing to do. The memories stir in your mind—the people, places, and conversations you recall, many years after they took place. How an abstract shape in a rock or cloud reminds you of something you once saw or owned long ago. Several times I pictured Eoghan out on his boat and hoped that he was okay. My parents, sister, and Lae were at the forefront of my thoughts—as they often were. Freyja and Angus. Anger washed through me again as I envisaged Freyja with another man. Images of her with him danced behind my closed eyes. Naked. In bed. Laughing. Kissing. Running his hands over her taut, muscular stomach, up her long legs...

Punching the rock nearest me to dispel the anguish that image provoked, the pain shot up my arm, and I swore, nursing my bruised and now rapidly swelling hand. Flaming hot, I seethed, unable to dispel the intimate images of them that flaunted themselves so vividly in my mind. I had never met Angus, but I could picture him. Tall, dark, handsome, and lithe, like a professional athlete turned model—chiseled jaw, perfect nose, and sparkling blue eyes. I set my teeth and clenched my jaw. Fury consumed me, which at least kept me warm from the freezing, howling storm outside. The betrayal and heartache threatened to boil over. My hand throbbed with pain, and my jaw ached from clenching it so tightly. Glancing down at my battered hand, a memory of Laetitia's tender nursing of my gardening scrapes and cuts flashed into my mind, making me cool somewhat. Her light touch and gentle words, the heartwarming feeling of being nurtured. The heat in my bones dissipated as I focused on Lae, realizing how much I missed her.

For hours, I sat there, sipping cider, thoughts of Freyja continuing to torture me, and I ran the full gamut of emotions. Anger. Betrayal. Anguish. Then finally ... forgiveness. I couldn't continue to blame her. It had been a year. Longer. It wasn't her fault. She had traveled by accident with no way of knowing that I would follow. She had gone back to August for me, finding me gone. If not here, then perhaps in the close confines of their yacht for all of those months, she had moved on ... with *him*.

"I forgive you," I whispered to the valley below, riddled with rocks and creeks that had sprung up spontaneously from the storm. Then with more conviction, as I realized I couldn't be overheard, I called into the raging storm, "Freyja, honey. You were my first love. I love you. I forgive you. Goodbye, my love."

Feeling sapped of energy but strangely more relaxed than I had felt in months, I fell into a deep, dreamless sleep, calmer than I thought possible in the dark, dank, rocky cave, crammed in between two large boulders.

CHAPTER 3

THE STORM PASSED DURING the night, and the sun glistened as it reflected on the damp rocks. Unable to stretch adequately in the cramped confines of the crevice, I wriggled out and felt my bones and joints crack as I reached with my arms overhead and arched my back, stretching my tortured spine. Quickly devouring the remaining food, I gave my bike a brisk shake to remove the excess water. It hadn't fared so well with no trees or bushes to protect it.

I made my way to the dome edge near Airidh a' Bhruaich, a small but widely spread crofting community. Cursing the wasted time, I searched for an entrance to the geodesic dome, able to see the green pastures so close, but unable to access. Making a bee-line for the entrance near Leurbost, far farther north than I had intended, at least I knew what I was looking for. The land here was so uneven and rocky that it was difficult to navigate with a bike and a large pack. But this was an access hatch I knew. It was where Lae had taken me through with our horses the day I searched for my aunt. Months ago, and yet in some ways, it felt like yesterday. If I closed my eyes, I could still see my Aunt Angela sitting there in her conservatory with her cat, looking so much like my mother, her iPad on the table next to her, the one she used to make videoconferencing calls with Mum.

I focused on getting the bike through the hatch without damaging either. Strangely, there weren't many bikes here, and it would be highly useful, so I planned to keep it in top condition. Once on the greenside, I carefully closed the hatch, checking the seal, and turned around to get my bearings. I was in the easternmost part of the community, many kilometers from the houses at Garynahine. Inside, the air was scented. The mingling fragrances of trees and grass were overwhelming. Despite my career choice, I had never realized the scents that grass and everyday plants gave off—gentle, wafting scents of freshness and purity. We take them for granted. But now that everything outside was dead, it was striking to my olfactory senses. My eyes were dry and sore from the salt wind, blinking after days of ocean travel and watching the morbid browns of death that dotted the islands we had passed on the way here, making it plain that there were no other communities in the vicinity. The colors immediately inside the shell were breathtaking. It was like going from a world of sepia to a world of brilliant color: the greens of the trees and bushes, the purple of the heather, the grays of rocks, and blue of the sky. A kaleidoscope of color—all because of water. Fresh, safe, water. The sounds were deafening. Despite the immediate lack of wind, birds were singing, and insects were buzzing. It was suddenly so loud. The assault on my senses was overwhelming. Scents, colors, sounds. All natural, and all wholly taken for granted.

Thinking of my aunt generated thoughts of the original residents of this area. Being able to see their world die, bleached of color and devoid of life, yet so nearby they could have touched the other world that was vibrant and alive, so close. Just on the other side of an impenetrable dome, muted a little as the colors were on the wrong side of the thick transparent fabric. But it was alive, thriving when the rest of the world had been rapidly dying and unable to be saved.

The motivation for hot food, a shower and a clean bed roused me from my stupor, and I kept riding, pushing through the pain. My ass spasmed. Stopping now and then to rub the cramping muscles, I looked around, taking it all in. Home. No matter how exhausted I was. My eyes stung, and my legs were throbbing, shooting pain up into my hips. I pushed on; I was here.

By late afternoon, I could see the village in the distance. The sun setting behind it and reflecting off the stone render of the original manor house made it glow a beautiful orange, a haze around the perimeter. No smoke rose from chimneys, yet I could see the light and movement. It looked familiar, yet somehow different, making me feel like a stranger, an intruder.

Hearing shouts in the distance, I knew they had spotted me as I rounded the last curve in the road, and I spurred up, my exhausted legs and sore butt screaming from the punishment. Soon a small crowd had gathered as I descended into the cluster of houses, and I heard a shout, "Cam!"

Lifting my hand to wave, I instantly recognized the rookie mistake as I wobbled on the rutted track and struggled to keep the bike upright. I didn't recall coming to a stop, getting off the bike, or taking the pack off my hot, sweaty back. The mob embraced me, my kin. I was being hugged, patted, and kissed all at the same time. Flushing with embarrassment, I recognized the feeling. I felt *loved*. I was with my family. Safe and nurtured.

That night I returned to my home with Lae, but not to my room. Despite my exhaustion, she pushed me toward the shower, herself turning toward the kitchen. Clean and being in fresh clothes revived me slightly, although my butt still spasmed. Cringing as I gently lowered myself onto the chair, once I was seated at that table, the one we had eaten at so many times before, just looking at each other but barely speaking, I knew I was where I should be.

It had been months since we were last together, but the familiarity came flooding back. Lae prepared a single plate that she placed between us, holding cheese, bread, some fruit from my greenhouse. We smiled shyly at each other, but with no words. There was nothing that needed to be said. I was here. As the plate slowly emptied, Lae stood and looked down at me, holding her hand upturned toward me. I rose and took her hand as she wordlessly led me to her room.

The morning sun woke me, streaming through the window and hitting the end of the bed. I stretched and rolled over to hug her. My arm hit her pillow, cold and empty. A pang of shock reverberated through my body as my arm rolled off the pillow and hit the bare mattress. *Has she run away? Does she have regrets?* The thoughts had barely escaped my mind when I registered the low, sweet voice coming from the kitchen:

Lae singing "Valerie" amid the muffled sound of pans and smells of cooking.

Slipping out of bed, I hunted around for my clothes, discarded slowly and deliberately the night before. Still on the floor where they had been dropped. Unimportant encumbrances at the time, but slightly more essential in the cold, harsh light of day.

She was standing at the biogas stove, cooking mushrooms that smelled divine, barefoot, and wearing a white robe. I crept up behind her and, stooping slightly because of my height advantage, wrapped my arms around her tiny frame, engulfing her. She lay her head back onto my shoulder to look up at me, and I leaned down to kiss her ardently, taking her breath away. Unable to stop myself from caressing her petite, yet womanly figure, I slipped my hands down the inside of the robe, reaching down to her ribcage.

"Oomph," she said when able to break away. "Well, I missed you too."

Sitting at the table as I watched her buzz around the kitchen, I realized how completely and utterly contented I was. Placing a laden plate of toast, eggs, mushrooms, and kippers and a mug of steaming coffee in front of me, she sat opposite me with her own meal. We ate slowly, watching each other, smiling occasionally but with no need for words. Being together was enough. We had all the time in the world.

"I brought you something," I said as we finished breakfast. "Please don't think I am daft. It wasn't like there were souvenir shops where I was."

Laetitia's face lit with such joy that I felt even more stupid. Perhaps I should have looked for a souvenir shop. After all, they were unlikely to have been ransacked. Who wanted Ugg boots or a Kiwi teddy in a time of crisis?

Heading back to the bedroom, I returned, carrying my pack. Suddenly I had second thoughts. "It is a dumb idea. Forget it."

Her face dropped, and I quickly recanted. "Here." I handed her my mostly empty backpack, having already removed the clothes inside, fearful of repulsing her with the stench of my filthy, sweaty clothes after nine days at sea. She looked at me, puzzled.

I nodded confirmation, and she fossicked inside. She came up with the bottle of cider first and looked at me, her head tilted slightly to one side, a little puzzled.

"Oh, not that. That was a gift from the community at Newgrange. I thought we might share it one evening with Fraser and Isla."

She smiled, understanding, and dove again. This time she came up with a roll of toilet paper, and her face lit like the sun had struck it and illuminated her for the first time.

"Toilet paper! Oh, I *never* thought I would see that again! Is it wrong to say I have missed toilet paper, wasteful as it is?"

Smiling, I nodded, gesturing that she should continue rummaging. This time she came up with several small packets of tissues, taken from the supermarket in Invercargill. She pulled one a little from the pack and felt it with her fingers.

"Tissues! I had forgotten how soft tissues feel. There is nothing quite as good as tissues when you need to blow your nose." She held the package to her chest. Then a look of horror crossed her face. "What about the plastic wrapping? There is no plastic here! What do I do with that?"

Laughing, I said, "It is okay. It is a tiny amount. I am sure no one will lynch you for that. Remember all the plastic bags we used to use? Shopping bags, bags for fruit and vegetables, cling film on trays of produce in the supermarket? One small piece won't hurt. We can bury it anyway, so no one needs to know. Keep looking."

Acknowledging this, she was standing beside the table, her arm down near the bottom of the pack by now. It was nearly as tall as she was. She froze suddenly, and her face went white, like something had unexpectedly bitten her. Slowly she withdrew her hand, grasping the three family-sized blocks of Whittaker's chocolate. New Zealand chocolate. The rest of my stash, taken the day I had left Hugh in the hotel in Christchurch. The look of utter shock on her face alarmed me as she dropped into the chair opposite me, and I rushed to her, falling to my knees before her. She held the bars in front of her face, staring at them. *Did I make a mistake? Does she not like chocolate?*

"Oh ... my ... goodness," she breathed.

"Do you not like it?" I asked worriedly. Freyja had loved chocolate. I had just assumed that Lae would also, but with none here, I had never had the chance to ask.

"I ... love ... it," she said with so much feeling that I knew she was telling the truth. She did. "It is just that ... well, I have never had foreign chocolate before."

"It is only from New Zealand. It is nothing spec—" I started, but she cut me off when she spoke, quietly, a faraway look in her eyes.

"When I was in primary school, a girl in my class went to Belgium for her summer holidays. When she came back, at lunchtime, she handed out small

36

Belgian chocolates. They were in a beautiful tin. It was painted like a multi-story shopfront—brightly colored items displayed on shelves in the windows and with a red roof. I had never seen anything like that tin. She took the lid off and offered a piece of handmade chocolate to each of her friends. They were raving about it, kept saying how delicious they were, *so* much better than British chocolate. I lurked nearby, hopeful, you know. Just watching. Hoping she would have one extra. Chocolate was a treat I rarely had." Lae paused, smiling wanly as I returned to my seat.

"She saw me standing there and held out a piece to me. When I reached for it, she snatched it away, laughing hysterically, telling me that a dirty little mouse like me wouldn't appreciate fine chocolate. Rodents couldn't tell luxury from rubbish. All her friends laughed and started chanting, 'Mousey, mousey. Here, want some?' I ran away."

Tears filled her eyes with the memory as she clutched the chocolate blocks to her chest. "But at least it was better than some other names they called me."

Too scared to ask, I said nothing as she kept speaking.

"The downside of having the word tit in the middle of your name is being called Le-titty-a, no tits, and a hundred other variations."

"I will never again let anyone hurt you like that," I promised, gripping her hands over the table, speaking slowly and assuredly, ensuring that she took it in through the hurtful memory that had momentarily engulfed her. "I am here now, Laetitia. Never again will you feel that way. I promise you."

Lae sat on my lap and threw her arms around my neck. "I love you, Campbell Mackintosh."

"And I, you. Laetitia ... Laetitia... Do you know I don't even know your full name? It just never seemed important before."

"Laetitia Katherine Rose," she replied shyly.

"Well, Laetitia Katherine Rose, I love you with all of my heart and soul. I have traveled across the world to be with you. I choose you above all others. Will you have me?"

A kiss was her answer. I took it to be a yes.

CHAPTER 4

IT WAS DIFFICULT NOT to groan aloud when I saw the state of the greenhouses. Weeds were choking the vegetables and seedlings. What was an edible plant and what was weed was nearly impossible to tell, even at close range.

Fraser looked abashed at my reaction. "I was busy. I had to do a lot of the outside work alone. More of the locals have moved off to crofts. Then Isla had the second bairn, and Iona was poorly for a bit… well, I didn't have enough time," he finished.

"The crops grew; people ate; no one bloody died. It was just the weeding I couldn't keep atop of," he added, a little defensively, his Scots accent deepening.

Begrudgingly, I knew this to be true. Fraser had two young children to care for. There also wasn't a team of committed gardeners here. But still. Gardening wasn't a one-off job. You can't plant seedlings once and then come back a month later and harvest them. Many times, I had spoken to people when I worked in the nursery in Melbourne and tried to explain that gardening was a process. You couldn't just whack some seeds in the ground, and *voila*! Instant vege-table patch. Care needed to be taken to prepare the soil, weed the garden beds, and thin the seedlings. I could spot them a mile off—the weekend gardeners—people enamored with the concept of new-age self-sufficiency but would invariably have died in the first winter in a place like this. Those who didn't read the labels but just looked at the pictures—usually those who purchased seedlings and not seeds. Sighing, I looked back at the greenhouses. I had a lot of work to catch up on.

"I am so glad you are back," Fraser said with gen-uine feeling.

"I am glad to be back. Now, where do we start?"

"That is terrible." Lae was genuinely shocked. Telling her about visiting Invercargill with Hugh, then Christchurch, had visibly upset her. The litter in the streets. The shops that had been ransacked. Houses were vandalized and never repaired, with no one left to care for them.

"I always just envisaged those places as we left them. I'd hate to think of Edinburgh with its beautiful stone buildings and cobbled streets covered in litter."

I shrugged. "I guess people were fighting for sur-vival. Litter doesn't really matter when you just want to live, to feed your family. Funnily enough, it didn't *feel* shocking, if that makes sense. After all we had seen, it just *was*. I imagine most cities in the world look like that now."

"I suppose. But why all the rubbish?"

"Hugh and I discussed it. That day we drove to his sister's house."

I had already told her about Hugh. I had needed to. Not to forget, I would never forget Hugh, but telling her was more about me processing what happened and seeking a sense of closure so I could move on and stop blaming myself for not checking on him sooner.

Lae nodded and indicated that I was to continue.

"We had done little talking—after. We decided that the rubbish situation was in part that bins hadn't been emptied. People had been conditioned to place rubbish in bins, so they kept doing so even though they weren't being emptied after the crisis had started. The bins started overflowing. It is likely the local council redirected all of its resources to life-saving matters. What value was a salary when you knew you were going to die? The deep piles of rubbish that lined the street gutters looked more like rubbish had blown from the landfill with no one to stop it or clean it up. With many of the trees dead and fallen, there was less of a windbreak."

"What do you mean?"

"There was light stuff flapping around everywhere: plastic bags, chip packets, chocolate bar wrappers, general packaging. You know how everything you bought came in a wrapper? Well ... that. Single-use disposable bags were banned in Australia many years before we left, and I imagine in New Zealand too, but you still saw them around. Now I guess they always will be. No paper that I recall, so that had decomposed at least. But cigarette butts were still visible too, on the footpaths."

Lae paused for a moment before asking, "Do you think we will ever be able to go back?"

"I don't know," I admitted. "I saw nothing in my travels that made me think the earth was recovering, either there or here. There was no rubbish here on Harris, but it was barren. Much like that day we went to find my aunt, just miles and miles of death. And do you know what? I am not sure that I want to. Go back, I mean. I am happy here. Things are ... better. Perhaps because we lost so much, the people here focus on each other, on helping their friends. Going back just showed me all the things we did *wrong*. Obsessed with *stuff*: phones, iPads, smartwatches, brand-name clothing, and shoes. Having a prestigious car or a swanky job with a business card. There were always sales, and you always felt pressured to buy new clothes, shoes, or car. We didn't focus on what truly mattered."

"And what is that?" she asked, an arm snaking around my waist and snuggling in close as she looked up into my face.

"People. Community. Family. Helping when someone has a baby. Bringing meals and cleaning their home, not just taking a gift bought in a store that was made in a sweatshop factory in a third world country. Wrapped in plastic that would never biodegrade. People here *care*. It was one thing that Australians did well. They always coped well in a crisis, although they went back to their normal lives when there wasn't a catastrophe."

"What do you mean?"

"In my lifetime, there were several catastrophic bushfires, bombings, tsunamis, and the like. Events that affected thousands of people. Australians don't offer thoughts and prayers. They *do* stuff. They offer rooms to the displaced, donate free accommodation in caravans or holiday houses. Aussies start food banks, take up collections of hay for livestock or accommodation for family pets. Despite the bad news, you would also see the good. The evening news was filled with these incredible stories of people putting koalas in their cars to save them from bushfires or making meals for volunteers and driving five hours to deliver them. People actively trying to buy goods and services from the communities affected so they could help just a little. Australians pull together when the going gets tough. That is one thing I love about all the survival communities I have visited. All four of them, to some extent, but this one most of all. I love that they *are* a community. A tight-knit group of people who look out for each other and who actually care."

"They do," she admitted. "They care about you too, you know."

"Do they?" I asked, feeling sheepish. It meant more than I would have thought to hear Lae say that. "I hoped they would … care, I mean. I desperately wanted to come back. For you, of course, but also … well … for everyone here. I wanted to be welcomed, but I was a little scared that I wouldn't be."

"Why would you think that? You will always be welcome here."

"By you, maybe. But by the rest of the community?"

"Yes," she replied firmly. "If nothing else, the quality of our food has taken a marked downward slide since you left. Don't you tell Fraser I said so. Also, I overheard some men planning a trip into Stornoway to track down mountain bikes like yours. There must be a shop there. They can't believe that they didn't think of that before, especially now that the community is more widely spread."

I smiled. "You are just trying to make me feel better."

"Partly," she teased. "You are responsible for a bit of change here, and people recognize it. We have a new baker, though. I'll take you to meet her. Her bread is incredible."

Lae was right. Juliette made the most divine sourdough bread. An electrical engineer by training, she had learned to make it for her family with the occasional loaf for trade with neighbors. But eventually it had become so popular that it had become her full-time job. Every morning, she rose at 4am to proof the dough and start the ovens fired by biogas.

"I would have liked wood-fired ovens," she sighed to me on my fourth morning back on Lewis as I brought her a basket of figs I had picked in exchange for our daily loaf. "The books I have read say the smoke adds such a rich taste to the bread."

"I'm afraid I wouldn't know," I admitted. "Bread was never really my specialty, although we had a wood-fired pizza place back home, and their pizza was amazing. Your bread is exceptional. It is far better than anything I could make."

"I'm not sure that is true." Juliette smiled at me. "You brought mangoes and macadamias to Lewis. Fresh mangoes are amazing, too."

Seeing my interest, Juliette generously explained the bread-making process to me and how she also had to look after the starter.

"Much like a child," she laughed merrily. "I need to keep it cool, then feed it flour and water every second day. If you don't look after it, then it dies. I've taken to calling it George, especially since I spend so much time with him ... it."

With the surplus of fruit lately, Juliette had been experimenting with different sourdough fruit bread:

figs, dried apricots, dried raisins, even honey, and oat bread. Great for breakfast, but also for using up the excess fruit, so I promised to collect the overripe fruit and drying them for her in the sun. With limited electricity and no dehydrator, the sun was the best drying agent we had. It was simple enough—laying them out on lined trays. Keeping the birds away was the most challenging part, although we had few bird colonies here. Most bird species had likely flown away as the dome was put in place and had perished. Those that had been caught under the dome and survived were now breeding. A memory flitted across my mind of when we first arrived on August, the birds flying into the dome, again and again, trying to escape. It had been a gut-wrenching sight and had made me feel even more trapped in those early days.

"What about some sultanas?" she asked me, pulling me from my melancholic thoughts as she ran her fingers through the figs, chopping them into meaty chunks ready for adding to the dough. "Can you make sultanas too?"

"You would prefer raisins," I advised.

"Why? Aren't sultanas just a different type of grape?"

I sighed inwardly, not wanting to make her feel bad. Very few people understood how foods were processed.

"Sultanas are grapes, sure enough," I admitted. "It is how they are preserved that is different. Sultanas are steeped in water, vegetable oil, and acid, specifically potassium carbonate to dry. Raisins are naturally dried."

"Potassium carbonate? That doesn't sound good."

"To be truthful, it is a type of salt, and while we used it in foods as an acidity regulator, it is also used in the production of soap and glass. Personally, I would stick with raisins."

"Done," she said. "Raisins it is. Can you get me some more figs though or perhaps apricots? They hold up well in the bread and give it a lovely texture. Any spices too?"

Promising to deliver on this request, I headed home, Jam appearing at my feet, squawking for some bread.

"Well, hello there!" I said, delighted to see her. I hadn't seen Jam in the days since I had been back.

Stooping to stroke her silky back, I realized she was plumper now.

"Little Miss Fat-Guts. Been on a mouse binge, have we?" I teased.

Oblivious to my taunting, Jam rubbed up against me, and I picked her up with one hand, holding the loaf at arm's length, struggling a little to balance both. Held against my chest, she rubbed her head under my chin, head-butting me for attention.

"Oh." The penny dropped as my fingers closed around her swollen belly. Her stomach was enormous, and her nipples distended. I could distinctly feel the multiple lumps in her belly.

"Well, missy, it appears congratulations are in order." As the words left my mouth, I realized there must be a male wildcat in the vicinity.

"Hmm... you aren't alone, then?" I asked her as I put her down again. It was too difficult to juggle her and the bread. She looked up into my eyes and made a loud *purrp* sound. I felt more than a little foolish talking to a cat in public.

"Well, of course you aren't. You were a kitten when I found you, and the community had been here for a few years. You must have had parents, likely siblings, too. I never really thought about it, but there must be a family of wildcats out there. Now then, what are we going to do with you?"

Jam followed me home. Placing the fresh loaf on the table, Lae walked into the room.

"Oh, that smells divine! Thanks for... *There* you are, you little monster!" she scolded Jam like a naughty child as she caught her lurking at my feet. "I have been looking for you for *weeks*! It devastated me thinking something had happened to you!"

"Something has," I said dryly, picking Jam up and flipping her over so Lae could see the enormous belly.

"Oh."

"Oh, indeed. Someone is not alone, although this is probably a good thing. Scottish Wildcats are endangered. Hang on. That is a stupid thought. I guess most animals are endangered or extinct now."

"I suppose they are. It is sad to think about it. Koalas. Pandas. Meerkats. Are they all extinct, do you think?"

"I don't know," I responded. "Anything under a domed community is likely okay. But everything else is likely extinct."

"When I used to go to the library in Glasgow, I had a favorite book about animals. I loved the koalas and wombats best. I always wanted to hold a koala in real life. Now I never will." Lae looked dreamy, yet sad. "What is a group of koalas called, anyway?" Lae asked curiously.

"I don't know. Maybe nothing. Koalas rarely move around in groups, rather solitary animals, koalas.

It is puffins I always wanted to see. I do hope they aren't extinct."

Jam, hungry and bored with the small talk, jumped up onto the table.

"Oh no, you don't," Lae scolded. "You are in enough trouble. Besides, I have told you a thousand times not to jump on the table!"

"Did she keep you company while I was away?"

"She did for the first two months. Then she started staying away for a few nights at a time. She disappeared maybe six weeks ago. I wasted days hunting for her, but she was nowhere to be found. I thought she was lost, had run away, or ... something had happened to her."

"Well, she seems happy enough now, though very pregnant. I wonder how long cats are pregnant for?"

About sixty days, we learned later that day from Isla, who confirmed that not only was Jam pregnant, she was due any day.

"She is having quite a few," said Isla as she palpated the enormous belly. Jam didn't seem to mind, purring away at all the attention. I suspected Isla too was grateful for the break from Niamh and Iona, the latter being only a few months old. We sometimes heard Isla soothing her in the middle of the night.

"What can we do for her?"

"Let her nest. It is what she will want to do. Give her a box and some old blankets, also a small litter tray with some sand in it. Place her food as far away from the litter tray as you can, but in sight of the nesting box. She won't leave her kittens for the first few weeks. After that, they are pretty much independent, and she will get back to her own life."

Thanking Isla as she left and making plans to catch up over dinner, we busied ourselves making a nest for Jam. Jam actively supervised the activities and climbed into the box, kneading the blue wool blanket.

"What a fantastic welcome home present. Kittens!" Lae laughed.

"*You* will always be my favorite kitten," I murmured to Lae as I pulled her close, my arms around her tiny waist and nuzzling her neck as we watched Jam moving the blankets around in the box to suit herself.

CHAPTER 5

"**DIDN'T YOU HAVE MICE** on August?" Lae asked me, hearing me muttering unrepeatable curses under my breath. For the third morning in a row, I had awoken to find mice droppings on the kitchen bench, and I was sick of it. With Jam out of action, there was nothing to slow the invasion of rodents.

"No. And a bloody good thing it was, too."

"I would have thought mice were everywhere. I mean, they are, aren't they?"

Thinking about that for a moment, I replied, "The difference, I guess, is that this was a community before. Most of the larger birds of prey would have had time to fly off, so the mice populations here have flourished. On August, it wasn't a community before, so there were only native species, and the ones we deliberately introduced like cows, chickens, and bees. There was a native mouse, kind of like an antechinus. Only it probably wasn't."

"An anti ... what?"

"*An-tee-kye-nus*. I sounded the word out slowly. To look at, it is like a cross between a mouse and a shrew.

But it was a marsupial, with a pouch, you know. Like kangaroos and koalas. Odd species. The males usually die after mating."

"Poor things."

"Well, not really. Mating can last up to twelve hours in some species, so they really do shag to death. Not a bad way to go, all things considered."

Lae giggled as I continued. "But antechinus were native to Australia. On August, there were several types of small rodent-looking creatures, but you rarely saw them. They seldom invaded our homes or sheds, unlike here."

Three nights later, we heard Jam yowling. Lae shot out of bed, barely waiting for me. "Should we get Isla?"

"I think so. We don't want to lose Jam or the kittens."

I dashed next door to get Isla while Lae made tea and got some water for Jam. Despite being the middle of the night, a dim light was on. Peering into the living room window, I saw Isla awake, feeding Iona.

"I'll come," she mouthed over the tiny head nodding off in her arms.

Returning to our house, I dropped to my knees to assist. Not that I had any idea how. Jam wouldn't touch the water, despite her tongue hanging out, panting.

Isla let herself in and kneeled beside the box, crooning encouragingly to Jam.

"Good girl. Aren't you beautiful?" she murmured, feeling Jam's belly. After some time, she looked up at us and smiled. "She is fine. But I will stay anyway."

Within an hour, three small furry bundles were lined up beside her, feeding. With closed eyes and folded ears, they were tiny. Jam had shown that she knew what to do, breaking each kitten out of its amniotic sac and chewing off the umbilical cord. There seemed to be a break in the proceedings now.

"Is that it?" Lae asked Isla worriedly.

"I don't think so. Cats usually have one at a time, and I am fairly sure she has more to come." Isla stroked Jam's belly in a downward motion. "No, there are a few more. I don't think she needs any help."

By dawn, Jam had given birth to eight tiny, spotted wildcat kittens. Four boys and four girls.

"What are we going to do with them all?" I asked Isla.

Isla frowned. "I will need to discuss with the other vets, but we may need to neuter some of them to ensure they don't interbreed. That could be bad for the bloodlines. We need to ensure that future generations come from as wide a gene pool as possible."

The selection of animals for breeding was a little out of my area of expertise, so I nodded but didn't ask for more information, hoping that they could soon help control our rodent problem.

Over the next few weeks, the kittens grew at an astonishing rate. Within a fortnight, they were moving around independently, their eyes and ears open. As active as Jam herself was in those first few weeks after she had found me in the cave, she surprised us, proving herself a relaxed mother, allowing her active offspring to clamber all over her, only occasionally batting one of them with a soft paw when they crossed the line between playfulness and bad manners. Soon they were all over the house, underfoot, into cupboards, and generally getting into mischief.

Isla dropped by daily to check them over, but it was clear she just wanted a cuddle. It felt like everyone in the village came by for their daily cuddle, commenting on how they were growing. Jam didn't appear to mind the steady stream of visitors wanting to pat her and cuddle her kittens. In fact, she plainly enjoyed the attention.

"Let's hope she doesn't make a habit of this." I grimaced to Laetitia one morning after the third group of visitors had left, and we still hadn't finished breakfast. "The village will be teeming with kittens."

"They can't be far away from being re-homed," she said kindly, looking me in the eye, recognizing the actual issue but kind enough not to state it out loud. "Let's ask Isla."

At eleven weeks old, Jam's kittens were widely spread across the community. Three went to crofters, one to Aidan, who now lived alone, north of the wheat fields where he grew wheat and operated the mill. He named her Gussie, short for Kingussie, where he was from originally. He was besotted with his kitten from the start, and she followed him everywhere: to tend the fields, to the greenhouse, to speak with me.

"I think she probably sleeps on his bed too!" Lae giggled one day, watching Aidan walk down the main road past the school, Gussie trotting along merrily behind him.

"Hypocrite! Jam sleeps with us!"

"Goodness, she is a nuisance. It is like she has a beacon for standing with all her weight on a single paw in the most uncomfortable place possible."

The remaining four kittens stayed in Garynahine with four families chosen to care for them. These were the four that were desexed to prevent in-breeding. No one really minded. Loyal and playful, they were also excellent hunters, a fact I was eminently grateful for, as they made quick work of the mouse infestation. The cats were great fun, pouncing on people as they walked past, prowling the sheds for prey. I even caught one recalcitrant kitten hanging from a neighbor's washing line one day, swinging from the corner of a bedsheet as it dried, dragging it into the dirt. Trying not to laugh at the kitten, who was having a world of fun, I left the scene of the crime quickly. I did not need to be blamed by association, even though I equally could not bring myself to extricate the cat.

It didn't feel possible that it had only been eighteen months since I had first arrived here, wet and bedraggled, distressed and alone. People say time heals all wounds. I am not sure that is true. While I didn't think I would ever get over losing Freyja and forget the agony of that time, I had learned to compartmentalize that chapter of my life and move on.

Lae and I had married at the winter solstice, marking the first anniversary of our meeting, and we were now expecting our own little person. I still couldn't believe Lae had taken me into her home in that knowing way of hers, just accepted me without question. We had grown to become friends, caring deeply for each other. Now we were that and more. Best friends, yes. Lovers, too. But beyond that, we were bonded, connected in a way I could not describe. There was that sense of utter contentment from knowing that I was complete, that someone always had my back.

She had asked me, just once, what happened on my trip back to August—about my journey back here to her. The day after I returned, she sat me down after breakfast. She ordered me to tell her everything, to leave nothing out. I had been immensely shy about telling her at first. She did not change expression or interrupt to ask questions, which made the story-telling easier. After a somewhat stilted start, my story flowed. Beginning with the passage through the portal, as awful as I recalled, I described the gut-wrenching, crippling frustration to find Freyja not there. Despite my happiness at seeing Di, Jamie, and Jacinda, my feelings of being isolated and alone, alienated from the community again, and my regret for leaving her. Learning about Freyja's relationship with Angus and her pregnancy. The overwhelming feeling of betrayal. Then my journey to New Zealand with Hugh, realizing that there was no life, that the world outside had perished.

I talked about Hugh taking his own life, and the memories of Sam that event had evoked, leading to me sinking into a deep depression, exacerbated by my longing for her. Being adrift, physically and emotionally, and my eventual arrival at the community on Bellcamp. I told her about Callie, Tadhg, and Blake, and the equinox passage to Newgrange. The night I had spent at Kevin's house, his theories of other sites, even his thoughts about the double spiral.

The long, painful boat trip with Eoghan followed by the day spent in the cave, so near to her and yet not *here*. My fears—had she met someone else? My anger—at Freyja, at myself. The path to forgiveness. Then, finally, the closure of that chapter of my life.

Laetitia sat silently, no expression on her calm face. When I reached the part about Hugh, I choked, not being able to go on. She placed her small hand on mine and nodded ever so slightly. A sign that I was to continue. She was here now. She made no movement when I told her about Freyja not being there, that my mission had not been fulfilled.

As I spoke, I realized the journey had been about seeking closure. Either reconciling with Freyja or ending it but moving on either way. The time I had spent here before had been necessary for healing, but in many ways, it had been a holding pattern, showing me options and alternatives. Being more intuitive, Lae had likely always known. Returning to August was a journey I knew I needed to take. I didn't understand *why*. But now, we both knew that I had done my best to reconcile my past, close the chapter on my previous life, and move forward. Create a new life here— with her. Despite not seeing Freyja, I had achieved this; I felt complete. The old was resolved. New experiences, opportunities lay ahead of me, ahead of us. Once again, I was happy and fulfilled.

CHAPTER 6

FEELING AS LIGHT AS a feather, I was chasing the wind. That feeling of being utterly free uplifted me—free of all restraints, from work, from any form of commitment. I was completely engulfed in that sense of utter exhilaration that comes with skiing at immense speed down a mountain firmly packed with freshly groomed snow. Every molecule of my being was poised, tensed, carving turns on a wide smooth piste, the edges of my skis rolling effortlessly. The wind rushed past my ears in a muffled roar. I watched the neat rows of evergreen trees whizz by, their boughs laden with snow, marking the edges of the run, looking like perfect rows of snow-capped Christmas trees. There was not a soul in sight as I tilted my face toward the sun, basking in the blue-bird day, tingling with energy. Cranking my legs into an epic turn, the snow spraying in a perfect arc from my outside edges, my arm vibrated slightly. Planting my pole more decisively, I drove my ski tips into the next turn, forcing them down the mountainside.

"Cam!" I could hear the voice, far off, but insistent. I looked around, confused, but there was no one on the slope with me. The sun reflected off the crystals, sparkling. It was almost blinding as I tracked my path down the hill. My arm was shaking again, more firmly this time.

"Cam!"

Jolting awake, I came to myself to find Lae doubled over in pain.

"Are you okay?"

"It's ... time," Lae panted. "Baby ... coming."

Falling out of bed, not even remotely awake, I hit the floor with a thud. Jam, who had been asleep on my feet, was sent flying with an indignant yowl. She had enjoyed the past months of being an only cat again and was blatantly unimpressed at this midnight caper, sauntering off into the kitchen with her tail held high in the air. By well-established community arrangement, I would call for our neighbor, and they would fetch the on-duty doctor. Scrabbling around in the dark for my jacket, I tripped over my boots and lay face down on the bedroom floor, recovering my wits as the darkness slowly gave way to shadowed shapes of furniture.

Great bloody help you are, Mackintosh, I thought as I levered my weight onto my hands to get up. Reassuring Lae that I was okay, I bolted out the kitchen door.

Fraser, Isla, and their daughters still lived next door, a reality I was eminently grateful for. With no concept of the time, I banged quietly, not wanting to wake the girls. After a few minutes of shivering outside in the cold, listening to the wind turbines drone far off in the distance, I pounded harder, spurred into action after hearing Lae's cries pierce the night. Her moans penetrated my heart, and I knocked loudly, no longer fearful of waking anyone. I had done this to her. *If she suffers...* I choked the thought off. I didn't want to think about that. We had doctors here, and good ones, although part of me fervently wished it was Sorcha here delivering my baby. *No. Now is not the time for that.* Blocking that out and refocusing my efforts, I banged harder on the door.

Isla finally answered the door, looking exhausted and disheveled. As soon as her eyes adjusted and she saw it was me, she spoke, her low husky voice over-shadowed by the piercing cry of pain emanating from our adjacent house. She pushed me toward home and said, "I'll send Fraser." I had performed the same community service for several neighbors in the past year: babies, overnight emergencies. We all knew exactly what to do.

Racing home, my eyes growing accustomed to the dark, I found Lae on the bedroom floor, on her hands and knees, a puddle glistening beside the bed. The membranes had ruptured. The baby was on its way. There was no turning back now, although part of me secretly wished we could.

Turning on the lamps, I sat behind her, encouraging her to lean back into me, to support her. She was tense and struggling. *She is so tiny. How on earth is she going to do this? Please, please let her be okay,* I begged silently to the universe. *She is everything to me. Please don't let her die.*

The next wracking moan of pain sliced me to the core.

"How can I help?" I pleaded as she cried aloud. Wishing fervently that we were back in the hospitals of home with sterile equipment and pain relief on tap, I glanced around the room, taking in the simple, rustic nature of it. Rarely did I genuinely believe that we had been better off "before" the pandemic, but at times like this, I wished we had more of the resources from the old world. The reassurance that came with a team of professionals, highly skilled and in a hygienic environment, was immeasurable. While logically I knew women had been giving birth since the dawn of time, it was the unknowns, the risks, that terrified me. Even in our time, women died in childbirth, especially in third world countries.

Within seconds, the contraction had passed, leaving Lae panting.

"Water," she pleaded, struggling to catch her breath. Bolting to the kitchen, I grabbed a jug of water, two cups, a towel, and after a second's consideration, the pillows from the bed, setting them up against the wooden foot of the bed to support us both. I sat behind her and laid her back into my arms, just in time for the next wave. That was quick. A vague memory stirred. *The closer the contractions, the sooner the birth. That is right, isn't it?*

I could feel the tension in her, the agony of it. She was splitting; I knew I was going to lose her. Then, as quickly as it hit, the contraction passed, leaving her sweating, exhausted, and limp.

The kitchen door burst open, and I heard Fraser's voice calling my name up the hallway.

"In here," I called and looked up to see Fraser and Hamish coming through the doorway.

Hamish swung into action, giving directions with such an assured air that I felt instant relief. Having someone assume charge of a tense situation made it more tolerable. As scared as I was for Lae, I was in awe of Hamish and his manner, his clipped instructions to

Fraser to fetch him items, his soothing words to Lae, and a few reassuring smiles at me.

Several tense hours later, I held my son in my arms, unable to take my eyes from him. Lae was exhausted, hair drenched in sweat, but with a sense of accomplishment and sheer bliss on her face as she watched me like a hawk as I held our child. Hamish lifted her effortlessly into bed and checked her over as I held the baby, speechless at the miracle I had just witnessed. Women were built to do this, I knew, but when it is your own child, it is entirely different. It is … magical. Watching as an innocuous bump transform into a living, breathing *person* was something quite indescribable.

Looking down at him, tiny and pink in the soft white wool blanket Lae had knitted for him, I couldn't wipe the smile from my face. Hamish touched my arm, and I looked up, the trance broken.

"She can feed him now."

Gingerly, I took the few steps across the room, terrified I would drop the most precious bundle I had ever been entrusted to carry. Sitting up in our bed, propped up with pillows, Lae held her arms open, ready to accept him. The purity of it, that sense of how natural she looked gazing down at our baby, took my breath away. I watched in awe as he fed for the first time. Hamish and Fraser quietly wished me well and left, slipping away into the early hours of dawn. They had arrived to find us as a couple. They had left us as a family.

CHAPTER 7

LIKE ALL EXPECTANT COUPLES, we had discussed names; for months, it had dominated our conversations. Despite having an ultrasound machine in the clinic, Lae wanted a surprise. I would have preferred to know. It was a blob. At least with an identified gender, it would have felt more real to me. I could be emotionally prepared. I believed technology was valuable—if it was there, then use it! We could plan, get organized. Not in a rushing out and buying everything in blue kind of way. There was a thriving community here in recycled children's clothing, toys, and other items like cots. No one cared about colors; most items here were naturally colored sourced from sheep and alpaca wool. Clothing dyes were not readily available because of the large volume of water coloring fabric required. Lae had insisted that all would be well, and I had relented.

We had agreed upon a shortlist of names, both boys and girls. But we both wanted to meet our little person before we completed anything. Peering down at the tiny, squished face in Lae's arms, I said, "I don't think he looks like an Edward … or an Eddie." Edward was my father's name. Lae knew I wanted to honor my parents, especially now that they would never meet their only grandchild.

"What about Douglas?" Lae asked, breaking the stillness. "Good strong Scots name that one, and there aren't many here."

Shuddering, I emphatically replied, "*No!*"

Lae glanced up from the baby, sleeping calmly in her arms, surprised at the force of my refusal, and raised her eyebrows enquiringly. Reluctantly, I felt the need to explain.

"One of Dad's closest work colleagues had been an older man with two sons, and we were forced to socialize with them occasionally. Not often but regularly enough. Kenneth, the older one, was quiet and studious. Well-mannered and reserved, you hardly noticed he was there. He sat quietly through conversations or often brought a book and would sit alone, reading. Douglas, though, a chubby little fellow, was a complete and utter drama queen. He strongly resembled a miniature blonde Michelin man. A feature significantly enhanced when he was dressed in white, which distinctly accentuated his little man boobs and belly rolls. God, he used to squeal like a stuck pig when he didn't get his own way. All I ever heard was him grizzling that it wasn't fair, like he was constipated and generally going through life complaining he was hard done by. His little hands would ball into fists at his side, and his shoulders would raise in anger. I have never seen a face go from freckled white to flaming red in a split second like Dougie's did as he screamed to get his way.

"Conversely, he could be a charming, social, and entertaining child with a flair for the dramatic, but it was like flicking an invisible switch, and he morphed into an insufferable pain in the ass. As a result, Sorcha and I did everything possible to avoid him. Dougie was also food motivated, meaning that you could get him to do most things by offering him food as a reward. A dangerous combination that—whiny and greedy," I concluded.

Lae was trying desperately hard to stifle her laughter, lest she wake the baby.

"Once, while watching him have a tantrum, screaming, 'You hurt me!' at me when I had accidentally bumped him, as I carried a tray of food, I contemplated which had come first. Had his parents despaired of his grizzling and fed him to shut him up, making him obsess over food? Or had he always been a gut, and the grizzling had started when he wasn't fed fast enough? Like the kid in McDonald's who threw a public tantrum having to wait for his chicken nuggets. He was as painful a kid as could be imagined, and Sorcha and I hated having them over, especially as we needed to be polite to maintain Dad's work reputation. 'Chungus' Sorcha called him behind his back. One time I could tell Mum was fighting to restrain herself when the kid screeched that his portion of ice cream was smaller than mine, smiling grimly as she rapidly tried to redress the situation to avoid him having a bigger meltdown. We all knew from experience that there was no point in trying to reason with him when he was in a mood—the fastest way out of the drama was to give in. But giving in was not in my mother's nature. I could tell it pained her to do it, and she did it under sufferance."

Lae laughed out loud this time, then tensed as it hurt her so soon after birth.

"Maybe not Douglas then," she agreed. "But I think we should honor your father. What was your grandfather's name again?"

"Louis."

"Louis then. But I want to include winter, to remind me of that cold winter's night when we first met."

At that moment, my heart filled with love for them both, I would have agreed to anything.

"Louis Edward Winter Mackintosh, welcome to the world." Laetitia smiled down at our miracle.

CHAPTER 8

"WHY DO YOU WANT to go back to work so soon? Louis is only eight weeks old. Isn't it a little early?"

"I don't know," Lae paused. "I just know that I want to make a difference in my students' lives. I want to be that one teacher that inspired them to be the best they could be. My Mr. Long, you know, the one who set me off on my path—I will never forget him. He changed my life."

Not wanting to point out the obvious, there wasn't exactly a plethora of teachers here to compete with, I understood what she meant. Lae had told me about Mr. Long before. He was the teacher who encouraged her to apply for the scholarship that had ultimately shaped her life and determined her fate. I recognized that feeling. I had been lucky enough to have several inspirational teachers, amid a few rather average ones. But for me, the most memorable teacher was different. With a strong family unit and access to quality education, my teachers had not pulled me out of a life of poverty like Mr. Long had for Laetitia.

"The person who affected me the most was Miss Davey," I started, then paused. I wasn't sure this was a story I wanted to tell.

"Go on." Lae looked at me encouragingly.

Reluctantly, I continued, "Miss Davey. She was my teacher in Grade 2. Well, she started as my teacher, then she got sick, so we had a series of horrible emergency teachers after that. What began as a wonderful year turned into an awful one. She was young and beautiful ... and she had leukemia. She went away after the first term holidays, and ... never came back. We were told that she was having chemotherapy. I was seven. I had no idea what cancer meant except that when grown-ups spoke about it, it was in hushed tones like it was something awful, something to be feared. It terrified me, like it was a monster that hid in the dark. I adored her, and then ... she wasn't there. One day, much later in the year, she came back to visit. She sat in the schoolyard at lunchtime on a wooden bench seat next to the flagpole alongside the basketball court. Kids were going up and saying hello throughout lunch, but I was afraid. Some kids were sitting with her, talking to her. I had overheard my Mum say to a friend that she had lost her hair, and I could see from across the yard that she was wearing a brightly colored scarf. She used to have gorgeous, long, brown, curly hair, but now she wore a scarf tied around her head. I was desperate to say hello, but I was so scared. Scared of her being bald, afraid of the illness, fearful of ... catching it, I guess. Maybe just afraid of who she was now. Just ... scared. I just lurked at the far side of the basketball court the entire lunch break. She saw me and waved, but I looked away, frightened, pretending I hadn't seen her. I had just about plucked up the courage to go over to her when the music started, and I had to line up to go back to class. I never got to say hello, or … goodbye, as it turns out. She … died … early the following year. I never got to say thank you. Thank you for being a wonderful teacher. Thank you for caring about me. She was so kind and creative, very artistic, I remember. She did these fabulous, funny little caricature drawings and made personalized birthday cards; all the kids adored her.

"I lost a tooth at school once, and she made me this gorgeous little cardboard box for the tooth fairy. I kept it for years until it fell apart. I used it every time a tooth fell out—it was like each time I used it; it allowed me to think of her and have that one happy memory of her making me feel special."

Shifting on the couch, my stomach churned from the unhappy memory. Lae put her spare hand on my leg.

"I was a painfully shy kid, and I didn't have many friends. I didn't know how to play in a group. The kids on my table took turns to pick on Cam. There were four to six kids per table in our classroom, and I was quiet, so I usually got seated with the naughty kids. When we had emergency teachers, that was the worst. They just didn't care. It was babysitting for them. But Miss Davey looked out for me. I felt like she cared about what happened to me. Even now, so many years later, I remember her and the guilt I still feel at not going up to speak to her when I had the chance. For the past twenty years, I have regretted that day and not being brave enough to speak to her."

"You were seven! She would have known how you felt."

"Maybe. Possibly. But even now, I *still* feel awful about it. I stood there on the other side of the basketball court, just skulking. Watching. I desperately wanted to say hello, but something petrified me. She looked different. Her face was bloated and pale. Then ... the chance was gone. I told myself that ... it would be okay. When she visited the next time, I would be brave and go over to say hello. But that is the kicker. I never got another chance. I never saw her again. She died, and I never got to tell her how much she meant to me. I had nightmares for months about how she must have looked when she died, seeing her pale and bloated. My mum went to her funeral. Lots of the parents did. But I wasn't allowed to go. I never got that closure."

Lae dropped her head into the cavity between my neck and chest. Her tiny head fit there so neatly, like it was carved out just for her. "What would you have told her? If she was here, now. What would you say?"

Pausing, I thought about her. A million words washed through my mind—all the phrases that could describe my lifelong feelings of regret, gratitude, sorrow. Finally, I picked two.

"Thank you. Just ... thank you. Thank you for being someone who made a difference in my life, even if it was for such a short time. Thank you for believing in me at a time when I didn't believe in myself. For encouraging me to be the best person I could be. And ... I'm sorry. I am so, so sorry that I didn't pluck up the courage that day to say hello. I will forever regret that."

"So, say it now. It isn't for her, not now. It is for *you*."

I closed my eyes, conjured up her image, and silently said, *Thank you. Sorry. Goodbye.* When I was finished, all the breath left me, leaving me feeling like a deflated balloon.

I lay on the sofa, my longer legs hanging over the armrest, and Lae curled up in front of me like a kitten. After a long period of silence, she asked, "What do *you* want to be remembered for?"

Never having thought about that concept, I considered as I looked over at Louis, swaddled up tight in his cot across the room.

"I think... I think I would like to be remembered as someone who made a difference. Made the world a slightly better place. Not just someone's husband, friend, and father, but someone who made people's lives just a little better. I'm just not sure how yet."

"If that is your goal, then I think you have already done that," Lae said with conviction.

"How?"

Lae rolled over to face me, snuggling against me. "Seriously? You traveled here from another place. You weren't the first traveler, but you were the one who *stayed*. The winters before you came, we survived, not lived. I mean, we ate, of course, it kept us alive, but that was all that could be said for it: potatoes, neeps, porridge. Stew, if the hunters had been successful. Now we have a veritable cornucopia of different foods, amazing things like berries, citrus, nuts, and tropical fruits. And it is all because of you. We are so much healthier for this. But it is more than the variety you introduced. Meals have taken on a whole new meaning now. People eat to *enjoy* food. Families welcome others into their homes to share meals. It is a *celebration*. We never did that before you came. We had celebrations, but they didn't involve food. Now, it feels like our celebrations all involve a feast.

Not to demean Fraser and his team. They fed us. No one was at risk of starvation, but now we have a wide variety of food, and it has changed the way we lived. *You* did that."

Blushing, I smiled at her enthusiasm.

"Because of you, we now have a mode of transport that isn't horseback. Perhaps the original planners of Garynahine didn't think of it. Maybe they didn't think we would want to spread out. But because of you, each home now has a bike, many with trailers for children. We can get around far more easily."

"I didn't bring them. We found them."

"But as silly as it sounds, it never occurred to anyone. Two trips to Stornoway, three bike shops, and now we are all so much freer. We can visit people in a fraction of the time. It has helped us be better connected."

"It isn't exactly curing cancer, is it? Besides, I didn't mean to come..."

"... well, I, for one, am delighted you did," Lae finished as she rolled off the couch to pick up a grizzling, hungry Louis.

"He is the most precious gift." I watched her as she cradled our son, preparing to feed him. "One I don't think I have adequately thanked you for."

Lae looked up, surprised. "You gave him to me, too. I guess he is a mutual gift. You've got that pensive look about you. You are thinking of your parents, no?"

"I am," I admitted. "I wish so much that they could have met him and you."

"Tell me about them."

Laetitia was a wonderful audience, listening without interrupting, able to make encouraging facial expressions. I always knew that she was enthralled by whatever I was telling her. With no experience of a traditional family, she regularly asked about mine and seemed to never tire of my stories, even though I knew she must have heard them all a thousand times. I described my father: tall and dark, large in build, but quiet, and my mother: small and fiery, redheaded to match her quick wit and fiery temper. Together, a team. Lae rarely spoke about her own emotionally absent mother. From what little she had said, I realized it was miraculous that Lae had even survived her childhood, riddled with neglect. Each time she questioned me about my family, I recognized she was trying to learn, in an academic sense, what it was like to *be* a mother, to live in a family—a concept as alien to her as being a dog would be to me.

"You are an amazing mother," I finished softly, knowing what she was actually asking.

"Am I?" she asked wistfully. "I just feel like I don't know *how*."

"Well, you are doing a damned fine job of it so far."

After some negotiation with the community, Lae returned to work ten weeks after Louis was born. The building team reconfigured the schoolhouse to have a small playroom with a cot for Louis, just off the primary classroom. After a few months of home-schooling, all the parents on Lewis were thrilled to have Laetitia back, even for short days. Trying to manage their own children while simultaneously tending animals, crops, or working jobs was hard, and more than one parent told me she should be paid for her work as a teacher. Smiling, I nodded in agreement, knowing that Lae adored her work and her students. She would never think of her role as more important than that of others.

Dropping by with some lunch one day, I found her, Louis in a sling across her front, reading aloud to a group of enthralled students. Scottish history, I soon discovered. She was telling them about the battle of Culloden in April 1746, the last battle of the Jacobite Uprising known as the '45. Her students were agape at the vivid description of the short, yet fierce battle, the boggy marsh across which the Scots charged the English cannons at Culloden field, and the smell of muskets firing. A natural storyteller, she mesmerized the children. She glanced up and registered my presence but didn't stop speaking. Smiling at her from the doorway, but not wanting to interrupt, I held the sandwich and apple aloft, then placed it on a table just inside the entrance and quietly tiptoed away before any of the students saw me.

Life was finally peaceful. It was everything I ever wanted: working in the gardens all day and coming home to my wife and son, having loyal friends and comfortable home. No stress of traffic, bills, or crime. Was it wrong to be almost *grateful* for the pandemic that had caused this? The pandemic that had killed my family but had also brought me here—to this place and these people—a place where I felt alive and valued in a way I had never felt before. Some days I felt overwhelmingly guilty for being so content, so utterly at peace. Was this just the nature of life—there could be no sunshine without shadow?

Laetitia was open in her feelings. Her life before moving here had been one of barely existing, whereas she was thriving here. My life back in Melbourne had been a happy one. My current life had come at significant personal cost: losing my parents, my sister, my home, friends, and everything I knew. This new life came with hardships. There were no cars, no shops, no holidays. We had limited access to the outside world, less technology, and less advanced medical care, and it felt constraining, limiting. People loved to talk to me as I had been outside, beyond the safety of the dome. They asked me again and again what it was like out *there*. Could we return one day? Or had the scientists who sealed us in here been right, and it would be at least two generations before the earth recovered? As an agriculturalist by training and now by choice, I often wondered how the earth would re-green itself. If all the plants and trees were dead, how would they reseed? Was this why we had been entrusted with the seed banks so that we could play a significant role in re-greening the planet?

Logically, it would never be the same. Many species of animal, mainly aquatic varieties, would have perished, never to be resurrected. Old-growth forests, rainforests, and thousands of varieties of plants were extinct. But while we were here, there was hope. We continued to live, to thrive, to grow plants and trees, to breed animals, and make the most of what we had.

CHAPTER 9

RUSHING FROM THE GREENHOUSE, the basket over my arm swinging precariously, I cursed myself. I was late delivering fruit to Juliette to use in her morning baking. She would wait for me, I knew, and I was cross at myself for letting her down and delaying breakfast for many. Louis had been screaming much of the night. Teething, Lae thought, although I had no way of knowing how she knew that. Our little man hadn't come with a manual.

We had finally fallen asleep, Louis firmly wedged between us, completely shattered, just before dawn. Forcing myself to spur up through my exhaustion, I could see the corner ahead, the turn from the path leading from the greenhouses to the bakery where Juliette would bake waiting for me. As I approached the intersection, I focused on my goal and slammed at full speed into a slight, balding, and bespectacled man who had the misfortune of turning up the path as I sprinted down. A dense hazelnut bush grew on the corner, shielding him from my view until it was far past the moment of impact. The man was significantly smaller than me, and my height advantage and increased speed had seen me stumble but hold my balance. By contrast, he had been ambling, his arms full of books and papers which flew everywhere as he fell, sprawling face down in a particularly muddy spot. The basket of apricots I had been carrying up ended with the impact. Apricots flew everywhere, splattering into the pathway and staining his books. Anger glowed on his reddening face, and I had a flashback of the first night I was with Freyja, knocking her flying in much the same way. Being familiar with everyone here, I was stunned for a moment, unable to place this man's face. Shaking myself out of my stupor, I picked up his mud-smeared glasses and offered a hand to help him up as I asked, "Are you alright? Ummm, have we met?"

"Nay," he snapped in a clipped, educated Edinburgh accent as he snatched his glasses and jerked his arm away. "Angus. You must be Campbell."

"Angus?" I crinkled my nose for a moment as my mind struggled to grasp from where I knew that common Scots name. There were a few men here named Angus, and it perplexed me. This man was a stranger, I was sure. All too slowly, the light globe illuminated.

Evidently, the look of puzzlement on my face had changed to one of disbelief as he retorted, "Aye, *that* Angus!"

My appraisal of this small, intellectual-looking man, more than ten years my senior, who smelled of stale coffee and fresh desperation, was not helped at all by the male pattern baldness, graying temples against his brown hair, and smeared glasses he now wore. He was not even remotely close to how I imagined him when I envisioned him in Freyja's embrace. Freyja was at least six inches taller. She would squash him like a bug. But plainly, she saw something in him, something she hadn't seen in me. Drawing myself up to my full height and towering over him, I tried to calm the stutter in my voice as I asked, "Is … is she with you?"

"Aye, she is." The worm might be half my size, but it was evident from the chilled tone and glare that he detested me. Nodding respectfully, I turned to leave. He called after me. "She'll want to talk with you."

Fuck. She would. Freyja didn't believe in keeping quiet for the sake of peace.

Leaving the squashed apricots in the path, I turned and walked away in the calmest, manliest manner I could muster, realizing that the cockroach was watching me go.

Advantaged with the length of my legs, I hit my stride and used the hillwalker's gait that my parents had taught me. Ascending the steep hillside, I was out of sight of the village within minutes. Without even realizing it initially, I recognized I was on the path to Jam's cave.

"Damn. Shit. Bugger. Fuuuuuuuuuuuuuccckk!" I bellowed to the surrounding silence.

Freyja is here. Laetitia is here. Laetitia and Louis are here. Fuck, fuck, fuck!!

Hang on. Reason took the upper hand as I caught my breath, slowing my stride. *Her lover, Angus, is here too. Their child is also here. How long has it been?* I tried to calculate but couldn't. My mind was racing. *Hang on, the baby, their baby. It must be born by now. I heard when I was on August Island, and that was ages ago. How long? Think, you fool! I returned here via Bellcamp and Newgrange, and it was several months until we married and Lae conceived. Louis is ten weeks old now, so Angus and Freyja's child should be nearly a year old. Okay. So, it might be alright. We can be civil to each other; we loved each other once. She moved on, and so have I. But why the bloody hell is she here, and why now?*

Ducking into the cave, I sat on the small ledge, panting as the thoughts steadily washed over me, unable to focus on any one notion in particular. *Why are they back? Why now? Thank goodness I saw him first and not her. Oh god, imagine if I ran into her first, and if I was with Lae. Oh, holy crap, Lae. Holy bloody fuck.*

With my bolting, Lae would likely have already heard of Freyja's arrival. Wife one and wife two. Bloody fucking hell. It was like being seated at a terrible dinner party and being surrounded by girlfriends past. *Shiiiiiit.*

As my heart stilled, my thoughts turned to my instinctive actions. *Why did I run? Why do I feel guilty? I have done nothing wrong. Freyja left, and I followed. She went again; I followed. I learned she was with someone else and pregnant.*

The anger was rising in me as I recalled that conversation with Heidi in our house on August. The home I had shared with my wife, Freyja. Remembering Heidi informing me Freyja was pregnant by another man, I punched the granite wall beside me. *Fuck.* My knuckles split and started oozing blood. I struck it again. And again. Wrapping my handkerchief around the bloody, bruised mess, I focused on the pain in my hand and not in my heart. She hadn't waited for me. She had come here, hooked up with someone else, and left.

Idiot. She didn't know you would follow, could follow. The reason in my mind soothed the raging beast. *She* was a world away and had no way to know if she would ever see you again.

She could have gone back through the portal, the niggling part of my mind taunted. *After all, you did. Obviously, she didn't think you were worth going back that way for. Why would she? She had met him by then. You can't compete with him and his superior intellect.*

The two competing voices in my head equally cajoled and taunted me.

With my head in my hands, I tried to focus. *Breathe. Think, Cam, think. Better to plan it and have it out in privacy than accidentally end up in a public scene that would be replayed and discussed throughout the community for months. Dinner. After dinner. She would be with him then. I can get her alone. And avoid Laetitia,* the niggling voice added with scorn.

Torturing myself for hours and waiting until dark, I steeled myself, left the cave, and made the short walk to the village. I knew which house was his. There were lights inside. Someone was home.

Knocking firmly on the door, he greeted me coldly, then stood and glared at me. He would not make this easy. Fine.

"I need to speak with Freyja," I asked in as civil a tone as I could manage without breaking his fucking glasses and bloodying his slightly dripping nose. This was the father of Freyja's child while we were still married. Damned if I would be pleasant to him. Friends, we would never be.

Angus turned from the doorway, grabbed a drab brown jacket from a hook on the wall, and left, muttering something about it being a pleasant night for a walk. If nothing else, he may have some sense of decency. He left the door open as he shoved past. Entering, I turned and bolted the door behind me. I would *not* be interrupted.

Taking two steps along the hallway, I turned into the room with the lights. Standing in the spartan lounge room, I waited. Framed, yellowed antique maps adorned the walls, and a worn black leather sofa was placed against one wall. I wiped a finger along the dusty coffee table surface. I knew no one lived here now, and no one had been in here since he had left. *Since they left,* I corrected myself. They had departed after living ... here. Together. The opposite wall was filled with floor-to-ceiling bookcases, laden with books. She would have heard the door, my voice. Like all homes here, the space was economically small. Standing awkwardly, I wasn't sure what to do.

Not yet invited to sit, I was uncomfortable doing so without permission in what had been their love nest. The house she had shared with *him* was one that I was unlikely to find any comfort in. Taking the single stride across the tiny room to the bookcase, I perused the titles. It was mostly academic texts, many leather-bound, some ancient and weathered. Running my finger along the spines, I stopped on one titled *A Statistical Examination of the Megalithic Sites in Britain* by A. Thom. A beautiful brown leather volume with gold embossing. In fine italic print, at the bottom of the spine, I noticed the year it was printed—1955. Pulling the book from its place, I opened it and read.

"You made me a promise. You gave up on me." The tone was angry, accusing.

Freyja was standing in the doorway, half in and half out of the room. Dressed in jeans and an emerald green top that highlighted her blonde hair and slim figure, she looked as beautiful as ever, but her rage was barely held in check.

"Sorry, what did you say? I thought you said I gave up on *you*. The way I hear it, you went there first. So, congratulations are in order? Girl or boy?" I responded, my voice low and restrained as I replaced the book on the shelf, a trifle firmer than necessary. If this was how it was going to be, it might be best not to have a weapon to hand. Freyja had hurled things at me when in a temper, and she had a good throwing arm.

She faced me full-on as she stepped entirely into the room. There was nowhere to hide from those beautiful emerald green eyes, her direct gaze now drilling deep into the marrow of my bones. Her eyes were blazing, her lips firmly pressed together, devoid of color, the tension in her high cheekbones evident. That stunning face that for so long had gazed at me with love was now filled with... what was it? Anger? Betrayal?

"Asshole!" she spat.

Wow. I flinched. That had descended rapidly. Just as I was conjuring the most hurtful insult I could muster, she hissed, "*I am not pregnant!*" with so much ferocity it forced me to sit down on the sofa. "I never have been." The rage in her was palpable, even from several meters away.

I was tightly coiled like a rattlesnake, ready to strike, but with those four words, all the venom in me dissolved.

"I'm sorry. *What* did you say?" The air and anger had dissipated with that single statement. All afternoon I had been rehearsing this conversation and the one to come later. In all the practice conversations I had held in my head, all the variations I had envisaged, never once did I imagine it would start with that.

"I have no child. I am not, and I never was *with* Angus."

"I'm sorry. *What*?" The magnitude of what I had been through over the past few years hit me like a cannonball to the pit of the stomach. I had followed her here, only to find her gone. I followed her back to August to find her gone again, but that time with another man. It had taken me a long time, but I was over her. I had moved on. I was happy. I had a family of my own. *Oh, holy fuck. Laetitia. What on earth do I tell Laetitia?*

Freyja sat down beside me on the two-seater sofa, a touch too close for comfort.

"Stop saying that!" she snapped in a tone that made it blatantly clear that she would rather tear my head off with her bare hands than have this conversation.

"Saying what?"

"Stop ... fucking ... saying ... *sorry!*" Absolute fury infused her words, making it hard for her to get them out. The ferocity was barely in check, her fists clenched by her side. I sat and stared at her, my mouth open in astonishment.

"What would you like me to say instead?"

After a moment, she managed in a slightly softer voice, but still edged with danger, "It isn't entirely your fault. She fooled us all."

"She?" I was beginning to feel like Cletus, the slack-jawed yokel struggling to catch up with the conversation.

"Heidi."

"Okay, you've lost me. I don't understand what she has to do with this."

"It was Heidi that told you I was pregnant and with Angus, wasn't it? Was anyone else around?"

"It was … and no, we were alone." I looked at her skeptically. "If what you are saying is true, why would she lie to me?"

"It *is* true. I *don't* lie!" The wrath was near the surface, and the volcano was close to erupting, daring me to argue further.

Recognizing this truth, I nodded. Freyja was not a liar. Freyja, realizing I would not fight with her, sighed, much of her heat dispersing.

"She isn't really Heidi."

"Okay, this is ridiculous. How is Heidi not Heidi? We lived with her for three frigging years."

"We did. Only *she* wasn't Heidi. Heidi was her younger sister, who *was* a vet student in Adelaide."

Seeing the incredulous look on my face, she held her hand up to prevent me from speaking.

"I'll tell you everything. But in my way."

I nodded agreement, stunned into silence anyway.

"The woman we knew as Heidi is named Lena. They were German, raised on a farm in the Adelaide Hills. She impersonated her sister, who was offered the place. The real Heidi passed all the tests, but Lena attended in her place. Lena had no formal training in veterinary science, and she was scared that would show up soon enough. She knew how to keep bees and chickens, so she took over those tasks. It made sense why she hated dealing with livestock."

Trying not to get caught up in memories of Fred and the marital bliss we had shared, I responded more gently, "I remember you mentioning once that Heidi was always missing when there was surgery or a birth to attend to."

"True. I don't know how I didn't see it earlier."

"You had no reason to suspect anything. We were all chosen. It wasn't our place to assess her skills. Assuming what you are saying is true, and I do..." I added hurriedly, watching the color rise in Freyja's face, "how did she fool everyone? We all went through the same selection process."

"The real Heidi, her sister, I mean, went through the tests and was chosen. Then she went home to tell her family, as we all did. This is where it is a bit vague. She ... Lena, that is, says that she took her place. In the madness of going through quarantine, getting out here, apparently, no one checked."

I wrinkled my nose, trying to remember that time over four years ago.

"They checked my ID. I am certain of that. They interviewed me too."

"Same. But evidently, she looked enough like her sister to pass as her. Katrin and I looked very alike. She used my ID to get into clubs underage. As for the interview, I don't know about you, but mine was more about, did I know what I was getting into. Once I had convinced them yes, it was about learning and training. After the initial testing period, there were no more medical tests or anything like that. I guess anyone could have passed that part."

Nodding slowly in agreement, I added, "But what a risk to take. She was clearly desperate. So, what happened to the sister?"

"Therein lies the mystery. All Lena says is swapped places, but with what we now know, we are not convinced. There is reasonable suspicion, but no hard evidence, that she killed her sister to take her place. Now that we know she poisoned you, we know she has homicidal tendencies and..."

"She ... *what*?" The shocks were coming hard and fast. I wasn't sure I could take much more.

"I was getting to that bit. It seems that Heidi, Lena, had a ... thing ... for me." Freyja blushed, the pink spreading across her glorious, tanned face. The most beautiful sight, and I remembered in a flood of longing how deeply I had loved her.

"She thought with you out of the way that she was in with a chance. I had no idea, truly."

I didn't know how to respond, so I remained silent.

"Then," Freyja continued, "when I disappeared, she tried to spread rumors that you had killed me to whip up a frenzy and have the community... I don't know. Lock you up? Banish you?"

"She succeeded there," I responded dryly. "Without doubt, that was the worst period of my life."

Freyja paused. "After I ... disappeared, initially she thought you had killed me. But she said she watched you closely and realized that you were truly heartbroken. I am sorry about that," Freyja whispered. "It was genuinely an accident. Me going, that is. I didn't mean to leave ... you."

Placing my hand on hers, I breathed more easily than I had all day. "I know. Go on."

"She watched you, especially when you didn't know she was. After a few weeks, she was convinced you hadn't hurt me. She said you roamed the hills day and night searching like a raving madman, filthy and your clothes in tatters."

I grimaced at the description but said nothing.

"She knew that if you had done me in, you would only pretend to search when you thought people were watching. Instead, she said you didn't eat or sleep and spent all your time looking for me. At first, she thought that was enough, but soon she realized that if I came back, she still had the same problem. You. So, she set about solving that problem. Rather than do it herself, she was clever. Malicious. Death by proxy. She spread little pieces of gossip that you hurt me. Nothing so overt, of course, just a story here or there that I had bruises on my arms from where you had grabbed me. That we had argued, and I had confided in her. That I feared you. That I was upset at not having a ... baby."

Her face contorted as she said this. Unmistakably, this topic was still raw. *Perhaps she heard about Louis?*

"Enough to sow the seed of doubt, anyway. I gather people distanced themselves from you?"

I nodded, recalling that awful time. "They did."

"Then, *you* disappeared. She told me she thought you had killed yourself."

Inhaling deeply, I confessed for the first time. "I tried to. That was why I was in the caves that night on the solstice. I couldn't bear life without you. They ostracized me. I was so completely and utterly alone. Trapped in that hell, unable to escape. You had gone, and everyone thought I had killed you. Eventually, I couldn't bear it anymore and..."

"Ahh. That makes sense. I wondered. Anyway, after you disappeared, Lena thought it was all neatly tied up with a bow. She thought I might have found a way out of the dome to go exploring the outer islands. She believed you had taken your own life out of despair. But then I came back, with Angus, looking for you."

"That isn't what she told me," I mumbled miserably, feeling sick knowing that she had deceived me.

"I know."

We sat and looked at each other in silence for the longest time. A year and a half we had spent together in a blissfully happy period of my life. But then it had been ripped away from me, from us. Heidi, and fate, had kept us apart ever since.

"Why didn't you choose Angus?" I asked tentatively, a little scared of the answer.

Freyja paused, looking at her feet. I could see her rotating her feet, the way she did when stuck for an answer. Lifting her head, she looked me directly in the eyes. "He doesn't bring out the best in me, the way you did," she finally whispered.

This statement floored me. Completely taken aback, I queried, "*Me?* How?"

Freyja sighed. "You made me more human," she admitted. "You care for others, regardless of who they are. You are unwaveringly loyal. You do things because they are *right*. I tend toward being rational, logical. Possibly a little hard-nosed and confrontational. So does Angus. He and I are alike in that way. But I... I was a better person when I was with you."

I had no response to this. How could I respond? There was no appropriate response to this statement. Instead, I held her hand, gently drawing small circles on the back of her hand with my thumb.

"I'm so sorry," I finally managed. "I followed you here. I waited that entire year, the six months on August and the six months here. Then I returned to August only to find you had left again. Then... then... *she* told me you were pregnant." I choked, struggling to recover. "Others had confirmed that Angus was with you, so it all made sense. I didn't question it. By that time, I believed you had moved on. Chosen someone else. It had been a year. I was alone, again. That is why I returned here and started over. I was accepted here in a way I wasn't on August. I couldn't stay there."

"I know," she said sadly. "I wish I could have gone back that way, but I couldn't. After my experience the first time, well, it took me weeks to recover."

"I heard. Head injury?"

"Fractured skull," she admitted, unconsciously touching her scalp. "By the time I had it x-rayed, it had started to heal. I swore Hamish to secrecy. I didn't want Angus to think I wasn't well enough to travel. Sailing, I was fine with. Slow and predictable. But heading back the way I came? No, thank you."

A thought occurred to me. "How did you know? About me returning, I mean. You got there first and then left before I arrived."

"The team planned to visit Melbourne, see if there were any survivors in Australia. Go back to where we did the testing and find what records existed. Angus knew from his role in planning these communities that the Melbourne headquarters managed most of the southern hemisphere, so there were likely records at that site. We had so many questions. Were there other communities in the region? We had found some other communities on our way from Scotland. But we needed to know. Had they found any breakthroughs in combating the spread of the protozoa? What research had they started that looked promising? That kind of thing. Anything that might help us resettle outside the domes when the time comes. We ran low on fuel on the way over, which reduced our speed, then we hit some terrible weather and were a few days late getting back to August. Needing to stay out of the rain in case it was infected. When we arrived on August, the first time, I looked for you, but Jamie told me you had vanished. I trusted him; he had no reason to lie to me."

The look in her eyes told me that Jamie had told her a lot more than that. I wasn't sure whether to be embarrassed or grateful.

"When he told me you went missing, I suspected you might have followed me through. But no one knew for certain *when* you had gone. I hoped you had followed me through and would come back. But it was weeks until the solstice. The team didn't see any point in sitting around, twiddling our thumbs when we could use that time to find answers. We didn't think it would be a drama. If you had traveled, then you would know that we had left Scotland and would have been told that we were heading to August. We didn't rush. I showed Jamie the cave and warned him to keep an eye out on the solstice, but we expected to be back ourselves. Then we were delayed. When we returned ten days after the solstice, we expected to find you there and had been told that we would be back. Instead..." She trailed off.

"I had already left," I finished her unspoken statement.

"And no one knew where you or Hugh had gone," Freyja added unhappily. "It wasn't until three days later when Heidi finally made her move on me, and we worked out why you had left. She locked me in and tried to kiss me. I rejected her. She attacked me. I was lucky. Luca came past at the right time. He detained her, and under some fairly intense questioning, well … it all came out. She had found Hugh's note and destroyed it. Poisoning you. Telling you I was pregnant." Her eyes glistened, brimming with tears. "It looks like she succeeded after all."

I could hear the wind battering the outside of the dome. I missed storms, wind, rain—the feeling of being alive, the electricity, the sheer power of it. I tried to ignore the emotion and focus on the story. "She attacked you?"

"She pulled a knife on me. In our home," she added as an afterthought, and I cringed. Our home. So, she had gone there, as I had, seeking memories of a happier time. Freyja rolled up her sleeve, displaying a freshly healed wound on her right forearm, over twenty centimeters long, a purplish red, raised, and angry-looking scar.

"It's okay. It was defensive. She was slashing at my throat. I put my arm up, and … well … it got in the way. Twenty-two stitches. It is all good. The guys from here are ex-military. They are good friends and very much enjoyed questioning her."

"I am so sorry," I spoke with feeling, looking at the nasty wound on her arm, desperately wanting to touch it. "I went back for you, then I heard… I thought… oh, Frey, it was awful. I couldn't do it again. Stay there after the weight of guilt, the suspicion. The memories of you, of us. Our home, our stuff. It was just too painful."

"I can't believe you went through *that,*" she shuddered, "twice."

"Three times technically," I admitted. "I did it for you. That said, I strongly believe that it has reduced my lifespan considerably."

We sat on the sofa in Angus's living room in silence. There it was. I had gone looking for her; she had gone looking for me. We had missed each other because of a set of unfortunate circumstances. But now, two years after she had disappeared, I had moved on. I had a wife I loved with every fiber of my being and a son I adored beyond reason.

She watched me closely. "Are you … happy … Cam?" she finally managed, though the words strangled her.

I answered without hesitation. "I am, Frey."

Despair etched her beautiful face as she responded, "Good. I wish you, Laetitia, and the baby all the best."

Standing to leave, I knew this was enough for now. There was more that I needed to know, to learn about the other communities she had mentioned. But for now, we had closure.

"I love you, Frey. I always will." Standing ready to leave, I kissed her softly on the lips.

Blotting the single teardrop that rolled down her cheek with my fingertip, she closed her eyes. I left.

CHAPTER 10

"**INTERMISSION. PART ONE OF** the day's dramas down. Part two yet to commence," I muttered under my breath as I stalled, delayed—torn between the confrontations. Which would be the hardest? Saying goodbye to my first love, the one I had been separated from by accident, by malicious lies? Had she never visited the cavern that day, this situation would never have happened. We would still be together, married, and possibly with children. I would never have traveled here and found my forever place. But now, how was I to face Laetitia? She had always been reasonable, rational. How did I tell her it was all a mistake? My first wife was still alive, single, and because I had been deceived by a psychopath? Because of that lie, I remarried and now had a child? With her. *Ahh... fuck!* I kicked a rock in my path and immediately regretted it. The pain reverberated up my right leg and into my knee, causing me to pause and wince until the stabbing pain had receded. My hand throbbed in sympathy, still wrapped in my bloodied handkerchief. *What have I done?*

Sitting on a rock under a large oak tree, I reflected on my life. Steps. Small steps, each seemingly insignificant but cumulatively, had taken me on a path, ending here. Without realizing it, each day, I had woken and made decisions that would lead me on a journey. Choosing a course at university. Saying "yes" to the offer of moving to August. Marrying Freyja when she had proposed. Now I was here and very much in love with my wife and son.

Within the dome, the landscape was varying shades of green: the darker green of trees, planted in rows along the edges of lush green grassed paddocks along with the purples of heather and the browns of peat. Thin gray paths, roads, and tracks snaked their way through, some planned in straight lines, others following the natural curves of the landscape. Dark blue-gray hills and mountain ranges rose in the distance, covered in trees and bushes.

As I sat there in the dark, I could hear the wind turbines humming in the distance, moving the air around within the dome. The occasional stone house or shed roof glinted in the moonlight from where I sat, but it wasn't possible to tell if they were inhabited or not. Increasingly, the population was spreading out to the old crofts to save them. Many of us felt it was wrong to let them disintegrate into nothingness. We tried to save them, restore, and renovate them. Laetitia and I talked about restoring a croft, but it was impractical at the moment, both of our workplaces being near the township, and it was hard to get around with a baby. We both wanted to honor the people who had been moved on but gave this space, albeit unwillingly, for us to live. Inhaling deeply, I felt the stillness envelop me.

But what made a place a home? People moved all over the world, changed cities, changed countries, moved houses within those places. People moved for jobs, to go to college, following a loved one. A house was not a home by simple definition. A house was a building with stuff inside. But what made a particular place a *home*?

Staring into the darkness, I tried to recall the few times in my life that I had felt truly at peace. Safe. With my parents in Melbourne. With Freyja on August. Now here, with Laetitia. The dawning sense of logic enveloped me. It wasn't a place or a particular house that made a place a home. It was the people. You could live anywhere, really, as long as you were content. Safe. Valued. That made a place a home. The people you lived with, people who supported you— your family. I considered what happened to those poor souls who had no family and lived alone. Did they feel the same sense of utter peace that individuals with family did, knowing that someone had your back, no matter what? Despite everything, someone would be there for you to pick up the pieces. I had felt that sense of utter serenity only three times in my life: with my family, with Freyja, and now ... here. Laetitia and Louis. My family. The family I chose and the family I made. They made this place home.

A growing sense of inevitability rose inside me, and there was no point in delaying it. Carefully making my way down the path in the dark, I could see our home, the lights shining through the window. Despite the dark, I could see movement through the window. Good, she was there. *Of course, she is,* I thought crossly. *Where else would she go with a baby in a domed village?* Laetitia wasn't the type to air her dirty laundry in public and tell other people about our marital problems, including the rather inconvenient fact that I already had a wife. That I was a bigamist. Instead, she would tell me what she thought and kick me out. She had been here first, after all: her community, her home. Pausing at the door, I closed my eyes and commended my soul to whichever deity would degrade itself far enough to have me. Inhaling deeply, I wished I had thought to go past the whisky store for a stiff drink, but I opened the door quietly and stepped inside. Closing it behind me, I turned to see Lae in the lounge room, pacing with Louis in her arms.

"Kitten," I started.

"*Don't* call me that! Did you call *her* that?" The undercurrent was one of hysteria, barely held in check.

"Laetitia," I fumbled, but it was too formal. I had never called her Laetitia. She hadn't turned to face me. She had been crying. I could tell by the way she kept her face down, snuggled into the warmth of Louis. She was moving erratically too, swift jerky movements, not the gentle swaying rhythm she usually displayed when carrying our child.

There was no point in delaying. Out with it then.

"She isn't with Angus," I said flatly.

Lae turned to look at me then, displaying her distraught, tear-streaked face. "I know. The entire village knows. Where were *you* today? Sympathy looks; that's what *I* had to endure all day. People thinking, 'Poor Laetitia. Cam is about to leave her for his newly resurrected first wife.' That is what I got. People looking at Louis and me, *with sympathy*!"

"I'm sure it wasn't..."

"It *was*." Her tone was final, shaky, yet angrier than I had ever heard. "I know all too well what a sympathy look is, Cam. I have been on the receiving end of them my entire life. Poor Laetitia, her mother is an alcoholic. Poor Laetitia, she can't afford new clothes. Poor Laetitia, she needs charity to buy her school uniform."

"I'm so sorry..."

"Don't. Don't apologize. Please, just pack what you came to take and ... go."

"Go?" The tone of astonishment must have been audible as she took a step backward.

"Isn't that what you came to tell me? That you had chosen her? Isn't that where you have been all evening? I was your second choice. I've always known, ever since that day when we saw the aurora out near the stones. I have always known that I was number two. You went back for *her*."

"Never," I whispered. "It just took me longer to find you, to reconcile my heart. My home is here. With you. With Louis. I never knew true contentment until I met you, and you shared my soul. I just needed to end things properly, that is all. I couldn't end it on August, so I ended it. Today. It is done, Lae. Truly. It is over."

She crumpled into a heap on the floor like a pile of rags, clutching the bundle to her heart. Sobbing. Then the tears really started, and I extricated the sleeping baby from her arms. Placing him gently on the floor beside us, I held her as she cried. Ugly crying, interspersed with hiccups. It sounded like her heart was breaking, but I knew it was the stress that she had held in all day. Then the wave of relief. Believing she was alone ... again. Then learning I had chosen her.

I whispered into her hair as she cried, "You will never be alone. Not while I still have breath, my kitten. You will never be alone. Louis will never, ever grow up without a father."

Between sobs, she whispered, "Why me? *Why* did you pick *me*?"

Smiling as I wiped away her tears, I replied, "That first time I saw you smile, I knew. Somewhere in my cold, broken heart, I knew I needed you in my life."

The tears turned back to sobs and finally to sighs, exhausting herself as the emotion that had kept her controlled all day finally ran out of steam. Picking her up gently, I carried her to bed, the one we shared. Tucking her under the covers, I held her as tight as I could without crushing her tiny frame.

"Kitten, I love you."

"I love you too." The tears were close to the surface, but I knew we would be okay.

"I'll take care of Louis. You sleep now."

Sitting on the bed, my son asleep in my arms, beside my sleeping wife, I was in turmoil. Why did I still feel so torn? Was happiness an emotion that could even be experienced without an element of guilt?

In the cold, dark hours of the night, Lae turned to me. "Really?" she whispered.

In answer, I pulled the nightdress over her head and spent the next hours proving my love, worshipping every inch of her tiny five-foot body. As she drifted off into a blissful sleep, I knew she would never question my commitment to her again.

CHAPTER 11

THE FOLLOWING NIGHT ANGUS and Freyja, along with the three others in their team, prepared to speak to all Lewis residents at the hall. News had spread like wildfire across the community of Angus's return, and everyone wanted to hear about their journey. Even those from the crofts were here. I was happy to see many people I hadn't seen in a while, including Aidan, Josh, and Orla.

Laetitia, clutching Louis like a shield, also attended. I had told Lae she didn't need to. I would give her all the details, but I knew she wanted people to see us together. A happy family. If that is what reassurance she needed, then if nothing else, I could give her that.

We entered quietly, holding hands, and sat in the back. Lae was not an exhibitionist. The community had seen us enter together, and that was the point. She didn't need to be front and center, a spectacle. That was not her way.

Angus started by telling the group about his trip from Lewis to August. I knew part of this from Heidi, Lena … whoever she was. But along with the rest, I listened intently to the story given, with far more detail, from the firsthand perspective.

After leaving Lewis, the team had sailed around the northernmost tip of mainland Scotland, past John o'Groats and down to Aberdeen, where they picked up a larger, ocean-worthy craft. The crew had then sailed down to Edinburgh, the east coast of England, to France.

If they had sailed along the west coast of Scotland, I mused as he spoke, *then the east coast of Ireland, they may have seen the dome at Newgrange.* Although inland on the River Boyne, the dome extended to the east coast, just north of Dublin. But from Edinburgh, where they departed, it made more sense to travel along the English coastline, where they saw nothing. If there was a community at Clava Cairns, inland from Inverness, following Kevin's theory, they would have missed that too.

I forced myself to pay attention to Angus's droning voice.

"While there are a lot of true antipodal points in Spain, there was no evidence of communities on the coast, and they knew they didn't have time to venture inland. There was no evidence it was safe or that there were any communities there. After all," Angus explained, "I knew from my important work with the government that there were only twelve communities in the world. We knew of two, so we assumed the others would be widely spread out and only one or two in all of Europe."

It wasn't until they had reached Gibraltar that they found another biosphere, green trees, and bushes. But no sign of human life.

"We could see the living plants from the yacht," he explained. "It made it easy to spot. We sailed until we saw greenery—plant life. We found that in Gibraltar, but it wasn't alive. Not quite. We found the remnants of a dome, but it was damaged. The foundations were still there, but there were great gaping holes in the fabric. The plants were all in a state of death, and there were no animals left. We also found..." He quickly scanned the room to ensure there weren't young children present. "We discovered *fresh* human remains. Not decay that was years old."

A collective gasp rose at this. We would still die if the dome were breached. It was a sobering thought.

Angus continued, "There was no sign of rain, so we explored. I don't know if many of you have been to Gibraltar?" Head shakes among the crowd mixed with the odd nod.

"Gibraltar is a small peninsula, covering less than seven square kilometers. It isn't an island exactly; it shares a land border with Spain. The rock is the most famous part, a 400-meter-high promontory over-looking the city. The Rock of Gibraltar? There was a cable car for tourists a few years ago. Well, after a few weeks on a boat, we tested our sea legs by climbing it. It took us a few hours. Despite its name, it isn't a single rock. Within the peninsula, there are hundreds of caves and tunnels, many used by the British military until the pandemic hit. Within the caves, we found food stores, clothing, and a seed bank. It looked like people had lived there until relatively recently. Gibraltar itself is an odd place for a domed community. It had very few natural resources and limited freshwater resources. But there *was* a dome. But it was tattered now and let the water in. There were so many caves that we couldn't explore them all. It was late November by this time, so we had a few problems.

"First, sitting around waiting for the solstice in an unprotected place. Second, not knowing where a potential portal even was. With hundreds of caves, we could well have missed it, anyway. As we know from the tomb within the stones at Callanish and the springs in the cave on August, the entrances to the portals are small, only a few meters across. We would have to know with some degree of certainty where the portal would open. Third, we knew for sure that there was a community on August, and we had reason to visit there. We decided the best course of action was to continue."

Lae shuffled slightly at the reference to having a reason for being back on August, but she held her head high, continued to watch intently, and said nothing. I placed my hand over hers as it rested on her lap, and she gently curled her fingers around my hand, grateful for the tactile reassurance.

"After we left Spain, we spent the next few weeks sailing down the west coast of Africa. That is when we made an enormous discovery. On the coast, just north of Dakar, there was a visible domed community built on the Senegal River."

Lots of mutters of excitement arose at this news.

"They were fearful of us, and it took us some weeks to build trust. But the miraculous thing was, there were three French speakers among them, paler-skinned men who didn't seem to be of African origin, unlike most of the community. Now my French is not great, but Nate here speaks reasonable French. They also spoke some English. After a few attempts, that is how we learned they were from New Caledonia.

A portal exists between Mauritania and the southern part, more mountainous part of New Caledonia, on the banks of Lac de Yate."

A collective gasp reverberated through the room.

Angus, considering himself quite the showman, settled the audience with an exaggerated shushing gesture with his hands, the lights shining off his greasy bald spot.

"So yes, we can now confirm that there *are* more domed communities, and they *are* connected by antipodean portals. What is interesting is that the portal between Africa and New Caledonia doesn't seem to be open on every solstice. The New Caledonians, who traveled by accident, have tried twice, unsuccessfully, to return."

This caused quite a stir. It was one thing to know that there were other communities; we had been told there would be at least twelve. Everyone here knew about my travels from Bellcamp to Newgrange. But to find out that there were definitely more, also linked, suggested something else. It wasn't just Callanish and Newgrange that were extraordinary places, antipodes. There were networks of these passages. It meant various governments had known about these portals for *years* and had kept them secret. The last part also meant that the passage wasn't stable. *Was I just exceedingly lucky?*

The chatter rose to a mild roar. Glancing at Lae, we both looked at little Louis, sound asleep in her arms. He didn't appear at all concerned with the noise. We smiled at each other over his tiny head. Angus took control once more. Holding his arms up for quiet, people settled, some loudly shushing others.

"Thank you for your patience," I could hear Angus say over the rumble of voices and finally quiet overtook the room again. Evidently, he had some experience in lecturing students. We were all made to feel like recalcitrant pupils. All eyes were on Angus, and he relished the attention. He was an insufferable show-off, a complete dick. Nothing like I had imagined. Feared.

"After we left Mauritania, we headed south, down the coast around South Africa. We searched abandoned cities and refueled and restocked. We didn't spot any other potential sites from the water, so we set sail for the western coast of Australia. According to the maps, there isn't much in that part of the Indian Ocean, so we headed for the only real landmark in between Africa and Australia, a French territory called the Kerguelen Islands or Iles de la Desolation."

"Desolation Islands," Lae muttered next to me. "How apt."

"These islands are among the most remote places on earth, over 3000 kilometers from Madagascar and another 6000 kilometers to Australia. They truly are in the middle of nowhere. Honestly, the only reason we planned to stop there was to break the journey. To stretch our legs on land. But then we found something quite remarkable."

Sitting up a little taller, I strained to hear what he was saying from my place at the back of the room. Being taller than most, I could see Freyja was sitting on the stage, a little behind Angus and to his left. She was surveying the crowd. Our eyes met, the gaze held a fraction too long, and then she looked pointedly at Lae, then away. I flinched and prayed Lae hadn't noticed. Surreptitiously glancing over my left shoulder, Lae seemed absorbed in watching Louis sleep.

"On Kerguelen," Angus droned, "we found another biosphere, but this one was slightly different. The Kerguelen islands have no indigenous population. Instead, the French government keeps a population of around a hundred professionals there, soldiers, engineers, scientific researchers, together with their families. This is the fascinating part. This community existed from *before* the Vienna Virus spread. They never went home. They were all French, but as professionals, most of them spoke excellent English, even if it was a little rusty. We learned that they had received word from France about the contagion, and they had dispatched a supply ship to them with a small crew, the equipment to build a dome, and supplies. A few of them left, but most, including children, stayed, along with most of the crew. Only the few that left sailed the supply ship home. While there are 300 islands in the archipelago, the settlement was on the main island, Grande Terre, which is roughly 6500 kilometers in size. Let me just say to those of you who think of Scotland as cold and dour, this place is far worse. It rarely gets above eight degrees and was a windswept polar tundra *before* they put the dome in place. On the main island, there is a glacier, and it is this that forms the freshwater supply for the community."

"Get on with it," I grumbled under my breath, frustrated at the superfluous information. We had been here for ages, and I was hungry. Louis was stirring; Lae was rocking him gently.

"They assembled the dome themselves, by hand, it appears. There is no airport on the islands. The only way in or out was, is, by ship. But," he paused dramatically, "they were sent instructions on how to activate the portal to Saskatchewan, Canada!"

Activate? Now I was intrigued. How had they activated it? That meant Blake and Kevin were right. The portals had deliberately been *de*-activated at some point.

The crowd was becoming restless. People were busting to ask questions, and Angus's delivery was boring as batshit, although the subject was not. I was desperate to ask *how* the portals had been activated by the community on Kerguelen.

Angus, finally recognizing the chatter in the room as frustration, spoke over the crowd once more. "There is one last thing, and I am sorry to raise this in a public forum, but it is always easier to let everyone know together. This is the primary reason we returned. We found evidence, and solid data, that the island and coastal communities are not the only ones in existence."

Puzzled looks flashed around the room, the chatter threatening to drown him out once more.

"When we were in Melbourne, we returned to the government building the Australians were initially assessed at, including Freyja here. After the initial candidates left Melbourne, we found evidence to prove that there were more rounds of assessment. They relaxed the selection criteria as time went on. As they realized that the domed communities were the only chance of survival, the Australian Government evidently planned more. Not islands this time and not linked to antipodes. They established *inland* isolated communities, near large bodies of fresh water with arable land. ISO they referred to them, and not recognizing the term, we overlooked it at first. Isolated communities. Rural areas, and in particular, near mountain ranges, the snowmelt being a pure source of water and a fertile area that could be used for the raising of crops and animals. We also found evidence to suggest that the Australian government extended the age ranges slightly and relaxed some medical conditions."

Being the only Australian here other than Freyja, I desperately needed to know. I raised my hand, caught Angus's attention, and asked.

"Where?" My voice faltered, but he heard me clearly enough.

"We aren't sure exactly, but we found evidence of at least three ISO settlements in north-east and south-east Victoria and another two in Tasmania," he admitted, looking over at Freyja. She nodded in confirmation.

More. More communities. My heart was pounding. *What if someone I knew is still alive?*

"We also found a list, which we believe to be the list of some of those candidates offered places at ISO 1 to 5. We have no way of knowing if there were other lists or even other communities beyond this. This list has pen marks all over it, some names scratched out, and check marks next to others. Our team has discussed it at length. Based on what we know, we *think* it was for the telephone operator to give the next steps. This appears to be the most likely scenario—those people who were offered a place, but not necessarily those that *accepted*. There was no additional identifying information, like a date of birth or address, so it is just a list of names. We know from our own experience that less than one in five people accepted those places, and that is mirrored on this list too, so it supports our theory. We also know, from Freyja's experience, that unlike the UK who dispatched successful candidates quickly, the Australians had more time, so they sent people home after the testing, and they set up a telephone hotline."

Sensing the crowd watching me, I nodded in agreement. That was precisely what had happened. I had been told what the offer was, had gone home to discuss it with my immediate family, then advised via telephone whether I accepted or not. Lae squeezed my hand, sensing my anxiety rise.

"We don't have the names of people who accepted, those living in those communities, but we *think* we know who made the short-list. It was sheer luck that we even found this. With no electricity and a bunker-like building, we didn't have access to computers. We found this paper copy by accident. We were looking for the locations of the other domed communities, specifications of the domes, perhaps even information about the portals and how they had been re-magnetized. But as some of you may have relatives or friends in Australia, I am sure you would like to check the list, so we brought it with us."

I released the breath I was holding. *A list. People I may have known. Family. Friends.*

Angus was still speaking, but the following words washed over me without really processing what he was saying.

"Based on this information, it logically follows that if the Australian government expanded the program beyond their original communities, other countries may have as well. My team's next logical course of action is to search more locally, mainly to find out if any of our own family and friends survived. There are over 750 islands off the coast of Scotland alone. Many are tiny and uninhabitable, but most *were*, even if it was for a few people, although it makes little sense that a government would establish a community for less than a hundred people. The fabric used to manufacture the dome triangles was prohibitively expensive to produce, and it wasn't readily available. We are now going to focus our search in the UK, seeking other communities, both island and on the mainland, before we spread our search more widely. We will look for teams to help us."

That made more sense. He hadn't returned here to find me and give me a list. They had returned to see if the UK government had also set up inland sites. More questions were asked, more answers, but it all passed in a blur. Then people were standing, pushing to get out. The noise hung low like a cloud of smoke, not loud, but a mid-level hum of chatter and hushed conversation.

More. How many more?

I could feel Lae's arm bracing mine, steering me toward the door. People were asking me questions. I could see their lips moving, but the chatter in my brain threatened to drown me. The words just intermingled. Lae's voice, calm and clear. I could hear that. Focus on that. She was making excuses, politely steering me outside, an arm now around my waist, Louis clutched to her chest.

CHAPTER 12

LAE STOOD IN THE doorway, looking at me quizzically. She had taken Louis to the bedroom for a feed and to put him to sleep upon arriving home, leaving me alone in the lounge.

"What are you doing?"

Lying on my back on the floor, feet up the wall, I looked utterly stupid, and I knew it. "Yoga," I mumbled sheepishly, swinging my legs down and looking up at her.

"I didn't know you did yoga."

"I haven't in a very long time," I confessed. "Mum took me when I was twelve for a year or so to help with the anxiety of changing schools. I used to get a lot of bad migraines too. My parents realized their choices were limited, meditation or medication. Dad, as a paramedic, knew that taking medication was long-term and likely had side effects. So, every Sunday morning, Mum and I would do a yoga class together. It helped a little. It was embarrassing being the only kid and the only boy in a class of middle-aged women, but ultimately Mum made me realize that who else was in the class wasn't the important part. It was about me. I struggled to relax and do the meditations, but then Mum told me it had taken her years to learn to relax and let go. Mum was also the most organized and forceful person I knew, so I realized that if she derived benefit from it, then I might too."

"Did it work?"

"For a while. Life got busy, and ... well ... we stopped going. That was over fifteen years ago. But sometimes, when I need it, I remember some poses helped. Anxiety and stress are some of my migraine triggers. It isn't something I like to talk about."

Lae smiled. "I would never betray your confidence. I think it is kind of cool."

"I'm not sure about cool, but it helps. A bit. And right now, I will take a bit over nothing at all."

"Have you noticed that your migraines have reduced considerably?"

Stopping to think about it, I realized I had only had a few since I had returned here and said so.

Lae smiled but said nothing. "Do you want to see the list? Under the circumstances, no one would mind if you went first."

"Not yet. I'm not ready."

"Fair enough. Let me know when you are. We can do it together if you like. Cam?"

"Yes?"

"I need to tell you something."

"What's that?"

"About yesterday. I have been thinking about it all day, and as silly as it sounds, it occurs to me that I have no idea how to disagree with someone."

I looked at her, my nose wrinkled, perplexed.

"What I mean is, I have never really seen relationships up close. I didn't have two parents or a sibling, so I never got to see how that dynamic plays out. Where I lived, in Glasgow, I could hear people fighting all the time. Often it ended when the police were called or an ambulance. When we … fought…" She struggled to overcome the emotion. "I just thought, 'Well, that is it then; it is all over.'"

"I never really thought about it, but … I guess … I guess navigating relationships is a learned skill," I admitted. While my parents had occasionally fought, they had shown us it was never The End. They always worked it out, and the good times outweighed the bad. Sorcha and I too. We argued constantly, but we still had to live in the same house, so we always reconciled. It never occurred to me that there was any other way.

"Kitten, people disagree. That is absolutely normal. But it rarely means that the relationship is over. It just means that they need to work the issue through, hear each other, understand both sides, and come to an agreement."

"Rationally, I see that. But yesterday, when I heard… Well, I just thought it was over."

"Never," I said with finality.

Angus's list tortured my every waking moment in the days of stress and sleeplessness that followed. *Who could be on the list? Neighbors? Friends? Do I even want to know?*

It was approaching five years since I had left Melbourne. What would I do with that knowledge, anyway? I had a wife and a very young baby. Would I feel the need to reach out or send a message? How? No one was going back there. Angus had clarified that he was spending his time more locally, not heading back to the southern hemisphere. Even if I found someone I knew, there was very little I could *do* about it. Realizing this, I was even more pissed at Angus. Why bring a list all the way here, but then dump and run?

Lae took charge eventually. Recognizing my conflict, I returned home one night after working in the vegetable gardens, dirty and exhausted, almost a week after the town meeting. She was sitting at the dining table, fiddling with a wad of paper held together with a bulldog clip on the top left corner. It was well-thumbed. Small rips were visible on the front page, complete with brown stains and curled-up edges. Jam was on her lap, purring noisily. Louis was asleep. I leaned over to kiss his cheek.

"Homework?" I asked. Lae sometimes brought home her planning work from the school when time didn't permit or when Louis needed her attention more.

"Sit," she instructed, pointing to the chair opposite.

"I just need to wash…"

"*Sit!*" she insisted with more force. I sat.

Watching me intently, she turned the wad of paper around so I could see that it was a list. *The* list.

Frozen, I looked at the front page but didn't move. Jam, sensing my presence, stretched from Lae's lap to my own, turned around three times, kneaded my legs slightly to get comfortable, and curled up again. Absently scratching her ears, I cast my eyes down the list. It was a well-spaced, typed list of names.

Alphabetical by surname. Broken down under headings, ISO001 through to ISO005. As Angus had mentioned, it was hard to read; they had scratched lots of names out. It was a mess. Some names had dots next to them, most of the legible ones had a mark. Some circled. Angus was right. It looked very much like a running list, a list someone had used to mark off names. *Thank goodness someone had printed a paper copy and not done this electronically*, I thought absentmindedly.

Adams, Andrews, and Armstrong. A long list of Ali. It required a great deal of concentration trawling a long list of partially illegible names, hoping one would pop out that you knew. Then there was the risk that it was just a common name, like David Anderson. There had been three at my school, in different year levels, but the same name. Lae, freed now that Jam was on my lap, was puttering around the kitchen. Louis still slept in a basket in the corner.

Hearing Lae turn on the biogas cooker, I looked up. "It is my turn to make dinner."

"Not tonight," she said firmly. "I'll do it. You read."

When she placed the bowl of chili con carne in front of me, just to the right of the pages I was reviewing, I looked up. "I was going to make burritos tonight. I know you love them."

"I know. I just thought you would like to keep reading. Burritos take two hands, aye? This way, you can spoon with one hand, and keep reading with the other."

I smiled gratefully. That was very considerate. Now that I had finally started, I didn't want to stop.

Scanning the list, I noted a few names of acquaintances, people I had vaguely known, from school, university, sports, friends of friends. But not particular friends. No one I would feel the need to reach out to, half a world away and with no email, telephones, or post.

Spooning the last few mouthfuls of rice into my mouth, I was midway through ISO003 when I saw it. I gasped audibly and dropped my spoon. It clattered to the floor as I used both hands to clutch the list. Lae looked up from her bowl, eyebrows raised, but said nothing.

My hands and voice shaking, I read aloud, "Mackintosh, Sorcha Anya."

Lae looked at me, her face unreadable. "Your sister?" she asked quietly.

I exhaled and tried to focus. Logic took over my initial heart lurch.

"It might not be," I tried to reason. "Mackintosh isn't an uncommon name, although there are very few Sorchas in Australia, I must admit. Likely even fewer with Anya as a middle name. She always complained as a child that she could never buy one of those items with names on them. You know, the keyrings, door nameplates, books of stickers."

"I know. Laetitia wasn't an easy name either. Not that we ever had money to buy anything. But every time I walked past one of those gift shops, I always checked."

"There is no guarantee it is her. Additionally, no guarantee she accepted the place. Although her name isn't completely scratched out. There is a tiny mark, like a hyphen, next to it. Is that proof that she accepted?"

Lae peered over my shoulder. "Look at all the other names. Many are scratched out. Some have clear ticks.

Others have dashes like this one. I think it is a yes, don't you?"

Putting the pen down, I closed my eyes and tried to focus. She *would* have accepted, I knew. Memories of Sam, of me leaving. Mum and Dad would have made her go. I knew that for certain.

Trying to review the rest of the list as Lae quietly cleared the dishes, I couldn't focus. After checking the rest of the Mackintoshes from each of the five communities several times, the names just blurred in front of me. Mum was a Campbell, had migrated from Scotland when she married Dad. She had no family aside from Auntie Angela and my two cousins, who had moved to London for university. Dad's family had migrated from Scotland to Australia when he was a child, but his brother, wife, and two nephews, all Mackintoshes, didn't appear on the list.

Louis woke, and Lae changed and fed him, then took him with her into the lounge room, singing quietly. "Row, Row Your Boat," I realized, a smile crossing my face. It was one of his favorites. One of mine, too, allegedly. Mum had told the story many times over the years that one of my first expressions as a toddler was row, row—requesting someone to sing the song to me. Sorcha had allegedly obliged for years. Closing my eyes and straining, I could still pluck the vague memory of her singing to me from the dark recesses of my mind. A sweet child's voice, singing to me, *for* me.

Oh Sorcs, I thought, overwhelmed with sadness. *Could it really be you? Are you alive? Are you safe?* I closed the half-read list. M to Z just didn't matter now. All I could think of was Sorcha. *Is she out there, somewhere? I was so much closer to the Australian mainland when I was on August or in New Zealand*, I thought wistfully. Now I was half a world away, with a new child, and it was insanely hard to get back.

Louis was an engaging little man with the sweetest smile that could melt any heart. Even Aidan, the gruff agriculturalist who had identified Jam as a Scottish Wildcat, was utterly under his spell. With his light fuzz of chestnut hair, chubby cheeks, and Lae's almond-shaped caramel eyes, he was a charmer, and he knew it. I walked into the lounge distracted, and he beamed up at me and squeaked, a signal to be picked up. I swung him up into my arms and caught Lae's sweet, gentle smile. I bent down to kiss her and threw Louis up into the air. He giggled with delight. That made me smile, and we played the throwing/catching game for some minutes before I sat with him on my lap, and he grabbed at my hair, eyebrows, and lips. Lae spread a mat on the floor for him to do tummy time, something he detested and screamed to ensure we were in no doubt about his opinion.

"We will need to babyproof the house soon," Lae noted, watching him. "He is going to be into everything."

Visualizing the shelves of baby-proofing gadgets available at every hardware and department store back home, I wondered for a moment what she meant. Plug stoppers for power points, plastic edges for tables, locks for cupboard doors. Here, babyproofing would mean ensuring nothing was on the floor for him to place in his mouth. With no chemicals and few electrical power points, the risks were far fewer in some ways but greater in others. As a young community, we had mostly thrived, with many new births since we had arrived. Counterbalancing that had also been some deaths, including some that would previously have been considered preventable deaths.

Looking directly at me, Lae asked, "Did you find any other people you knew?"

"I stopped looking after ... her," I confessed. "Lae, this is pointless. I mean, what can I do? I can't just call her up and say, 'Hey, guess what! I'm alive too!' Besides, there is no guarantee it is her, and even if it is, I don't know where she is. I can't just hop the next portal express to August and then find my way to Melbourne, then overland to wherever she might be. There were no boats on August, not one capable of making it to Melbourne, anyway. Add to that, I have absolutely no way of getting to her community, assuming she: one—accepted, and two—is in one of the protected communities in Victoria. Didn't Angus say there were also communities in Tasmania?"

Lae nodded but looked a little vague. Australian geography was not something taught in Scottish schools. Slowing somewhat, I pulled an old atlas off the bookshelf—one of Lae's reference books for the school.

"Look, my family lived in Melbourne, the capital of Victoria. See ... here. Angus said that these isolated communities were in regional areas. The list Sorcha's name was on was ISO003. But we have no way of knowing where that community even is. Victoria, as a state, is only slightly smaller than the size of the entire mainland United Kingdom. Even if Angus's theory is correct, and ISO001 to ISO003 are in Victoria, she could be anywhere within a five-hour drive from Melbourne, and that is assuming that there aren't any communities up in the north-west, the hotter parts of the state. It is roughly the equivalent of arriving in London and trying to find someone who could be in the Scottish Highlands or Cornwall. Large area, much of it rural, and while there are towns and regional cities, the communities are most likely a long way from Melbourne. I have absolutely no idea of where to even start. Add to that Tasmania is an island state, twelve hours by ferry from Melbourne, and not an area I know well at all."

Lae nodded, looking up from the map, beginning to understand the complexities of the problem.

"What will you do?"

"I have no clue. I don't think I can do anything except maybe write a letter and send it with Angus, hoping one day it might make it to her. Assuming it even is her. It is almost impossible that there is a portal where she is. If she is in regional Australia, then there are no antipodean points anywhere on the mainland despite the size of the continent. Bizarrely, all the antipodal points from mainland Australia fall in the ocean, Kevin told me. We also know that most points seem to be linked to ancient sites like Callanish and Newgrange. As Angus said, it looks like the Australian government, with the benefit of time, decided just to try to build as many communities as possible to protect people from the protozoa spread. The first ones like August and Bellcamp might have been strategically placed to account for antipodes, but it is unlikely the latter ones were. They were just built to save as many lives as possible."

Lae looked quizzically at me. "If the Australian government did this, do you think others did too? Built lots of communities, I mean?"

Pondering this for a moment, I responded, "Well, I assume so. Angus does too. I can't imagine he returned only to show me the list."

Lae nodded slowly. "You would think so. But inland, obviously, with a fresh water supply."

I had another thought. "When I first came here, Mike told me you didn't arrive here until March, yet we were in place nearly a month earlier, in February, despite Europe being affected sooner. He also said, and I am sorry to bring this up, that you saw the last people outside in July of that year. I am wondering, at what point did the Australian government extend the program? If we left in February, was it soon after or a long time after? Our last broadcast was the following December, so nearly ten months after we were settled."

"I wonder if Angus knows that?"

Pondering that for a moment, I countered, "He likely knows ... from Freyja."

Unwilling to dwell on the touchy subject of my former wife, who was still nearby, I hurriedly continued, "But what he probably doesn't know is that I have traveled across the south island of New Zealand, and I didn't see any evidence of other communities. I wasn't exactly looking, mind you, but I am fairly sure that I would have noticed an enormous geodesic dome looming on the horizon."

"It is 25 November, you know." Lae's eyes were downcast. I knew what she was thinking. Just over three weeks until the portal opened, and I could travel again.

"No." My response was firm. "No. I am not doing that again for *any* reason. I told you when I returned, I was here for good. I returned to you, and I won't do that again. Besides, the solstice is our first anniversary."

"She is your sister, Cam. Family. You would do it for Louis and me, wouldn't you?"

"That is unfair. You know I would do it for you and Louis. There are no guarantees it is her, and even if it is, so many things could have happened. It has been *years* since I left."

"You have to try." Her tone was calm yet resolute. She had me, and she knew it.

"But you … Louis. You are my … my everything."

"I promise we will still be here when you get back," she whispered as she led me to our bedroom.

CHAPTER 13

"**YOU KNEW. THAT IS** why you came back."

Freyja spun around at the sound of my voice, momentarily startled, but then registered the question. She looked around to confirm that we were alone.

"Yes. I saw the name on the list. Her name. I suspected..."

"Why didn't you just tell me? That first night, at Angus's house. Why didn't you just tell me?"

"It wasn't the right time. It also wasn't my news to tell. Angus wanted to tell everyone about the list at the same time. I didn't know if you would even look. I thought... I thought it might make you anxious."

I sniffed. "Well, that it did. But then I looked."

"And ... you want to go?"

"Oh Frey, I don't know what to do. But you must think the list is genuine, or you wouldn't have brought it all the way back here."

"What does Laetitia think?"

I caught the ever so slight inflection of glibness on Laetitia's name, just a touch, that would have been lost if I hadn't known her so well. I paused. *Do I call her out on her disrespect? No. Ignore it.*

"Lae says I should go. She thinks I should at least try."

"So, will you?"

"Probably. Maybe. Oh, goodness, I don't know. I have traveled that passage three times in the past few years. I would rather tear off my fingernails than travel through that bloody hellmouth again."

"You are a better person than me. I have only done it once, and that was more than enough."

After a pause, Freyja asked, "Does it get easier?" Her words pulled me back from my nightmarish vision, standing on the brink of the portal.

Pondering the question for a moment, I replied slowly, "Actually, yes. Not that the passage is any easier, it is just that you know *what* to expect. You know you will spin until you puke your guts out and feel you are being turned inside out. But you know it will end, and that you will survive."

Freyja nodded, looking unconvinced. "I can go with you, you know. You need help. You can't make that journey alone."

I genuinely appreciated her offer. I knew how mortally afraid she was of the portal. "You don't need to do it," I replied quietly. "I can do it alone. It wouldn't be fair to you or to Lae."

Freyja nodded, seeing my point.

"Not that I don't appreciate the offer, though," I hastened to add. "Maybe I am just stupid for contemplating it. So, back to my original question. Is that why you came here? With the list, I mean. You know me pretty well. You guessed I would be here if I had left August so quickly. I had somewhere to go. I don't see any other reason Angus would come *here* first after traveling from the other end of the earth. He seems intent on exploring the rest of the UK, searching for domed communities, which makes sense. People here want to know what happened to their loved ones, and he would want to bring evidence of that. So, why else would you come here first?"

"First, you aren't stupid, just ridiculously loyal. Second, I convinced Angus to come here first. When I saw her name on the list, like you, I just *knew*. I felt I owed you that. I was the one who caused this mess. If I hadn't decided to warm up that night after hunting for Fred, none of this would have happened. That reminds me—did you ever find Fred?"

"Jamie found him. He came ambling out of some bushes, not distressed at all. I found your torch in the cave but couldn't remember if we had left it there from one of our previous visits. I didn't know for sure you had been there; there were no clothes. Besides, it was daytime before we realized you were missing. I had fallen asleep on the sofa waiting for you."

I was heading into dangerous territory, touching on the many blissful nights we had spent alone at the hot springs, swimming, making love, baring our souls. It had been our sanctuary, where we had pledged commitment to each other. I steered us back to safer conversation matter.

"That bitch had killed him by the time I made it back. Some bullshit about not allowing for enough diversification of bloodlines."

"Fucking cow. She always hated Fred. Not that I could have done anything, but I loved that goat," Freyja whispered.

"I loved him too. He was like..." I stopped.

"A child to us?" she prodded gently.

"Yes. It is painful that he ended up that way. Are … are you okay?" I asked tentatively, unsure I wanted a truthful answer. It must have been hard for her, too, knowing that Heidi had deceived me, and I had believed it and moved on without her.

Freyja sighed. "I will be. The new mission will keep me focused."

"Mission?" I was a little startled at the terminology.

Freyja chuckled. "I told you that Luca and Jake were military. I picked up the lingo from them and a few other cool skills. Great fun they are, and they were bored here. We will keep moving now that we have shared our news. Resume our search for other survivors."

"What will you tell people?"

Freyja shrugged. "That they aren't alone. But that it isn't safe, not yet, to live outside the protection of these communities. Maybe in time, but not now."

"Did you get any other takers to join you?"

"No, everyone is happy here. That is okay. We are an excellent team. But I can help, a little, with your passage with the tech we picked up from the scientists on Kerguelen. It isn't smooth sailing, but they swear it helps."

"I'll take even a little less chunder-inducing over nothing," I confessed.

CHAPTER 14

MY HEART HURT BEING so far from Lae, Louis, and Jam. My family. Flashbacks of my parents talking about how they had placed their family first, over their respective parents and siblings, infiltrated my every thought. Had I just broken the cardinal rule of marriage? Leaving my wife and child to hunt for my sister, who may or may not be alive? Lae's voice echoed in my head: *you have to try.* I did. I knew I had to find her. It was such an unusual name, especially in Australia. It had to be her. She met all the criteria, and if they had lifted the restriction on medical conditions, especially asthma—surely she was the perfect candidate? Young, fit, medically trained. She had told me once that she would have accepted. *But would she have left Mum and Dad? They would have been alone without us. Would she really have left?* Recalling Mum's iron resolve that I would go, I realized that … yes. Our parents would have insisted that she accept. The chances she was in a safe community, somewhere, were reasonably good. The question now was—where?

A few minutes to midnight on the winter solstice, I kissed my wife and sleeping son goodbye, now aged sixteen weeks. Our first wedding anniversary. We should have been spending it with a romantic meal and precious child-free time alone. I hadn't been sure about the timing of the wedding. I wanted her. That was not in doubt. But the solstice? Laetitia had been adamant that the solstice had brought us together, and she couldn't imagine a more perfect time to be handfasted. With the entire community as our witnesses, standing under the stones at Callanish, but carefully timed for an early afternoon ceremony so that none of our guests accidentally disappeared between speeches, we had pledged our lives to each other. A traditional Scottish handfasting, complete with ribbons binding our wrists together, symbolizing the intertwining of our lives. Thirty-six weeks later, a slightly early Louis had arrived. Little Louis, our solstice gift.

For the millionth time, I questioned my decision to go. *My sister or my family?* Louis was active and alert. He recognized me when I came into his view and smiled. That broke my heart, realizing that he wouldn't see me for at least six months, possibly twelve. A mental picture of an older Louis flitted into my mind. He would be walking and speaking by the time I saw him again. Missing a critical part of his childhood filled me with angst. *This is my family, here, now. What if I am chasing a ghost? No. I have to try. Time will only make it harder to leave.*

The passage through the portal was less traumatic this time, in part thanks to the research discovered by Angus, Freyja, and their team and the heat suits they devised. Unlike electricity, there was no insulator for magnetic force. They learned about the heat suits from the group on Kerguelen, who had reactivated their portal. That community consisted heavily of scientists, and they generously shared all the information that they were provided about the science of the antipodean portals. They learned that temperature affects magnetic force, heat weakening it, and cold strengthening it. Angus theorized that was perhaps why most of the portals they knew of had at least one base in a freezing climate, strengthening the poles, and why the African one appeared unstable. Temperatures of 80 degrees Celsius could demagnetize objects. Called a Curie temperature, this could be permanent if the heat was sustained for a long enough period.

Research provided by the Kerguelen residents confirmed that governments had collectively deactivated the antipodean portals in the early 1900s. This was to stop unauthorized travel during the mounting tensions across Europe that ultimately ended in the Great War, World War I. Many had been reactivated at various points in history, including Newgrange and Callanish during the 1800s. Because they were considered top-secret, only very few of the upper echelons of government officials even knew that the portals existed. More than a hundred years had passed since their deactivation, and eventually, they became a legend, something known by very few until the outbreak.

Documents later found by Angus and Freyja's team showed it was the Bellcamp-Newgrange portal that had been re-magnetized first, although August had been settled first, a week before Bellcamp. Scientists had built an electromagnet coil connected to a bank of capacitors. Charging the capacitors and then discharging them through the coil produced a brief but high magnetic field and re-magnetized the poles. The troubling part was that the antipodean portal on Bellcamp had been tested only two months before our settlement to ensure they worked. Two crates had traveled each way on the night of the southern hemisphere summer solstice in December, proving that the re-magnetization process had been successful. Because of time constraints, they had not tested the other portals prior to settling the communities.

I realized with a gasp that this meant that Freyja had been the first traveler through the August/Callanish portal, decommissioned for over one hundred years and untested. She, and I only six months after her, were so very lucky, remembering the New Caledonians stuck in Africa. *If one end had not been re-magnetized properly...* I cut that thought off.

Three of us traveled, arriving on August Island on the southern hemisphere summer solstice. The two others, wanting to establish trade relations, were hopeful I could introduce them. Like last time, I was thrown clear of the springs, landing on the rocky edge. The suit was heated and padded and protected my fall to some extent, but I knew I had bruises on bruises as I hit the rocky steps in our cave. Angus had been right, though. It was by far the least traumatic journey through the portal I had taken, the heat generated by the suit protecting me from the worst of the vortex's spinning.

The following night, we hosted a community meeting. August had split relatively early into separate communities, so it took time to get everyone together. Recognizing Angus's logic, it made sense to explain it to everyone at once. Like Garynahine, there was a stunned silence initially, followed by much chatter. People were intrigued yet wary. There were a lot more survivors than we originally thought. Asked about Hugh, I gave a sanitized version of the truth. He had made his choice.

We had made ten numbered copies of the original list brought back by Angus to distribute them among the population. Technology was limited, mainly because of the electricity supply, but Lewis had a scanner and printer. Paper was also limited, but we considered this a matter of the utmost importance. I loaned the ten copies out, tracking who they were with. Unlike six years ago, when any home could run copious copies of anything, now printed paper was a precious resource. We couldn't afford to lose any copies. We needed to take them to Bellcamp after this and then to Australia.

A week later and after what felt like a million conversations, three other Australians had found names they wanted to investigate, one of them being Diana. Diana had found the name of her only cousin, Kendra Chan, on the list, someone she had been especially close to.

I was beyond thrilled to have welcoming company in Diana, the other two people planning to make this expedition not being people I was close to. Colin was one of the men who had tried to take Kai's aquaponics pond after he had defected to the new community of Green Island. He kept his distance from me, recalling the day he had held Kelly hostage and I intervened. The other was Florence, known as Floss, one of the cooks, whom I had overheard gossiping about me killing Freyja. While this had proven blatantly untrue, I still held the distinct impression that she believed the truth was spoiling a great story. Still resentful of the treatment I had received at the hands of the August residents, I was cool with them, and they kept their distance from me. Fortunately, Diana lived alone, so I stayed in her spare room. Freyja's and my original home was now occupied by a young family. My two companions from Lewis were welcomed, and Jamie and Jacinda promised me they would care for them.

With only four of us traveling, the plan was to replicate what Hugh and I had done two years prior and paddle a small rowboat to the mainland of New Zealand, then find a decent-sized vessel to take us across to Melbourne. Our path was to detour past Bellcamp Island, advise the residents of the list and see if any of them wanted to join us.

As is the law of averages, a significant percentage of the August residents had found names on the list. Still, in most cases, they were too preoccupied with their new lives to investigate distant relatives and friends. Nearly everyone was married with small children now. Some found family members but claimed that the ties weren't close or admitted that they weren't willing to risk leaving the safety of August. We knew beyond doubt the virus was still rampant, and the reality of being infected was inevitably a painful death.

On our last night on August, Jamie, Jacinda, Di, and I had dinner together, a proper farewell, the one we had been robbed of with my two previous departures. After a delicious meal, Diana produced a small wooden box. Sliding it across the table to rest in front of me, she said coyly, "I have something for you."

Wrinkling my eyebrows in confusion, I opened the box and gasped. Inside the box lay the photographs I had so carefully curated but had left behind in my accidental departure and hadn't thought to ask about on my return, being so devastated over Freyja. All of my photos were there: my parents, my home in Melbourne, our garden, friends, old pets, family holidays, even one of Sorcha and Sam. That one was especially precious now with the journey I was about to undertake.

Overwhelmed with emotion, all I could manage was, "Thank you, Di. Truly, thank you."

Jacinda threw her arms around me in a bear hug. "We will miss you, Cam, again."

CHAPTER 15

FOUR PADDLERS MADE SHORTER work as we set out for Bluff, despite Colin vomiting most of the way. This time I was better prepared and suggested we find a small boat to take us around the coast to Invercargill. Diana had laughed hysterically at the image I verbally conjured of Hugh and me, both tall men, riding kid's bikes along the dead, dusty roads to Invercargill. I caught a smile on Floss's face, but she turned away when she realized I had seen it. Colin continued to ignore me, stony-faced and silent.

The marina was just as I remembered it: gray, dead, and decaying. We split up, trying to find a boat we could start. After an hour, we heard the engine of a small diesel boat start, and we all made our way onto the pier to see Colin throttling the engine. He looked like he would have much preferred to have taken the vessel and left. My suspicions were confirmed a short time later. Colin was from western New South Wales. Despite a good working knowledge of engines and machinery, he had no experience with boats and nautical navigation. The vomiting started again as soon as we hit the open water, and I tried not to smirk.

"Karma," Diana mouthed silently at me as he heaved his guts over the side of the boat for the umpteenth time. Floss was a sympathetic vomiter and looked green, even though Colin was only dry retching.

Diana and I navigated the small craft up the coast to Invercargill. It wasn't hard to find our way. A decent-sized city at one point, it was nestled at the head of a protected bay. Memories flooded back of Hugh as we walked along the main street, and I saw the camping shop we had raided, the glass still shattered across the street.

"Come on," I sighed. The others followed me into the store, fitting ourselves with new clothes and sleeping bags. A sense of déjà vu washed over me as I thumbed the rack of jackets, seeing the exact jacket I had taken last time and had left in our home on Lewis. The house I shared with Laetitia and Louis. *God, I miss them.* Snapping my attention back to the task at hand, I chose a different jacket, pants, new boots— goodness knows I needed them. I looked up to see the others doing the same, choosing new clothing, trying on shoes.

I could feel Hugh here, sense his presence. *I'm so sorry*, I thought, picturing him trying on his backpack. *If only I had known, maybe I could have talked you out of it.* But I knew his mind was set when he had agreed to come with me.

I had told Lae about Hugh's story that first day back on Lewis. She listened intently and listened to me wish, over and over, that I knocked on his door sooner. Maybe I could have changed things. Lae looked at me in that unwavering way of hers and said, "What makes you think you could have changed the outcome? Don't you realize he was already dead on the inside, living a half-life on August, regretting his decision every day?"

She had never met Hugh. *How did she know it was a half-life?* I wanted to argue with her but paused, my mouth open. She was right. He was a quiet, solitary man, a family man. Perhaps they were not his biological children, but they were his responsibility. He had shouldered that burden intensely. Much like I did now. A wife and a child. My responsibility, my family. They were Hugh's family. One unconsidered decision, and he had left them to die. He had never forgiven himself and had righted past wrongs.

Finally, I met Lae's eyes and nodded. She was right. I could never have saved him. He had been building the boat anyway. Leaving was his plan all along. Sam though. Sam, I felt responsible for. He had wanted to talk, to spend time together, but I had blown him off. But I had delayed, stalled too long. By the time Sorcha and I found him, he had taken the ultimate step, and it couldn't be reversed.

Walking back to the marina, we scouted each of the boats we passed. Most vessels were fishing trawlers, but they all seemed larger and likely slower than the small craft we had. It was a long way to Melbourne from here. Days, possibly weeks, depending on how fast we could go. We needed shelter to avoid storms and water splashing in our faces. Our route was to detour us past Bellcamp, but there was no guarantee that the *Sea Witch* was there. It was likely they were off exploring. Sighing, I suggested we take our small boat around the coast farther to the east, back past

Bluff, and head toward Dunedin, a larger city with lots of places that could have yacht clubs and marinas.

"Why not go south? Isn't that closer to the other community, Bellcamp?" Colin asked.

"It is," I agreed, pointing at the map we had taken from the shop. "But the west coast of the southern island of New Zealand has no major settlements. It is mountainous terrain and mainly national park. Dunedin is the only other major city here other than Christchurch. At least if there is nothing in Dunedin, we are closer to Christchurch, and I know for a fact that there were large yachts in Christchurch less than two years ago when I took the *Sea Witch*."

Colin sniffed audibly but didn't argue any further. I assumed he agreed with the plan, or at the least, he wasn't planning to press his case. Loading everyone back on board, we chugged out of the harbor and toward Dunedin.

Hugh had been on my mind all day because of the identical journey across to Bluff and then around to Invercargill. I knew we needed to stop, to rest, but I couldn't bear doing it in the camping shop. The memories were too immense. I felt sick realizing that he and I were the last people to stand in that street, in that shop. It could be decades before someone did again. Diana, sensing my angst, placed a hand on my arm and looked up at me expectantly. I nodded. It was getting dark, and we needed to find a place to stop. There was no point in overshooting Dunedin altogether. It wasn't like there was electricity anymore. We couldn't just look out for the town lights to guide us. Being summer, the daylight hours were long. We had just passed Bluff again, so we had a few hours of daylight left, but I knew we were all exhausted.

"Let's look for a sheltered cove and a sandy beach," I whispered to Diana. "It is time to stop. It isn't going to rain." As the only one of us with any seafaring knowledge, and even mine was extremely limited, I had assumed command of the small vessel. But I was struggling too. Weary, unable to focus, my thoughts kept returning to the last time I was here: seeing Hugh's still form in that bed.

Looking up at Diana, I could see that she was observing the coastline.

"There!" she pronounced. Peering over the side of the lurching vessel, I could see what she could see. I nodded in agreement. The small, protected cove with a sandy beach was perfect. The tall trees that had sheltered the inlet were long dead, along with all the vegetation, but at least they were still in place. They hadn't eroded the bank and collapsed into the sea. Steering the craft into the tiny harbor, the others looked at me for instruction.

"We are all exhausted. Let's rest for the night."

General murmurs of agreement met this announcement, and everyone piled off the boat, shoes and socks in hand, slowly wading through the shallow waters to the beach, trying not to splash water in our faces. Dry, dead wood was in abundance, so we started a fire, not because it was cold, just because we could. It was such a strange feeling, a hot live thing. It had been years since I had sat around a beach bonfire. With the dome fabric's breathability, it was dangerous to have anything that generated smoke. Even candles weren't permitted. The last fire I had enjoyed was the night before I had returned to Lae, but that was a small campfire, mainly fueled with smoky peat. But here we were free, out in the open.

"I wish we had marshmallows," said Floss wistfully, and we all looked at her and laughed uproariously, as much from exhaustion as the comment. She looked stunned, then smiled. "Such pointless things, weren't they?" She giggled. "I mean, they were basically sugar balls."

"Not as pointless as fairy floss," Diana added. "You know, in French, it is called *barbe a papa*—Dad's beard. And in Dutch, it translates as *sugar spider*."

For the next few hours, we amused ourselves while cooking cans of baked beans and soup, leftover from our original settlement of August, talking about the most pointless things we could think of from our old lives. This morphed into what we missed, the silly, pointless things we had once owned.

"I miss cafes," sighed Floss. "Sunday morning breakfast after a night out."

"Online shopping," Diana said with a smile. "We lived out of the city, so online shopping was a godsend for me. I loved to click and buy. My purchases arrived in a few days. Being able to try clothes on in the privacy of my home, accessorize with things I already had, and not feeling judged under the ugly lights of a department store."

"Ugly lights?" Floss questioned.

"You know, those hideous fluorescent lights they use in change rooms that distort color and tone. I loved trying on clothes at home, then returning what I didn't want. No snotty sixteen-year-old sales assistant bursting in to see if I needed a larger size. I had a wardrobe full of clothes, shoes, jewelry." Di sighed. "I miss it. Being able to dress for an occasion: a party, the theater, a long dress for the beach, jeans and a t-shirt to go shopping. Here I am with two pairs of pants and two tops!"

"What would you do with heels, anyway?" I asked.

Diana laughed. "You are such a man, Campbell! It was a different time. I was so sad, leaving behind my little house with all my *stuff*. My kitchen fully stocked with saucepans, a nice dinner set, matching glasses. The funny thing is, I haven't thought about any of it—until now. I just don't miss it. I'm kind of ashamed now to admit how many hours I spent choosing my dinner set, looking for the perfect pattern, the right size plate, and the number of settings. Checking around for a good price, getting a matching gravy boat and platter."

"Seriously, *you* owned a gravy boat?" I asked, astonished, trying not to sound like I was ridiculing her.

"I did," Di responded, a little haughtily. "I liked to host dinner parties, and it was important to plate up my food nicely."

I snorted, which caused more laughter.

We watched the sun plunge into the ocean far out on the horizon and the sky darkened, and the conversation became more wistful. Even Colin warmed up, realizing that he was stuck with the three of us whether he liked it or not. We talked cautiously at first about our homes and families—just little snippets—but eventually warming up and sharing more. After listening to Di and me speak of our families and homes, Di and Floss encouraged him to tell us about his life. He declined, looking embarrassed. I would have left it at that, but the girls kept needling him, and he relented.

He had grown up on a farm outside of Mudgee, in regional New South Wales, and Colin's father had died in a farm accident when he was six.

"He was a good man. Hard-working, gentle, and he loved me—and Mum. My earliest memory is of him letting me sit on his lap as he drove the old farm ute," he said, a note of bitter sorrow in his voice. "He would always wear a blue flannel shirt. I loved the smell of it. It smelled of *him*. Dad. One day he was there. The next … he was gone. Mum and I had gone into town, and he was alone. The police said he hit a rock. The tractor rolled, crushing him. Mum never forgave herself. If she had been there, she could have called the ambulance. We might have saved him. I was too young to know all of that."

"Were you an only child?" Diana asked gently.

"I was, for a time. But Mum struggled after Dad died. She couldn't run the farm alone, so the bank took it, and we moved into the cheapest rundown house she could find in town. When she met another bloke, she married him pretty quickly. She had two more children, but they were his, and I … well, I wasn't. He hated me. Called me a little black bastard. Beat me for the slightest thing. Mum turned a blind eye usually, or he would start in on her too. Dad had always been so kind, never laid a finger on either of us, so it was quite a shock."

Diana flinched next to me. I felt her move in the shadowed darkness. The comment had cut me, too. I had never realized Colin was part Aboriginal, indigenous Australian. It was painful to think people still used racial insults, especially to children.

"I don't blame her," Colin continued quietly. "She was protecting herself and the young ones. I left when

139

I was fifteen. Troy and I had a blazing row over something stupid. Leaving the door open or something like that. One punch and I knocked him out. Mum was screaming hysterically, telling me I had killed him. I picked up my jacket and just walked out the door. Didn't take a thing. Never looked back."

"What do you mean, never looked back?" Floss asked, astonished. "You mean you never saw your mother again?"

"I did. Twice. After the fight, I went into town for a few weeks and stayed with friends. Then I got offered an apprenticeship in Narrabri with a friend's uncle. I saw Mum the day I was getting on the bus to Lithgow to meet up with the guy giving me a ride. I was sitting in the bus shelter, and she was walking up the other side of the street. She saw me, stopped, and stared. She had a ripper of a black eye and was wearing a long-sleeved shirt in the heat of summer. Even I knew what that meant. I ran over to her and begged her to come with me, but she told me to go. She was fine. The kids needed her. Go. Live my life. She would manage things. I didn't want to go, but she made me. It wasn't safe for me there. Troy was after me. He wanted revenge. I told her I would write. She told me to write to a friend of hers. She would pass the letters on. It was best that he didn't know where I was because he would hunt me down. Vicious bastard he was, even when he wasn't half gone with drink, and that was most of the time."

Colin moved uncomfortably with the memory. "The coach pulled up then, and she pushed me on. I stood on the step, towering over her, and had to squat to hug her goodbye."

We all sat in silence, taking in Colin's story.

"You said you saw her twice. When was the second time?" Floss asked curiously.

"The last time was in Dillwynia."

Silence. "Dillwynia?" Di questioned gently.

"Dillwynia Women's Correctional Center." Col spaced the words out, each dripping with sarcasm. "Jail. She killed the bastard."

Silence filled the space between us.

Diana finally spoke. "I'm so sorry, Col. Truly."

Colin paused for a long time before he spoke again. "He deserved it. She didn't. She was trying to protect the kids, my little brother and sister. She had stepped in when he was giving one of them a thrashing and hit him full in the face with the frypan. But he tripped, fell backward through the kitchen window, and the broken glass cut his brachial artery. It was quick—for him. Too bloody quick. It was them who suffered. Mum and the kids."

"Foster care?" I asked gently. My mum had taught kids in the foster system. Not always but the older ones usually learned to be hard far too quickly—to defend themselves and not be victims again.

"No. They were lucky. My grandmother took them. They lived in a Warlpiri community near Katherine, where Mum was from. Poor but loved. They were tainted by having a murderer mother, though. I wanted to take them, but I wasn't even twenty. I barely had the money to feed myself, let alone help them. Put them through high school and such."

Colin shook his head and continued his story, more gently this time. "It is my little sister's name that came up on the list. Harriet. That is why I needed to come. To see ... what happened."

I put an arm around his shoulder. He stiffened for a moment, then melted. His head slumped, and his entire body caved. I wondered how long it had been since he had experienced human comfort.

"We will find her. Harriet," I vowed. "We all have loved ones we left behind in the chaos. My sister: it is her name on the list. I need to know. To find her, my parents. To know what happened."

"It is my cousin Kendra," Di confessed. "I was an only child, and so was she. We were raised together. We were like sisters. I felt so awful leaving her, but it happened so quickly... I never said goodbye. She had gone to Bali for a holiday. We were mobilized so quickly. I always regretted that. Now, I feel like I might have a second chance."

"I suspect that was deliberate," I answered. "To stop people from regretting the decision, taking too long to choose, and realizing what and who they would leave behind. Maybe to prevent us from telling people and causing a ruckus."

"What about you?" Di asked Floss. "Who are you looking for?"

"My son," Floss whispered, and we all looked at her in astonishment. She saw our shocked faces and continued. "I fell pregnant with my first boyfriend. I was only fourteen," she admitted. "My parents were devout Maronite Catholics and considered themselves pillars of the Lebanese community. I humiliated them. They spent months screaming at me, calling me a slut and a whore, my mother crying about how much I had shamed them. They locked me in the house under the pretense of home-schooling and forced me to give the baby up for adoption. But I saw his name, just once, on the adoption records when I was in the hospital.

They kicked me out when he was born, cut me off, so there was no proof of my dishonor. I moved into Newtown in Sydney and got a job in a café. After a while, I was offered an apprenticeship in a restaurant and trained as a chef while living in the women's refuge. I was twenty-nine when I left for August. He was sixteen. But then the age restrictions changed, I guess. I was at the upper end, he at the younger. But somehow, we both may have made it. If it is him. I can't quite bring myself to believe it. Besides, he may want nothing to do with me. I gave him up."

We all took a deep breath as we pondered the mission we were embarking on. Those two letters—*if*. Such a colossal meaning for such a tiny word. *If* it is them. We were all making an enormous trek, placing ourselves in danger, hoping ... wishing ... it was someone we love. A fresh wave of alarm swept over me. *What if it is a different Sorcha? Have I left my wife and baby for nothing? No.* I corrected myself. *Not for nothing. For family.* Lae and Louis were my family, but Mum, Dad, and Sorcs were also my family.

I knew the reality was that Mum and Dad likely didn't survive. They were too old to have been accepted into a protected community. But Sorcs— aside from asthma, she was a perfect candidate from what I now knew. I had visited four sites in the last few years: August, Bellcamp, Lewis, and Newgrange. From what I had seen, I genuinely believed that she was a prime candidate—single, healthy aside from asthma, which could be controlled with medication. Medically trained, resilient personality. Why wouldn't she be chosen? Nothing I had seen in my travels had indicated that any government, Australian or otherwise, had accepted just anyone. Clearly, it had been a question of resources. With limited resources in the time available, they needed to set up as many safe communities as they could. It made sense to choose young, intelligent, and resilient people to ensure the survival of humanity. People who would become the founders of a new world order at some point, when it was safe to leave. When would that be? In my lifetime? In Louis's? When would the earth recover? I knew from my science training the world would eventually recover. We would have saved enough animals, trees, and vegetation to repopulate the planet in time. Once the water was safe. When there was nothing to feed off, would the protozoa starve and fail to reproduce, ceasing to exist, allowing us to spread the living plants and animals outside of the communities once again?

Silence had overtaken us as we sat there in the dark, contemplating our lives. After a while, a muffled snore punctuated the silence. I stifled a snigger, and Diana, somewhere to my right, whispered, "I didn't think it was you!"

Col whispered back, "Not me either!"

The three of us listened to Floss snore peacefully.

"Will you come back? To August, I mean. After?" Col asked, after a long period of silence.

Realizing that he was asking me, I responded without thinking. "Never." It came out blunter than I had intended, and I tried again. "No, there is nothing for me there. My life is on Lewis now. I have a wife and son."

"I think August was your liminal place," Di spoke softly, partly to not wake Floss and partly as it was such a serene location. There was no need to be raucous, even though we were all alone, sitting in the darkness, watching the embers burn down.

"What is a liminal place?" Col asked, sounding intrigued. Secretly, I was glad he asked. I didn't know the reference either, but I didn't want to ask and appear stupid.

Di collected her thoughts for a moment before responding.

"A liminal place is a time or place between the 'what was' and 'what comes next.' The root word is Latin for threshold, and that is how I always think of it. That idea of 'the space between.' It is a place or a time of transition, of waiting, and not knowing. The way I personally see a liminal space is that it is the place where the transformation happens, making us ready for the next chapter. There is even a group of gods in mythology called liminal gods, those that preside over doorways, thresholds, gates, or boundaries. In Cam's case, August was the place between his first home, Melbourne, and his forever home, Scotland. But the time on August was necessary for the transition into his next chapter, for him to grow and develop into a husband and a father. It really is the space between your major life events."

"I like that," I murmured as I pondered what she had said. I had never really thought of August as an experience that *had* to happen. Di knew about Laetitia and Louis and how blissfully happy I was. But as Di talked, I accepted that it had needed to take place in that order. Without August, I would not have known how to be part of a community, to be a husband. It was the place where I overcame my grief of losing my family. I hadn't grasped the importance of con-nection to others until I was estranged from that community. August had been a vital stepping-stone to the next stage of my life. I could never have stepped from Australia straight to Lewis. My years living on August were a step that, albeit extraordinarily painful, I needed to take to end up where I was now.

"Is there a period you need to spend in this liminal space?" Colin asked Di.

"No. It isn't a concept of physical time. It is… it is like … if you think of your life as a novel, and the major changes in your life form the chapters, you *do* live between the chapters of your life. They often aren't memorable or even that pleasant. But they do need to happen in order to move the story along. Colin, from what you told us, your early life was wonderful. Then a not-so-pleasant part happened. But it was necessary to get you on your life path—here. You learned skills, resilience, tenacity because of the liminal space. It can often be the healing process after a death or a divorce that is the liminal space. The event itself is catastrophic and fundamentally changes who we are and what we seek, but it is what comes between the major events that are equally important. We often just don't recognize it."

The wisdom of her words resonated with me. Lying back in my sleeping bag, I thought of the significant chapters of my life: childhood, university, August, Lewis, then back to August, and finally home. *I wonder if this period of travel is a major event or just filler?* I pondered as I was pulled down into the depths of sleep.

CHAPTER 16

WITH NO DOME FOR a filter, the sun woke me, hot and painful on my face. The dry, banging sound of the wind blowing through the dead tree branches above sounded like rattling bones.

"I miss wind," Diana blurted, looking up. The boughs were creaking and rattling, though there was no fear of them breaking off. The loose ones had fallen long ago and had formed the bulk of our bonfire the previous night.

Smiling, I said, "I can't tell you how many times I have thought that."

A quick breakfast of more canned food, and we were back on the boat, heading north to Dunedin. A friendlier mood pervaded the silence now—a comfortable silence, not the awkward one of the previous day. Colin and I had never spoken directly about the incident at the aquaponics pond, but now that I knew his family history, I realized he was unlikely to have hurt Kelly. He was a follower, just doing what he was instructed.

Several yacht clubs lined both sides of the narrow bay, mainly with small, somewhat dilapidated craft moored to a pier. Halfway from the bay entrance to Dunedin, we sailed past Port Chalmers Yacht Club. Moored there were two large, ocean-capable vessels. Both looked in reasonably good condition, considering the number of years they had stood still with no maintenance. Colin and I took one each and tried to start the engines.

After a good thirty minutes of struggling with mine, I kicked it and swore. As I did so, I heard the roar of a boat revving into life in the distance.

"Fuck," I muttered. "That's two for two."

I emerged looking rather grimy and climbed the stairs back up to the deck and up to the pier. The girls were already loading our gear onto the yacht Colin had started. *Pamplemousse* was painted in now somewhat faded black lettering across the white bow.

"Good job," I muttered as I carried the last bags onto the large three-level boat, now purring with life. "How much fuel do we have?"

Colin looked blankly at me, and I derived a slight sense of satisfaction that I still knew something he didn't. Looking around, I saw the fuel pump at the end of the dock. It was locked. My heart sank.

Floss, seeing my face, turned to the group and asked, "Anyone got a Swiss army knife?"

We had all been issued one upon settlement, and we laughed as all of us fossicked in our pockets and produced one. Taking both Colin's and mine, Floss astounded us, demonstrating how to pick a lock within a few minutes.

"I don't want to know, do I?" I questioned playfully.

She smiled and replied, "Probably not. Let's just call it a misspent youth."

Within moments we were filling the *Pamplemousse,* and like the *Sea Witch*, I watched the ludicrous value tick by as the 11,000-liter tank filled. Who on earth had tens of thousands of dollars to fill a boat? This wasn't as big, nor as luxurious as the *Sea Witch*, around the fifteen-meter mark at a guess, but it would do. It wasn't like we were sailing to Scotland in it. We entered at the upper deck: white tables and deck chairs were weathered but still useable. The middle-deck contained four bedrooms, two bathrooms and a large open-plan kitchen, a dining and living room, and a small separate captain's area. Storage and the engine room were on the lower deck. Not that we had much to store. Concerned about the distance to Bellcamp, I wondered if we shouldn't try to find supplies. We had quite a lot of the remaining tinned food brought from August, but it made sense to find a supermarket in Dunedin.

In a vessel this size, it should only take a week to travel to Bellcamp, ten days at most. The variable was how long we stopped at Bellcamp Island. I pondered this. Unlike me, who had been to Bellcamp before, the others were keen to get going to Melbourne, and I suspected, rather resented this side-trip. We would need to wait for the Bellcamp residents to review the list, decide if they wanted to come, and put their affairs in order. A week maybe? Then perhaps another two before we reached Melbourne. Then what? Visit the headquarters and try to find out where the communities were? Angus thought they were in regional Victoria and Tasmania, but Angus likely had no clue how big Australia was. Like many, his scale of reference was by UK standards. Upon arrival, we didn't even know in which direction to travel.

After raiding some homes on the waterfront and filling the lower deck with food and water, the *Pamplemousse* was full, and I didn't see any reason to delay. It wasn't yet midday, so I found my way to the navigation equipment and plotted coordinates for Campbell Island, which appeared on the GPS. *Bellcamp,* I smiled to myself, remembering Callie telling me how they had named their new home.

A pang of guilt struck me when I realized they had placed my bag in the master bedroom. While I was doing the lion's share of piloting the vessel, I wasn't expecting that they would recognize it, and I wasn't planning to fight for it. A bed was a bed, and I didn't care. The master bedroom was significantly larger than the others, so it was quite a generous act.

My best guess was that the smaller *Pamplemousse* could cover about 150 kilometers in a day. Ruapuke was quite close to Dunedin, but I didn't mention this to the others. There was no way I was going back to August by choice. The days I had spent there this time were several days too long. I had caught up with Jamie, Jacinda, and their daughters, Aroha and Kara. I had also avoided Heidi/Lena, only glimpsing her from a distance three or four times. As she hadn't succeeded in poisoning me, there was no proof she had killed her sister, and lying about Freyja and Angus wasn't strictly illegal, the only crime she had committed was cutting Freyja. The penalty imposed had been community service as there was no prison. I found this a great miscarriage of justice. A person would at least be tried for attempted murder in Australia for attempting to kill two people. If Di was correct,

August might have been my liminal place, but I didn't need to spend any more time there than necessary.

According to the GPS, the Campbell Islands were 745 kilometers from here, so at least five days. The *Sea Witch* must have been faster. I made it in four days last time. At least I think it was four days. I was so out of it after Hugh's death, memories of Sam, Freyja, and the news that Freyja was pregnant, combined with copious alcohol consumption, and ... well, I wasn't really paying attention. Five days. I had better tell the others that it could be this long. They didn't seem to have any idea how far the communities were from each other. It was an absolute fluke that I found them last time. Of all the islands, I found the inhabited one.

Setting our course on autopilot, I went up to the top deck to find the others reclining on deck chairs and enjoying the view. Sitting upright when I approached, they all looked guilty. My first thought was that they were talking about me behind my back. It took me a moment to realize that Di would never engage in that, instead recognizing that they felt guilty that I was doing all the work navigating the craft when they were all relaxing up here. *Little do they know*, I thought, *I much prefer solitude to inane chatter*.

After delivering my estimated timeframes, I sat and chatted for a bit, accepting a beer from Floss. The conversation turned to the holidays we had taken and the places we had visited. Di turned to me and asked, "What is Bellcamp Island like?"

"Cold and dark!" was my immediate response. They all looked at me in surprise.

"I just assumed that I would be much like August, Ruapuke, I mean," Floss said in astonishment.

"Not at all. It is much farther south, sub-Antarctic, I believe. One of their scientists told me that the temperature only ranges from five to twelve degrees, so even though the dome makes it warmer, it is still significantly cooler than August. The residents named it Bellcamp. They were fairly sure they were on Campbell Island and wanted to honor the name, but recognize the fresh start they had been given, so they mixed it up. It has distinctive geography, mountainous but a large fjord nearly bisects it east to west. That was what made one resident almost certain that it was Campbell Island. He was correct, and my GPS proved it. One of the unique aspects of Bellcamp is that 215 days per year, nearly 60 percent of the year, they get less than one hour of sunlight. But they make do. Not that it affects them, but apparently, it rains over 300 days per year too. But to look at, well, the scenery looks much like Scotland. Very green, mountainous, and spectacular. Different from August but the settlement is disturbingly the same."

"What do you mean by that?" Col asked.

"I mean, it is *exactly the same*. The dome, the housing, the layout. It is a precise replica of August, disconcertingly so in fact. But over the years, they made adaptations as we did. Extensions, minor modifications. But it was a standard template."

"If there was a standard template, it makes you wonder how many more there are?" Diana mused.

"It does," I replied darkly. "I have wondered exactly that. Now we know that there are likely some communities inland, too, not just islands. It makes me wonder if it was a far more common occurrence."

Walking along the deck back to the stairs leading to the cabin, I stopped and leaned on the railing, looking out over the glistening water. *Oh Lae, how I wish I could show you all of this.* Her sweet face appeared briefly before me, then flickered away. Lae, who had never been out of Scotland, would have loved seeing New Zealand, the coastal towns and cities with rising blue mountains behind, snow-capped in winter; the ocean with blue sky as far as the eye could see meeting blue waves, the colors merging, blending, subtly changing. I wanted so badly to share this with her, but equally, I was pleased that she was home, safe, caring for Louis. For someone who had never had a nurturing parent of her own, she was intuitive in caring for him: responsive, loving, gentle, a natural mother. My thoughts turned to my mother. How she would have adored Louis and Lae. She would have fussed over them both and made them feel part of the family. Memories stirred of her buzzing around the kitchen, serving food up to my friends, anyone who visited. An image of her seated on the couch in our living room, cradling baby Louis, broke my heart. Louis would never know his grandparents, and she would never know that she had become a grandmother.

Feeling eyes on me, I looked up to see Di watching me from the other end of the deck.

"Okay?" she asked cautiously.

"I'm okay," I replied wearily. "I miss Lae and Louis. My parents too."

"I can't imagine how hard this must be for you, leaving your family behind. You must be fairly certain it is your sister."

"I had to." I shrugged. "I could never live with myself if I hadn't tried."

"That's much how I feel. If it isn't Kendra, I will be sad, but at least I will *know*. Not knowing what happened to them all... well, it eats me up inside. I feel like I can't move on. I need closure."

"I feel much the same. Did I tell you about my aunt?"

Di shook her head.

Sighing, I stepped inside and sat on the curved red velvet couch, moving the cushions to get comfortable. Seated beside her, I told her the story, all of it, ending with me in the dirt and realizing on the trip back to Garynahine that Laetitia was the one.

"Are you kidding?" she asked incredulously. "*That* was your epiphany?"

"It was," I confessed. "There I was, spewing my guts out with Lae holding my hair back, distraught at the realization that I was alone in the world, and yet amid all of that, I had this moment of absolute clarity. *This* was the woman I wanted to spend my life with, have children with. This was the woman who would support me through good times and bad, would love and nurture our children. That single thought hung over my head like a firefly all the way home. Her. It was *her.*"

"That is possibly the most beautiful thing I have ever heard." Diana smiled fondly. "So then, if I can ask, if you had found the love of your life, why did you travel back to August to find Freyja?"

"Obligation, I guess. Closure. To see if I still had the same feelings about Freyja. We had been apart for a year by that time. Freyja chose *me,* and it happened very quickly. I was madly in love with her. I fully admit that. She was stunning, intelligent, magnetizing. But with Laetitia, it is different. We were friends for a long time first. She treated me in a way that I can't quite put into words. I knew she accepted *me.*"

"Did you feel you couldn't be yourself with Freyja?" Di asked gently.

Sighing, I pondered that. Di had been very close to both Freyja and me. The last thing I wanted to do was to disrespect Freyja. None of this was her fault, and I knew that part of me would always love her, but it was a part that I couldn't allow myself to feel anymore.

"Maybe it was just me being insecure. I don't know. But I often felt that she was beyond me, an unattainable standard. We were happy together, that you know. Freyja is very rational, very logical. She and I were very different, and while it worked, with Laetitia, it is like we are two halves of the same whole."

Di's eyes glistened. "I've never felt like that," she whispered.

"You will," I assured her.

Having Diana here made the journey tolerable. Someone to talk to. Someone who understood me. Col and Floss were civil enough, but we could never be friends. I had friends on Lewis. I just needed to get back there. After I found Sorcha, that was. In my gut, I knew it was her. But it had been nearly five years since I left. *What if I have changed? What if she is married with kids? I would never want a child to go through the portal. What then? Do I just leave and say, "Good luck!"* My head hurt from thinking about it.

CHAPTER 17

FIVE PAINFULLY BORING DAYS later, we spotted Bellcamp. Slowing the yacht to a crawl, I brought her in slowly, not wanting to take the Bellcampians by surprise. Far better to have them see us and be waiting. The New Zealand flag flying from the mast was little more than rags and not identifiable as any country in particular, although it was still a faded blue. Spotting the cove where I had docked the *Sea Witch*, I carefully moored the *Pamplemousse* in toward the beach. The *Sea Witch* wasn't there. Either they had moved her somewhere more convenient, or Blake was off exploring. As suspected, a small crowd gathered nervously on the cliffs overlooking the beach, watching. Popping out on the deck, I waved madly, looking for familiar faces.

Callie's Irish husband Tadhg spotted me and shouted, "Ahoy there!"

Beaming, I waved back. He turned and said something to the crowd, who visibly relaxed and started moving down the path to the water's edge. Ushering the others onto the deck, I gently returned to the wheel and nestled the boat against the dome.

"Drop anchor!" I called, and Col dropped the anchor, securing our berth.

Callie was running down the beach, her long black hair streaming behind her, her two young daughters in her wake. She caught up to Tadhg, and I could see the joy on her face spotting me. Several others were opening the access panel in the dome so we could pass through.

Callie rushed me as I stepped through the panel and nearly knocked me over.

"It is *so* good to see you!" she squealed as she squeezed me so tightly that I couldn't breathe.

Tadhg clapped me on the back, and several other people I had met a year ago came and greeted me warmly. Di, Col, and Floss were hanging back, a little taken aback at this overly familiar greeting.

Turning to them, I introduced the Augustinians to the Bellcampians.

"We have a lot to tell you," I said to Callie when people had left the beach. "The sooner, the better. Can we have a community meeting, and we will tell everyone tonight?"

Callie recoiled slightly, but quickly recovered her poise. "Sure. I'll organize it. Blake is away on a mission with a few others, but I can do that for you."

"Thanks. It is important."

Callie started to ask a question, but at that moment was interrupted by one of her children, Aislinn, tugging at her top. Taking the opportunity to escape, I supervised removing our bags from the *Pamplemousse* and began the walk into town. Like Garynahine, the hospitality here was wonderful, and we found ourselves billeted with families, a shower, and a hot meal within the hour. Callie insisted I stay at her house again but dropped me off and left.

Callie returned just as I was finishing a delicious dessert of apple crumble, delivered by one of her neighbors, and I looked up to spy her standing in the doorway watching me. It was the first non-canned meal I had eaten in over a week, and I was savoring each delectable mouthful.

"Do you recall when we met, and I was stuffing my face on cakes and sandwiches?" She grinned.

"How could I forget? The food was the only decent thing to happen in that entire bloody facility. Well, aside from meeting you," I hurriedly added.

Callie smiled. "You were pretty keen to scoff the cheesecake, too, if I recall!"

"I was starving! For some ridiculous reason, I thought it was going to be a quick test or something. I had hopes of getting to my ecology class that afternoon. I never went back to university," I said wistfully. "Never thought I would miss it, but so many days digging fields, I would think of how much easier it was just to go and listen to someone speak."

"I know what you mean. Studying to become an engineer was an awful lot easier than having the entire community rely on you to construct new housing and hook them up to a power supply. We used to complain about assignments and exams. Walk in the park compared to this."

"Are you a civil engineer now? I thought you were an electrical engineer. I never thought to clarify. Between all the cakes, I mean."

Callie slapped at me jokingly. "I *am* an electrical engineer, but much of that here is providing power to homes. There are so many hours of darkness here that we need efficient batteries from what little solar we can generate as well as hydropower. There are a few engineers here. It takes a lot of effort to counteract the natural darkness. Oh Cam, I am so glad I met you that day. Now, tell me all about you and what you have been up to. Did you make it back to Scotland and that pretty lass you were madly in love with?"

I gazed at her in astonishment. "Madly in love? How did you know? I said nothing!"

"Are you completely daft? It was written all over your face whenever you spoke of her."

"Only I was the last person to realize it."

"Usually the way."

I wished I had a photo of Louis and Lae. I described the reunion, the wedding nine weeks later, and the joy to discover we were expecting a child, conceived on our brief but wonderful honeymoon at Dun Carloway Broch on the west coast of Lewis.

"His name is Louis. He is four months now. So many things will change while I am away," I said nostalgically.

"It must be something vitally important to bring you back here—with friends."

"It is. It really is. Did you arrange a meeting then?"

"I did. Seven o'clock in the hall."

"What time is it now?"

"Just after five. Plenty of time."

Callie sat down and looked at me expectantly. Sighing, I gave a quick precis of our mission. The list. My sister.

Speechless, Callie looked at me for a long time. "More?" she finally croaked. "More communities?"

"We think so. Not with portals, but under domes, we are fairly sure. On the mainland. Who knows how many more there are?"

"Oh, God." Callie stared at me blankly as we looked at each other over the table, both unable to speak. Standing, I walked into the bedroom to retrieve one of the copies of the list from my backpack. A book really, a double-sided inch thick booklet of names, now well-thumbed from its time on August. Placing the paper on the table in front of her, I looked down at Callie, who was still seated, and nodded at it.

"Go on. I need to rest anyway." I was far too keyed up to rest but recognized that this was a personal journey. We would all likely recognize at least one name on the list. But whether that person had been important enough for us to make the trek... that was the entirely private part of the question—a decision we needed to make, alone.

Bellcamp, like August and Lewis, had experienced its share of joys and tragedies since I was last here a year ago. Many marriages and births and a few deaths. We still struggled with death, being so sheltered from it in our pre-settlement lives.

The community was still buzzing about the most recent tragedy, a woman named Bec, who had died of suspected dysentery only a few days before. Her home had been found filthy with bloody diarrhea in the bed and across the floor, illustrating that it had been a slow and agonizing death after being infected by a parasite. This had proven that as a community they were not immune from disease and suffering. She had lived some distance away from the main village, preferring to live in isolation. Described as a woman with no friends and not liked, it had taken some days for the community to realize that she had even passed. I knew enough about dysentery from Sorcha's time in Papua New Guinea to realize that she had likely been in agony for days but could not get herself to someone who could help. Because of the distance, no one had noticed that she was missing or ill until it was too late to save her. Found on the floor of her home, surrounded by her vomit and feces. It was an awful way to go. Her home had needed to be destroyed due to the contamination. A fire would have been best, but not possible under the dome as it would generate smoke, and that affected the breathability of the fabric. Instead, it was knocked down and buried.

The primary concern now was *how* she had contracted the illness. If it was through water or food source, other people could contract the infection too. I didn't remember Bec from my last visit here. No one seemed to have been close to her.

"A malicious, self-obsessed maggot who cared more about her appearance and self-interest than the welfare of others," was how Callie described her, in a tone that made it clear that this description didn't come close to describing her true nature. Her death appeared to have caused more concern about the potential spread of disease than the distress of her passing.

Speaking to the community about Angus's findings that night, the reaction was much like August. Shock, then fear, and finally intrigue. We answered questions as best we could, distributed the lists, and left.

We would leave in three days and happy to take any others seeking family or friends with us, noting the physical restrictions of the boat.

Callie, Diana, and I left together, seeking a quiet place away from the chatter. Tadhg, not being a local and thus with no family in Australia, was looking after Aoife and Aislinn, leaving the three of us free to talk without interruption.

We settled in under an enormous tree, Callie having had the foresight to bring a large blanket to sit on. Callie filled us in with her news of the past year, the technological advances, the exploration by Blake and his team on the *Sea Witch*, a new pregnancy, too early to be public knowledge. Hugging her, I shared her joy. We regaled each other with stories of our lives and children's development. I could see past the smiling facade and knew that Diana was sad. Still single, she was smiling along with Cal and me, but I sensed her feelings of isolation.

I hope she meets someone special, I silently wished to the starry universe. *Someone who recognizes her for the wonderful woman she is. Someone to share her life with.*

I shared the news from Lewis and mentioned the knowledge around the portals that Angus had discovered from Kerguelen, including the heat suits. Callie, recognizing the importance of this information, promised to schedule a time for me to talk to the scientific team here.

The conversation moved onto more neutral topics, life on August and Lewis versus life here. Topics that Di could contribute to: how the communities were similar yet different, and as the years went by, how the differences were accentuated. August was a mixed economy with three distinct communities, some goods and services owned by individuals and some by the collective. There was trade between the distinct groups, but relations were tense. Bellcamp was primarily a capitalist economy. Nearly everything here was traded, sold, or bartered with the individual setting their own price. Lewis and Newgrange were predominantly socialist. All work was shared and done for the good of the community, for everyone's benefit. It intrigued me that the societies I had the most significant experience of had developed into different economic models. No model was right or wrong, and none were better than the others. It just ... was.

Callie and Di, both with Chinese ancestry, started talking about what they missed, foods and celebrations. I hadn't realized that Callie, being Mauritian, was half-Chinese, but it made sense. She had been raised speaking Creole and English but understood some Chinese words from her father's family.

We had been talking for hours; the sun had gone down long since. Despite being summer, it was freezing, Bellcamp being situated close to Antarctica. Traveling from Scotland in winter, I was immune to cold, but I could see that Diana was struggling but not wanting to be rude.

Yawning, I exaggerated the motion so we could excuse ourselves and get to bed. We had billeted Diana with a friend and neighbor of Callie's, so we dropped her off on the way home.

Callie wanted to talk more but could see that I genuinely was tired.

"Tomorrow," I promised her. "We have plenty of time."

We had told the community that we would leave in three days, and any residents that wanted to accompany us were welcome. Based on the small number from August who were willing to disrupt their lives for a ludicrous adventure with absolutely no proof that these communities even existed, I had a reasonable assumption that very few would want to come. *It is a shame Blake isn't here,* I mused as I fell asleep. I would have liked to talk to him directly about the re-magnetization process and the heat suits we had worn while traveling.

Di came over for breakfast, and we stayed at the dining table, talking for hours. Callie would not work that day, and I was secretly thrilled that they got along so well. So much so that I was sad to realize that we would be gone soon.

Angus's list was just that—a list—a stained wad of paper with names on it. We had no idea where these communities were, assuming they were even established. Our first port of call would need to be the Department of Innovation and Science offices to see if we could discover more detailed information. The genuine risk was that it was all electronic, and there was no electricity anymore. Was it lost forever? Had they deleted all the data before closing the facility?

The day before our departure, I expressed this concern to Callie. What if all the records were on computers and we couldn't access them? Callie nodded but said nothing as we were interrupted by a woman in her late twenties whom Callie introduced as Katya, one of their doctors. Katya had found a name she thought could be her sister Nadja on the list and wanted to discuss our plans in greater detail. Soon another man joined us, and Callie slipped away as we discussed how we would travel to Melbourne, then the plans thereafter.

Over the course of our visit, I spoke with over thirty people who thought they knew a name on the list. Eventually, it was whittled down to only five wanting to make the journey, bringing our party to nine.

"Nine people," I told Callie and Diana the night before we set out for mainland Australia. "That will be quite a squash on a small yacht with only four bedrooms."

"Ten actually," Callie replied with a knowing smile. "Tadhg is going too."

Perplexed, I looked at her. "Really? He knows someone in Australia?"

"No," she admitted. "But he is a whizz with technology. He has rigged up a battery pack and plans to spend some time in the Department headquarters where you and I met, trying to get as much information as we can. He can access the computers and help you find the site locations, then wait there for you to return."

Finally, the neurons in my brain fired again, and I tried to talk her down. "It isn't necessary. Besides, he is needed here. You and the kids."

Inadvertently, I glanced at her midsection, and she caught the look. "Campbell Mackintosh, I have done this twice before," she scolded. "It is very early days, and his part in this business is done, at least for a while. Promise me you will have him well back before I need him. But he is my gift to you, for being a friend. Besides, the knowledge he may find may assist all communities and humanity as a whole, not just you."

Hugging her, I whispered, "Thank you." Having a tech genius with us would certainly make the process much smoother. Feeling much lighter than I had in weeks, I went to bed, dreading the journey ever so slightly less.

CHAPTER 18

THE MORNING DAWNED CRISP, cold, but clear—a perfect day for sailing. The ten of us waved goodbye to the community, many of whom turned out to wave goodbye. Strange how this community was there to bid us farewell and wish us luck. Previously, only Jamie and Jacinda had wished Di and me bon voyage. *The Bellcampians are like the residents at Garynahine,* I mused. There was a genuine sense of community, wishing each other well and genuinely caring about what happened. With Tadhg now with us, we had the potential to learn something beneficial for us all.

Diana was keeping a log of our travels and noted the time and date of departure along with the names of each passenger. Trying to spell Tadhg's name was hilarious and had us in fits of laughter.

"How on earth do you get 'Tige' out of T-A-D-H-G?" she asked for the third time. "I just don't get it." A laughter-filled hour passed trying to replicate the tongue-twisting Gaelic names of Tadhg's family—Caoimhe, Saoirse, Ruairidh—leaving the Augustinians in fits of laughter. Tadhg was a natural comedian, and everyone was relaxed and enjoying the journey.

That evening, a wild storm blew up quickly, directly in our path. An inexperienced sailor, I struggled with navigation and steering in the wild winds. To my surprise, Katya proved herself a master sailor and was more than capable of navigating us through four hours of dangerously stormy seas. Gratefully, I shared the captain's duties with her. This enabled us to split shifts and travel day and night, reaching the mainland in seven days rather than the two weeks we had envisioned. It also allowed me the alone time I needed. Sometimes a passenger would sit with me while I was controlling the vessel at night, but they were often asleep. While I secretly liked this arrangement, it meant I didn't come to know our new companions like Diana did. But she kept me informed of issues and concerns.

With limited space aboard the *Pamplemousse*, this logically meant that Katya and I shared a bedroom, as one of us was always at the helm. The smell of another woman in my space was confronting and not one I particularly liked. Strange as it was, and despite being careful to never be in the bedroom together, it felt like I was cheating on Lae. Katya's scent wasn't offensive. In fact, quite the opposite. I found it somewhat arousing, and that concerned me more. How could I be attracted to another woman when my wife was at home with my infant son? Lying in my bed, the scent of another woman on my sheets, I felt like I was betraying my family. *Don't be a dick*, I reprimanded myself. *It is just a working arrangement.* But I couldn't shake the overwhelming feeling of infidelity, not aided by the fact that Katya was a beautiful and highly intelligent woman.

Mooring in Melbourne, the strangely familiar sight of the deserted foreshore and abandoned houses stopped me in my tracks as we pulled up at Station Pier in Port Melbourne. This was my first trip home since my departure. Regularly, I rode my bike along the beach, walked the dog, or met friends for coffee. But now, like Christchurch, it was bleak, gray, and dead. The foreshore was a mess of dead grasses, leaves, and trees rotting into the sand. The houses were crumbling from lack of care and attention, gutters and doors falling, and paint flaking. For a busy street in a thriving city, it was still. Too still. The lingering eerie silence struck us all, and we stood on the pier, haunted by the magnitude of what had hit our home. Millions of people dead, no birds singing, insect noises, or traffic.

"Breakfast first," I suggested, trying to be cheerful despite the darkness that had permeated my mood. "No point making decisions on an empty stomach."

We each took a single bag of clothes, enough to see us through several days. We would also need to find a clothing store for the Bellcamp residents. Like those of us from August, they were in dire need of new boots and quality waterproof jackets and pants to keep them safe outside the dome.

Leading the way onto the foreshore, turning, I faced the group. As the only member of our group originally from Melbourne, it appeared, with no formal consultation, that they had appointed me the quasi leader of this mission.

"We should look for food first." Nods of affirmation. "I hate to say it, but our best bet is probably private houses. The risk is that we may find ... uh, the former residents."

"I am sorry." My voice was barely audible over the shocked gasps from the Bellcampians, but I knew they had heard. "But we need food, canned and packaged food especially. Supermarkets and stores are likely to have been looted as the ones we saw in New Zealand were. Our best bet is private homes. I know you all feel horrible about it. Believe me, I do too. Breaking into someone's house goes against everything I believe in. But it has been nearly five years. They are all gone, and well ... we need to eat. Goodness knows how long it will take to find where the communities are and travel there. We don't have a lot of food left. As you can see, this was a wealthy part of Melbourne, so it is likely that those who stayed stockpiled food. But if anyone has any other ideas, I am happy to hear them."

Glances passed among the group, but within seconds everyone was looking at their feet, ashamed to admit that I was right.

"Let's go then."

Heading toward the affluent-looking houses in the streets behind the apartments in the main road, I advised, "Let's split up into groups of two. Stay together, but get as much as you can."

Diana stood firmly by my side, so I assumed this meant that she wanted to come with me. That suited me just fine. Floss partnered with Col, Katya and Tadhg, Ian and Dave, and Daniella and Iznayah.

Di and I chose a large, well-restored Edwardian with a vast, now dead, weeping cherry tree in the front garden and what was once a neatly manicured lawn. The wrought iron electric gates were open, covered in so much dust and dirt that it was hard to tell the original color. We walked up the long driveway to the right of the house, noting the many cameras mounted on the eaves and around the back. As ridiculous as it was, I felt the need to knock on the expensive-looking stained-glass French doors. While logically I knew that everyone here was well gone, I still experienced a sick feeling in the pit of my stomach, queasy at the thought of breaking into someone's home.

Di watched me and smirked. "I always knew that you were a good boy."

Casting about, she picked up a large rock used as part of the garden edging and smashed the doors at the back. I stepped back, careful not to fall into the swimming pool, now filled with rotting leaves and branches. The reverberating sound of glass shattering was deafening, and I froze, waiting for someone to come running to see what the noise was. A few doors down, I heard another smash with no traffic or noise of the living to disguise it.

Wrapping my arm in my jacket and reaching through the now-empty frame, I unlatched the door and carefully stepped over the millions of pieces of glass—never to be cleaned up. A momentary jolt caused me to pause, awaiting an alarm to go off. There were cameras inside, including one pointed at the door through which we had entered.

"Fool," I muttered under my breath. With no electricity, an alarm was entirely redundant. Even if it had a battery backup, it would be flat by now.

The overwhelming stench of the stale locked-up house engulfed us, and Di and I paused as we coughed from the dust and stagnant air, waiting for the fresher air from outside to lessen the odor. Dad, in all his years as a paramedic, had said that there was a distinct smell of death and one that was unmistakable. Sniffing cautiously, I cast about for the scent of death, but nothing was obvious over the reek of dampness and dust.

Searching the ground floor, we found the kitchen quickly, but it was empty. Diana and I split up and went searching through the house.

"Here!" Di called, and I headed toward her voice in the dining room. Neatly placed in the floor was a trapdoor to a cellar, a small ring-pull recessed into the floor. Once opened and the small torch we had prudently brought with us switched on, showed that it was originally an insulated wine cellar, lined from floor to ceiling with wine racking, many bottles still there.

"Shame we can't take those," I said wistfully. "I haven't had decent wine in years."

"We can take a few. There." Di pointed to the boxes of canned food and packets, stacked neatly, enough to feed us all for many months. Some boxes were opened and partially used, but there were many cases still sealed. Realizing that we had nothing to carry our stock in, I climbed the stairs back into the kitchen and opened the pantry. Inside were dozens of reusable shopping bags in a variety of colors.

"Perfect!" Di exclaimed as I dropped them down the hole in the floor, ahead of my return descent.

We started loading up bags of pasta, rice, lentils, and cans, as much as the bags would hold. Diana was filling, and I ferried them up the stairs: beans, soup, stews, anything that would feed us.

"Jackpot!" Di exclaimed as she moved a box and revealed several piles of bottled water. Slabs of 24 bottles. "Goodness, there must be 50 boxes of them!" she exclaimed.

On my third descent back into the cellar, I said, "Di, there is so much here, maybe we should call the others. No need to break into other houses if there is all we need here. We could even start loading up the ship for our return trip with all there is here."

Looking over at Di, she smiled in agreement. Despite her playful taunting, she too was uncomfortable with stealing from others, even if they weren't alive to know it.

Nodding, she climbed the stairs out of the cellar, leaving me to load the bags. I heard the back door open and her calling. A few minutes later, I could hear the faint sound of conversation, then resounding footsteps of boots on the polished wooden floors above my head. Stairs creaked as Diana and three of the team from Bellcamp descended. Daniella looked down at us, pale and sickly even from this distance and in poor light but made no effort to assist. Stepping out of sight in the cellar, I beckoned Di to come closer.

"Is she okay?" I asked quietly.

"Saw some decomposing bodies," Di replied equally quietly. "Guessing it was her first experience of death."

Glancing back up at her, I saw she was definitely spooked. While I hadn't spoken to her much, the opinion I had formed of her from the week we had spent on the yacht was that she was straitlaced and uptight, always played by the rules but happy to sell you out if you didn't do things in the way she thought was right and proper. From personal experience, I thought she was the type of person you don't turn your back on. There wasn't anything I could do to make her feel better, so instead, I resumed carrying bags of food up the stairs, out of the cellar, and into the kitchen. A thought occurred to me as I lugged my sixth load of heavy bags up flights of stairs. If these people had a lavish home, they were the type to have a luxury car.

Dropping the bags against the wall in the kitchen, I called down, "Be back in a minute" and went in search of keys. Nothing was hanging in the kitchen. Fossicking around in the drawers, I turned up a can opener, which I thriftily popped in one of the food bags in case some weren't ring-pull. Heading toward the front door, I saw a hall table with a drawer. Bingo. A remote garage opener and a ring of keys.

Heading out the front door, I could see the garage was on the opposite side of the driveway to the path around the back we had taken to break in, complete with a large, paved turning circle. The remote control was dead. Not surprising to have a dead battery after all this time.

Heading back through the house, I walked around the back and found a single locked door in the luxurious laundry, complete with a dusty set-up ironing board.

The third key opened it, and I found myself in the garage with a luxury European 4WD—black, with a sunroof and white leather seats. Rolling my eyes, I thought of what Mum would say. A particular person drives a large luxury 4WD in the city, the model of capable vehicle that has never been on a dirt road.

The automatic control for the garage door was not working, so I manually unlocked the latch and tried to lift the heavy double door manually. With the roller door now open, more light was cast on the dust-covered vehicle. What rapidly became clear was that none of the keys I had was a car key. Great. Returning inside to track down keys, I noticed Daniella was sitting in the lounge, looking more green than pale.

"Are you okay?" I asked kindly.

"No!" she snapped. "We are breaking into people's homes. Stealing from them. You are nothing but a criminal!" she spat.

Recoiling from the venom she had just unleashed, I was speechless for a moment.

"That's fine," I responded in a calm, even tone. "I assume you don't want to eat tonight. Let me know when you find a shop where you plan to buy your own dinner." Walking away, I caught her open-mouthed reflection in the large mirror hanging over the fireplace.

Keys. Where would I find keys? Logically, upstairs.

Sighing, I headed upstairs and found myself on a bright, open landing with several closed doors.

"Behind door number one," I muttered to myself.

Door number one turned out to be a study. Too tidy to be an actual workspace, it was one of those studies people keep for displaying the "right" books, conversation starters, but books they have never read. Door number two was a bathroom. Number three: a child's room, but no evidence of the resident child, thank goodness. I really couldn't deal with a dead child right now. Number four was the charm. A large master bedroom. The stench of rotting death hit me as soon as I opened the door. Trying to hold my breath to keep the dry retching at bay, I saw the family, decomposed masses now, huddled together in the bed at the far end of the enormous room, thick dust on the quilt cover covering them. *It is incredible how dust is one of the few things remaining,* I thought, then realized that was the most bizarre, irrational thought under the circumstances.

The stench and heaviness in the air was unbearable. From the relative safety of the doorway, I held my breath and cast around wildly until I spotted a woman's handbag on a dresser beside the large bay window, complete with a window seat and matching floral cushions. Holding my breath, I took the four steps required to reach the bag, grabbed it, and bolted before I lost what remaining stomach contents I had, having the sense to close the door behind me. My stomach had been full at breakfast just a few hours before. Losing it all over the once expensive Turkish rug on the second-floor landing wasn't ideal.

Entering the large tiled bathroom, I sat on the edge of the spa bath in the relative cool, and exhaled, then inhaled. The air was musty, and the lingering stench of rotting flesh seared my nasal passages. Choking, I tried to clear it as I checked the bag. Bypassing the embossed black leather wallet, I couldn't bear to look at the ID, knowing that these people had names and faces was more than I could take. Shaking the bag, I could hear my prize: keys. Fossicking around, I felt the keys and withdrew them triumphantly. Looking at the expensive black handbag, I wondered about these people. This beautiful home was like a display home complete with carefully curated artwork, multiple bathrooms, a pool, manicured lawn, and a black European car. Lovely furniture, clothes, and private schools for their child, as evidenced by the professional school photos I had glimpsed walking up the hallway but had tried not to look at too closely. They had it all. Yet, when the last breath was taken, it was the same as everyone else. Rich, poor, married, single. The end is the same for us all. If they had known that their lives would end in this way, what changes would they have made to their lives?

Looking around the large white bathroom, it occurred to me that someone had cleaned it. Dusty as it was, it was neat. Towels neatly folded. In the last weeks, someone with all the knowledge that the protozoa had spread and would kill them had still troubled to clean this bathroom. Cleaning wouldn't be on my list of things to do.

Freyja flitted into my mind. This was the kind of house she had grown up in: decadent, expensive, grand staircase—a showpiece in a wealthy area. Freyja hated cleaning; she had grown up with a cleaner, a gardener, and a nanny. She had struggled to perform the most basic of tasks until I had taught her. Gorgeous, gentle Laetitia replaced the image, and I smiled seeing her face, clouds of soft dark hair with highlights surrounding her pretty, heart-shaped face. Lae had grown up in a tiny drab two-bedroom high-rise council flat in Glasgow with barely enough heat and food to survive. She was neat. Caring for her alcoholic Mum had been her sole responsibility from a very young age. She had once described where she lived as a rat-infested hellhole filled with syringes and rubbish piled up the hallways, violent disputes and police visits a regular occurrence. Lae cleaned by necessity, but I couldn't see her stopping to clean a bathroom if she knew her days were numbered.

Standing from the edge of the cold bath, I took one last glance around the white and mirrored bathroom and descended the stairs, my trophy in hand. Daniella was still sulking on the previously white leather sofas. She would have been an attractive woman if she didn't have a perpetual scowl on her face.

Ignoring her, I went out the shattered French doors overlooking the feral pool and dead garden and into the rear door of the garage. Realizing that using the remote was probably futile, I just put the key in the lock. Old school. The audible click indicated the unlocked door, and I opened it. Surprisingly, the interior light came on, proving that there was some battery life left. Arranging myself on the dusty cream leather seats, I needed to adjust the seat. A shorter person than I had driven this last. Four, maybe five years ago. Seeing the push-button ignition, I pressed the button and waited with bated breath. Nothing. Shit. Exhausted, I dropped my head onto the steering wheel, and the horn went off. *Does everything need to be so bloody hard?*

"Try it again," a voice near my ear said.

Startled, I jolted upright and saw Tadhg at the driver's window. Without questioning his instruction, I pushed the start button again, and the car struggled, but then, with my foot full on the accelerator, chugged into life.

"Don't turn it off," he warned.

I did as he suggested. Leaving it in park, I let the car idle as I slid off the now warmed leather seat.

Looking at him, he saw my unspoken question and shrugged. "Old engineering trick. If there is enough juice to power the light and the horn, then sounding the horn can sometimes start the car. Not sure why, but it works."

The team was gathering around the front of the garage, interested to see what was going on. None of us had heard a car horn in years, but the noise was unmistakable. Waving them out of the way, I moved the car into the short driveway, but left it running as we loaded up with food. Despite only having five seats, we could easily make two trips or just cram everyone in. It wasn't like the police were going to stop us. The thought made me smile. Ten people in a car, laden down with groceries and being pulled over. Funny how laws only exist when there is someone there to enforce them. All those things you are taught to do, or not do, suddenly don't seem important.

Di saw me and said, "Why are you smiling?"

Unable to repress the smile, I cracked and grinned, "I had an image of all ten of us wedged into a BMW and cruising down St. Kilda Road being chased by police."

Diana smiled too. "Not really the car for it, is it? Though, I have always wanted to drive down the beach with my head out of the sunroof."

Daniella was glaring at me, too far away to hear what I was saying, but unimpressed that I found something entertaining.

"Goodness, her face might crack," Di whispered in my ear.

With half of the bags of food loaded into the back of the BMW, we decided, perhaps sensibly, to make two trips and take all we had sourced. Knowing Melbourne reasonably well, I offered to drive the first half of the team, leave them with Tadhg, and return for the second half. Diana offered to stay, along with Floss, Ian, and Dave from Bellcamp. Daniella, I noted, was in the first group with Col, Katya, Tadhg, and Iznayah, the perpetual surly look staining her face unattractively.

Arriving at the Department of Innovation, I had a momentary concern for breaking into what I remembered as a highly secure facility. But when we arrived, the gates were open, so we drove straight in. The more significant issue we faced was where to start. There were many buildings, some of which I had been in, but most I had not.

"They fed us while here," I recalled. "I just don't remember where the dining room was."

It would be as good a place as any to set up camp. Smiling, I thought of Callie and how we had bonded in that room. I must remember to tell Tadhg that story. Describing the windows, we found it without too much trouble. The door was locked, but we could see through the window.

"May as well break one," Col suggested and picked up a can of baked beans. Hurling it through the low window, it shattered the glass. Col kicked the broken glass from the frame and carefully climbed through. A moment later, the door opened to reveal Colin, pointing rather sheepishly at the broken window on the opposite side of the large room.

Carrying in the food, I instructed the first group to portion it into ten manageable parcels while I returned for Diana and the others. One package, for Tadhg, needed to be much larger, containing enough food to feed him for several weeks. Tadhg was keen to get to work and would have little time to go looking for food. Without knowledge of where the other communities were, we were just wasting time sitting here. Then those from Bellcamp could find an outdoor shop, get kitted out, and provide Tadhg with a camp stove, saucepan, and basic utensils. Those of us with gear could move the tables and chairs to make this a living space for Tadhg and room to sleep tonight.

Six hours later, we regrouped to eat and make plans.

"It seems likely that the large water sources make the most sense to base the communities," Floss noted. "Surely you would just be better off finding the largest lakes on a map and heading there?" It was a logical question. It was Tadhg who knew the answer.

"Too big," he explained. "For a body of water that size, it is hard to dome the entire water resource plus a large settlement area, and the risk of infection is too high. It is easier to choose a small, self-contained body of water on fertile land and keep the community completely sealed. Besides, we don't need that much water. Remember that the water evaporates and then is reused. Some water is lost obviously, but as long as there is enough..."

"I was told that there was enough water for several hundred years," I mused aloud.

"Callie said they were told the same," Tadhg added. "It was a little different in Ireland."

I nodded. I had been there. Tadhg saw the look. "That's right. You have been there. Well, we didn't have a lake, but we were near the River Boyne. The engineers made a dam adjoining our community. It was fully self-contained so that no water could flow in or out. It kept us safe, but it is not enormous. I wondered at the time why they had chosen that place. The land is fertile all over Ireland, and there are plenty of lakes. Some sizable ones like Lough Ree in the center of Ireland. Of course, once we discovered the portal, we knew why that particular location was chosen."

After dinner, Tadhg rigged his battery enough for essential lighting. He was keen to begin his research, and I went to help him. There was no point sitting around here. Like the others, I was eager to be on my way. Tadhg would stay here and try to work out the technology behind the domes, how they had re-magnetized the portals, and see if there was a reference to other communities around the world. But for now, all we needed to know was where the other potential communities in Australia were located.

I was being shaken, rather roughly. Annoyed, I pulled away and slowly opened my eyes. Rolling my stiff neck, I realized I had fallen asleep with my head on the desk where I had been reading by the dim lights. Tadhg had a laptop in his hand and was rabbiting on about finding them. My brain defogged to the point where I could decipher his excited speech, delivered in a heavy Irish accent, making it difficult to interpret. He had decoded enough to work out roughly where the communities were. He had also found a list of who had been sent to each community. We knew about August and Bellcamp, but there were several other islands. Within the southern states of Australia, there were two in Tasmania, and three in Victoria. Poring over the lists, I scanned for Sorcha's name.

"Come *on!*" Tadhg was keen to wake the others, and I dragged myself back to the dining hall, where the others were curled up asleep on the floor.

With one screen, it was difficult to review when we all wanted to read it immediately. Soon we determined it was the three Victorian communities where the nine relatives of our team had gone. That was a stroke of luck. Thank goodness we wouldn't have to split up over the mainland and Tasmania. Sorcha and Diana's cousin Kendra had both gone to Kiewa, the community in Northeast Victoria in the valley at the foot of Mt. Bogong on the Kiewa River. I had visited Mt. Beauty many times as a child and knew the area well. One community was Glenmaggie, on the banks of Lake Glenmaggie in Gippsland. Colin's sister, Floss's son, and Daniella's brother were there. The third community, Kinglake, was north of Melbourne, and the remaining four were noted as having moved here. Excited chatter filled the room. All of us were thrilled that we had made the journey, and it was looking likely that our relatives had survived.

We were all too excited to sleep, so we stayed up making plans. Kiewa was geographically the farthest. The four heading to Kinglake would be dropped off by Diana and me, as it was roughly in the same direction, with only a minor detour. We would take the car, but they would find their own way back. There was no point relying on us, just in case something happened. The remaining three, led by Colin, would try to find another vehicle to get to South Gippsland, which was in the opposite direction. Colin, with his mechanical skill, was reasonably confident of hot-wiring a car. Tadhg would remain here. We agreed on a date to reunite in six weeks. We would wait three days, then the people at the yacht would depart back to their respective communities, August, Bellcamp, and for me, back to Scotland.

We spent ages discussing ground rules, Daniella proving my earlier suspicion that she was wholly inflexible and unwilling to negotiate. I was looking forward to traveling in a different direction tomorrow. After much discussion, we agreed that if we didn't show up at the rendezvous point and on the agreed dates, we wouldn't go looking for each other. It was too risky and the variables too many. Everyone was in agreement, although I could tell that Daniella wasn't happy about it. Nothing seemed to make that damned woman happy.

Trying to get to sleep was excruciating, and it wasn't the cold, hard floor with the sleeping bag that kept me awake. *Sorcha is alive, and only about five hours away. Probably less, as there is no traffic, no traffic lights. Tomorrow. I will see her tomorrow!* I badly wanted to leave now but realized that traveling in the dark wasn't the smartest of choices. Fragmented images of Mum, Dad, and Sorcha filtered through my mind as I drifted off.

CHAPTER 19

I WOULD HAVE RECOGNIZED HER anywhere. From the back, the thick red plait that reached her hips, swishing as she moved, could have been one of only a dozen people. But that poise. The straight upright carriage was so like Mum, only taller. I gasped as she turned slightly, so I saw her in profile. My goodness, she looked like a taller version of Mum. Her coloring was Mum's, although our height had been inherited from Dad. Unable to move, to speak, I watched her from across the open space, a distance of thirty meters. So far. I had traveled so very far to find her, and now, here she was, and I was yet again the little brother humbled into submission by his dominant older sister.

She was kneeling in front of a garden bed, weeding maybe, or pruning. Yes, pruning. She was cutting something. She pivoted, sensing someone watching her. Sorcha always had cat-like senses. She looked at me, through me, then like her world suddenly came into focus, she was upright and running, sprinting into my arms. Five long years we hadn't seen each other or spoken, me believing her dead. But that familial bond was still there. Tears were streaming down her face. Holding each other as tightly as we could, I could feel the wracking sobs in her smaller frame engulfed by my much larger mass. Eventually, her breathing slowed, and she looked into my face. As tall as she was for a woman, I still had several inches of height on her—the little brother, but no longer smaller.

"Is it really you?" she gasped.

Between gulps, I managed, "Well, it would be rather awkward if it wasn't!"

Sorcha punched me in the arm, and we both dissolved into giggles, punctuated with sobs.

Intermittently we hugged, held each other at arm's length, trying to work out how we were the same and how we were different. Her hair was longer, and she looked, well... sadder, despite the enormous grin she wore. Her face was like Mum's, only slightly more angled. Mum's face had softened as she aged.

"It was so hard," she rambled through the streams of tears. "Knowing you were most likely alive but no idea where or how to get to you. How on earth did you find me? My goodness, you have grown! That beard is positively awful! My god, you look so much like Dad! How *did* you get here?"

"All in good time," I soothed. "We have plenty of time."

"Is it safe ... out there, I mean? Are there others? Can we leave?" Her questions tumbled over each other in an attempt to get out. Rather than answering her questions, I asked the most important one.

Inhaling deeply, I broached it, "Mum, Dad?"

Sorcha's face fell as she looked at her feet. Her head shook in negation. Seeing her distress, I said,

"It's okay—another time. Tell me everything ... later. It is not important now."

Her eyes filled with fresh tears as she threw her arms around me briefly, then led me inside the tiny house. Located with many others, I noted, intrigued that here they used existing homes and townships for the protected settlement. I wondered what happened to the original residents but didn't want to distress her by asking right now. Time we had plenty of. She picked up the sprig of basil she had been cutting. I smiled to myself. That is something Mum would have done. Never wasted a thing.

Glancing around the living room, I noticed children's books and toys. She saw me looking and nodded, beaming with pride.

"You are an uncle. I have a little boy. He is nearly four."

My heart melted for her. I looked into her eyes. "You are a Mum? That is amazing, Sorcs. I am so happy for you. What is his name?"

"Sam Edward," she said wistfully. Then added, "I needed to."

Nodding, I smiled. I got it. "Well, brace yourself. You are an aunt. I, too, have a son named Louis Edward Winter, after grandpa, Dad, and the night Laetitia and I met. He is nearly five months old now. I left when he was three and a half months. To find you."

"Did it take so long to get here from your island, then?" Sorcha looked a little surprised.

Snorting, I responded, "That is a long story and one best told over a drink. But first, where is your partner and Sam?"

Sorcha's eyes filled with tears yet again. Kicking myself, I felt like such a clot. *Have all I done in the minutes since I arrived is bring her pain?* Seeing the look on my face, she rushed to defend her reaction.

"It isn't your fault; you weren't to know. Tomori, my partner, died about eight months ago. Snakebite, tiger snake. Of all the stupid bloody things. We survive an apocalypse, yet he dies of a fucking snake bite. Something so easily preventable with anti-venom, but we didn't have any, you see. Medicines and equipment were in short supply by the time we came here."

Seeing the quizzical look on my face, she continued. "You left in February. Things started getting pretty hairy by April, especially food shortages. We used to go to the supermarket every few days. It was bedlam once everyone realized there was a problem. We were lucky, thanks to you. We knew and bought most of our stuff well in advance. It was only fresh fruit and vegetables we wanted, milk and eggs. But even that was rationed eventually—one item per customer. Shops were being raided as people stockpiled food and water, preparing for the worst. Toilet paper, of all things! It was impossible to get after the first few weeks, and people had to adapt. Pasta, tinned foods, pet food, bizarre stuff all went first. People wanted to bunker down, I guess. Everyone stopped going to work and stayed home to protect their families. There was no international travel by March, and by April, most people had stopped going to work. There was no point. Pharmaceutical manufacturers stopped producing medicines. States closed their borders. There was a shortage of everything. By June, things were really tough. It wasn't safe to leave your home. The elderly and disabled were hit the hardest. You saw people on the news fighting over cans of soup and toilet paper. But the elderly couldn't line up, couldn't fight for a can of soup. Some supermarkets tried. They set an hour each morning, early, for people with pension and disability cards. It worked for a bit, but eventually, there was just nothing to buy. No food was being delivered. Trucks hijacked. No people prepared to work. Everyone just hunkered down in self-quarantine, trying to survive.

"Just when Mum, Dad, and I were about to take Merlin and head to the block, they changed the rules, and I got the call. They admitted me to the program. That was the first week of July. It was the hardest thing I have ever done, leaving them. I thought you had it easy when you left, but at that moment, when I got the call myself, I understood what you went through. Live yourself and deal with the memories, or all endure the pain together? Mum decided. There was no way she was going to let me suffer. I cried and pleaded to stay with them, but you know Mum. They both drove me to the drop-off point, hugged me, and left. Didn't look back. I knew they were as distressed as I was, probably more so. But Mum was so stiff upper lip about it. Mum and Dad had loaded the car and planned to go out to the block with the last tank of fuel. There hadn't been petrol stations open for months. They had already taken most stuff. House invasions were common. Lawlessness was rife. They took Merlin and just planned to ride it out as long as they could. We knew it was the end. There was no coming back."

Merlin. My buddy. Technically, a family cat, but he had always been mine. Long and lanky, black with a white chest and feet, he looked like he was wearing a tuxedo. Very chilled and calm, he was the most relaxed kitty I had ever known. If I was in bed or even just sitting down, he was with me. Not that annoying kneading thing that many cats do. Merlin just liked to be leaning against you, touching you. He eased my anxiety only by being there.

"Poor Merly," I murmured. "I hope he didn't suffer."

"You know they would never have allowed that. They had a plan for the end. If either of them was infected, they would both take drugs they had. Because of you, they knew earlier than most people, and they prepared early. Besides a lot of water and food, Dad had secreted some drugs. I didn't ask what. Something to make them both sleep and not wake up. They were prepared for the end and were planning to meet it head-on. Neither of them would have cowed. They were fighters. You know that."

I did. I nodded, unable to speak. It was too real.

"They planned it out. Dad constructed a mini dome out of plastic. In the days immediately after you left, Dad researched, and then he bought as many of the strongest industrial tarpaulins as he could and glued them together. It took him several trips to transport them all. I went and helped him a couple of times. On fine days they would lift the edges and let the air flow. The tarps weren't breathable like ours, but on a dry day, it was safe to let the air in and out. It was only the water that was dangerous. He knew what he was doing. It was an insurance policy, buying them extra time. They wouldn't sit back and take it, but they knew it wasn't a perfect solution.

"In the days before most people even knew, Mum and Dad secretly went shopping and bought up all the bottled water they could, medications, tinned food, generators and fuel, solar panels, and batteries. They set themselves up at the block with four large water tanks, seeds, plants, and garden tools. They both quit work, drew down on their retirement funds, and quietly started buying up survival equipment. Not enough to draw attention to themselves, but enough to get by for a few years. Knowing what you had taught them about plants and pollination, they even installed some bees and hives."

"Really? Dad finally invested in hives?"

"And the expensive flow hives, too. Goodness, I laughed when I saw the boxes arrive. He always refused, telling you they were too expensive."

"I suppose when the end of the world is nigh, you don't really care, do you?"

"I can tell you from personal experience, money is one thing you don't care about," Sorcha replied quietly. "I think about them all the time, but so much more since little Sam arrived."

"Same," I admitted. "Nothing like becoming a parent yourself to make you think about how you were raised. The choices they made, the values they instilled in us."

"Loyalty was one they got right with you. Thank you for coming to find me. Now the big question, how did you know?"

Two hours later, Sorcha and I had filled in some of the gaps of the past years and were on our way to the community meeting, little Sam at her side. Diana met us on the way there, her cousin Kendra beaming by her side, arms interlinked, unable to stop smiling at their unexpected reunion.

Kendra was much like Diana in both looks and personality. While I knew they were cousins, they looked like sisters and completed each other's sentences or spoke in a bizarre half English, half Chinese dialect. It was fascinating to watch and impossible to follow.

Our third community meeting passed much like the other two—incredulousness, suspicion, and finally a little joy at knowing that others had survived. Di and I were questioned, tested, and a little revered at having traveled all this way to find *them*. The saddest part was advising the people here that in my travel across Australia, New Zealand, Ireland, and Scotland, nowhere had I seen any sign that the earth was yet recovering. Silence met this news. But they were not alone, and we had proof. We *were* proof. We left the two copies of the list we had, along with another list of those living on August and Bellcamp, and left quietly, amid loud chatter and a buzz of excitement. The difference here was that this was our endpoint. A sense of relief lightened my spirit as I left the meeting.

Life in the Kiewa community was more independent than on August or Lewis. There were two small towns here, linked by a single road running along the valley floor. Fertile farming land with neatly planned paddocks of crops, fruit trees, and grazing livestock, ran along both sides of the road, rising into the lush green hills with several industrial-looking buildings at the edge. The houses existed from before the pandemic, mostly with empty blocks in-between, split between the adjoining homes and allowing each household enough space for a vegetable patch, chickens, and small livestock like a goat. Each home had its own small aquaponics setup, I noted, along with solar panels, water tanks, and an outside toilet. They had removed every second house from the original settlement, allowing for more space.

As we explored, Sorcha told me they equally shared the fields of crops and orchards between householders. People kept much more to themselves, the way we had grown up. There were social activities, but people grew their food, kept chickens, and some, a hive or two for honey. It was much like a small village where people were self-sufficient and traded excess produce. Like the other communities, everyone had a specialist skill to share. Sorcha, a doctor. Kendra, like Di, had followed in the family's market garden business.

Never in a million years had I thought I would end up here, back in Australia, and in a place that our parents had adored. North-East Victoria reminded Mum of Scotland, and she loved the autumn colors, the snow-capped mountains that ringed the valleys, and the proliferation of wildflowers. I often wondered why they hadn't bought their weekender block here, but being nearly five hours' drive from home caused problems for a holiday house.

Most days, I tagged along with Sorcha, watching her work. She was paid in food usually, so we regularly took a bag to carry home whatever random item they gave her. Di and I had spent some time with Kendra and the agricultural team, sharing what we knew. But for us, knowing we would leave, this visit was about spending time with our loved ones.

Several weeks after my arrival, we were walking back from the other town, where I had accompanied Sorcha to suture a nasty wound. I stopped dead in the road, stunned.

"Oh, my goodness. Is that...?"

Sorcha, standing beside me, smiled. "A koala? Yes. They took great pains to ensure that most of the native species would survive: kangaroos, wallabies, wombats, koalas, possums, kookaburras, and lots of species of parrot. They are all here. Sadly, snakes too. But that wasn't deliberate, I don't think. They were just here when the biosphere was placed. But with so few birds of prey, they have endured too."

"I can't tell you how irrationally happy it makes me, knowing that these special animals persisted. Not many, of course, but that some *did*."

"They have survived, thrived even. With limited predators and knowing that they won't be harmed, many animals are quite conditioned to us now. No cars to run them over, no foxes. We co-habit happily for the most part."

"Tame, you mean?" I held my hand out to the koala sitting on the side of the road.

"No, conditioned. It is a little different. These animals will never be tame, domesticated, I mean. That takes generations. These animals know they are safe. It is kind of like a wild animal in a zoo. They have learned that the keepers care for them, but they aren't tame. You can never trust them. They are still wild animals."

Withdrawing my hand rapidly, I looked up at her from my position, crouched next to the koala.

"Laetitia. I wish she were here to see this. She has never seen a koala. I wish I could take one back to Scotland."

"Not many eucalypts in Scotland!" Sorcha laughed. "Besides, you have wildcats!"

As we approached the outskirts of town, I stopped and pointed to the industrial-looking buildings in the distance, usually sitting in the shade of the hills. But today, the afternoon sun reflected off blocks of what looked like square glass tanks filled with fluorescent green water, making it glow, alien-like.

"What on earth is that? It looks like slime."

"It is algae, of course!"

"It is … what?"

Sorcha sighed in her typically exaggerated fashion. Internally, I did too. This meant I was up for a lecture, but I had an inkling that it might be an interesting one.

"Alllll … geeeee," she enunciated slowly, making me feel like a toddler. "Don't you produce your own algae?"

"No. Why would we?"

"Because algae generates half of the world's oxygen! Those tanks over there produce oxygen the same as plants, via photosynthesis, only they are far more efficient at it. Each of those bioreactors contains micro-algae. Each milliliter contains about 5 million cells—or individual plants. In each 500-liter tank, the algae produce about as much oxygen as one hectare of forest."

"Wow. Seriously?" Di asked. She had walked up behind us and was now listening intently.

"No, I am joking. Of course, I am serious."

"Do you know how they set it up?" Di asked.

"Sure. That one was there when we moved here, but they gave us a briefing on it, along with other things. It was Tom's job to build more photobioreactors. He was working on a smaller system so they could power each house. There is already one at our house, so I learned quite a lot."

"Who is Tom?" I asked without thinking.

The look of disgust was instantaneous. "You are so … so … dense!"

Despite the stink-eye Sorcha was giving me, I couldn't help but laugh raucously at that. "Sorcs, I haven't heard that expression in twenty years. Only you could still make me feel like a toddler."

Her face softened a little.

"I'm sorry," I said, as genuinely as I could. "I didn't mean to..."

"It's okay," she cut me off. "But yes, Tomori was studying his Ph.D. in environmental science. A geek, like me."

"Well, that explains why Sam is so smart," Di interjected, "with two overachieving parents."

Sorcha rolled her eyes, but I could tell that she had accepted the compliment good naturedly. "Tom was a good man," she said sadly.

"I'm sure he was. Now tell me about these bioreactors. I'll bet the team on Bellcamp would love to know about those."

It turned out that the algae did an awful lot more than just produce oxygen. It also produced biogas which could be used for heating or cooking, and for the Kiewa community, this was used to complement the biogas bladder systems. It was while working on the tanks that Tom had stepped backward and was bitten by the snake. Being late afternoon and working alone, he had needed to walk the several kilometers home.

"By the time he reached the path outside, he was feverish," Sorcha told us as we entered the town, her voice dropping, even though Sam wasn't with us. "Thank goodness I was even home. He was in so much pain he could barely walk. He was struggling to breathe, vomiting, and was disoriented and confused. He couldn't recall what had happened, making assessment difficult. He had been wearing long pants, so by the time I realized it was his leg and managed to get a look at the wound ... well ... the venom was already circulating in his bloodstream. There was nothing I could do except make him comfortable. He died in my arms."

"Oh, Sorcha... I am so sorry."

"It's okay. It was a while ago. Sam took it hard. Cried every night for his dad. What could I tell him? He was there for breakfast but gone by dinner."

There was nothing to say to that. Just the overwhelming feeling that I was helpless to ease her pain for the second time.

CHAPTER 20

"**WHEN DID YOU ARRIVE** here?" Di asked, a little tentatively, one night over dinner. She and Kendra had joined Sorcha and me for a late meal. Sam was already in bed. Kendra's partner, Arjun, was caring for their son, Sanjiv.

"July," Kendra replied. "This was one of the last communities to be set up, I believe. Things were fairly dire by that stage. They transported us here using armored personnel carriers with a military escort."

Sorcha nodded in agreement but said nothing.

"July?" I said, more thinking aloud than continuing the conversation. "Five months after Di and I had relocated."

"Did they run out of potential sites, people to migrate into them, or just resources?" Di asked. "I mean, they stopped moving people if you say this was one of the last, but we received communications until mid-December."

"Resources, I would think," Sorcha said. "In one of my medical briefings, the guy kept apologizing for the lack of medical supplies. We had no basis for comparison. But it made me think that other groups, earlier groups, had been better resourced."

"There was a lot of fighting by then, too," Kendra said softly. "It was hard to get anywhere. Nothing to buy, even if you got out. But it wasn't safe. Going out, I mean."

"Someone continued to broadcast to us," I pointed out, as much as a distraction from the awful times I knew my family experienced and me not there to protect them. "From where I wonder?"

"Who knows, but I can tell you that the world you left was not one you would recognize: lockdowns, curfews, no paid work, no fresh food. Then there were riots in the streets, lawlessness. The police had all quit too, to stay home. Even the military was struggling with deserters. If we were all going to die, they just wanted to be home with their families too, so there was no one to stop it all. Each night we would lock our doors and windows and wonder what we would wake to."

The four of us lapsed into silence at that: Sorcha and Kendra reliving those times, Di and I feeling incredibly guilty that we hadn't been there. Breaking the melancholic mood, Di asked Kendra a question about the family business, and they morphed into a conversation about their family's market garden. Sorcha and I looked at each other with a mixture of horror and shame when Kendra described the racial attacks their family had been subjected to. Their warehouses were raided, and one burned, racist graffiti sprayed in red paint on their white house.

"Why?" I asked incredulously. "Didn't you say your family had been in Australia since the 1800s?"

"I did," Diana agreed, "and they have. Our several times great-grandfather arrived in 1860."

"Didn't matter in the end," Kendra said sadly. "We were outsiders, and when it is every man for himself, they saw us as alien. I was yelled at, spat on in the street, told to go back to my own country. Many times, I pointed out that I was born here. I *am* Australian. But it didn't matter. It took me a long time to realize that *everyone* was struggling. Lashing out at each other. People who were perceived to be hoarding. People who had more. But our difference was our physical appearance, so it was just easier to blame us."

"Blame you?" I asked. "Surely not."

"Oh, definitely. People blamed us because we owned a market garden, so we had sheds filled with fruit and vegetables waiting to go to market. Our family still tried to keep going while the produce wasn't infected. They kept working, trying to help feed others. Then one of the sheds was deliberately burned down. Fortunately, it was mostly empty, but that was when we realized it was serious. Two days later, the offer came for me to come here."

"Nai Nai?" Di asked gently.

Kendra's eyes dropped.

Sorcha and I looked at Di quizzically.

"Grandmother," she translated. "Specifically, our father's mother. There is a different word for maternal grandmother. But Nai Nai, our father's mother, was the matriarch of our family. If she told Kendra to go, then Kendra would go. No one would question it. It was she who ordered me to go too."

Kendra smiled at the memory. "She said they had chosen me. It was a great honor, and she was pleased to know that someone from our family would remain."

Diana and Kendra smiled at each other. Nai Nai had said the same to her.

"Though, I am not sure what she would think knowing I had married an Indian man!"

Arjun was a lovely man who idolized Kendra. I didn't think their grandmother would mind. But not knowing much about Chinese traditions, I said nothing.

"Our mother said something very similar to me." I smiled at Kendra.

"She said it to me too," Sorcha spoke in a low, husky voice. "I have never thought about it before, but I wonder how many other families are lucky enough to have two people survive?"

Silence lapsed over us again as we contemplated our losses, but how fortunate we were, not only to survive the catastrophe that had befallen the earth but to have each other.

Three weeks later and two weeks before our curfew, I broached the thorny subject over dinner. Taking a deep breath, I let it all out in a rush.

"Sorcs, I need to get home to Scotland. To Lae and Louis. I am needed there."

"I never thought you would stay."

"Will... will you come with me then?"

Sorcha gave me that exasperated look, the one that is so effortless to older sisters. "You know we will. I can't believe that you even needed to ask!"

I thought my heart was going to burst. I hugged her tightly. "Really? You want to leave your life here? Your work?"

"You are my family."

"Lae is going to love you and Sam. She never had a family of her own. You know Sam will need to travel through the portal? It isn't fun—let me warn you."

"I know. I know. You've told me. I have a fair idea of what it will be like. But I can strap him to me, and if there is one, place us both inside a heat suit. You said they made the passage less daunting, didn't you? But Cam..." she started cautiously, observing my face, "you have a car. I need to find Mum and Dad first."

Nodding in agreement, I said nothing. What was there to say? I had come all this way. Lae's words were ringing in my ears. We had to try.

Over breakfast the following morning, I addressed the subject of leaving early with Diana, delicately. We had been friends for years. Being reunited had been such a joy, and I would miss her terribly. She and Kendra were like twins, finishing each other's sentences and so alike to look at, I often had to check the clothing to ensure it was Diana I was speaking to. To my utter astonishment, she told me she would return with me. Her cousin Kendra wanted to stay here. She had roots, a partner, and a child. She was part of the community and didn't want to leave.

"Are you *sure* you don't want to stay?" I asked Di, bewildered by her response. She seemed happy, settled. More at peace than I think I had ever seen her.

"No," she responded firmly. "I will return with you."

"But we need to leave a few days early, to see what happened to my parents. We... we don't know what we will find."

"I will come with you," she said purposefully, still looking more content than I had seen her in years. I hadn't realized that she was so happy on August. Maybe it was closure, knowing her cousin was alive and well. Despite missing my family, seeing Sorcha again had filled me with a lightness of spirit that I didn't think possible. I had told Sorcha everything. For so long, I had thought I was alone, the sole survivor of my family. Now I knew for certain that not only had my sister survived, but she also had a child. The joy was overwhelming, and I couldn't wait to introduce Lae and Sorcha. Vastly different women, but I hoped that in time, they would become friends. Sorcha wasn't really a woman's woman. Much like Freyja, she was tall, assertive, and confident. Men admired her; women felt threatened by her. Secretly, I suspected that Freyja and Sorcha would have more in common than Lae and Sorcha but dismissed that thought. It wasn't likely that they would ever meet. Fortunately, despite also being vastly different in personality, Sorcs and Diana seemed to get along fine. Di was staying with Kendra, but often I woke to find her at the table, sharing breakfast with us each morning. Waiting for me. I hoped that I would have the chance to introduce Sorcha to Callie, Jamie, and Jacinda, those people who had been a support to me over the years.

Sorcha publicly announced that she was coming with me. Raf, the community leader, openly scowled at me when he heard. None of the Kiewa community was thrilled about losing one of their best doctors, but most understood that she wanted to be with her family. After all, which of them wouldn't make the same decision? Unlike Lewis, people here co-existed, but it didn't have the same sense of community as Lewis, that sense of cohesion and unity.

Di's emotional farewell with Kendra was far more difficult. Sorcha, once she had decided, was adamant. Nothing short of explosives would budge her. Like Mum, she was fierce and determined. Only a fool would take on that battle. But Di was floundering. I could see the emotion on her face. For the thousandth time, I couldn't fathom why on earth she would want to leave Kendra to return to August, but I could see that emotionally she was in no place to discuss it. Perhaps she didn't want to be a burden on Kendra's family? Be the third wheel in their marriage? Di and I had discussed the lack of solidarity here, but personally, I found it no worse than August. Yet, she clearly had her reasons. Watching her as she gave Kendra a last squeeze, tears streaming down her face, she turned and got into the back seat of the car, looking miserable.

Sam, who had never seen a car, let alone get in one, was permitted the front passenger seat so he could see the landscape ahead. Quietly, I had promised Sorcha that I would do my best to shield him from anything gruesome along the way, but it was likely a better choice that she sat in the front as we entered Melbourne. Di and I had seen some pretty grisly scenes on our way here.

Heading south, I set a cracking pace along the Snow Road and Hume Freeway. With no other cars, no police, it didn't matter at what speed we drove as long as we were safe. Once we were past the winding parts, it was a long, flat, and tedious road. Any obstructions were visible from quite a distance and easy to avoid. There were dead trees in abundance, the occasional abandoned car, but mostly the road was clear. Sorcha and I glanced over at the Brown Brothers winery as we traveled through Milawa, just off the main road. Our parents had been members of the wine club, and we had often stopped there for lunch while Mum and Dad sampled the cellar releases after a ski trip. But the vineyards were brown and decaying, fences half fallen and the buildings deserted.

I programmed the GPS, although I surprised myself by remembering the area well. While the freeway was mostly clear, once we started on the B-roads through small, abandoned country towns, it was slow going. Hours of frustration passed as we were forced to stop and move trees blocking the road and dodge enormous potholes from the road not being maintained. We passed through Mansfield, previously a thriving tourist town. Smashed shop windows, litter everywhere, and vandalized cars littered the main street, making passage slow going.

Sorcha took Sam to use the public toilets in the main street, and I could hear her laughing as his innocent voice drifted over the top of the stalls, asking where the sawdust was. Returning to the car, the landscape became more familiar, despite the dead trees and washed-out appearance. We fell into silence. Everything around us was lifeless, washed out, devoid of color. The engine purr sounded like a roar in the silence. The only other sound was the rustling sound of wind in the dead branches. The leaves had fallen and disintegrated years before. No birds singing, no insects chirping. Sorcha had been ensconced in her community for nearly five years and hadn't left. While they could see the deadened landscape through the surrounding dome, she didn't have any idea that it was this apocalyptic and barren.

Diana and I had traveled around the coast of part of New Zealand, then overland from Melbourne to Kiewa; thus, we had some idea of the destructive nature of this simple protozoon. What damage it had done to the formerly lush green landscape. It wasn't the sight of death that was affecting Sorcha. It was not knowing what we would find. Stopping as we turned off the main road, we switched Sam, who looked exhausted, to the back seat. Sorcha took the passenger seat as we braced ourselves for the last leg.

Ten minutes later, we came to the turnoff from the road to our private driveway. I stopped the car, looking over at Sorcha. She looked searchingly into my eyes, and I nodded assent. We would walk from here. It was a long, rutted, dirt road, one we had walked and ridden many times. It had been heavily treed, and likely some had fallen, blocking the road now that they were dead.

Diana made no move to get out of the car. She knew this was something we needed to do alone. Sam was nearly asleep in the back seat, stretched out beside Diana. Good. He didn't need to see this, and we didn't want to answer his questions about where we were going.

Closing the car doors as quietly as we could to avoid disturbing Sam, the soft slam still echoed through the eerily silent forest. Previously this area had been deafening, alive with birdsong, chirping, and tweeting. Flies would buzz and insects click and hum as the backing track to life. Occasionally, we would hear a koala call in the evenings, a sound akin to a motorbike in the distance. But now, it was like we had stepped into a bubble of unnatural, muted silence.

The driveway was a little over a kilometer long, and after a while, I regretted not trying to drive closer. Most of the branches across the road were light enough that we could have moved them. Sorcha was silent but sensed my frustration and looked up at me as she walked.

"We needed this time. This is for us and us only."

As the driveway opened out into the turning circle Dad had bulldozed years ago along with the house site and home garden, we could see the patchwork of multi-colored tarpaulins Dad had used to build the dome. Not visible from the road, they were isolated from the world. Lifting it at the base, with a bit of effort, we pulled the fabric out toward us and climbed underneath. From the inside, we could see that the tarps were held down by curved concrete garden edging laid in an enormous ring along the ground, leaving the tarp secure at the base and a long thin metal frame forming an arch up and over in a matrix. Dad had welded the frame. It appeared to be light metal bars joined at the ends to form the structure, the tarpaulins taped together on the inside and outside, and the frame embedded into holes drilled into the concrete base. It was simple, yet effective. *Could they still be here? Alive?* A glimmer of hope sparked in me.

"Mum! Dad!" I called, projecting my voice.

Sorcha joined in, "Mum!" Her high, clear voice rang out through the open space. "It's us, Cam and Sorcha!"

Scanning the dome above, I thought it appeared intact. Glancing around at ground level, I saw there was greenery all around us, with the marked exception of a central patch, like a bullseye, roughly ten meters across, of dead plants and trees. Amid so much life, that area was in various states of death, leaves brown and falling. The dome integrity had been breached, just not visibly. I sucked in my breath audibly, and Sorcha turned to look at where I was. Following my gaze, she saw the small grave at the foot of a nearby large eucalyptus tree, the tree still bursting with life. The small mound was edged with sandy-colored river stones and a simple carved wooden marker at the end.

"*Merlin,*" I read aloud as my eyes filled with tears. I sniffed and angrily blinked them away. Logically, I knew he wouldn't have made it, but somehow having it proven was different. More traumatic somehow.

"Come on." Sorcha started walking hesitantly toward the house, patches of green on one side and the contrasting brown foliage on the other side of the path.

It was exactly as I remembered it. A small, neat cabin, timber-lined on the outside and plastered on the inside with a gray colorbond roof, now sporting a bank of solar panels, fully guttered and filtered into a large tank at the back. A wide porch around the perimeter surveyed the length of the bush block. On the side of the house we were approaching, there were two wooden chairs to the right of the door, each chair with a worn tartan cushion, a small square table between them. Sorcha and I paused as we took the two steps up onto the deck and reached the door, closed. Neither of us wanted to go in first, fearful of what we would find.

Exhaling sharply, I muttered, "I'll go," and knocked loudly. The sound reverberated through the porch and around the cabin. No response. We hadn't expected one. I pushed the heavy door open, creaking on its hinges, and entered.

Coughing from the light layer of dust my boots had disturbed from the timber floors, I removed my hand from my mouth and cautiously looked around as the dust settled. Daylight illuminated the house with the large windows along each side, curtains open, dust dancing in the sunbeam. Opposite the door, the oiled solid red-gum kitchen bench Dad had crafted with a single deep farmhouse style sink ran along one wall, plumbed to the outside tank. Dad had built more cupboards, I noted. An additional row of timber cabinets now hung above the bench. A new, larger fridge was facing me, silent. The generator had stopped. Turning, I could see a double bed at the other end of the cabin, nestled into the nook, the bed neatly made with a slightly dusty navy print duvet cover, a throw blanket across the foot for Merlin. The pillows were propped up, awaiting someone's use, and two half-filled water glasses sat unloved, one on each bedside table. The old blue three-seater couch had been pushed to one side to allow a clear path, the table and two chairs against the opposite wall. They had removed our bunk beds. Instead, there was a double bookcase laden with books. There was no tv or radio, but the bookcase was two or three rows deep with books. Two books, with both sets of reading glasses, sat on the coffee table. I smiled slightly at the realization that I could still recognize my parent's reading habits. Several dead plants sat in unused corners, the dead foliage making a mess. Scanning the room, I could take in the full view of the cabin; there was no one here. Taking the two steps back to the door, I opened it wide and looked directly at Sorcha, shaking my head.

Sorcha stepped inside behind me, and together we looked more closely around the room, careful not to disturb the dust. The bed was made, but no sign of how long ago. They had washed the dishes, and they sat on the drainer beside the sink. Afraid to speak, to disturb the silence of this place, I caught Sorcha's eye and walked outside, circumnavigating the house. On the porch at the back was a box of canned food, random items, like someone had been shopping. There was another small shed, one I hadn't seen before, beside the large vegetable patch. Pumpkins ran on vines trailing all over the yard. Corn grew in tall husks, tomato bushes tipping over from the weight of the ripening fruit, not yet staked. Opening the door to the small shed, I saw boxes of canned foods in enormous quantities: beans, vegetables, soups, even canned ravioli, and tuna. Sorcha was right. They really had prepared. The stash of food here, combined with the enormous supply of fresh fruit and vegetables, would have lasted them for years.

Next to the food storage was a chicken coop I had never seen, now empty, scraps of straw still scattered over the ground. Bees still buzzed around, and I wondered how they could still be alive. Dad's old green Range Rover was barely visible under a tarp, protected by the trees at the back. They had cleared far more of the block since I was last here.

A movement caught my eye, and I glimpsed Sorcha's cornflower blue top walking around the side of the house and out of sight. No point in going that way then. Skirting the vegetable patch, I headed through the now much-enlarged orchard, one side ripe with fruit and the other side dying, leaves brown and lying on the ground. How strange. Looking up, I noticed that Dad had used clear plastic here. Closer to the ground and over the house, they had used the colored tarps, blues, and greens. That was logical. The clear plastic allowed the sun to penetrate and the plants to photosynthesize. A few steps to my right and I was in a forest of death. Trees looked like they did in winter. Brown leaves rotted into mulch at the bases of leafless brown branches. I flexed a twig, and it snapped, dry and brittle. My heart lurched as I heard the blood-curdling scream from the far side of the house. With no conscious thought, I ran, sprinting toward the sound of Sorcha's terror.

The sound of Sorcha's anguished screaming is a sound I will never forget. Breathless, I rounded the house and found her on her knees in front of a cherry tree. One of the original trees we had planted when we first bought the property, now nearly twenty years ago, before we had planned the gardens with some sense of order, the Stella cherry was planted in full view of the side porch and the bedroom window. It had been one of Mum's favorites in spring, its stunning pink blossom adding a touch of color to the garden.

Sorcha's body blocked from view, just for a moment, what became rapidly apparent. Freshly turned earth in a mound, not yet flattened or lightened by time. Back against the tree was my father, watching over his wife. An inconspicuous small white bottle lay against his jeaned leg, and an empty glass still beside him. He was wearing his peaked black wool cap, a cap I had bought him for his birthday many years before, his face partially obscured, dropped into his navy tee-shirted chest. Dried mud caked the soles of his

Blundstone boots. My stomach churned, and I had to look away. Scooping up Sorcha blindly, I carried her weeping form, curled up in my arms like a toddler, the kilometer back to the car in a daze. We didn't look back.

Diana saw me coming down the road and opened the back doors of the car. Gently, I deposited Sorcha into Diana's care. Sam had woken and was distressed to see his Mum crying.

"It's okay, buddy," I told him gently as I moved him to the front seat and put a seatbelt on him. "Come and help me drive." Sam still looked at the seatbelt with fascination, and it occurred to me he had never seen such a thing. Showing him how it opened and closed that morning had fascinated him. Carefully closing the passenger door, I climbed into the driver's seat, put the car in reverse, and maneuvered back onto the road. In the rearview mirror, I could see Sorcha's head in Di's lap, Di stroking her hair like a child as she sobbed. We drove in silence, interspersed with Sam asking me questions about our surroundings: street signs and electricity towers, mailboxes, and graffiti—things he had never experienced. My mind naturally wandered to Louis and our life on Lewis. He, too, would never see a skyscraper, a cinema, a petrol station, or a shopping center.

As we arrived in the outer suburbs, I paused, contemplating which way to go. Freeways would be best, with fewer shops and hopefully fewer blockages. We were lucky to find the car with a full tank of fuel and still had nearly half left—enough to get back to the *Pamplemousse*.

An accusing voice fired from the back seat. "We should have gone sooner. We might have been able to save them."

Knowing from years of experience that this wasn't likely to be a brief conversation, nor one I wanted to have while distracted navigating my way through parts of the city I was unfamiliar with, I pulled the car over to the curb and turned in my seat to face her.

"Sooner. How much sooner? Come on, Sorcs. We couldn't have known. I didn't even know that there were other communities in Australia until Freyja arrived, and that was only a few months ago. I had to wait for the next solstice. There was no alternative to that. Would the few weeks it took to travel from August to Melbourne have made a difference? The few weeks I spent with you at Kiewa? Would we have made it in time?"

"He hadn't been dead that long," she sobbed.

"What do you mean by that? Weeks, months? Surely with fewer insects to speed up decomposition, you can't really tell."

"No, I can't. But it was less than a year."

"A year ago, I didn't know that there were other communities here. I had no idea that *you* were alive, let alone them. And you. You were safe, caring for your child in a community several hours away by car but with no vehicle to use. You also had no way of knowing if it was safe out here. I think we have learned today that the contagion is still active. Some trees in the orchard were alive, some dead, and some still dying. What should you have done? Traveled here, risking yourself and your child? They wouldn't have wanted that."

"What would *you* know about what they wanted? You left us! Abandoned us! You were long gone before things got bad. The first opportunity and you bailed. You don't understand what it was like. Gangs roaming and people being mugged in the street. Windows being smashed. Pets being stolen, likely to eat. Being too scared to go outside, shower, or drink water. Only Mum, Dad, and I left to deal with it all. I had to help them fortify the house, get enough food and bottled water. You were off living the high life, hot springs, and romantic rendezvous with hot Norwegian chicks. Meanwhile, we had to take it in turns to sleep so someone could always guard the house. You. You were off having a glorious time." Sorcha's voice was getting louder and higher, signaling, warning.

Sam began to cry, and Diana got out of the car to retrieve him from the front seat. Despite having no siblings of her own, she recognized a sibling dispute and knew enough to stay well out of the way. Sorcha also exited the car, slamming the door as hard as she could. I also got out and faced her, slamming my door equally loudly.

"Left you?" My tone was low and mocking. "Abandoned you? I'm sorry. Were you actually there? Do you not remember Mum *telling* me to go?"

"I was there. I remember perfectly. You didn't fight very hard." The shrill, angry voice had turned to a low, menacing hiss. This was getting dangerous.

"Maybe I didn't. I didn't *want* to go. I didn't want to leave you at all. How was I to know what would happen?"

"You knew more than we did! You knew, and you bloody well left us to *die*!"

"I did," I admitted. "I thought you were all dead. And not a day went by that I didn't think of you all and questioned, why me? I wasn't special. Why did I get chosen?"

"Don't play your psychological mind tricks on me, asshole," Sorcha sneered, fury radiating from her. "You knew, and you still left. It doesn't matter why. You *deserted* your own family. You thought you were a big shot. You thought you were more important than us, and you *left*."

The last word was spat with such contempt that some of her saliva hit my cheek.

Ignoring her insults, I took a deep breath and wiped my cheek. "I did leave, but that isn't why. Don't you remember Mum saying she wanted something of our family to remain?"

I was trying hard to keep my emotions under control. When we were younger, Sorcha and I would regularly disagree and end up in a shouting match. It took me many years to realize that she simmered down a lot faster if I could stay calm. The problem was, inevitably, I fired up too, and it always ended badly.

"I know she did, but you didn't have to *go*." These last words were delivered with such anger I knew where this was going. She was looking around wildly. Years of sibling conflict told me that this was for a weapon, something to hit me with, or preferably, throw at my head.

I started to respond, "Well, you did too." I sensed the trap a fraction of a second before I put my foot in it. Catching myself, I paused and replied as quietly as I could while still being heard. "I shouldn't have gone. I should have stayed. I should have been with you. I'm so sorry."

The wind visibly plummeted from her sails. She was waiting for me to blame her for going too, then she could be justified in her anger at me for leaving first. At this admission, she didn't know how to respond. Uncomfortable silence sat between us like a black cloud as we looked at each other.

Finally, she begrudgingly admitted, "Mum wanted you to go. She said so many times. Whenever things were bad, she said she was happy to know you were safe."

"Then I am assuming then that she wanted you to go, too?"

"They both did. But I feel so *guilty*. Mum and Dad were out here, alone, all this time. *They* were alive. Knowing that we were both out there, somewhere, but unable to get to us."

We had made it to the point, and she knew it. Guilt. Overwhelming, all-encompassing guilt. We had both abandoned them to their fate. Putting my arms around her, I held her as she cried. Tears of loss and tears of forgiveness. Years of pent-up emotion. Tears flowed down her cheeks. I had already beaten myself up for leaving, years before, when wandering around the forest after Freyja's disappearance. I blamed myself for leaving my family, for abandoning them. It had taken seeing my Aunt Angela to realize that is how we all would have ended up. With Laetitia's help, I had finally forgiven myself. Now Sorcha needed that forgiveness, too.

Between sobs, I spoke softly, words of support and encouragement. As she slowed, when I knew she could hear me, I whispered, "They forgive you. They forgive me. It is what they would have wanted. Their end was on their terms. Together."

Sorcha's tears overwhelmed her again as she recognized the truth in my words. She cried and cried until she ran out of steam and lay limp in my arms. We were seated at the side of the road, abandoned shops with filthy smashed windows behind and opposite.

After a while, Di and Sam returned, Diana looking apprehensive and Sam looking scared. Glancing up, Sorcha held her arms out to Sam, and he ran to her. Arranging him on her lap, she cuddled and snuggled into him. I held my hand out to Diana; she came and sat between us. Sam lay his head against Diana's shoulder, and I realized how quickly he had become fond of her and how natural she seemed with him. I had never really seen her as the motherly type, and it astonished me how quickly she had adapted to a nurturing role. Although it was late summer, and the days were long, we still had some way to travel.

"Come on," I urged gently.

CHAPTER 21

BOARDING THE YACHT, WE were the first to arrive. We were early, several days before the agreed rendezvous date. We had allowed some extra time, just in case we ran into trouble. Or in the faintest hope that Mum and Dad were still alive. It was time we could have spent with them, convincing them to come with us. Sorcha looked up at the yacht, its sails flapping in the breeze, alive amid so much death. Sam was fascinated, never having seen the ocean or a sailing vessel of any kind.

Showing them around the yacht, I noted that there were only four bedrooms. Without knowing who would return, we would need to share. Di had shared with Iznayah on the way over, taking turns to sleep in the king-single bed or on the tiny amount of floor space alongside.

"We will need to shuffle rooms around so you and Sam can have a room to yourselves," I explained to Sorcha.

It was Di's voice, quiet and calm, that responded. "Sorcha will sleep with me. Sam can have the trundle mattress on the floor."

Remembering we had found a kid's mattress on the boat, I looked at Diana, puzzled.

"That's right. We have a half-size mattress. But there won't be enough room on the floor for them both. How will you... ohhhh!" My face flushed crimson as realization struck, and I realized precisely what she meant. Sorcha stood stiffly beside her, evidently uncomfortable, but steadfast. Both were glaring at me, daring a response.

"Got a problem?" Di snapped defensively as she reached for Sorcha's hand.

"Nope. None," I hastily replied, the words tripping over themselves in a rush to get out. Never in a million years had I seen *that* coming. In all the years I had known Di ... and my sister... never had I even suspected that... that... My head was spinning out of control, and I needed to sit down to stop the feeling of vertigo.

Di and Sorcha left me to my bewilderment and went down to the bedrooms to set up. Sitting on the deck, dumbstruck, staring out to sea, it made perfect sense. There had been something between Diana and Sorcha since we had arrived five weeks ago. A spark, something indescribable. They had connected instantly, bonded, but I hadn't given it any thought. Naively, I just thought they got along, much as Di and Freyja had. I thought it over: Di always being there for breakfast; the looks they shared. I was too caught up in my mess, my trauma at leaving Lae and Louis, learning that Sorcha had been through yet more loss, and I hadn't been here to support her. I felt inadequate, a failure. I felt guilty taking her away from Kiewa. Sorcha was settled there, part of the medical team. But over the past few weeks, we had reconnected and realized that we couldn't be apart anymore. Sorcha had few ties in Kiewa. Sam would come with her. I was integrally linked to the community on Lewis. My wife and child were there. My friends, my future. To leave with me, with Di, meant a fresh start for them both.

Since I had returned to August, I had been thinking of potential partners for Di, even considering Aidan or Kevin in Newgrange. Never in my wildest dreams had I considered my own sister. Down the open walkway, I watched them prepare dinner together in the galley, really watched them. It was blatantly apparent—they were in love. With Sorcha's outward confidence and Diana's kind and gentle nature, they were the perfect match and brought out the best in each other. Diana softened Sorcha's sharpness, and Sorcha made Diana's personality shine ever more brilliantly. Watching them, I saw they were perfect together.

Somewhere in the early hours of the evening, Diana came to find me up on the deck as I watched the sunset, holding the rail, a million thoughts drifting like a tunnel through my head, but unable to process any of them. They flitted in and then out without any interaction. Random thoughts.

"Are you sure you are okay with this?" she asked shyly from behind me as she placed a plate of food on the small table.

Startled, I turned to look at her. "Okay? Why on earth wouldn't I be? My best friend and my sister in love? What more could I ask? I am thrilled. No, beyond thrilled. Though, you had better not hurt her..." I mock warned Di. "She is my sister, and she has had her heart broken twice now. I am *not* picking up the pieces again."

"She told me about Sam," Diana whispered. "The other Sam, I mean."

Nodding, I acknowledged the trust that had taken on Sorcha's part. It was serious then.

"Will you go back to August?"

Diana shook her head. "I have no desire to return to August. I would much rather accompany you back to Lewis."

"But you said you wanted to return to August?"

"No. Actually, what I said was that I would return with you. You assumed August, and at the time, I didn't correct you. It was new between Sorcha and me, and we weren't ready for you to know. But I want to be with you. Both of you. We all want to come to Lewis. If... if that is okay, I mean," she asked hesitantly.

"To have you *and* Sorcha with me? Nothing would make me happier."

"The other people there won't mind?"

"Fairly sure they would be thrilled to have another doctor and agriculturalist. Lae won't mind another student in Sam. I would be so happy to be working with you again."

Di hugged me, and I heard a throat-clearing noise behind me.

"Get your grubby mitts off *my* partner." Sorcha's warning emanated from the darkness.

Her face glowing in the sunset, Diana blushed at the word partner but said nothing.

Wrapping my arms around Diana protectively, I retorted, "She was my friend first."

A deep, guttural growl emanated from Sorcha's throat, making both Di and I look at her in astonishment.

"Fine." I let Diana go, and she hurried across the deck to Sorcha, who protectively placed an arm around her waist. Sorcha towered over Di, but they *fit*.

"I don't think I could choose anyone better for either of you," I admitted. "I would never have even considered it, but I am thrilled for you both."

"Thank you." Sorcha's husky tone proving she had been genuinely concerned at my reaction. "That means a lot."

After they went to bed, I ruminated on my life. I was happy for them both, but it made my heart ache for Laetitia and Louis. How long until I could be back home, safe in the arms of the woman I loved? Had I placed Sorcha, Di, and now little Sam in danger? We had a treacherous ocean crossing, then a portal to endure. If nothing else, the discovery of our parents had illustrated that the threat had not passed. In my travels over the past few years, I had just been lucky. Was I thoughtless, spending so much time outside of the security of protected communities? I had been careful, but it took just a drop of infected water to be ingested to become infected. It didn't take a forensic scientist to see what had happened with our parents. A few drops had entered their protected space, started killing trees and plants—perhaps before they even realized it. Maybe Mum had just eaten something that had been infected. I doubted they would have drunk infected water.

The only wholly safe places were the domed communities. But even then, what had happened on Gibraltar? The dome there had failed if Angus was to be believed. How? An overwhelming need to speak to Blake consumed me. He seemed to understand the technology behind the domes better than anyone.

Well, except Angus, and hell would freeze over before I spoke to him voluntarily. But goodness knows where Blake was. Likely on the *Sea Witch*, and I was here in Melbourne. As an engineer, Blake was fascinated with the mechanics of the portals, the engineering. But he was someone in whom I could confide my fears. If the Gibraltar dome had failed, what was stopping ours from failing also? I couldn't shake the uneasy feeling that I was leading my sister and her family to certain doom.

CHAPTER 22

OVER THE FEW DAYS we were alone, we filled the hold of the *Pamplemousse* with as much as we could find: food, water, tools and furnishings, batteries, torches, bikes. Anything that could be useful to any of the communities. Sorcha and I, originating from Melbourne, did most of the scavenging, while Di, who didn't know her way around, looked after Sam.

We had no way of knowing how many people would return, and we didn't want to waste time later. With visions of snarky Daniella judging me, the uneasy feeling of invading someone's home didn't get any easier, especially when we were occasionally confronted with the deceased owners. Despite this, we knew. We needed the goods, and they didn't. Part of me wished we had just brought some fresh fruit and vegetables from Mum and Dad's place. But we couldn't. Sorcha and I had been in no fit state to think about raiding our parent's stash. There was also the genuine risk that they had been contaminated.

Watching the pink-orange glow of dawn as the sun rose over Port Phillip Bay, we had officially reached the agreed three-day waiting period. A heightened sense of tense alertness made us jumpy, wondering who would return and who wouldn't.

Not wanting to hang around waiting, Sorcha and I paid a visit to our family home. Our street looked like a war zone with smashed windows and burned-out cars. Our own home had fared little better. Our parents had installed metal roller shutters many years ago to block the light and noise when Dad was sleeping during the day, accommodating his night shifts. The shutters were dented, rocks and paint cans in the front garden bed used as weapons. Mum's pride, her standard roses, were little more than sticks in the ground. The fruit trees, carefully espaliered around the fence lines, were gone, rotted away. A flash of anger struck when I noted the Buddha head statue, used to mark our pet's graves, had been stolen, likely used to smash a window. The house itself appeared to be intact, and Sorcha, remembering the location of the hidden key safe, disappeared for a moment, then returned, brandishing the key.

"Are you sure you want to do this?" she asked with some hesitancy.

Nodding, I unlocked the front door. I planned to return to Lewis. The likelihood of me ever returning here was minuscule. Not really recognizing the distance and the difficulty in the journey, Sorcha was unlikely to understand.

Slowly we entered, and like wraiths, crept through the house. The strangest feeling washed over me. Familiarity, but somehow, I was an intruder. This wasn't my place anymore. Standing in the doorway to my bedroom, I felt uneasy, out of place. An adult standing in a child's room. It was familiar, but no longer mine. My thoughts flitted to Louis as I scanned my formerly treasured possessions. Louis would likely never have posters of pop stars on his walls or a stereo with CDs. Not even a trophy from local sporting competitions. As I absorbed my past, I realized how lucky I was to have had these experiences. My son would never sit in a cinema or have a favorite band. He would never have a wardrobe filled with clothes. Sitting on the edge of my bed, careful not to dislodge too much dust, I took it all in: the things I had collected and valued at some point but valued no longer. Feeling the movement, I saw Sorcha in the doorway, looking down at me. She was holding a photo frame, a strange, conflicted look on her face.

"What did you take with you to August?" she asked.

"Photos," I admitted. "Just photos. Di gave them back to me on my last trip to August. They are on the yacht. I couldn't bring myself to leave them behind. You?"

"I left in such a rush that I took nothing other than all the salbutamol we had. We got the call at 2pm, and I was to report there by 5pm. I'm ashamed to admit that I spent most of those hours crying and fighting with Mum, not wanting to leave them. But now... now I want to show Sam where he came from."

Standing, I started collecting the few remaining photos from my room. Moving to the lounge, I could see Sorcha was collecting those in frames on the walls and on display. Those pictures had humiliated me but now captured the family that we once were. Some were missing, evidently taken by Mum and Dad doing precisely what we were doing now.

Returning to my room and digging around under my bed, I found a large duffel bag I used for ski gear.

Tipping out the goggles and gloves, I gently placed in my treasured photos and moved into the lounge to assist Sorcha. Together we collected albums, framed photos, and loose prints. A single bag filled with memories was all we had left.

As I loaded them into the car, Sorcha went into Mum and Dad's room. I watched her as I re-entered the house.

"What are you looking for?" I queried.

"I don't know," she admitted. "I just want something ... of them."

Moving into the wardrobe, I flicked through the now dusty clothes, but nothing evoked memories. It was just cloth. Sorcha was methodically going through drawers but closing them as she opened the next. I watched as Sorcha pulled out an emerald green merino scarf, finely knitted into a diamond pattern, and wrapped it around her neck.

"Mum loved that scarf," I acknowledged. "It suits you. She would love that you have it."

Sorcha fossicked around in the drawer and came up with a small box. Opening it, she looked inside, taking out an object before closing it again and handing it to me.

I opened it, and inside lay a silver piece of eight coin made into a pendant and mounted on a silver chain. Many times, our father had told us the story of buying it on the Scilly Isles, a small archipelago off the coast of Cornwall, only a few months before he met Mum. A treasure chest had been salvaged there from a shipwreck off the coast, containing Spanish coins dating back to the 1500s. He had bought the best piece he could afford as a backpacker. It wasn't a whole coin, yet mostly intact after centuries under saltwater. But he had treasured it. He had worn the pendant to special occasions over the years, including to his wedding. Slipping it around my neck, I vowed to one day give it to Louis in memory of his grandfather.

Sorcha was gazing at Mum's aquamarine ring, now on her middle finger. It had been made from an older brooch owned by our grandmother. The unset stone was initially bought in South Africa by our grandfather. Mum treasured it, a memory of her parents who died when she was young.

"She always said she wanted you to have that."

Sorcha closed the drawer.

That night I brought out the photos Di had given me on August and showed Sorcha. Combined with the images we had taken from the house, we laughed, cried, smiled, and sobbed our way through the evening. Diana understood. Sam, who had never met these people, was mesmerized, begging for more stories about these people and events, making me even more homesick for Laetitia and Louis. Sorcha pointed out his namesake, the other Sam. Granny and Grandpa. Sorcha and I when we were young. Sam was fascinated by a photo of Sorcha and me standing behind our two Saint Bernard dogs. With no dogs in the Kiewa community, Sam had never seen one and was captivated by these enormous, magnificent beasts.

"Thank you," I whispered to Diana as she showed the photos to Sam for the fifteenth time while Sorcha went to the bathroom and to refresh our drinks. "Thank you for bringing me those photos."

"Thank *you,*" she replied. "When you left, I found them in your house. It was strange. I knew somehow that I was supposed to keep them safe. That I would see you again. The other thing was...."

"What?"

"As soon as I saw the pictures of your sister, I knew."

"Knew what?"

Di shrugged. "That she was the one. For me."

"From a *photo*?" I asked incredulously.

"I just ... knew."

"Knew what?" Sorcha asked, watching us as she entered the room, another bottle of red in hand.

"Nothing." Di smiled, reaching her glass out for a refill.

CHAPTER 23

DAY TWO OF THE agreed waiting period dawned, and it was still only Sorcha, Diana, Sam, and me. Tadhg had dropped in the previous afternoon. He had nearly finished downloading all the data, but he hit some technical hurdles and needed a little more time.

"Am I glad to see you!" he gushed in his thick Irish brogue after embracing me in an enormous bear hug. "Six weeks with no human contact is like being in solitary confinement. You end up talking to yourself and going half-mad!"

Remembering those months on August thinking Freyja dead and the community ostracizing me, I knew that feeling all too well. Add grief to the mix, and ... well, that was a long time ago. Thrilled with the bike we presented to him from a shop we had raided, Tadhg returned to the offices for a final download of the data he had recovered, which he promised was worth it.

Late in the afternoon, we heard a motorbike, a sound I had not heard in years. Stunned momentarily, it took me a second to recall what the noise was. Sam, still struggling with the gentle movements of the yacht, looked terrified, never having seen nor heard a motorbike. Walking out onto the deck, we saw Col with a woman behind him, her hair flying behind her. She looked very much like him with stunning copper skin, long black hair, and dark eyes.

Their mother must have been beautiful, I thought, seeing them together.

As the engine stopped, Col helped his sister off and unstrapped the deep panniers on either side of the bike. Sorcha was holding Sam on her hip. He wasn't quite brave enough to approach the enormous noisy beast just yet, even though Colin had killed the engine. Diana was already racing down the gangplank, and I wasn't far behind her, beaming at the sight of them. As I made the final descent onto land, I saw Di fly at Col, and after a brief introduction, hug the younger woman, too.

"This is Harriet," Col introduced proudly.

"Lovely to meet you." I greeted her warmly as I clapped Colin on the back. "Good to see you, too." I was just about to ask about the others when we heard a car engine drone in the distance. The silence here heightened all sounds, and it was some time before we saw the dirt clouds billowing in the distance, approaching the dock. A chocolate brown Peugeot 404 came trundling down the road, looking very out of place. We could see two figures inside but were unable to see who it was.

As the 404 neared the dock, we could see that it was two of the team from Bellcamp.

"It's Ian and Katya!" Di exclaimed as they got out of the car to join us.

"Where are Daniella and Floss?" I asked Colin and Harriet.

"Floss found her son." Colin smiled.

"Assuming it went well then?"

"Better than well. Their reunion was really ... touching."

It must have been, I realized. A taciturn man, he was positively gushing with emotion.

"They hit it off straight away, and we could barely get a word in. Goodness, he is like her, both in looks and mannerisms. They just clicked. She stayed at Glenmaggie."

"That is good news," Di said. "She was worried about the reunion, so I am glad it went well. The community didn't mind?"

"Not at all. They have had a bit of a population explosion and were happy to gain another cook, and Floss proved herself capable almost immediately. The community there is very bonded to each other. She fit in just fine. Besides, they gained one and lost one!" Col beamed at his sister, standing at his side.

"Fantastic. And Daniella?"

Colin's face dropped. "That isn't such good news."

"Why not? Was she not welcomed?"

"Oh no, it wasn't that. After we left you, we looked for a car. We found one, an old Corolla. Usually, they were reliable, mechanically, but apparently, this was the exception. Well, we made it out of Melbourne and were on the Princes Highway. Then it broke down somewhere on the other side of Warragul, and we couldn't get it started. Literally in the middle of nowhere. We tried everything, but the piece of shit would not start. I've got a bit of knowledge with engines, but something had seized and would not give. With no tools, there was little I could do. We started to walk, not wanting to waste any more time. We were lucky. There was a flat verge along the highway that had been grassed once, and it was mostly flat and clear, even if it was littered. We knew the community was somewhere north of Traralgon, but not precisely sure where. None of us had ever been there. We figured we would see the dome from a distance, but knew it was a few days' walk. Daniella insisted on walking with no shoes, said the new boots she had taken from here were heavy and made her feet blister. She had left her old shoes with Tadhg at the government offices. Floss and I kept telling her to wear her boots, but she refused.

About four hours after we started walking, she stepped on a rusty nail hidden in the dead grass. She screamed and carried on. Floss was great. She pulled the nail out, cleaned it up, bandaged it with strips we tore from my t-shirt. I offered to help her walk, piggyback her, but she wouldn't let me touch her, said she was fine. All good. Then a day or so down the road, it got infected. We didn't have any antibiotics, no Panadol. Nothing. The puncture wound was red, swollen, and pus-filled, so we knew it was infected. We cleaned it again and kept moving, an arm around Floss and me so we could support her.

That night she spiked a fever, constantly sweating and short of breath. We were still quite a way from Glenmaggie by our calculation, bearing in mind we didn't know exactly where it was, nor where we were. She couldn't move far, and we were fearful of rain. Floss stayed with her, and I explored the areas surrounding the highway. Finally, I found an old farmhouse. We carried her there to keep her comfortable. Aside from our backpacks, we only had a small amount of bottled water left and not a lot of food. We had expected to reach Glenmaggie sooner, so we hadn't rationed the food. Then the muscle aches started. She complained of contractions in the neck and told us her jaw ached something terrible."

Sorcha's mouth had dropped. "She didn't make it, did she?"

"No." Col's voice dropped even lower. "We buried her in the farmhouse yard, less than a day's walk from Glenmaggie. The worst part was, Floss and I had no clue where we were. Had we known we were so close, I would have walked it. Run even to get help. They had doctors there. But we didn't have a clue. We thought we were much farther away. So, we watched her die. In agony."

"From an infected wound?" I asked, turning to Sorcha incredulously.

"Not the wound. Tetanus," Sorcha pronounced like a doctor solving a medical mystery.

"Tetanus?" Puzzled, I looked at Sorcha. "Surely, she was vaccinated."

"She wasn't." It was Col who spoke. "She was an anti-vaxer. I asked her at the beginning when she first stepped on the nail, and we removed it. She thought vaccinations were toxic, full of chemicals, and believed in homeopathic supplementation."

Sorcha snorted audibly in a way that reminded me so much of Mum. I knew what she thought of such things.

"I have never seen a full-blown case of tetanus," she admitted. "Apparently, it is hideously painful. They used to call it lockjaw."

"Well, from firsthand experience, I can tell you why." Colin looked green while telling the story. "It was nasty. Painful, too, at the end. There was nothing Floss nor I could do for her."

"We all had our vaccination status checked when we departed," I mused. "I remember having to ask Mum."

"She lied, apparently," Col interjected. "No one bothered to check in the panic."

"That's twice," I growled quietly, recalling the systemic failure to identify Heidi as a fraud that had caused me so much personal pain.

"Did you find her brother?" Di asked.

"We did—Ward. He was mighty upset to hear that she had been so close but hadn't made it. He was a lovely man, too. Dare I say nothing at all like her."

Silence fell over the group. Colin looked at Ian and Katya, who had been listening intently to Colin's story. Being from Bellcamp with Daniella, they likely knew her better than anyone.

"Where are Iznayah and Dave?" Col asked.

"They both stayed in Kinglake. Dave caught up with the girl he was seeking, an old girlfriend it appeared, and they...well...reconnected. Not without a little drama."

His tone indicated that there was quite the story behind this. Responding to the quizzical looks, he supplied the rest of the information.

"Marina may have already had a husband. He wasn't best pleased with her leaving him for a new man. Especially when you can't really leave. Fireworks is an understatement," he supplied somewhat theatrically.

"Ohhhh... And Izzy?"

"Izzy, well, Izzy met up with her cousin and was happy to stay. Said she didn't care which community she was in, and it may as well be on the mainland."

Murmurs of acknowledgment, but our thoughts centered on Daniella and her painful demise. Admittedly, none of us had found anything redeeming about her and considered her uptight and prudish, but it was still a nasty way to go.

"So, this is all of us then and a day early too." I looked around the group. Sorcha, Diana, and little Sam. Colin and Harriet. Ian and Katya. Tadhg was returning in the morning, and we could be off. Bellcamp first to drop off Tadhg, Ian, and Katya. Colin and Harriet were returning to August. Then, in a few weeks, Sorcha, Di, and I could travel to Lewis.

Di produced several bottles of good quality whisky, vodka and wine liberated from one of the raided homes in Brighton. We sat on the deck and talked well into the night. At one point, Diana disappeared and returned with food, which we consumed as we exchanged news of what had happened in each of the communities. Glenmaggie was thriving, with low death rates and high birth rates, to the point where they were becoming concerned about sustainability. Kinglake had not fared so well. An unknown virus swept through the community in the second year and killed over a quarter of its 400 inhabitants. Of those who had died was Katya's sister Nadja, and the distress still visible. Losing one hundred and three highly trained individuals had been a monumental loss to the establishing community, and they were still struggling to return to a sense of normality. Ian's

half-brother was there, but like him, he was established and didn't want to leave.

"You didn't think of staying there?" Sorcha
asked Ian.

"It was funny. The entire time I was at Kinglake, it
felt like I was on holiday. You know that feeling when
you visit a place, and it is fun and all, but you know,
deep down, that it isn't *home*. As bizarre as it might
seem, Bellcamp is home for me now. I'm used to the
strange climate, the long dark days, and the people.
It is where I belong."

I realized Katya was struggling, despite the brave
facade. To believe your family is dead, then someone
comes along with a glimmer of hope that they might
just possibly be alive, you take a leap of faith, leave
your life and home to take a risky journey only to get
there and find that your sister had survived the worst
of it but had died later—died of something that likely
could have been cured a few years ago with hospitals,
pathology labs, medical technology, and a wide range
of medications. Katya had been dealt the worst hand
of us all, I knew.

On my right, I watched Di and Sorcha snuggled
close on a sofa, little Sam asleep beside Sorcha. She
was gently stroking his hair and appeared the image of
domestic contentment. It was such a strange feeling
seeing her as a mother, a role in which I never envisaged her. Spying on them surreptitiously, I thought
of Lae and Louis, snuggled up on our couch at home,
Lae singing softly to him. How I missed them both.
Closing my eyes, only slightly drunk, I had an image of
them in the greenhouse, picking tomatoes and beans
for dinner. Louis in a sling on her hip, Lae's long thick
hair cascaded down her back, and Louis grabbed for

it, making her laugh. The sun was shining. It would be nearly spring there now. The fields and paddocks would soon be green with new life. I should be there. It was my place, my home. Sorcha caught my eye and smiled. Smiling back, a pang of guilt washed over me. I had abandoned them. But my mission had been successful. I would bring Sorcha home, and she, Di, and little Sam would be welcomed.

The conversation grew slower and quieter, and eventually people drifted off to their cabins below. We had a long journey ahead of us and were keen to get started. Insisting Katya sleep in the bed, I spent the night uncomfortably on the couch.

Tadhg arrived bright and early in the morning, thrilled to see that most of us had returned safely. We proudly shared the stash of coffee beans and tea leaves that we had found in one of the homes we had raided. The tea lovers swooned. The coffee addicts like me were equally thrilled with the beans, albeit slightly stale. After a hearty breakfast supplemented with fresh hot tea and coffee, Tadhg asked after each of those who had not returned and nodded grimly when he heard of Daniella's painful demise. Being Catholic, he insisted on saying a prayer for the repose of her soul. Standing on the beach, Tadhg solemnly recited the words in Gaelic, then in English. They were not familiar to me. Our parents were lapsed Protestants, and Sorcha and I had been raised in an agnostic household. The few times we had been to church were for christenings, weddings, or visiting religious sites with historical or cultural significance on our travels.

I always felt a sense of peace in a holy place. I recognized the feeling but had never been drawn to study religion. Laetitia was also not religious, so we had not discussed Louis and having him baptized or christened. I didn't know the difference. Besides, there were no ministers or priests in any of the communities I had visited. Tadhg, originally from Ireland, had told me that most of that community were practicing Catholics, and thus, his children with Callie had been baptized, Catholics allowing a layperson to perform such rituals in the absence of a priest.

On August, and Bellcamp too, there had been a preference for sending people with no religious affiliations, and there had been no conflict motivated by religion. Strange, I contemplated, that the population on August had instead divided along social lines instead of religious ones. Perhaps people would always find a point of similarity or difference. If not religion, then something else. Studying history in high school, I firmly believed that religion caused most wars and conflict. With my experiences of the past five years, I reconsidered this position. While there wasn't exactly war on August, the clear divisions along economic lines had caused considerable conflict and discontent. Not physical violence, nor expansionism, but I could envision a time in the not-too-distant future where challenges over land boundaries could occur.

Similarly agnostic in outlook, Sorcha had come home from her aid work in Papua New Guinea with a revised opinion. Missionaries, she had said, had done so much excellent work. While initially, she had viewed them with skepticism, thinking their role was to convert the masses to follow Jesus, the reality was somewhat different. They had set up medical clinics for children and pregnant and nursing mothers that saved lives. They built schools and universities, providing education and the potential for a middle-class income for children who would previously never have been able to go to school or for only a few years to a village school. The church assisted those village children, through scholarships, to earn a degree to study teaching, engineering, nursing, or medicine and earn enough to buy a home, live comfortably, and afford education for their own children. Sorcha, while not changing her opinion on religion for herself, saw the good that missionaries did.

Realizing that Tadhg was no longer speaking, and that everyone was boarding *Pamplemousse*, I followed them all aboard, taking my place with Katya at the helm, thrilled to be on my way home.

CHAPTER 24

GASPING, UNABLE TO BREATHE, the sheer agony of eternal loss echoed through my bones. The gut-deep physical ache of losing her felt like a hole plunged into his chest. Opening my eyes in the dark, I could still see my father's face in the shadows, the ravages of grief etched into the lines of his face. The image was pulsing in and out as the mottled sunlight flickered across his face, but I could still *feel* his physical pain at losing Mum. He had believed that they would die together. That had been the plan. But she had gone first, abandoned him, left him all alone. After they lost Merlin to the virus, they knew time was short. They agreed to pass together, so neither of them had to live alone. But she was infected first, she thought after eating a peach from the tree, and being smaller, its destructive infectious nature affected her faster—only three days from the first symptom to the last gasping breath. He tried to relieve her pain, mostly unsuccessfully. She begged him to save her; she didn't want to go. But that was beyond his capacity for healing. He buried her under her favorite tree and sat down to talk to her, a glass of infected water in his hand. When the symptoms affected him, he hadn't moved, just kept talking to her as he swallowed the tablets they had carefully saved, telling her his favorite shared memories. He would join her soon. He had. Less than an hour after swallowing the pills, he joined her. Together and at peace. It had been his choice.

Blinking the fog away, I could see them standing there, together, his large arm around her tiny shoulders, beaming at me. They were proud of me, I sensed, but for what, I couldn't quite tell. "Take care of them, Campbell. All of them," Mum told me, distinctly, before they turned, slowly, but in complete synchronicity, and walked away, fading from sight. Mum's hair fanned across her back. Opening my eyes, I saw the light touched the edges of the room, casting shadows across the wall and illuminating the writing desk in the far corner. Even with my complete lack of belief in heaven or an afterlife, I had an overpowering sense of serenity. They were together and happy. Despite missing my home and my family with an intensity that physically hurt, a sense of grace filled me as I dressed and slowly climbed the narrow stairwell to the deck to face our second day on the open seas.

Tadhg, like myself, missed home, Callie, and his children. Keen to get back to Bellcamp, he sat with me as I piloted the vessel during the day, spending hours talking. Katya once more shared the navigation of the yacht with me. The news of her sister's death had hit her hard, leaving her quiet and despondent, feelings I knew all too well. I offered her the night shifts, and she accepted gratefully, recognizing the gift. Being alone with your thoughts and avoiding conversations with people by being awake at night when the majority were asleep was the kindest option. Ian was also quiet and kept much to himself, thinking of his half-brother who he had left behind. His brother had not wanted to go, and Ian had not wanted to stay. But his quietness was infused with peace, a sense of closure. It was Katya's pain that I understood.

The second evening, after dinner and Sam being put to bed, Sorcha forced Tadhg to tell us about what he had discovered in the facility in Melbourne. Making ourselves comfortable on the three-sided ring of sofas, we cracked open some wine from our stash from Melbourne and settled in. Katya excused herself, claiming that she needed to pilot the vessel through the dark. A quick, pointed glance at me secured my silence. I knew very well that the yacht was on auto-pilot. We were in absolutely no danger of crashing. She just didn't want to be social. If anyone under-stood this, it was me.

"Thanks, Katya." I raised my voice over the chatter. "Sing out if you need a hand?"

Disappearing into the front room, she closed the heavy door firmly behind her, leaving the seven of us to share the wine and listen to Tadhg's adventures.

Like all Irishmen, Tadhg was a natural storyteller and relished having a captive audience. His humor stimulated by the free-flowing wine, the night was all his. We had nothing to do, nowhere to go. Tadhg's first task had been to use the battery he brought from Bellcamp to fire up the backup diesel generators and generate enough electricity to turn on lights, the IT systems, and the servers. He had carefully chosen the computer he believed belonged to the most senior official.

"It wasn't hard," he chortled. "I wandered around and picked the poshest office with the most expensive-looking furniture and a secretary's desk outside!"

Hacking the password was a little more challenging and had taken several days.

"That might sound like nothing, but let me tell you, two days of running fecking algorithms to crack a sodding password is as boring as batshit."

We all laughed at his Irish accent with that quintessentially Australian expression, and the words bat shit, which came out as 'bartshut.' Callie's influence, no doubt.

"So here I am in the big boss's office, sitting in his handcrafted brown leather chair. Soft as butter on my weather-beaten old ass, I tell you. Photos of this austere, balding man in uniform, decorated with ribbons, all the colors of the rainbow. The pretty, young, blonde wife and two picture-perfect kids, bookends, you know, one girl, one boy, all over his desk. Degrees lining the walls in perfect alignment. The absolute epitome of the perfect life. Anyway, so finally, after much cursing and threatening to throw the sodding thing out the window, I manage to access his computer. Let me tell you, no grown man should use Kylie as his password, especially when his lovely wife's name is Sarah."

We roared with laughter at his story, but I knew Tadhg well enough to know that this was a cover. It had been a stressful time. Alone, pressured to access information, the world's resettlement potentially rested on what he could find.

Tadhg was enjoying himself and took another swig of his whisky.

"Finally, I open his personal files, and what do I find? The entire back catalog of Kylie Minogue albums, that's what. So here I am, bored out of my skull, and all I have to choose from is fecking 'Locomotion' or 'On a Night Like This.' I mean, seriously. How is a man to choose?"

He shook his head in mock mournfulness. He had to wait for the laughter to subside before he could continue. We were hanging on his every word, in part as he was an entertaining storyteller, but mainly as we were dying to learn what he knew.

"So, Melbourne was the base for establishing five separate island communities on behalf of the Australian government partnering with New Zealand. There were also ten others within Australian borders. Well, ten official ones," he countered. "Even before they officially closed the office, they were aware of small communities, families, small groups, you know, setting themselves up, isolating themselves from the world."

Glancing over at Sorcha, our eyes met. Mum and Dad had done this.

How many more existed? I wondered. *How many survived—the first year, the second? Were they still out there? Waiting for it to be safe? Would it ever be safe again?*

Sorcha was still watching me, and I knew my face had betrayed my thoughts. *Damn.*

Returning my attention to Tadhg, I struggled to catch the thread of the conversation.

"Did he know where they all were?" Ian was asking.

Yes. He had plotted them all on a map. The known locations anyway.

"How many are there?" Col asked cautiously. "Was it twelve, like we were told?"

Tadhg smiled. "Well, that depends now. There are twelve linkages. But twenty-four actual communities, twelve pairs if you like."

"Well, now I don't feel quite as special!" Di joked in mock outrage.

"You will always be special to me," I punned, amid deafening groans. Sorcha raised her eyebrows, and I made a show of relinquishing Di to my sister.

As Tadhg plunged his forearm up to his elbow into his satchel to retrieve the map, I asked the group, "Do we have a moral obligation to find them? To tell them they aren't alone?"

Silence echoed through the room as we all pondered that.

"I think..." Di said, then stopped.

"Say it," Sorcha urged gently. "We are all friends. You are entitled to your own opinion. No one will crucify you for it."

Taking a deep breath, Diana tried again with a little more certainty. "I think while there *is* an obligation to find these other survivors, it isn't necessarily *ours*."

Feeling the stares on her following this unexpected sentiment, she tried again, stammering a little, the words falling over themselves in her haste to not be misunderstood.

"What I mean is... we came back here with a single purpose, which we have now fulfilled. We all have commitments elsewhere. Tadhg has a wife and children. So does Cam. Sorcha has a young child. I don't doubt that we need to ensure that a message gets to these people to let them know they aren't alone, that there are other survivors. Quite a few other survivors. Potentially safer places for them to be. Share the knowledge we have about traveling through the portals, the technology behind the domes. But I am not sure that it needs to be *us* that does this. When we get back to Bellcamp and August, people may be willing to take up the mission. Cam, didn't you say that there was already a team from Bellcamp who were exploring?"

I nodded. "There are two that I know of. Blake from Bellcamp and Angus from Lewis both have exploratory teams and well-fitted out yachts capable of long ocean voyages."

Di smiled at me, grateful for my support. "The communities we come from or have just visited, they all know that there are others out there. They may take up the work. It isn't necessarily *our* responsibility."

Tadhg was nodding along as he smoothed the large folded map onto the central table, adjusting it so we could all see. There were black pen marks at random points all over the map.

"I agree with Diana here. Part of the reason I didn't tell you all about these communities before we left Melbourne is that I can't help but feel that it is not our place to spearhead this mission. It has been what … seven weeks now? I, for one, really want to get home. I know most of you do. Sleeping in my bed, in my home, with my beautiful wife. We can regroup and make a plan. It is not time critical. Not to mention that some of these settlements are a bloody long way from here."

Glancing around the group, it appeared this viewpoint was mostly unanimous. Di and Sorcha wanted to travel with me to Lewis. Sorcha wouldn't want to place Sam in any danger. I was desperate to get home to Louis and Lae. Colin had found Harriet, and I suspected that was all he cared about. Ian looked like he wanted to challenge it, but a wave of resignation washed over his face. Plainly he recognized he was outnumbered six to one, so wisely remained quiet.

Tadhg looked around the group, and realizing that no one wanted to divert the return home to search for other communities, he continued.

"So, as we suspected, there are confirmed antipodal communities all over the world. It is reasonable to think many of them have found each other by now."

"Where are they?" Harriet asked with interest.

Tadhg started pointing to various circled reference points scattered all over the map.

"Let's start with the ones we know and close to home. Ruapuke Island, New Zealand territory, linked to Lewis, Outer Hebrides, Scotland—we know of this one." He grinned, looking at me. I nodded. Now known as August Island. Initially, the experience of living there had been painful, but it had only taken a few months for me to embrace the benefits of my new life.

"Campbell Island, New Zealand sub-Antarctic territory to Newgrange, County Meath, Ireland." He looked up, beaming. "On a personal note, I am very thankful for this one. Without the glorious Bellcamp community, I would not have met my beautiful wife, Callie."

"Then we have Mauritania, Africa to New Caledonia, South Pacific."

I had heard of this one from Angus and Freyja and had told Tadhg previously.

"Angus and Freyja's team visited the Mauritania point," I advised those I may not have told. "There were people from New Caledonia already in Africa, so we know that as of a year ago, both communities were active, knew of each other, and after Angus's visit, they also know that there are other communities."

"That's good, isn't it?" Colin asked.

Pondering this, I responded. "I would assume so. They know they are not alone. Angus held concerns about the stability of the portal. As the story goes, it doesn't always open, but they have activated it. I don't see any need to interfere."

Refocusing my attention, I listened with intent interest as Tadhg continued his list.

"Easter Island, or Rapa Nui to use its official name, to Jaisalmer, India."

We all looked at each other. This was the first we had heard of a site in Asia.

"Didn't you tell me that Kevin was working on the assumption that ancient sites were indicators of portals?" Sorcha asked me.

"He did," I agreed. "The stones at Callanish, Newgrange."

"The Rapa Nui Moai, you know, the monolithic human figures, date back to 1200AD, so Easter Island fits the profile," Tadhg added.

"Wow. How did you know that?" Di queried.

"Read it one of the reports!" Tadhg laughed. "I'm a tech, not a historian! I have never heard of Jaisalmer, though."

"I have," Harriet piped up unexpectedly. We all turned to look at her, and she blushed, a pretty rose tint on her honey-colored complexion.

"I traveled through Asia after high school and spent some time studying yoga in India. It is a fascinating place. They call Jaisalmer the golden fortress. It is a medieval fort or perhaps a citadel. I don't remember which. It has been years since I have thought of it. From what I remember, it was an enormous sandstone complex with temples inside. It was huge, covered kilometers."

"Did you go there?" Col asked curiously.

"No. It was in the desert and hundreds of kilometers from the major cities and all by bus. When I was in Mumbai, I stayed in an ashram with a guy who had just been there. He raved about it, how immense it was, and so old, yet unchanged. Fairly sure he said it was over three thousand years old. His enthusiasm made me want to go there, but by that time, I had received word from home, and ... well, I needed to leave." She broke off. Judging by the look of discomfort on her face, it hadn't been positive news.

"Desert? Now that it is interesting. How do you think they would survive if it were a desert?" Di asked.

"Well, it depends, doesn't it," Sorcha interjected. "If they started with water stores and there was a geodesic dome, then does it matter they are in a desert?"

"Sustained heat would test the integrity of the dome," I countered. "We know the fabric can cope with rain and wind. But excessive heat? Surely it would evaporate more of the water?"

"Water evaporation and dome integrity are one issue, but there is another one," Tadhg interjected. "The earliest communities of Bellcamp and August were set up around portals. That was the priority. Survival of humanity. When they chose the initial sites to be settled, they did so with the full intention of reactivating the portals. They placed great emphasis on linking communities along with ensuring a long-term, safe water supply. What I learned in Melbourne was that they held grave concerns for the stability of the portals between the warmer sites. One file contained the results of a battery of tests they had completed, and one night, bored as I was, over a can of disgustingly bad Irish Stew, I read it. The scientific teams had proven that sustained heat weakens the antipodean points, a situation likely exacerbated by the dome itself acting like a magnifying glass, so they deliberately settled the cooler sites *first*, and tested those with what little time they had. They hoped that they could supplement the integrity of the fabric to cope with the sustained heat, but ... well, time ran out. It made me realize the stroke of luck that saw me settled on Newgrange, linked to another cold climate portal."

We all pondered that. Luck. Pure luck that the original settlers had been on August and Bellcamp, cool sites and linked to similarly cold climes. The later ones, like Kiewa, were to ensure the survival of as many people as possible. Nothing to do with antipodean portals.

"It makes you wonder why there are antipodean portals in hotter places, doesn't it? Did the weather change that much over thousands of years?" Di asked.

Sorcha corrected her ever so gently. "Not weather—climate. Weather is the atmospheric conditions that occur locally over short periods of time: hours or days. Climate refers to the long-term average of temperature, humidity, and rainfall patterns over years or centuries. Global climate patterns have changed drastically over the millennia. Major glacial or cold periods and interglacial or warm periods are initiated by changes in the Earth's orbit around the Sun called Milankovitch cycles. These cycles have occurred at different intensities on multi-millennial time scales."

"What is multi-millennial?" Harriet asked, blinking, in awe of Sorcha and her vast scientific knowledge.

Sorcha smiled. "Periods of between 10,000 and 100,000 years. Those orbital changes that occur slowly over time, influencing where solar radiation is received on the Earth's surface during different seasons. If these portals really are as old as we believe, then it seems possible that they were once linked when the local climate was somewhat different."

"That makes sense," I interjected. "Do you remember when Mum and Dad took us to Mungo National Park in far western New South Wales?"

Sorcha nodded. Harriet's ears pricked up, too. "Ooh, I've been there! We went there once on a camp. That wasn't too far from where we used to live."

Colin laughed. "Harriet, it was nearly 800 kilometers away!"

"So just down the road then?" she replied, deadpan.

The Australians laughed uproariously at this. Poor Tadhg just looked confused.

Once the laughter died down, I continued.

"One thing I remember was that while Mungo is dry and desert-like now, thousands of years ago, there was a chain of freshwater lakes which supported a lot of aquatic and land life. Then there was tectonic movement and climate change which resulted in the semi-arid environment that exists today."

"If they were concerned about the stability of the portals, why did they settle the hot sites then?" Harriet asked. "Why not just settle the cold ones?"

It was Tadhg who answered this. "It was in the research papers. They just wanted to give as many people a sporting chance as possible. They knew it wasn't ideal, and they knew that those sites likely wouldn't last as long as the others, but to have two communities linked was still seen as better odds than a single community going it alone. If something happened in one community, they could go through the portal to the other without placing themselves at risk of going outside. That is why the communities weren't jam-packed with people. The second reason was to diversify the gene pool. They knew that a comparatively small group of intelligent young people likely couldn't bring themselves to have lots of children. We all come from a time in history where we can choose, if and when, to have children. From a sustainability and resource-use perspective, this was good, but it also meant that the gene pool would be quite restricted, and this could cause genetic inbreeding within a few generations. So, they knew if people could travel *between* communities, they would. It is human nature to be inquisitive and want to explore."

Tadhg looked at me and grinned. Both he and I had met our beloved partners from another community and had done precisely this.

"What other communities did you learn about?" I asked, intrigued by the idea of different climates and their impact on antipodean travel.

Tadhg returned to his map and pointed to South America.

"Raqch'i Temple, Peru, near the Machu Picchu region, to Da Nang Marble Mountain Vietnam."

"Well, Machu Picchu, I think we have all heard of," said Ian. "We know that is old. Incan?"

"Some notes I found..." Tadhg fossicked around in his satchel again and brought out a wad of papers with a flourish, "said that it was an Incan site, but that there were known civilizations settled there prior to the Incas. Hang on... where is it? Ah. The Tiwanaku, based near Lake Titicaca."

Col snorted his beer and spilled it down his top.

"Sorry," he apologized. "That name has always made me laugh. Childish, I know."

"So not Incan then?" asked Diana over the giggling, trying to stop this from descending into drunken chaos.

Tadhg handed her the notes. "I read a bit but not all. Like most ancient civilizations, other Andean civilizations preceded the Incas. Like the Celts and the Picts. Successive settlements recognized these places as special."

Di, taking the notes, flicked through them but placed them back on the table. "Where else?" she asked excitedly. "This is like an Easter Egg hunt! What is at the Vietnam site? A mountain, you said?"

"Da Nang Marble Mountain," Tadhg enunciated slowly. "This one is interesting for a different reason. The Marble Mountains are a cluster of five marble and limestone hills in Ngũ Hành Sơn District, south of Da Nang city in Vietnam. But it was, at the time of the outbreak, a densely populated area. Made me wonder how they cleared the area to place a geodesic dome.

All I could learn was that the mountains contained several Buddhist and Hindu grottoes or caves that held religious significance."

"Gee, I wonder what that significance could be," Sorcha asked sarcastically.

"Quite." Tadhg grinned widely, returning to the map. "Also in the cold category is Chita, a regional center in the far east of Russia linked to the Falkland Islands, off the coast of Argentina."

"The Falklands are supposed to be beautiful," Harriet said dreamily. "Friends of mine went backpacking through South America a year before the virus hit and raved about how beautiful it was, especially the Patagonia region."

"If it is under a domed community, it likely still is beautiful," Ian chipped in.

"Makes you wonder if that was why they had a battle over the islands, doesn't it?" Di spoke softly. "When was that—the early 1980s?"

We all looked at her in astonishment.

"Good catch, Di," I exclaimed. "They did too. The problem is, I can't remember who won."

"British," Tadhg interjected through a mouthful of peanuts. "The islands are self-governed but remain a British territory, although I understand it is still a matter of some dispute, especially to the Argentinian government."

"Well, if the British and Argentinian governments both knew that the islands had an inactive portal, *and* that portal linked to Russia, *and* it was during the Cold War…" I started.

"Both governments would do anything they could to control the islands," Ian finished.

"I can't see any other reason the British would relinquish sovereignty of so many nations around the world but fight to maintain control over a tiny group of islands," Sorcha interjected. "Let's face it, at their peak, the British Empire controlled something like a quarter of the planet. Why relinquish some places and yet fight for a small group of fairly insignificant islands, albeit strategically located and with only limited natural resources?"

We sat in silence as we let that sink in.

"Makes you wonder what else they knew, doesn't it?" Tadhg asked, voicing what we were all thinking. "Moving on then. Next, we have the Cocos Keeling Islands, which are the third of the five Australian/New Zealand colonies, which are antipodal to Gran Isla del Maiz off the coast of Nicaragua."

"What does Gran Isla del ... whatever you said, mean?" Harriet asked curiously.

"Large Corn Island, apparently," replied Tadhg, rolling his eyes. "Very original, don't you think?"

"Anything interesting about Corn Island?" Sorcha asked. "Archeologically speaking. I'm going to hazard a guess they grew corn."

"It was a British Protectorate originally in an area called the Mosquito Coast."

"Attractive," I muttered.

Tadhg, ignoring my comment, said, "I tried to research them a little, but with the limited time, I needed to focus on other matters. But the quick answer is not that I know of. That goes for the Cocos Keeling Islands too. Interesting history, but not archeologically. Also, neither of them fit into the cold category, so likely less stable portals."

Returning to the map, Tadhg pointed out the Chatham Islands.

"An archipelago about 800 kilometers east of New Zealand, linked to Toulouse, France. The Chatham Islands are a little interesting. Apparently, they are the only part of the now submerged continent of Zealandia still above sea level."

We all sat back a little at this.

"Zealandia?" Colin asked. "Is that a place?"

It was Ian who responded, much to my surprise. "It was. About 23 million years ago."

We all looked at him in surprise.

"I started off studying to be a geologist before switching to geotechnical engineering," he said, deliberately emphasizing the Kiwi accent I hadn't noticed.

"I didn't realize you were Kiwi!" I said, surprised

"Born and raised," he said proudly, sticking out his chest for emphasis. "But then I traveled to Australia to go to university and, well, never really went home. Stopped ordering 'fush and chups' and tried to pass as a local."

"What is it?" Di asked.

"Zealandia is an almost entirely submerged mass of continental crust that subsided after breaking away from Gondwanaland, the supercontinent. Gondwanaland also broke up. But much of it is still above water. It makes up South America, Africa, Australia, and Antarctica. Parts of the Indian subcontinent and the Middle East too. That is why there are similar fossils found in such diverse places as Africa and Australia."

"Agreed," said Tadhg. "Well, the Chatham Islands are the only remaining part of Zealandia. Ancient and with a long history of Moriori settlement, the indigenous people of the islands. At the other end, the Toulouse region is famous for prehistoric cave paintings and other Neolithic art. Where the portal and community is, there was a small village named Saint-Sernin-sur-Rance, which is famous for, wait for it, Neolithic menhirs, carved in the Celtic style."

"Call me stupid," I said sarcastically, "but I am starting to see a pattern forming here."

"Absolutely," Tadhg agreed. "Moving on, we know of Gibraltar. You said Angus and his crew stopped there?"

Nodding in agreement, I didn't want to interrupt.

"Gibraltar is antipodal to Great Barrier Island, known to the Maori as Aotea, about a hundred kilometers northeast of Auckland. We know from Cam here, who learned from Angus, that the Gibraltar community has already been abandoned. There was evidence that the dome had been breached. The crew reported seeing it in tatters. The question remains: what happened to the residents? If they had already found the link to Aotea, then they may have gone through and be safe. The opposite may also have happened. The Aotea residents may have come through and attacked the Gibraltar community. Or the dome's integrity was breached, and they left or perished. It is impossible to say."

Silence met these options, but the truth was, there weren't likely many others.

"Surely the Aotea community didn't attack," Ian put in. "After all, none of us attacked our antipodal neighbors."

"True, but we don't know the circumstances, do we?" Tadhg responded. "Maybe they couldn't make themselves known. History shows many a battle has arisen out of miscommunication or an accident."

"But it was Gibraltar," I protested. "Spanish speaking. Surely someone spoke Spanish or English for that matter."

"I don't know," Tadhg said, wanting to move on. "The next communities are Inverness, Scotland, to the Auckland Islands, another New Zealand territory. The Auckland Islands and the Inverness communities were settled last. These are notable because they were settled by scientists and officials from all over the world, not just Australia and New Zealand. Strangely, that one too is not a direct antipodal point, but the strong magnetic fields in that region appear to account for the difference."

"No way!" I exclaimed excitedly. "Tell me, the Inverness site, is it near the Clava Cairns?"

"Actually, it is," Tadgh responded. "Well done."

"You aren't going to comment on the fact that the scientists kept two sites for themselves?" Sorcha asked, sarcasm dripping in puddles. "Is there anything to be gained from that knowledge, or that it is the only site we know of that links to mainland UK?"

Tadhg pondered that. "To be perfectly honest, I hadn't given it a great deal of thought. I was a little distracted by all the diva tunes I was spinning. But yes, it is a little odd that they used mostly islands. Well, except Antipodes Island."

"Really, there is an island named Antipodes?"

"There is. Right … there." Tadhg dropped his finger on a tiny speck of land. "It is a similar distance from mainland New Zealand as Campbell Island. There under our noses all along, and no-one thought to question it. That one doesn't have a settlement or a portal. The teams didn't believe it and wasted a month searching for one. Uninhabitable, it was declared."

We were all silenced for a moment, then broke out laughing. To have named an island Antipodes, surrounded by antipodal points that were portals, yet the island named Antipodes wasn't? Exhaustion or wine. Either way, we found this hilarious. When we eventually settled down again, it made one thing apparent. It was clearly a sign that these portals between points on the earth had been known for many thousands of years.

"The last links are New Amsterdam Island to a prehistoric site at Mesa Verde, Colorado, USA and Kerguelen Islands that link to Saskatchewan, Canada."

"Angus visited the Kerguelen Islands," I interjected for the benefit of the others. "The residents were given a lot of technical information about the portals as they reactivated the passage themselves. It was them who told Angus's team about the heat suits I wore traveling this time. I will tell you about that later."

Tadhg nodded and continued the explanation. "That would make sense. Kerguelen is in the middle of nowhere, between the west coast of Australia and Madagascar. Although it is relatively close to New Amsterdam Island and similar in that they are both French territories, and both settled by scientists and researchers, not permanent residents, it seems likely that the New Amsterdam residents were also taught to reactivate the portal themselves. Anyway, one of the many incredibly boring scientific papers I read to lull myself to sleep each night cited twenty-four original sites. That would make twenty-four, no?"

Checking the black marks all over the map, I counted aloud. Twenty-four communities, each under its own protected dome, but each paired with another site, at the opposite end of the planet—twelve linkages in all.

"What did they mean by original sites?" Ian quizzed Tadhg. "Twenty-four with antipodean points in total, and the rest are isolated settlements? Or twenty-four they settled first, but knew of others that could be linked?"

"No clue. If I meet the author, I'll let you know. Time was ticking by, and I needed to learn more about the re-magnetization process, when and how. Specifications for the dome in case we ever have a breach and knowing how to fix it. I figured we weren't going looking for these communities, so I didn't need to know how to get there immediately. I did, of course, bring the details along with me. No point in making someone go back now, is there?"

There was a general agreement at that.

"So, did you? Find out about the magnetizing?" Colin asked.

"Ahh, that I did," Tadhg announced proudly. "Now pour me another glass, and I'll tell you everything."

CHAPTER 25

TRAVELING FROM SCOTLAND ON the northern hemisphere winter solstice meant I had barely enough time to return on the southern hemisphere fall equinox. While I had planned to be away for six months, twelve weeks separated the two points where it was possible to travel.

Katya, not wanting to return to her doctor role immediately, offered to drop us at Bellcamp and then take Colin and Harriet back to August. We accepted with enthusiasm and much gratitude. Getting home sooner would be wonderful.

"The equinox is in four days," I said to Sorcha, looking up at the darkening sky, threatening a storm. "If we don't make it through on the fall equinox, we will need to wait another twelve weeks to the solstice."

"And you don't want to do that?" she teased gently.

"The alternative is to sail all the way home, and honestly, I don't think we have the fuel, nor I the skills to do that. But I am glad we didn't go to August first. It is much closer, but they haven't worked out how to open the portal on the equinox yet, only the solstice.

Besides, I promised Callie I would return Tadhg as soon as I could. She is pregnant, plus I wanted to say goodbye and thank you."

"We will make it," she assured me. "You can do this. I have faith in that. Besides, if we don't make it, we can always go on the solstice. Diana never really got to say goodbye to her friends on August."

The shock I felt must have registered on my face as Sorcha laughed uproariously.

"It is okay. I am teasing. She is fine."

"I am such a shit friend. I didn't even think to ask her. When she left August to find Kendra, I just assumed she would stay in Kiewa with Kendra. Then she didn't, so I assumed she would go home. Then … well … the situation changed, and you both said you would come with me. But I didn't even *think* she might want to wrap things up there. Collect her things. Does she? Does she want to go back to August first?"

Sorcha laughed again. "*No*. Really, I mean it. She tied up her loose ends, thinking she might stay with Kendra. This is a slight deviation to the plan, but no, she doesn't want to go back."

The tension easing, I exhaled with relief. I didn't want to wait another twelve weeks if I could help it. On Bellcamp would be bad enough, but on August? That said, at least I would travel through at Callanish and not have to endure that North Sea crossing again.

"Do you remember what Mum used to say when you were antagonizing me?"

"No, what?"

"If you stir the shit, at some point, you will need to lick the spoon." Sorcha smiled sweetly and looked so much like our mother that I had to look away.

When the storm hit, we slowed our speed and kept everyone in their cabins. Katya and I spent several tense hours navigating our way through, hoping we wouldn't need to stop. But it passed, and two days of beautiful calm weather followed, allowing us to run at full speed. While the storm had slowed us somewhat, the mood was still peaceful. The return trip was much calmer in both weather and emotion. We had achieved our mission and were far more relaxed, spending the time getting to know each other better rather than ensconced in our world. Colin was far more comfortable now that he had found Harriet, and she proved to be hilarious, regularly having us all in fits of laughter with her impersonations. Colin proudly boasted that she had been studying at the Victorian College of the Arts, offered an acting scholarship. Harriet was a natural mimic and comedienne. Colin differed vastly from the Colin we had known. Having her here had mellowed him beyond what I thought possible. He was amiable, and I found myself, to my complete disbelief, liking him.

Sorcha and Di were infatuated with each other and spent far more hours below deck than strictly necessary. Sam was a highly inquisitive child who enjoyed running around the decks, talking to everyone about anything. Not being able to swim, he was forced to wear a life jacket during all waking moments, something he detested and protested loudly about. Still, he was well tolerated, and everyone included him in whatever they were doing. When he learned some rather crude words one day and repeated them, in singsong fashion, to his mother, Sorcha vowed to pay greater attention to where he was and who he was with.

Stressed, exhausted, and filthy, we finally arrived on Bellcamp the evening before the fall equinox. I had never been so happy to see land. Falling off the boat and onto the sand, I silently expressed my gratitude to whatever earth spirit had let us make it in time. I would be home—soon. Callie hugged me briefly before throwing herself at Tadhg, swamping him in her embrace. Their children clamored to be picked up, and Tadhg broke himself free of his wife to pick up a girl in each arm, kissing them each in turn. They squealed with joy, both at having their father back but also at the game. Tadhg reminded me so much of Fraser, outgoing, jovial, and intelligent. But around their daughters, both men were teddy bears.

Quick introductions of Sorcha, Sam, and Harriet, and we were ushered into the village, and accommodations provided. I stayed with Callie again, but Di, Sorcha, and Sam were shown to Iznayah's house. She had lived alone, and with no warning that she was not planning to return, no one had cleaned out her home. They showed Col and Harriet to Dave's house, also now unoccupied.

"You know..." I began, as Callie fussed around, preparing her spare room for me.

"I know. Tomorrow is the equinox. But we will make the most of one last evening together, my friend, even if it means using toothpicks to pry your sleepy eyes open."

We did. Putting the children to bed early, we ate, drank, and laughed until our sides burst. Tadhg and I took turns to tell her about our journey, what he had found and what I had seen on the mainland. There was a hushed silence as I told them about my parents, but nods of agreement with my summation. Losing any family member was devastating. But they had lived several years longer than most and had been fortunate enough to have lived, knowing that both of their children had survived. As parents ourselves, we finally understood. We would do anything for our children and would place their safety above our own. I knew now why my parents had insisted that I go, and Sorcha after me. If there were even a slim chance at survival, I would want that for my son.

Blake was back and happy to see me in the morning. Between a late night with Callie and the stress of impending travel today, I hadn't slept well. He was dying to learn everything he could, but he also recognized the urgency in Sorcha, Di, Sam, and I crossing to Newgrange that evening when the portal opened.

"I have a memory of you doing this, what, a year ago?" he teased. "Developing a bit of a habit, aren't you?"

"A year and a half ago," I corrected.

"Ahh, and to think I consider myself well-traveled," Blake joked. "Now, let's share intel. I understand you have learned quite a lot in the past year."

There were five of us traveling: myself, Sorcha, Diana, and Sam, and Fionn, a Newgrangian returning home, whom Tadhg and Blake had been filling with information all day so it could get relayed to Kevin at Newgrange. They included me in the briefing, only the more technical components going over my head. For me, it was the locations of the other sites I found fascinating, especially Easter Island and the Clava Cairns. Kevin had been right!

There were four suits. Sorcha and Sam were to share one. Diana would take the second. Fortunately, that left one for me and one for Fionn.

"Hold him facing you," I advised Sorcha as she and Sam were zipped into the suit together.

A large silver foil suit, it looked much like a spacesuit, excluding the helmet. Instead, it had a hood with a clear soft plastic face shield, zipped up at the last moment. Heating pockets throughout the suit were then used to heat the suit and the wearer. As uncomfortable as it was being heated, like standing in front of a furnace or an overheated sauna, I also knew from experience that it was far preferable to traveling unprotected.

Callie hugged me goodbye before I stepped into my suit, her tummy now barely showing the new child. I was to go second, after Sorcha and Sam. If the portal closed suddenly, as it occasionally did on the equinoxes, it was less critical for Di or Fionn to go through this time. While not ideal, they could wait the twelve weeks.

As the portal in the cave crackled and static electricity hovered in the air, I heard Blake yell, "*Now!*" and saw Sorcha step through and disappear. Barely waiting to see them through, I leaped in after her, too scared I would lose my courage if I didn't just go. With the vision of Lae and Louis firmly in my mind, I closed my eyes and endured the passage once more.

CHAPTER 26

THE TENSION WAS SO thick you could cut it with a knife. Two wildcats, circling each other, preparing for attack, neither willing to relinquish their position. Sorcha, the older sister, who had known me all my life, knew my deepest darkest secrets and was my only remaining family. Then Laetitia, sweet Laetitia, she who held my heart and soul in the palm of her hands, the woman for whom I would walk through fire and back again—the mother of my child. Introducing them was always going to be difficult.

The journey from Newgrange had been long and arduous, just as it was the first time. Kevin had been ecstatic to hear of the other communities linked to portals and especially about Clava. We stayed an additional night so he and I could catch up on what we learned in Melbourne. After Kevin promised that he would contact me soon, we left early on the morning of the third day.

Eoghan, no more communicative than during my first journey, at least dropped us closer this time, recognizing that we couldn't walk long distances with Sam. Less than two weeks after we made the journey from Bellcamp, we walked into the village at Garynahine.

The first night had been all tears and laughter. Happy tears of reunion. Sad tears at the confirmation that our parents had not survived. A wonderful dinner with my extended family: Lae, Di, Sorcha, Sam, and me, and Fraser, Isla, and the girls joined us, too. Sam and the girls were running around outside, playing. Little Louis didn't leave my lap, Jam at my feet.

But this morning, it was different. I woke to find Lae gone and heard muffled voices in the lounge. Judging by the light outside, it was mid-morning. I had overslept.

Dressing hurriedly and arriving in the kitchen, I found Sam and Louis sitting on the rug eating bread and honey. Louis was coated in it, and Sam was visibly enjoying feeding his younger cousin. The voices were guarded, tense. Sorcha and Lae, I realized, pricking up my ears. Poking my head into the lounge, I saw them standing, facing off. Sorcha was drawn up to her full height to be intimidating, but Lae, barely reaching Sorcha's armpit, was not backing down. Neither had noticed me.

Recognizing that they needed to battle it out, I quietly left them to it and returned to Sam and Louis in the kitchen, cleaning Louis's sticky hands and sweet face. I could hear and intervene if matters got entirely out of hand. Sorcha would need to approve of Lae in her role, representing my family, and there wasn't much I could do about it.

The interrogating tone was brutal as I heard Sorcha speak. "So, I hear you married quickly."

Despite her soft, homely appearance, gentle manner, and speech, Lae was sharp. She knew perfectly well that she was being tested, probed to see if she was worthy. Sorcha had missed years of my life and was putting Laetitia through her paces. Lae correctly interpreted the unspoken question. *Did you marry him for love or just for companionship? Did he choose you, or were you just lonely?*

"We married quickly when he returned to me. He lived with me for six months before that."

We were friends first. He didn't act spontaneously. He chose me.

"He must feel very comfortable with you."

Do you know about his Asperger's? His other wife? Has he told you everything?

"We were close friends for a long time. It was a natural progression."

Yes, I know everything. I have been here for him all this time.

And on it went. I gave up listening after a while. It sounded like Lae could hold her own. Perhaps it was better if I wasn't here. Sam, Louis, and I finished up our brunch, and I looked at them. "Who wants to go to the greenhouse?"

Sam grinned up at me. He loved being outside, playing in the mud. Sorcha wasn't an outside person by choice. Watching Sam as he put on his jacket and hat, I wondered again what his father had been like. Japanese, obviously, but what had his personality had been like? Almost immediately after Sorcha and I had been reunited, she had hooked up with Diana. This had unceremoniously put an end to any questions about her former relationship. Perhaps stupidly, it felt wrong to ask a woman in a relationship with a woman what her former male partner was like. After her fiancé's death, I had watched her slump into a morose state for months. She sleepwalked her way through life with no passion, no drive. She had distanced herself from everyone, including me. Not nasty, just remote. But in Kiewa, she had fallen in love again, or at least cared enough to make a life with someone and have a child. I was just curious what this man Tom had been like.

Sam squealed with delight as he splashed in the puddles that formed on the floor of the greenhouse. Louis squawked in my arms, but there was no way I was putting him down. Like the dome itself, the greenhouse had a light sprinkler that watered the plants, which then evaporated and formed condensation on the plastic-lined roof and arched walls. It dripped onto the convex floor, caught in gutters along the edge, and was recycled to begin the process again. Water was so precious here. The sight of Sam playing in the water made me remember my father and the dome he had built on our bush block. Just the way the light caught the highlights in his hair was enough to remind me of my father. Tall, dark-haired, and solid. Sturdy in a reassuring way, Dad was dependable and honest. You always knew where you stood with him. There was no bullshitting. He told it as he saw it, not to be nasty, but because he hated time-wasting. Outgoing and friendly, he also didn't tolerate fake people or liars. You knew his opinion, even if you didn't share it. But he never tried to push his will on others.

Sam moved, and it broke the spell. His eyes differed from Dad's and his mouth too. Sam's eyes were green. Dad's had been blue, like mine. Sam had

Sorcha's eyes, our mother's eyes. Eyes like emeralds, glittering green that sparked with fury when either of them had lost their temper. *Eyes like Freyja's*, I realized. If eyes were the window to the soul, they also gave a clear warning of when the owner was about to explode. Like Mum, Sorcha had a ferocious temper. Mum had learned to control hers, while Sorcha as a child was a veritable nightmare. Screaming, throwing things. She was like a banshee on steroids. But Sam had been a happy, compliant child.

Glancing up at the shadow that had fallen over the planter box nearest to me, I saw Lae's face, shadowed and guarded.

"Alright then?" I asked, not wanting to get into a discussion about Sorcha in front of Sam, although a quick look in his direction proved he was still happily playing in the pile of hay we used as compost. He had bits of hay stuck in his hair, throughout his clothes, and looked thoroughly disreputable. I smiled, watching him, thinking how much Sorcha would be cranky when she saw it.

Lae followed my glance and nodded but not convincingly. Something was up. "Was she awful to you? Do you want me to talk to her?"

"No, that wasn't it. I mean, she tested me alright, but I expected that. She is your sister, your only blood relative. It is her job to look out for you, to test me, to see if I am the right one for you. I mean, it isn't like your parents can do it, so she needs to."

For the millionth time, I looked at Lae in wonder. How could a child of an emotionally remote mother and no father, with no siblings or family, be so insightful into family dynamics? I had asked her this once, and she admitted that being small and non-intrusive, she spent much of her time observing the dynamics between people, watching interactions in cafes, train stations, shopping centers, and parks. It was what made her want to become a psychologist.

She was right. Sorcha had nothing against Lae personally. Not that I could ever have seen them as friends in the old world. They were too different. Sorcha wasn't a bitch for the sake of it, but she came across as forceful and direct.

"So, what was it then?"

"Well, she talked about … her."

"Her?" I asked stupidly.

"Frey … ja." Lae stumbled over the name.

"Sorcha never met Freyja," I replied incredulously, but Lae interrupted.

"Diana knew Freyja well, didn't she?"

That was true. Diana had regularly eaten with Freyja and me, and we spent time together several times each week. Di and I worked together, but we socialized as a trio. Many a night, Diana had stayed over in our spare room after a long dinner, lots of conversation, and wine. Diana still lived in the dorm, so she appreciated the time with us in a small, quiet house. We were so close that people often laughed that we were a threesome and how lucky I was. It hadn't occurred to me that Di would tell Sorcha about Freyja.

"She did," I admitted. "We were all very close."

Lae's lips tightened at that, and her fingertips turned white as she scooped up Louis, his red jacket clinging to her hip.

"How … close?"

"Di was my best friend on August," I admitted. "Other than Freyja."

Laetitia and I had never really spoken about my relationship with Freyja. When Freyja was here the first time, before I traveled, she had spent most of her time with Angus. Many residents had told me she had little time for the people here. I doubt she had exchanged more than a few words with Laetitia. That was just her way. She had planned to leave here as soon as she could. She wouldn't have thought it worthwhile to waste her time making friends when she planned to go. Her time and energies would have been best spent on pursuits to further her goal. Ever practical, rational Freyja. Then Freyja left, and I arrived, and Laetitia met me. Had it not been Fraser that found me and Fraser's friendship with Laetitia... well, perhaps I wouldn't have grown to know her either. Because of them both, I had tried to meet people, be part of the community. Whether that was because I had been ostracized on August, I couldn't say. But I wanted to belong here. My family was from this land. I felt at home here.

A gentle snore from the haystack proved Sam was asleep, and we were safe to talk. I smiled, watching him.

"Where is Sorcha?" I asked abruptly, not wanting a deep and meaningful conversation to be interrupted by my nosy sister.

"She went to find Diana."

"Good." That meant she wasn't likely to come looking for Sam for some hours yet.

Gesturing to a wooden bench nearby, Lae and I sat, Louis fast asleep in Lae's arms, sucking on his thumb, looking angelic.

"What is it you want to know?"

"Nothing ... everything. Oh, I don't know."

Sitting down beside her, I waited, letting Laetitia catch her thoughts. I could see the multitude of emotions flooding her face, struggling with each of them: doubt, fear, betrayal. One would fight for supremacy soon, and I would know when it had.

She turned to face me.

Game on, I thought grimly, awaiting the onslaught. Years of living with Sorcha and then Freyja had taught me to expect anything and never, ever let my guard down.

"I guess what I want to know is … well … why me? I saw her when she was here. I mean, I never spoke to her directly, but I saw her around. She was tall and queenly, like a Viking. She commanded attention. She is so beautiful."

After a halting start, the words were coming more rapidly now, like a trickle of rain expanding into a torrent. She was babbling, distressed.

"Intelligent too. A vet, you said? So beautiful *and* intelligent. The men here were absolutely obsessed with her. If she walked down the street, they leered after her like puppies drooling after a meaty bone. If she dropped something, they would have squabbled over who would pick it up. That night they told us about the settlements in Australia. The entire community was buzzing about her. What I can't work out is, if she was … *is* your … wife," the word choked her for a moment, "why on earth would you settle for *me*?"

"Settle? What do you mean *settle*? I chose you, Laetitia Katherine Rose Mackintosh. I didn't settle for anything."

"You know what I mean!" Anger was getting the upper hand now, and she was struggling to keep herself in check. I had never seen Laetitia angry before, so I was watching her facial expressions, carefully ensuring that I had a calm blank expression on my face, despite the emotional rollercoaster churning away in my stomach.

"She entered a room, and everyone turned to look. The girls were jealous of her—her long legs that went up to her armpits and flowing blonde hair that made her look like she was in a shampoo commercial. The men just flat-out desired her. It was plain in every single one of their faces. No man has ever looked at *me* that way. Not even *you*."

I was a little taken aback at that last insult.

"What do you mean, I have never looked at you that way? With lust, you mean? No, I suppose…"

"A-ha!" The look of triumph on her face signaled this would not end well. "Of course, you haven't!"

She was all but shouting now and would have been if it wasn't for Louis, miraculously still asleep despite the turmoil.

"I get it. Why on earth would you lust after me the way you did her? She was so elegant, so beautiful, so … so … so *fucking perfect*!" At this, she burst into a flood of tears, dropped her head into Louis, and I was sure I could hear her heart shatter.

Trying to remain calm, I spoke loudly enough to be heard over the sobbing. "Do you know what lust is?"

She looked up at me, tears and mucus streaming down her face, streaking her red face with white. "Of course, I do. I'm not a fool. Or do you think I am stupid and ugly?"

Ignoring this last irrational comment, I continued. "Lust is a fleeting emotion. You see the doughnut or the cake, and you know logically that you shouldn't have it; you know it isn't good for you. But there is something in you that makes you *want* it, just for that moment when it is in front of you. When it is there, even if it isn't attainable, probably especially if it isn't attainable, you *want* it. The funny thing about lust is that it is much like greed. Once it is no longer in front of you, you no longer want it, and you don't give it a second thought. It is like seeing a gorgeous hot red sports car and desperately wanting it. You long for it as it is passing and are envious of the person who has it. That feeling of envy is worse if you know the owner, I think. But once you are back in your own life, you don't think about it again. Yes, those men lusted after Freyja, but only the *idea* of her. They didn't know her, what she was really like. Once they were home with their wives and partners, I doubt they gave her a second thought. She wasn't attainable, but they wanted the *concept* of her, much like the convertible. It looks amazing as it is driving down the coastal road with the roof down, but once it is out of sight, it really is out of mind. You, on the other hand, I couldn't forget you. I sailed across the ocean, dreaming of you. Your dark brown hair with golden highlights where the sun hits it. Your soulful eyes that make me feel like I am the only man alive. That face. Your gorgeous, beautiful face, so sweet and gentle. From the moment I first saw you in your kitchen making me breakfast, I wanted you. That day you took me to find my aunt, I knew. I didn't care what it took to get back here to you. That isn't lust. It is something far more powerful. That ... is love."

"Why did you leave me then?" she wailed. "I thought you had gone for good. I mourned you, as stupid as that sounds. You weren't mine, but I grieved for you. More than I did, even for my own mother." The anger was dissipating rapidly.

"I had to go." I shrugged. "I had made a commitment. I needed to see it through."

"But you didn't resolve it, did you?" Tears were brimming in her eyes as the truth kicked in. "You went back, and she wasn't there. You came here and settled for me. You hadn't resolved matters between you at all. You chose her first, so she still wins."

I blinked slowly. "This isn't a ... *competition!*" I finally managed, dumbfounded at her irrational logic. "Yes, I came here by accident. Then I went back, as I had made a vow, a promise. I hadn't seen Freyja in over a year by the time I returned. I wanted to resolve things so I could move forward. I didn't always want to be wondering about what happened. When I got back to August, and she was gone, well, I was free to let go and move on. Part of me will always love her, I admit. But I didn't need to keep hunting for her. I never wanted to have that shadow lingering over us. If I stayed here the first time, and she had come back, then you would always wonder, and I would too. I tried to do the right thing, and I went back. But she had gone, and it was so damned hard to get back here the second time. You were here, and all was well. And now there is Louis, too."

I touched his sleeping cheek, and the corners of his lips turned up in the sweetest of smiles.

"I crossed the ocean and traveled through the portal—for you. Freyja came here, and I still chose you. I only went away the second time to find my sister, and I returned yet again—for you *and* him. Tell me how you want me to prove my love for you, and I will do it, willingly."

All the heat washed out of her then. I saw it as if I had turned a tap on and the water ran out. The emotion was gone, and only Laetitia was left.

The small face looked up at me. "Really? Di told Sorcha that she had never seen a couple so much in love as you and Freyja. She made it sound like I was rebound. Your second choice. I have to ask: do you truly love me?"

"More than anything in the world," I assured her.

She melted into me then, and I held them both as she shed the tears of anger and distress, loneliness, betrayal, anger, and finally relief that she had been holding in for the months of my absence.

Stroking her thick dark hair, I murmured, "It is all okay now. I am here. You are here. We are together. We are a family. Nothing will separate us again."

CHAPTER 27

AFTER FIVE NIGHTS IN our tiny spare room, Sorcha and Di moved into a new home of their own. Another family had recently moved out to a croft, raising sheep, cattle, and pigs. Their small house was quickly freshened up, and we all helped them move. Coming from Kiewa and August, they had nothing in the way of homewares, so in typical Lewis manner, everyone contributed something: a few spare plates, a set of sheets, a mattress. Within hours, they were fully set up. Over time, the potter would make them pottery of their own. The cutler would make them a set of cutlery and knives. But for now, it was much like a twenty-something moving out for the first time. Furniture and homewares were mismatched, but it was their home, their place, and they were exhilarated.

Desperately happy to have my home back, I begged Lae to take a day off from work so we could spend a day together as a family. With a child, this looked a little different from pre-child, and after a rare and indulgent sleep-in, we went for a picnic to Dun Carloway Broch, where we had spent our honeymoon, on a rare sunny day, the light streaming in through the dome's fabric. Louis loved crawling around the grassy verge, picking flowers, turning over rocks, looking for insects and small lizards. Lae and I lay on the grass under the dome, chatting and enjoying the sunshine but watching him. The cliff edge was near, but he showed remarkable awareness as he clambered over the rocky hilltop near the broch.

"Do you like her? Sorcha, I mean," I asked cautiously, not wanting to start an unpleasant conversation.

"I don't think she likes *me,*" Lae responded immediately, although that wasn't what I asked. "I feel, well, I feel like I have been judged, and I haven't quite made the grade."

"What makes you say that?"

Lae paused, thinking. "It is nothing she says. It is just a feeling I get. That she expected *more.*"

I wanted to argue, tell her it wasn't true. But if I was honest, I had detected the same vibe from Sorcha. Unsure how to continue, I was glad when Lae spoke instead. "Di though, she is lovely. I like her."

A sense of relief relaxed my tensed shoulders, causing them to drop. "Di is lovely. I am so glad she is here. I really missed her."

"She is so kind and thoughtful. She even stopped by the school yesterday to help. For no reason at all."

"That's Di," I agreed.

"I have to ask," Lae blurted. "Di is lovely. You were single. She was single. Why didn't you marry *her?*"

"You know, I have thought about that many times. We met on the second day and were good friends from the beginning. We worked together and enjoyed each other's company. For a while, I am sure people thought we would hook up. To be perfectly honest, I considered it too, in an academic sense."

"An academic sense?" Lae looked uncomfortable.

"In that sense that we thought we were alone in the world. In our departure briefings, it had been clarified that our role was to survive and reproduce. Keep humanity going. After a few months, everyone was pairing up. I felt I needed to do my bit. But … it was *Di*. She was like a sister. I just couldn't see her that way. We were great friends but nothing more."

Lae nodded, understanding. "Well, I like her."

"Me too."

Sorcha and Di slotted in like they had always lived here. Di came to work with me, and it was just like August. Not feeling like work, we chatted and laughed our way through the day, anticipating each other's needs with tools and workload. Sometimes Fraser joined us, or we assisted him with the outside garden beds, working as a team. Every Friday night, they came for dinner with Sam, and over time, Lae became more relaxed around Sorcha. Sorcha, to her credit, was kind and did her best to include Lae in conversations and regularly had both Di and Lae in stitches, telling stories of me as a child.

Not for the first time, I regretted bringing my sister here as she was regaling the girls with a story of me learning to ride a bike, the bike having no brakes, and her pushing me downhill toward a brick wall. I could see that Lae was torn between laughing hysterically and being loyal to me. Di, traitor that she was,

was egging Sorcha on, begging for more stories and details. Wracking my brain, I tried to think of humiliating stories from Sorcha's childhood but couldn't help but feel mean at the prospect of telling stories about her worst moments. Willing to tolerate nearly any degree of taunting, I just smiled, thrilled to have my sister and my friend here.

"Can you build a swing?" Lae asked without preamble one evening as we sat watching Louis play with a wooden car on the lounge floor.

Thinking about it for a moment, I responded slowly, "I guess. The concept isn't that difficult. An A-frame with rope or chain and a seat. I am assuming you want him buckled in?"

"Of course."

"Why a swing? Did you like swings when you were a girl?"

Lae smiled. "I did. I loved the feeling of the wind in my hair and the swoosh as I flew. It made me feel ... alive."

"Did your Mum take you to the park?"

"Sometimes." Her face darkened. "More often than not, I just went by myself. It wasn't until years later that I realized how lucky I was."

"Lucky? How is that? There is nothing lucky about going to the park alone!"

Lae sighed, and I could see the distress flicker in her eyes.

"Hey!" I embraced her as she collapsed onto my shoulder. "What is wrong?"

She sniffed audibly and drew back, looking at me. "I think I told you once that when I was at university, I volunteered with disadvantaged kids?"

"You did. I told you what an amazing person you are."

"Hardly. Well, there was this woman who volunteered there, too, Nilmini. Older than me, maybe early thirties. Small, silent, kept to herself. Haunted."

"What do you mean ... haunted?"

"She had that *look*. The look of a terrible tragedy in her past."

More than once, I had seen that look and knew what she meant. Sorcha had sported it herself for months after Sam's death. I nodded for Lae to go on.

Laetitia continued, "There was nothing remarkable about that day, well, except perhaps it was sunny. Sunny days in Edinburgh are rare, ye ken? Anyway, this particular Saturday was a glorious day, and some kids wanted to go to the park. There were a few of them, so two staff needed to go because it meant walking there and crossing the main road. Nilmini was the only other one there, so I asked her. She refused. Then the children crowded around her and started begging. She eventually relented, but I could tell she *really* didn't want to go."

"Did she say why?"

"Not at that point. We walked the few streets to the park, and I could see that she grew more and more agitated as we walked. I was holding the hands of the youngest ones who were chatting away to me, so I couldn't do much, but I could see she was struggling. Emotionally, I mean."

I nodded but said nothing, wanting her to continue.

"We set the kids up on the swings, see-saws, slides. Soon the kids were all engrossed in their play, so I sat next to her on the park bench that overlooked the small playground. She was shaking. I don't know why I did it. Instinct, I guess. I just hugged her. She froze and stiffened in my arms. Just as I was about to withdraw, thinking I had made a huge mistake, she dissolved. She just softened and collapsed, sobbing in my arms. I held her and watched the kids playing nearby. She cried for what felt like ages. Then finally, it slowed and stopped. I continued to hold her, saying nothing. Eventually, she sat up and looked me in the eye. 'Thank you,' she whispered."

"What did you do?" I asked gently.

"Nothing. I just sat there. Slowly she opened up, told me the story of her past, how she ended up volunteering at the shelter, and why."

"Why?" I was intrigued.

"Nilmini had been a drug addict and an alcoholic. Then she had fallen pregnant. She didn't know who the father was. She was out of it most of the time and staying in squats. But she had tried to get clean for her little boy. She did well for a few years, but when Ryley was three, she had struggled. They had needed to move house, away from all she knew, and she was struggling emotionally. He was a rambunctious little boy, and they lived in a tiny council flat with no money to buy toys. She often took him to the park. He had loved the swings especially and would spend hours on them, swinging backward and forward. She said that most days, she had to fight him to get off the swings, to let other kids on, or to go home. He just loved swinging.

One day she took him to the park and took a needle with heroin in it with her, hidden under the pram. He was happily playing, so she shot up, needing the release from the pressure of parenting. Just once, she told herself. Just one shot to help deal with the stress of life, of bills, of an energetic child, of being a sole parent struggling to buy food and keep the place clean. Just one hit."

"So, what happened?" I asked, intrigued, a million possibilities drifting through my mind, equally recognizing the similarities with Lae's upbringing.

"She woke hours later, and it was dark. The park was empty, and Ryley was gone. She was lying on the grass, the pram still there. She sat up and took a little time to come to her senses. It had been years since she had used, so it hit her hard. When she realized where she was, she looked for Ryley. She ran around, calling his name, becoming more and more frantic. The park was deserted. Homeless people were drifting in, looking for a quiet place to sleep. One saw her running around wildly and asked if he could help. Soon there was a small group hunting for little Ryley. A small dark-haired boy in a red parka and blue pants. There was no sign of him. Finally, someone called the police, and they came. But by that point, she was hysterical and incoherent. They took her to the station, and she gave a statement. They sent out a team to hunt for Ryley but found nothing. Without a trace, as they say. Media coverage of the missing boy started but soon faded as there was no sign of him after a few weeks, and she didn't have the money or the profile to keep him as front-page news. She was ostracized, vilified by her neighbors for falling asleep and leaving him. While the media didn't report her drug use, that she had fallen asleep in a public place was bad enough. That he loved the swings and wouldn't have left the swing voluntarily haunted her. Someone must have physically removed him, screaming, yet she hadn't heard him.

"Eventually, the world moved on, but she didn't. She visited the park every day, looking in every pram she passed on the street, staring into the face of every child she met. Then she became a recluse, leaving only to buy food. One day a sympathetic neighbor took her to the shelter, not accepting no as an answer. It was kindly meant, to get her out of the house where she was slowly dying of grief. She thought she would hate being surrounded by kids, by life, but was surprised to realize that she didn't. It gave her purpose. She admits she volunteered at the shelter in the early months and years to see if Ryley came in, but he never did. Then she realized it was her penance. Payment for her crime. She had lost her child through her selfishness and weakness, so she felt the need to help others."

"Payment. That is a little harsh."

"I thought so too, but she was adamant. She had ruined his life. She needed to make amends by improving the lives of others."

"How long did she volunteer for?"

"Well, I think it had been ten years by the time I started there."

"Crumbs. Ten *years* of guilt. Did she ever use drugs again?"

"Never. Not drugs, not alcohol. I never even saw her take a simple aspirin. She cleaned up her life but forever paid the price for that one mistake."

"That poor woman. I cannot imagine…"

"I can," Lae interrupted. "That could so easily have been me. I wasn't quite that young, but I was visiting the park alone at five and six. I was a tiny little thing, underfed as I was. Any adult could easily have picked me up."

"So that's what you meant by being…"

"Lucky," she finished. "I am so damned lucky."

Watching our little boy play on the floor, I gently rested my arms around her and sat and watched him, counting my blessings. I had it all, a wonderful childhood with opportunities and experiences, a wife, child, and hopefully more to come, living in a safe place, away from the death and destruction. I was the lucky one.

"Yes, I can build him a swing."

CHAPTER 28

THE PAIN WAS EXCRUCIATING. I barely made it outside the front door before the vomiting started in earnest, making my stomach cramp more than ever.

"Something you ate?" Lae questioned as she watched me creep back into the bedroom and curl up in a ball on the bed, grimacing in pain.

"Don't know," I managed between moans.

"Should I get your sister?"

"No," I croaked, wishing the pain, cutting me like a knife from the inside would stop.

After four months, they had welcomed Sorcha to the medical team, and she was now on rostered shifts like the others. She didn't mind the night shifts. Sam was nearly five, and he adored Di, so she had someone to care for him if she was called out. Babies, it turns out, love to make an appearance in the middle of the night. People also seem to get sick more frequently during the night.

"Why is that?" I had asked her one day on my way to work and seeing her as she trudged home from an overnight call out.

Sorcha, exhaustion written all over her, had mumbled, "Usually they are no sicker than they were at 6pm the night before or at 9am the following morning. The difference at 2am is that they can't sleep. They aren't distracted by work or things to do. They lie there and think the pain is worse when it usually isn't. But when they can't sleep, I can't either."

Remembering this conversation and realizing that it was likely well past midnight, I didn't want to disturb her. I could wait until morning.

Lae didn't look convinced as she watched me curled up in pain but didn't ask again. She went and got me a glass of water and watched over me, concerned. "Do you want me to get something for the pain?"

I nodded. Anything. Anything to make the sharp stabbing pain stop.

Another wave of nausea overcame me, and I bolted upright. Lae quickly thrust the bucket under my nose as I lost my guts, realizing as I did so it wasn't a pretty sight. Maybe she loved me.

When the vomiting ceased, Lae sprang out of bed with the bucket. A few moments later, she returned with it clean and a warm wet towel, which she used to wipe my face.

"I love you," I mumbled as I lay there, completely incapacitated.

"And I, you," she beamed. "I am going to get you something for the pain. Are you okay for a bit?"

"Not. Going. Anywhere," I gasped, curling up like a woodlouse, trying to minimize the distance between my stomach and ribs.

Lae bustled around the room, putting on shoes and a jacket. I vaguely heard the door close and wondered why she needed shoes to get medicine that we kept in the kitchen, out of reach of Louis.

Twenty minutes later, I had my answer. Sorcha stood over me, annoyed, and started firing questions. *When did the pain start? What was I doing at the time? Where is the pain? Was it getting better or worse? Rate it on a scale of one to ten.* The questions kept coming, and I was struggling. The pain was overwhelming, and I struggled to focus on her words.

Forcing me to lie flat, she palpated my abdomen, and I bellowed, bolting upright and projectile vomiting as she pressed on a tender spot. A look of concern crossed her face, quickly covered, but I saw it.

"What? What is it?" Lae asked, concerned.

"How long have you been in pain?" she demanded.

"All day," I muttered. "Maybe yesterday too."

"Why didn't you say something sooner?" she barked.

"Busy," I muttered, in too much pain to care what she thought.

"What is it?" Lae asked. "I'm assuming not food poisoning?"

"Appendicitis," Sorcha pronounced. "Fairly severe too, I'd say. Can you get Fraser? Hamish, too. I will need help to carry him to the surgery. This can't wait until morning."

I tried to protest but was drowned out by her next set of instructions to Laetitia. The pain was crippling. I couldn't focus on anything else.

The next period passed in a blur. Focused only on the pain, I vaguely recall being carried somewhere. Then a needle, followed by sleep, blissful sleep.

Daylight hitting me in the eye woke me, and I tried to shield my eyes from the glare. Sorcha saw me move and jumped up to adjust the blind. Resettling herself in the chair beside me, she questioned, "How do you feel?"

"Like a truck hit me," I croaked, my throat sore and terribly dry.

Sorcha, recognizing my plight, poured me a glass of water and handed it to me, helping me lift my head from the pillow as I drank.

"Arrgghh," I bellowed as the pain kicked in from my belly. That part hadn't been a dream then.

Sorcha turned to the small metal side table, and I watched her prime a syringe, a small amount of a clear fluid popping out of the tiny needle tip.

I must ask her why they do that, I thought abstractedly through the fog of waking and pain.

Sorcha deftly swabbed and injected the syringe into my upper arm before I could protest. "You were lucky," she said. "If Lae hadn't called me when she did, you may be in a far worse position."

"Huh?"

"Your appendix ruptured while Hamish and I were operating. It is a fairly simple procedure, normally. But not when the appendix has ruptured. Then it can spread the bacterial infection throughout the abdominal cavity and cause abscesses."

"Will I be okay?"

"You will be fine. But next time you are in pain, bloody well do something about it sooner, will you? We are rapidly running out of most medications, and I would hate to come all this way to see you die of a simple infection."

Sensing a movement in the doorway, I glanced up to see Lae and Louis. Lae, looking extremely worried, Louis beaming at me.

"Dadda!" he sang happily.

"You can't hug Daddy," Lae told him. "Daddy sick."

"Sick? Why sick, Dadda?"

"Stupidity," I heard Sorcha breathe but loud enough for me to hear. I wasn't certain Lae had heard the taunt but suspected she had.

"I'm okay, Louis," I soothed, watching his smile turn into worry. "I'll be home soon."

Lae looked at Sorcha.

"A few days," Sorcha said, catching the look. "We need to watch him and ensure he doesn't get a secondary infection. You did well, waking me when you did."

This was praise from Sorcha, and Lae recognized it.

"Thank you. For saving him."

Awkwardness filled the room, both women looking at the other, unsure of what to say. My sister, who had saved my life. My wife, who had also played a part in recognizing the emergency that this could have been.

It was Louis who broke the silence. "Cuddle Dadda?" he asked Lae.

Sorcha answered him. "Gently," she advised, plucking him from Lae's arms, placing him carefully on my left side.

The morphine was taking effect, and the edges of objects looked hazy. Feeling pleasantly removed from my body and the pain, I smiled at Lae. I could still feel the pain, but it no longer bothered me. It was like I recognized it; it was still there, but I was distracted. My eyes were getting heavy, and I fought to stay awake.

"Rest," I heard someone say as I plunged into the depths.

CHAPTER 29

"**I HAVE SOMETHING TO** tell you."

Rolling over, I emitted a muffled moan as I pulled the stitches in my stomach. I had been home for a day and had not recovered from the surgery.

"I'm pregnant."

Sitting bolt upright, I banged my head on the shelf above our bed. "Arrgghh!" I exclaimed, rubbing my head and looking at Laetitia in amazement, clutching my stitches with my right hand and the rapidly swelling lump on my head with my left hand.

"I thought you couldn't ... while you are feeding Louis, that is."

"So did I, but breastfeeding isn't foolproof, it seems. Are you ... happy?" she asked cautiously.

"Are you mad? I am the happiest I could be! Another child? Another miracle that combines the two of us? Yes! Yes, I am happy! Thrilled. Ecstatic. Over the moon!"

I threw my arms around her, ignoring the pain, and squeezed so tightly that she pounded me on the back.

"Oxygen," she wheezed.

"Oh! Sorry!" Withdrawing, I couldn't help a tiny pat of her stomach. "Hello there! I wonder if you are a boy or a girl? Ooh, how many weeks?" I asked.

"I'm not sure, really, but around sixteen, I think. Because of feeding Louis, it took me longer to realize."

"Reunion baby?" I asked with a smile.

"Seems so."

"Best. News. Ever," I pronounced as I rubbed my throbbing crown.

We lay snuggled together. Lae's head rested on the space between my collarbone and arm. Content and at peace. Blissfully happy in the life we had made together, filled with love and partnership. We had overcome so much. Had so much yet to look forward to. A new child, maybe a girl this time?

"Do you feel okay?" I asked. "I'm sorry I have been no help for the last few days."

"That's okay. You couldn't help it." Then after a long pause, "Cam, can I ask something?"

"Anything."

"What was it like?"

"Like?" Carefully rolling over to face Lae to avoid exacerbating my wound, she looked shy, embarrassed almost.

"What was it like, outside of the dome?"

Pausing, I tried to recall. It was like all the other days I had been outside. But for Lae, who had spent just a few brief hours outside, the day we found my aunt, she hadn't been out there in years.

"Dreich," I responded, which made her smile, with my use of a peculiarly Scots word. "Tedious, damp, wet, and gray. Dead. No sound, no life. Very depressing."

Her face fell.

Trying to interpret the look, I asked, "Did you want to go somewhere? Before the baby is born? Louis is old enough that we could leave him with Sorcha and Di for a night or two."

"No, not that. I just … well, I just wondered if the world would recover."

As she moved to lie flat on her back, I noticed Lae was just developing a tiny pot belly. I stroked it and envisioned the person who would be, wishing there was a window, a sunroof through which I could peek in and see him or her develop.

"I can't wait to meet you," I whispered to my child, then looked up at Lae's face. "I mean it. We could have a few nights away from here. We could take some horses or just walk. Slowly, under the current circumstances, but we have time. We could go to Stornoway or even south to Tarbert. We really can't go much farther. It would involve boat travel, and that means being exposed to water."

"No. It is okay," she replied. "I mean, I want to go to these fantastic places that you have described: Australia, New Zealand. But my home is here, with you, with my boys."

"Are you sure?"

"I am. One day we will explore together. But when our children are older. Maybe one day it will be safe, and we can see all those places I never got to, but just imagined what they looked like. Places I have seen in books and on the internet. I realize it is likely pregnancy hormones making me melancholy, but I regret never traveling when I had the chance. I would have made an effort had I known. I could have caught a train to London, or York, or Inverness. Even just for a day. But I was focused on my studies, on my volunteer work. I have never been on an airplane, not even on a boat, until they brought here us. I always just thought there was time."

"We all did. None of us knew."

"And that's the sad part, isn't it?" she asked, looking up at me from her pillow. "We all thought there was time to say the things we didn't say, to visit places and people. When the end came, it happened so quickly. I didn't even realize it was the end until later."

"This isn't the end," I assured her. "I have been to so many thriving communities. I know it is hard as you haven't seen them, but I believe humanity will survive. Blake, Kevin, even Angus: they are all trying to help the earth recover. Hey, did I tell you there are koalas in Kiewa?"

Lae's face lit like it was illuminated from within. "No! They survived? What else?"

"Oh, lots of Australian wildlife. Not a large number, just a few breeding pairs of each."

"Like an ark?" she asked, smiling.

"I guess. Sorcha said the science teams had carefully chosen breeding pairs, unrelated, to diversify the gene pool. But the other animals were already there in the settlement. That reminds me, do you know if the vets here ever neutered any of Jam's kittens?"

Jam, hearing her name, lifted her spotted head from where she lay at the foot of the bed and emitted a purrp of inquiry.

"They did. Just after you left, once they had grown to full size, but everyone is asking when she might have more."

Goodness. Babies galore, I thought.

CHAPTER 30

RECOVERY WAS SLOW AND frustrating. I was desperate to get back to work, conscious that I had dumped it all on Diana and Fraser. Still, they got along well, much as Jamie, Di, and I had on August.

Fraser, Isla, Sorcha, and Di regularly joined us for meals. Isla and Sorcha got along well, both being scientifically oriented women with children of a similar age. Fortunately, Di and Lae also got along fabulously. As I had suspected, Sorcha and Lae were on friendly terms but not friends. They were just far too different. But there was a deeper level of respect now. Lae was grateful that Sorcha had saved my life. Sorcha recognized that I truly loved Laetitia, and she me. Secretly, I was glad that Freyja had left with the crew before I left for Australia and hadn't yet returned. I wanted Sorcha and Di to become comfortable with Lae and me before introducing the complicating factor of Freyja to the mix. Di and Freyja had been good friends. It would be difficult for Lae to compete with that existing friendship. She was struggling enough as it was: me returning with my dominant older sister and a long-term friend, now in a relationship and both looking to catch up on lost time with me. She said nothing, but I suspect she felt left out of conversations. Sorcha bringing up childhood memories, and Di talking about our lives and people on August. I did my best to steer conversations to something where Lae could be included wherever possible, but it was difficult.

"I wanted to have a chat about using some woodlands on the western side of the village. It is in the open, and it would make fantastic pasture lands. We wouldn't need to clear too much of it," Fraser commented one evening, over a bottle of wine, looking at Di and me. It was our first dinner together since my surgery. While I was in the hospital, Isla had given birth to their third daughter, Kari, assisted by Sorcha. Tiny Kari slept in a basket beside the table. Louis was asleep in his cot, the older children in the lounge playing. It was Louis's first birthday, and we had been celebrating all day, although I spent it sitting on the sofa. Everyone brought him a gift, hand-made with love. We shared our joy at the news of our new person to be born in the winter.

"You want to clear old-growth forest?" Sorcha asked in shock.

"Just a small area. There is lots of land."

Sorcha looked at him incredulously. "Why do you think it is we can breathe under here?"

"Duhhh ... oxygen?" Fraser replied in a perfect imitation of Fred Flintstone.

"Yes, but what about what we exhale? Carbon dioxide? Did you know that carbon build-up was an enormous issue facing the planet when this all happened? Scientists have known about this since the

1970s. The Greenhouse effect, global warming, El Nino, climate change were all words for the build-up of excessive carbon in our environment. The fossil fuel companies were responsible for the campaign of misinformation back in the early 1990s. We know that. That was proven. But the issue remained as no one wanted to take on the global mega-corporations, so as a result, we all watched as the world argued. But at the core, it was the production of carbon that was the issue."

"Okay, but surely there are other ways of addressing the carbon issue. I'm just saying that it is a simple piece of land to..." Fraser tried to backpedal, recognizing what he had started.

"I know what you are saying!" Sorcha was getting worked up. Leaning back in my chair, I tried not to smirk as I waited for the fireworks that inevitably occurred when Sorcha got on her academic soapbox. Di had seen this side of Sorcha and was also edging herself away from the action. Lae had not and was watching, her mouth open in astonishment. Wishing I could warn her, I tried to catch Lae's eye, but she was mesmerized by the rapidly agitated Sorcha. Isla strategically chose this moment to leave the room and check on the other children.

"There are several methods that could remove carbon from the environment. Before the outbreak, the company where Tom worked investigated using biomass for energy in the industrial, power, or transportation sectors, capturing carbon before releasing it back to the atmosphere and storing it underground or in long-lived products like concrete. But for obvious reasons, that wouldn't work here."

"What do you propose we do, then? I assume we need to address this?" Fraser asked cautiously, unsure that engaging with the enemy was a wise move. Especially without his wife present.

"There are several options. Direct air capture is chemically scrubbing carbon dioxide directly from the ambient air and then storing it. It is relatively straightforward, but when we needed to come here, the technology was costly and energy intensive. Seawater capture is much like direct air capture, except CO_2 is extracted from seawater instead of air."

"Can we do that?" Di asked cautiously. She had seen enough of Sorcha in action to know that, at times, Sorcha could be an insufferable know it all.

"Not without a lot of work and probably technology we no longer have. It leaves us with the simplest process and the most natural. Good old photosynthesis removes carbon dioxide naturally—and trees are especially good at storing carbon removed from the atmosphere by photosynthesis. Back home, they were expanding forests and managing forests to encourage more carbon uptake. Did you know that every acre of land restored to temperate forest can sequester three metric tons of CO_2 per year? Before Tom died, he was researching which plants were the most efficient at photosynthesis. He was researching black plants ... but he never got to finish that project." Her voice trailed off, the memory of Tom still recent.

Di placed her hand on Sorcha's knee and looked up at me. "Did you see anything in your travels that made you think the earth was recovering?"

I shook my head sadly. "No. Everything was dead, devoid of life. The strangest part was the wind blowing, but no leaves to fall or branches to sway. The branches just banged together like rattling bones. It was a very disconcerting sensation."

Lae sat quietly, not interrupting. Feeling her stir, I turned to look at her. She was bursting to say something but didn't want to be labeled a fool.

"What is it?" I encouraged gently. "We are all friends here."

I shot a glare at Sorcha, a look she knew well enough. *Don't be a bitch*, it said, *or you will pay.*

Sorcha smirked back at me. *Message received.*

"Well, if we need to clear the forest, and still deal with the carbon issue ... I thought maybe Di and Sorcha could set up algae tanks here. Didn't you say they had algae tanks on Kiewa? With Di's agricultural knowledge and Sorcha's experience with the bioreactor on Kiewa, surely working together, they could..."

Boom. Still in the honeymoon phase and utterly obsessed with each other, Sorcha and Di wanted to spend as much time together as possible. If that meant being away from other people, all the better.

"Do you have access to the algae you need?" Lae asked.

"I guess so," Sorcha responded cautiously. "There are algae here, right?"

I nodded. "Freshwater or saltwater?" Freshwater would be simple. Saltwater, not so much, the dome only extending to the beach in a few places and not to the water.

Sorcha thought for a moment. "Freshwater algae are best. The concept is easy enough. I just need clear panes of glass so I can make a large vessel in which to keep them in so they can reproduce."

"We likely have the right algae. There are plenty of rocks and streams with algal blooms. What we don't have here is glass, Sorcs. To make glass, you need to heat sand to something stupid like 1700 degrees. We have no capacity to do that without creating smoke."

Sorcha's face fell. "Where can I get glass tanks?"

"No clue. We are on a remote island. Not exactly a glazier on the street corner."

Silence fell over us. So close, yet once again, something we didn't have here.

Again, it was Lae who came up with an idea. "How big?" she asked. "I mean, does it matter, from a scientific perspective, how big the tanks are?"

"Well, no, not really. What are you thinking?"

Lae looked at me and blushed. "The day Cam and I went outside the dome. To... to your aunt's house." She was stammering slightly with nerves.

Placing my hand over hers, I encouraged her. "Go on."

"Well, as I was waiting for Cam, I poked around. There were several old aquariums outside—seven or eight at least. I didn't look closely, but they looked intact. Would they do?"

Sorcha's face lit up. "I remember now. Uncle Malcolm loved tropical fish."

"I don't remember," I admitted. "But I wasn't paying much attention under the circumstances. Are you sure?" I asked Lae.

"Positive. They were dirty and full of rubbish, stacked up outside a shed. But I don't recall seeing any broken glass."

"That is so like Aunt Ange." Sorcha grinned at me. "Never got rid of anything. Easy. We will go tomorrow."

"Are you sure you want to do this?" I asked, worried. "It isn't a pleasant sight."

"She was my family, too. I need to pay my respects. Besides, I think she would have liked to know that Uncle Mal's tanks came in useful. Mum always teased her about hoarding useless crap in that shed. Ange would feel somewhat vindicated."

We both laughed at that. I grimaced as it hurt my wound.

"Are you sure you should lift heavy things?" Lae asked, concerned. It had only been a few days, and I was still struggling to get around.

"I can do most of it," Sorcha responded briskly. "I won't let him damage my handiwork."

It was settled. The following day, Sorcha and I would take a horse and one of the few wagons out to Aunt Angela's and collect the tanks. Lae wasn't convinced so soon after my surgery but saw that arguing with both of us was futile.

The next day it was raining, so the expedition was called off.

"I'm sorry, Sorcs; it is just too dangerous."

"I know. I just wanted to get started."

"You will. But we need to stay safe. I just found you. I will not lose you now."

She smiled at that. "Fine. But tomorrow."

The following day was overcast but not raining.

"How far is it on the other side of the dome?" Sorcha asked, looking at the sky. It could rain, but it didn't appear to be imminent. If we moved quickly...

"An hour, maybe. I think we can make it if we don't hang around."

"Let's go then."

The sight of my aunt looking so like our mother was no less harrowing the second time. We stood there in silence, staring, wondering if that had happened to Mum, too. Despite being thousands of kilometers apart, and their demise years apart, had their death ultimately been the same? Refusing to go inside the house, Sorcha still looked distinctly unwell as we fossicked around the garden for tanks. Eventually, we found ten good-sized ones in usable condition. There were more, smaller ones, or some needing repair. Likely some in the house, too. We could come back for those later. For now, this was enough. Sorcha lifted them onto the cart. I helped strap them down, only the occasional twinge of my stitches jarring my movements.

The ride home was far quieter, Sorcha replaying the gruesome scene in her mind.

"I'm glad Mum and Dad went on their own terms," I mumbled.

Sorcha dropped her head onto my shoulder as I drove the horses, the tanks strapped on securely behind us.

Di was there to greet us and helped Sorcha unload the tanks. We had agreed that the most logical place to set them up was on the brick wall behind the row of houses in direct sunlight. When operating efficiently, not only did the algae absorb carbon and produce oxygen, they could also be used as a biofuel. Di and Sorcha chatted excitedly about collecting the algae from the ponds and how they would set them up, each slightly different, so they could assess which was the most productive. Recognizing that my role here was now redundant, I slipped away. Fraser needed my help in the greenhouse, which I could do standing, freeing him up to work in the fields. With more mouths to feed because of population expansion, we needed to keep up with the cropping.

CHAPTER 31

EVEN THOUGH IT WAS only September, Christmas memories swirled in my head, warm and fuzzy fragments of my childhood. Roasting meats, visits to family and friends. Gifts under the tree. Family traditions like driving around to see houses lit up, the Christmas windows in the city. Crepes at the French stall in the center of Melbourne. Walking through Chinatown and watching chefs hand make dumplings filled with deliciousness. I had missed Christmas with Lae last year because of my travels to find Sorcha.

"What did you do for Christmas as a child?" I asked dreamily. I could have kicked myself as I saw Lae's face fall.

"Shit. Oh, kitten, I am such an idiot. I spoke without thinking. I am so very sorry."

"It's okay. Please tell me about yours."

"No, I can't."

"I want you to."

"Are you sure?"

"Absolutely. As odd as it sounds, I don't mind because it reminds me you don't pity me. You aren't constantly thinking, 'I can't talk about my child-hood memories in case she doesn't have any.' I have some, mainly as I got older and explored the city more, especially during my years in Edinburgh. I loved the Christmas decorations in the streets, car-olers out singing. Enormous trees with lights. Some years, Mum bought me a small gift, when we had little money to spare. Mine were usually homemade for her. Some years I would find a small pine tree and deco-rate it with paper chains I had made at school. A few times, we even went to one of the local churches for a Christmas lunch. I enjoyed those very much. There was singing and more food than I had ever seen in one place. But I need to know what you did. I need to know what to do for Louis, don't I?"

Smiling, I started, hesitant at first. Then I described all the amazing events of the season: Christmas lights, carols, and windows. Shopping for others. Gifts for children who otherwise wouldn't get any. Making food for a charity to serve on Christmas day. Our Christmas Eve box.

"What's that?" Lae interrupted.

"Every Christmas Eve, once we had eaten dinner and cleaned up, Mum gave us a Christmas Eve box. It always had a new movie or two and new pajamas for Sorcha and me. Popcorn and hot chocolate, sometimes some other treats, too. On Christmas Eve, we would sit down as a family and watch a new movie, usually a tacky Christmas one when we were younger, eating popcorn in our new PJs and drinking hot chocolate. Then we went to bed and waited for Santa to come."

"That sounds divine," Lae said wistfully. "Maybe we can do something similar for Louis but with books rather than movies. We would need to call him Father Christmas, though. I never really understood Santa."

I laughed. "My Mum had to adapt to that term, too. Mum still said Father Christmas, although Dad, being raised in Australia, used Santa."

"But are you okay with the idea of a Christmas Eve box?" I asked. The Christmas Eve box was one of the many traditions I had loved.

"Of course!" Lae smiled. "What else did you do?"

"Well, on Christmas Day, we opened our presents early, then had a special breakfast, usually croissants or Danish pastries. Spent some time looking at our gifts, and then lunch was always with our extended family. My father had one brother in Australia, so they took turns to host. Originally it was the brothers, their wives, and children. There were always cousins to play with. As we grew, the cousins brought partners too, and some of them started having children. We were unusual because it was always a hot meal—turkey, ham, and pork with all the trimmings and plum pudding with custard. We ate so much we couldn't move afterward."

"Why wouldn't it be a hot meal?" Lae asked, intrigued.

"Remember, it is mid-summer in Australia. It can be swelteringly hot, up to 40 degrees on Christmas Day. Many families we knew adapted to the climate and served a seafood lunch with salads and fruit. Summer fruit in Australia was exceptional: chilled grapes, cherries, raspberries, mangoes. But our family was traditional and insisted on a hot lunch. One year my aunt, not wanting the work involved in a roast lunch, suggested a cold buffet. I thought there would be a

riot! Mum was beside herself. No turkey at Christmas!"
I smiled, recalling her face when Dad told her.

"After lunch, we would all flop into chairs and open the gifts we had bought for each other. The youngest had to hand them out. It took me years to realize that it was a ruse, as the adults were all too full and too drunk to move. We did a Kris Kringle for many years—you know, when each person buys for one other person. But eventually, it just ended up that presents were bought for the kids, me and Sorcha, and our cousins. I still wonder what happened to them..."

"Your cousins?"

"I looked on the list, but they weren't there. Two of the three had children, so they would have been ineligible, anyway. Do you have any relatives? I never thought to ask."

"Honestly, I don't know. I must do, somewhere. Mum refused to speak of her family, although I tried to ask her often enough. Just once, when I was about eight, she saw something on the telly that set her off. She started to rant, 'my brother...' and then stopped when she saw me. I prompted her, but she clammed up and never spoke of it again. When I asked her the next day, she pretended that she didn't remember, but I could tell by the look in her eye as she turned away that she did. She just didn't want to speak of it. I have an uncle, it appears. Had an uncle, I guess that would be. But whether I have cousins or grandparents, I have absolutely no idea. A bit late now, isn't it?"

"Did you ever think to look? Births, Deaths, and Marriages, I mean. There must be a record somewhere."

"I thought about visiting the National Records of Scotland office. It was in Edinburgh, you know, not too far from the university. When I first moved to

Edinburgh, I planned to do it during my university break. But I worked several jobs most years to pay for my board and living expenses. Cleaning hotel rooms, waitressing, that sort of thing. A scholarship paid my tuition, but I still needed to live. Working and studying left little time for personal research. I always thought I would get around to it, but well..." She shrugged. "I never did."

"You found time to volunteer."

"That was my way of giving back," Lae responded.

"I know. Maybe one day, we could still look. Those records are likely still there, you know."

"I would like that, to know where I came from. It was never imperative to me until now. But now that I have Louis and this little one, I want them to know."

Lae, like Sam, had devoured the photos of my family, asking questions about people, places, items in the background. Where we were, what we had done there. We had spent weeks going through them each night, sometimes with Louis, sometimes after he was in bed. Not once had Lae seemed sad. She just wanted to know these people. People who I had been close to. One day I hoped to give her a sense of her own family, the people she originated from, so she could discover her place.

CHAPTER 32

"HAPPY BIRTHDAY!"

Lae opened her eyes and saw Louis, freshly changed and dressed, with a small green leaf-wrapped parcel in his tiny paws. She smiled at him as he sat on the edge of our bed.

"Give it to mama," I coaxed gently.

Louis, fascinated by the small object in his hands, didn't want to relinquish it.

"No!" Louis stuck out his lower lip obstinately.

"Louis," I tried again with exaggerated patience. "That is for Mummy. It is her special day. Can you give it to Mummy?"

"No! *Mine*!"

Lae, desperately trying not to smile, was entertained by the power play between the willful toddler and the adult trying hard not to lose his cool.

Trying a firmer voice, I coaxed, "Louis. You need to give it to Mummy *now*."

Instead of handing over the package as I had expected, Louis threw his head back and howled. He screamed so loudly that I was confident that the neighbors could hear him. He sounded like we were stabbing him in the eye.

I looked at Lae, defeated. She laughed both at me and the situation.

"Get his teddy," she mouthed over his head.

Wondering what on earth she was up to, I complied, admittedly, in part, to get away from the noise for a short time. As I returned, she gestured I should pass it to her under the blankets so he couldn't see.

Watching intently, I saw Lae ignore Louis and his tantrum completely. He was red in the face, with snot and tears streaming down his face at this point. He had lost all knowledge of why he was angry. Now he just *was*.

Lae continued to ignore him as he raged. Without speaking, she slowly pulled the teddy out from under the blanket and stroked him gently.

Louis, mid-tantrum, didn't notice at first. When he did, he bellowed, "*Mine*!"

"Oh dear," Lae responded calmly, not looking at him but continuing to stroke the teddy. "Ted doesn't like noise. Ted likes quiet, he told me."

Louis sniffed loudly and repeated, "*Mine*!" with a fraction less intensity.

Lae stayed stroking the teddy and ignored Louis. Louis looked completely bamboozled, unsure what to do. Finally, he offered the parcel to his mother.

Lae, propped up against the pillows, turned her dazzling smile on him as she took the present. "For me? That is lovely, Louis. Thank you. Would you like your teddy?"

Louis took his homemade teddy and began gnawing on its rather ratty ear. Lae smiled up at me and said nothing. Words were not required. It was clear who was the better parent.

She slowly unwrapped the gift. I waited, holding my breath.

I watched as she pulled out the silver pendant with a small blue sapphire glinting in the center. Laced on a delicate leather thong, it swayed back and forth slightly and caught the sunlight coming through the window.

She said nothing, and I watched, waiting. Finally, I couldn't bear it anymore and burst out, "Do you like it?"

She made no sound, just stared at it as the swinging slowed. I was a little taken aback. Watching her face, I tried to interpret the emotions but could not work them out. Her face was still, emotionless.

"I found it, the stone, I mean." I was babbling a little, but I was so taken aback by her lack of response that I felt the need to break the ice that had inexplicably formed between us.

"I was out by Loch Roag collecting algae, and I kicked a rock, and that was underneath. In its raw form. I nearly missed it, but Jam was with me. She tapped her paw against it like a marble. When she moved it, I saw the blue, so I picked it up. I took it to Toby and asked him to make something for you. For your birthday... Lae?"

She finally looked up at me, looking tortured.

"What is wrong?"

"My mother," she admitted in a strangled tone. "My mother had a pendant very similar to this. It fascinated me as a child. She never took it off. But once, she did. She left it in the bathroom. I found it there and played with it. I took it to my room, put it on, and played dress-ups. I must have been seven or eight. She came in and saw me. She beat me for it," she ended, a strange bitter tone entering her voice. "Banged my head against the wall. Once the headache had subsided, I couldn't sit down for days without being in pain. The bruises lasted for weeks. I never touched that *thing* again."

The last sentence was delivered so coldly I was stunned that this was Lae speaking. Lost for words, I picked up her hand and held it, waiting for her to talk again. She rarely told me about her childhood, and what she had told me wasn't good. Neglect, but she had never described such blatant abuse. I didn't think I had ever heard her recollect a positive memory, yet she still seemed to miss her mother. Genetics, I guessed. We were bonded to our earliest caregiver, no matter how ill-equipped that caregiver might be in raising us.

"Would you like Toby to make it into something different?" I finally asked gently. "Or would you rather I take it away and get you something else?"

"What would you do with it?"

"Give it to someone else, I guess," I said logically. "Toby put in a lot of work. No point in wasting it."

Lae rounded on me. "Give it to Freyja, you mean?"

Stunned, I was utterly unable to speak for a moment. When I found my voice, she was already shouting at me, saying that my lack of response had proven it.

"That wasn't what..." I started, but she had thrown the bedsheets back, narrowly avoiding hitting Louis, and was already halfway across the room.

"Lae, don't be silly..."

Whirling in the doorway with more grace than a woman five months pregnant should, she screeched,

"Silly? Now I am silly too? Wonder what you see in me at all."

She hurled the pendant at me and stormed out, her small, hard belly visible through her white nightgown. Louis, still on the bed beside me, started to cry.

Pausing to pick him up and comfort him, I heard the front door slam.

Completely confused, I tried to settle Louis while replaying the conversation in my head, trying to work out what on earth I had said or done to make her go off like that. Had I accidentally implied something? Was it that just that the sapphire had brought back the terrible memory? Was it pregnancy hormones that the men always laughed about, but I had never experienced? Had Freyja and Angus's return two days prior set something off? Had Freyja spoken to her? Had Di said something about Freyja and me in front of Lae? More importantly, *What do I do about it*?

Pottering around the kitchen, I made Louis some porridge, unable to eat myself, feeling sick in the stomach. After breakfast, I changed him into some non-porridge-strewn clothes. In my confusion, I had forgotten to use a bib. I sat him on the rug while I dressed. Looking down at his sweet, chubby face, I said, "Want to go visit Auntie Sorcha, buddy?"

"Sor-ka, Sor-ka," he chanted.

"I'll take that as a yes, little man." Swinging him up into my arms, I looked down at the pendant I had placed on the bench. Pocketing it, I took it with me. Probably safer than leaving it behind. While it held no monetary value, I didn't want it to distress her further, as evidently it had.

Dropping Louis at Sorcha and Di's place with minimal explanation, I checked in at the greenhouses and tried to plan my work. Thoughts whirring, I couldn't focus. After a few hours, I needed to get out. A walk, I decided. As I wandered the mountainside, my brain droned with the argument of the morning. It was silly. Arguing over something… honestly, I don't even know what. Why on earth would she think I would give the necklace to Freyja? Freyja was in my past now, even though she was physically here at the moment. Di had been overjoyed to see Freyja and the crew arrive a few days before, and the two had spent hours together since her return catching up. Perhaps that had upset Laetitia—seeing Di and Freyja together?

Yesterday, as Lae and I passed Sorcha and Di's house on our way to drop Louis and Lae at school, Di had drawn me into the conversation with Freyja before I could escape. Likely not realizing the distress she was causing to Lae in her joy at seeing Freyja again, Di was overly friendly, not at all malicious. She talked about things we had done together, people we had known, like Jamie and Jacinda, reinforcing to Lae that I had been married before. Happily. That I had a life before her. I loved Freyja, and I always would. But I loved Laetitia more than life itself. The way the light caught her hair, her warm caramel-colored almond-shaped eyes, the golden flecks more visible when the sun was in her face. Gentle and loyal. When she sang to Louis to make him smile. Catching her stroking her rapidly expanding stomach when no one was watching. Her kindness, her sense of warmth and caring that exuded from every word and every action. That was why I loved her.

Realizing I needed to tell her this rather than sit here and catalog the reasons I loved my wife, I carefully picked my way down the slope as the sun dropped below the horizon, leaving the soft blues of twilight. Berating myself for the long walk here and now needing to walk home in the dark, I tripped heavily at one point. An enquiring meow sounded behind me, and Jam escorted me home. I scratched her behind the ears, and she weaved her way precariously between my legs as I descended, thinking about Lae, Louis, and the new baby. My family. Truly, I had it all.

Like her first pregnancy, Lae insisted that we not use the single ultrasound machine here to find out the gender. It used so much power that it was relegated to medical emergencies only.

"After all," she laughed when I wanted to find out the gender, "for thousands of years, women have given birth and not known what they were having. We will be fine, too."

Recognizing the logic in this, I had not pressed my case. But secretly, I wanted to know if it was a girl or a boy. We agreed that if we had a girl, she would be named after my mother, Cairstine. Perhaps we would change the spelling to the more phonetic Kirstine, though, to make it a little simpler. I could see my mother rolling her eyes as she spelled her name aloud, frustrated, for the millionth time on the phone. She had always complained that it was too complicated, and she should shorten it. But none of the traditional abbreviations, Kirsty or Tina suited her. It was also the name her parents had chosen, parents she had barely known. Cairstine she remained, despite the difficulties of a traditional Scots name in Australia. Remembering that Callie and Tadhg had named one of their daughters Aoife, pronounced Ee-fah, I realized that our little lady, or man, I corrected myself, wouldn't have the most difficult name in town.

As I cleared the last curve in the path, I looked over toward our house, smiling at the thought of soon being home with my wife and child. We could sort this out. We rarely fought and never, ever went to bed angry at each other.

A wave of chilled panic enveloped me as I cast my eyes over the village. Something was wrong. Really wrong. People were running all over the place, yelling, crying. I froze, not sure if I should enter the melee or run from it. I had never seen this sight before, so I watched, mesmerized, unable to make out what was happening. I could hear people crying, groups of them. *Did someone die?*

Knowing I couldn't stand here forever, slowly, I took the final few steps into view and paused.

"He's here! Cam is here!"

"Oh, thank goodness!"

Someone was against my chest, hugging me tightly. My head was swimming, fuzzy with the noise. It wasn't Laetitia. No. It was Diana. *Why was Di hugging me?*

I pulled back and looked at her tear-stained face.

The blankness on my face triggered something in her, and she started to cry. Loud, ugly crying interspersed with gulps as she struggled to breathe.

I joggled her to get her attention. "What? What is it? Is Sorcha okay?"

She nodded but was so overtaken by crying she could not get more than a few broken words out. "Sorcha, okay. Laetitia…"

Not waiting for her to finish, I let her go and ran for our home. Sorcha was in the kitchen with Louis. I swept him up into my arms and rounded on

Sorcha, only then noticing her blood-stained clothes and hands.

"Where is she? Where is my wife?"

"Cam..." she choked, barely able to get my name out. "Cam, sit down."

"*No*." I was getting frustrated now. "What is going on? Where is Laetitia?" I demanded.

"Gone." The word was so simple, so soft. I almost thought I hadn't heard it. A whisper on the breeze. *Gone*.

"What do you mean, gone?" I asked, fear making my voice shake.

"She was ... taken," was all Sorcha could manage.

My brain hadn't yet caught up. It was whirring and churning. "Taken? Taken where?"

"I don't know."

I looked at my sister, her clothing soaked through with blood but not her own. She dropped her head into her hands and sobbed.

Realizing that I wasn't getting anything more from her, I whirled out of the house and started banging on doors. Someone must know. *Where is she?*

Door to door, I raced. Friends greeted me, crying, hugging me, but no one told me what was going on. I broke away and started running. But running where? Where would I go? I found myself at the greenhouse and fell onto the bench seat. So many times, Lae and I had spoken here, about our lives, about Louis, our dreams for the future. With my head in my hands, I wept out of sheer frustration and anger. Sometime later, an arm crept around my shoulder, and I looked up into Freyja's clear green eyes: gentle, concerned. She pulled me in and held me in her powerful arms. I could see the scar along her forearm, blurred.

"Tell me," I croaked. "No one will tell me."

The moon was rising, the orange light infiltrating the corners of the greenhouse, golden shadows falling on the leaves and creating speckled shadows on the floor.

"From what I can gather..." Freyja whispered, then paused. She started again, this time more firmly, both in tone and words. "Raiders. Raiders came. They found the portal near the ocean at Carloway. Laetitia was there. She saw them coming, and she waved. She thought they were friendly. By the time she realized they weren't ... it was too late. They grabbed her and took her. Angus saw it all. He tried to stop it. He ran to help, but there were too many of them, and they attacked him. Your sister, she saved him. If he survives the next few days, that is. They took several ... people. All women."

"Women? Why would they take women?"

Freyja just shrugged. "I don't know. It makes no sense."

Standing, I turned to face her, responding stiffly, "Thank you for telling me."

I was gone before she could speak, out the door and moving wraithlike toward our home. Fraser was sitting on his doorstep, a statue in the late evening light. Approaching slowly, he looked up as he heard me approach. His face fell slightly when he saw it was me.

"I thought ... I thought it might have been Isla."

"Isla is ... missing?"

"Aye. She is. Since this morning."

Sitting next to him, I put my arm around his shoulder. I knew how this felt. Even mired in my own grief, I could see his plainly etched on his face. I knew this pain all too well, and I knew pain shared was pain halved. I wished someone had done this for me when Freyja was missing.

"I don't know what to tell the kids," he finally managed to say, his Scots accent becoming stronger as it always did when he was emotional. "They keep asking for their mam, and I don't know what to tell them. How do I tell them she is missing?"

"You tell them the truth as much as they understand." I remembered my Mum giving this advice many times to people who sought her guidance on children and grief. "My mother always said that you do not shield children from the realities of life, but you break it to them in language that they understand."

"That is probably sound advice," Fraser acknowledged quietly. "What about you? I heard Lae was ... taken ... too." Fraser stumbled, raw emotion at the surface for us both.

Comforting Fraser had lessened the stabbing pain in my stomach, at least for a moment or two. Now it was back with a vengeance.

"Louis is too little to understand, for now." I choked, unable to comprehend what I would tell my one-year-old. Channeling my fury, I spoke again, more forcefully.

"What I want to know is, who were these people? Where did they come from, and where are they headed? I mean to get my wife back."

"They took four women that we know of. At least there are four women we know are missing: Isla, Laetitia, Lucie, and Mairi. There could be more if they were from one of the crofts, and we don't know about it yet."

"No men?"

"No. Not taken. Three were ... killed. Angus is fair badly wounded too. Freyja said it is a miracle he is alive, the way they gutted him like a trout. They didn't mean just to wound him."

I sucked in sharply. This was planned then. To have weapons, know the access points, kill the men, and take the women screamed premeditated.

"But why? Why take women?"

"Who knows? But they did."

Escorting Fraser inside, I made a late supper as his daughters clamored for their mother. I tried not to listen to the sobs and cries coming from the other room as he spoke to them, just focused on making tea and pikelets.

Leaving them, I wandered home, alone. Louis was best with Di tonight. The house was cold and dark. Laetitia had been back after our argument. She had taken her clothes, cloak, and boots. Lying on our bed, I held her nightdress that carried the scent of her. All night I lay awake, haunted by the sound of her crying filling the room.

CHAPTER 33

A MEETING WAS HELD THE following morning, and all became slightly clearer. Five women had been taken. A largish fishing trawler had been seen the previous day. It had approached the island at several points, but it was evident that they didn't know precisely where the access points were.

"But they knew how to open them?" asked a male voice.

"Aye, they did." It was Hamish speaking. "I watched them go past slowly, heading south down the west coast looking for something. I saw them, but they didn't see me. Just as well. I was high on the cliffs above Dalmore Beach, cutting peat for the still. My first thought was that they could be from Newgrange, so I planned to attract their attention as they got closer, but as they neared me, something struck me as not quite right. Maybe it was the craft itself. I can't say. It was nothing obvious, just a gut feeling. I dropped behind a bush and watched. There were at least six men on deck, but goodness knows how many more below."

"What did they look like?"

"I couldn't tell from the distance I was at, but men is all I could say for sure, large burly men, all with beards. By the time I got back here early evening and learned that they had taken five of our women... I wish I had done something." Hamish's voice shook from emotion.

Is it anger or regret? I wondered abstractedly.

"It wasn't your fault." It was Aidan's gruff voice speaking. "You weren't to know."

As the only witness, Angus had the most knowledge. Woken from his induced state of unconsciousness and relayed via Freyja, Angus had seen the men take Laetitia and confirmed that he had also seen Isla, Mairi, and Lucie on board, tied and gagged and on a corner of the deck. He couldn't guarantee that they had also taken Orla, but it seemed likely, especially when she had last been seen pursuing an escapee goat in the vicinity of the coast. A pang of shock struck me when I realized she had left not only Lillian at home, a gorgeous toddler now with red ringlets that cascaded down her back, but a new baby, Liam, too. Poor Josh.

"When he saw them grab Laetitia, he yelled out and started running toward her. He made it as far as the beach when three, possibly four, men blocked his access. Two held his arms back as another ran his knife across Angus's belly. He laid on the beach, bleeding, and saw the boat leave though, heading north at speed," relayed Freyja.

North? Even through my fog of sleeplessness and anguish, this struck me as odd.

"What is north of here?" I asked. "I mean, aren't the Hebrides fairly far north as far as it goes?"

"Angus said if they were headed north, then it is likely that they were headed for the Orkneys, Shetlands, or even the Faroes. When we were in Edinburgh last time, we found evidence of more communities that we didn't know about previously."

"So, what are we waiting for?" Hamish asked. "We need to follow."

I could tell he felt guilty. Guilty that he had seen the boat and done nothing. Guilty that he was alive, and three others were not. Guilty that his wife sat by his side when five others had been kidnapped.

I stood up. "I'm going."

Sorcha clutched at my hand. "You can't. You have a child, and you haven't long had surgery."

"I'm fine. The surgery was nearly three weeks ago. I don't want to. Hell, I don't want to go. I don't want to leave this place again. But it is Lae. I must."

I was trying hard to keep my emotions in check. I wanted to scream, to cry, to punch something.

Sorcha, sensing my distress, placed a hand on my shoulder.

Freyja, overhearing my outburst, said quietly, "I'm coming, too."

Wanting to protest, I was easily swayed as she insisted and pressed her case. I saw the logic. She knew how to sail better than I, she had a vessel with which she was familiar, and she had been to other communities. The crew knew her. She had no ties here. She could leave immediately. Sorcha and Di could look after Louis. It made sense.

Nodding, I assented.

Freyja started barking orders, and soon people were scurrying everywhere, fetching, carrying, packing. *She would have been quite successful in the military*, I mused. *Tall and commanding, with a clear, crisp voice and a manner that brooked no argument.*

I promised Fraser to bring back Isla to him and their children when we set off from Garynahine. He stood watching me go, holding the hands of his children, the youngest Kari, only a few months old, in a carrier on his back. Three distressed little girls, now with no mother. The adage "it takes a village to raise a child" was so true here. Children were the responsibility of the entire community in a way I had never seen before. We all cared for each other's children, and often they slept the night at someone else's home. Louis would be well cared for by Sorcha and Diana in my absence. It was Laetitia I was terrified for. Five months pregnant, she was awkward and unwieldy. Morning sickness had continued into the second trimester, and she regularly felt unwell. Spending days, possibly weeks, on a boat would be torture, especially when she had no sailing experience.

By early afternoon, Freyja's crew of Luca, Nate, Jakob, plus me, were packed and ready to go. Mike gave us his fastest horses, and we galloped the distance from Garynahine to Stornoway where the *Selkie* was moored. Sorcha accompanied me to the dock and would return the horses. She hugged me in farewell.

"Do not to pop those stitches," she ordered, the stern façade hiding her distress. "They aren't yet healed. Nothing strenuous, okay?"

Freyja was already on board, overseeing the last of the food, water, and supplies being carefully stowed below decks. Luca finished filling the *Selkie* with fuel as I carried my backpack aboard. I carried a single change of clothes for myself and Laetitia. I wasn't remotely concerned about the food situation. All I wanted was to get moving, to get my wife back.

With no actual knowledge of where they had gone, the *Selkie* hit open water, veered east, then north. Under Freyja's watchful eye, the men took turns to man the cruiser, running it as fast as we could.

The *Selkie* had been moored on the opposite side of Lewis to where Lae and the others had been taken. We argued the merits of circumnavigating the northern part of Lewis and heading back south toward Carloway. But the raiders had nearly twenty-four hours head start on us now, Freyja reasoned. They weren't likely to hang around waiting for us to follow, even if they thought we couldn't. From the description of their boat that Angus had given us, a rusty fishing trawler, we had a larger, more capable craft. If we were headed in the right direction, we would catch up in a day or two. But in which direction had they gone?

Sticking as close to the shore as we could, partly for navigation and partly to see if they had stopped anywhere else, we passed the Port of Ness and the Butt of Lewis lighthouse, still white and steadfast on the northernmost tip of Lewis. The choice needed to be made. East, toward the Scottish mainland? Or north, toward the Orkneys?

Islands, Freyja contended, made more sense. They must live in a domed community too, and they had access to a boat.

We veered east toward the northern tip of the Scottish mainland, just to check on our way to the Orkney Islands. It was a rugged coastline with lots of small coves and inlets in which to moor a vessel. We would hate to learn that we had passed them. As night fell, brilliant stars lighting the sky, the western coast of mainland Scotland came into view. The light thrown off by the stars and moon was barely enough to see by, the single spotlight on the *Selkie* faintly illuminating the distant rocky crags and cliffs. Tiny islands scattered off the coast meant we traveled slowly, keeping a close eye on the coastline.

The crew predicted each other's needs and worked seamlessly. We slept in shifts. Always one person on the deck acted as a lookout, and one operated the craft and engines. Three shifts, two people awake. Lying in bed, I tried to rest, realizing it was pointless. There was no way I could switch my mind off enough to sleep. My heart broke for Laetitia. I knew where she had gone and why. She had gone to Carloway nominally to spend the day with one of her school families who lived on a croft near Doune. The mother had recently given birth and couldn't get the older two to school. Lae had offered to give up her Saturday, despite it being her birthday, to take a few months of learning resources to the children so the mother could homeschool them while their father handled the farm.

The broch was like a magnet for Lae. It was her favorite place and where we had spent three blissful nights as newlyweds on our honeymoon. We had camped beside the broch on a grassy patch overlooking the windswept bay with the broch immediately beside us, protecting us and blessing our marriage. I have no doubt it was where Louis was conceived. Right on the edge of a cliff, overlooking the North Atlantic Ocean, Lae would stare out to sea, mesmerized, conjuring places she had never seen. She loved the windswept nature of it, the history, the broch itself dating back to the first century. She told me she had often gone there, watching for me, when I had left the first time. Closing her eyes, she dreamed that she was with me, sharing my adventures. She prayed I would return across that vast open sea.

The argument we had yesterday morning was playing on my mind, too. No amount of wishing I had gone after her instead of disappearing up the hills and licking my wounds would bring Lae back. She was jealous of Freyja; I knew that. Now here I was, in close company with the very person who had caused the argument—sending Lae goodness knows where and me after her.

Tossing and turning, I knew achieving sleep was not going to happen. I slipped up to the deck to keep the watch company. It was Freyja. Inwardly groaning, I slunk back to the stairwell when she turned and saw me.

"Couldn't sleep. Thought I would keep you company," I mumbled.

"But you didn't realize that it would be *me* you would keep company?" she guessed.

"Something like that," I admitted sheepishly. Other than Lae and Sorcha, Freyja knew me better than anyone else in the world. At least she had. Once.

The familiar look, the scent of her: the memories came flooding back. It was the first time we had been together, alone, and not angry in a very long time. I turned and looked around for another deckchair.

"Over there," Freyja gestured toward the pile stacked up against the opposite side of the bow. Unfolding the wooden chair beside her, I sat quietly, watching the shoreline pass in the dark. The single spotlight was shining on the banks of the coastline as we cruised past. Occasionally Freyja moved the light to get a better view. She took her job seriously. That was good.

"Why did you agree to do this?" I asked suddenly. "It isn't like you know any of the people taken. Wouldn't you rather just look after Angus?"

Freyja paused, and I knew she was choosing her words.

"For you," she responded simply. "I know, rather, I heard, what you went through when I disappeared. Hell, from what Di told me. The thought of putting you through that again... well, I can help."

"That you can. And I am so very appreciative, Frey. Really."

She held my hand for a few long seconds, searching my eyes, then turned back to her duties.

Comfortably, but in silence, we sat together.

"I'm sorry..." I began, but she held her hand up to stop me.

"No. Not now and not here. Shit happened, and it was neither of our faults. It happened, and here we are. I went, you went. We missed each other and lies were told. But life is different now, and I won't have you apologize for any of it. We are here to get your people back. We can't lose focus from what is important now: our mission. We can talk when we get back to Lewis—with your wife."

I nodded in agreement. Freyja had said "your wife" like she was saying "your book" with no emotion. I was so thankful for that. It was a good plan.

"Agreed. Where do you think we are?"

"We are passed the mainland, and I am fairly sure that is the Orkney Islands over there."

She gestured into the distance, but I couldn't see in the dark. I said so, and she laughed. She had always had better night vision than I had. So many times, we walked back from the hot springs in the dark, and I tripped on a rock or tree root. Yet she could see like a cat in the dark. Shaking my head, I tried to remove the vision of that time. That was not helpful.

"Hang on a second," she muttered, more to herself than me. She turned and flashed the light three times through the front window of the cabin. Nate, the engineer, slowed the motor, and we slowly putted in closer to shore. I could see it now, shadows looming in the dark.

"That would be the island of Hoy," she murmured. "We are close."

"Close to what?"

"Well, Angus believed if the stones at Callanish were a portal, and Newgrange, and your evidence from Melbourne shows that the Clava Cairns are, then there was a reasonable chance that there was one on Orkney. There is a ring of standing stones of Brodgar on the main island but also a prehistoric village at Skara Brae. We were planning to head here next week as one of our next ports after we had stopped in to resupply and have some R&R on Lewis."

As the sun rose in the eastern sky, illuminating the ocean and small islands, Freyja turned off the spotlight, and we strained our eyes, searching for any sign of life. Slowly, Jakob and Luca ascended the stairs to the deck, spacing themselves out, assisting us in our quest.

It was glaringly obvious. The brilliant green of life was blisteringly clear from a long distance. Surrounded by the grays and browns of death, the green was a beacon, the dome visible too. *No wonder they found us so easily*, I thought crankily. I was irrationally annoyed at the geodesic dome designers for making us so visible to the outside world. If you were going to create secret communities, why place them so close to the coast?

Mooring carefully on the coast near Stenness, we could easily see the triangles of the dome in the early dawn light. The five of us anchored the craft and started hunting for the nearest opening. Stepping inside and closing the vent, I looked at them, unsure of what to do next. Time was still against us.

"Stick together," Freyja and Luca said in synchronicity. She smiled at him.

"You never leave people behind," Freyja said firmly, looking me in the eye.

We had barely taken three steps when we heard shouts from a nearby hill. Looking up, we saw a small group of four people. We waved, hoping that they would not think us the enemy. We, in turn, hoped like hell that they weren't the raiders. We approached cautiously, like two packs of dogs advancing on each other, slowly, each afraid to make the first move.

"Who are you?" the call came, hostile, fearful.

Looking around at the others, I shrugged and called back, "We are from a settlement on the Outer Hebrides. Some of our people were taken. We are looking for them."

A moment passed as they assessed this information. The only female among us, Freyja, sensibly took this moment to fluff out her long blonde hair, illustrating her gender. They froze as they saw her and the tension, even at a distance, dissipated.

The group descended, then stopped and watched us warily. Still fearful. *Are we the first outsiders they have seen?*

"Hi, I'm Cam," I ventured. "Originally from Australia, but I have been living on Lewis with my wife for the last few years." I felt Freyja bristle behind me but tried to focus.

"Two days ago, a ship came with some men. They killed three men from our community and kidnapped my wife and four other women."

A murmur spread between the four as they looked at each other in astonishment. The tall blonde man had been appointed leader.

"They came here yesterday. They took six of our women, too. Do you know who they are?"

I shook my head sadly. "No. But one of our people saw them heading north. This was the first community we have spotted since leaving Lewis. The dome, you know. Everything outside is dead, inside is green. It is fairly obvious…" I trailed off lamely.

"Will." The tall blonde guy stepped forward to shake my hand. "I'm Will. I'm from Tarbert. Did you say you were on Lewis?"

"I did. Our community is centered near Garynahine."

Looking around at the others, I wondered if I should explain about the portals.

"Come with us."

As we walked, Will kept talking, reminding me ever so much of Fraser on our first meeting, nearly three years ago when I came through the portal, dazed and frozen.

"Where did you say your community was again?"

"Garynahine, but the dome spreads to the west coast, near Carloway. Do you know it?"

"Och, aye. Near Callanish, aye? I ken it well. I went off to college a few years back in Inverness, never went home. Ended up here. Didne ken there was a community on Lewis, though. Perhaps I should put in for a transfer," he joked feebly.

I was unsure how much to tell him. As it turned out, I didn't need to. He asked me. "Is there anything special about Callanish? The stones, I mean."

"Ahh … well, yes." I wasn't sure how much to tell him, lest he suspect I was insane. Not a great way to start a new friendship.

Will nodded. "I wondered if that was the case. De ye ken Maes Howe here?"

"I have heard of it but never been there. A Neolithic chambered tomb, isn't it?"

"Aye, it is. A little unusual it is."

Getting a little sick of the dance and the time-wasting, I asked bluntly, "Is it an antipodean portal?"

Will looked at me. "Antipodean?" he asked cautiously.

I sighed. *Here we go*, I thought and took the plunge.

An hour later, we were sitting in the main village, eating shepherd's pie and washing it down with a rather good ale. The raiders had been here too, the previous day. Six women were missing, all of whom had been working near the coastline. No one had seen them go, and they weren't missed immediately. It wasn't until dark when none of them had returned that a search party had gone looking. Eventually, a young boy had admitted that he saw a ship and was scared. He had never seen a boat, being born here. Terrified, he had run home and thrown himself into bed, where he had fallen asleep and missed the ruckus as the community pieced together what had happened. He had woken, hearing the noise, and cried, thinking the boat was attacking them. Finally, he told his mother what he had seen. She had rushed outside to tell the others.

"There are no boats here, you see, so we knew it was outsiders. The problem is, we don't know what to do."

"Well, we have a vessel," said Freyja, her clear voice piercing above the low din of conversation. "And we intend to do something about it."

The chatter stopped, and a single voice asked, "What do you intend to do?"

"Go after them. Get our people back and yours too."

A chorus of chatter rose at this.

"How?"

"We work that out along the way. But if any of you want to join us, we won't say no. We need to leave soon to keep up with them, but we would very much appreciate some more hands."

Three men agreed to come. One, a former police officer, had that solid, no-nonsense build. The other two were big, burly, quiet sorts. One reminded me of Hugh. Not so much in looks, but in manner. That calm, quiet yet capable demeanor. Freyja started rounding up what she needed, and I took the opportunity to probe Will some more about the portal.

The Orcadians, it appeared, had discovered the portal in the same way we had; someone had gone missing. But that person had returned six months later, raving about a freezing island and being all alone.

"He was raving mad and barely alive," Will admitted as he explained that the island that Ross had traveled to was uninhabited but also not protected. He had discovered a series of caves, some of which had fresh artesian water. This had proven safe to drink, and he had found fish, breeding them in some of the larger pools, keeping himself alive.

"When he got back, he was in a terrible state—scurvy, malnourished. A diet of raw fish and water keeps you alive but only just. He was raving, unable to string words together coherently. He had gone six months without speaking to anyone, you see. I guess it does things to you."

Since then, no one had traveled through the Maes Howe portal, unsure where it led. Hurriedly, as I knew Freyja wanted to go, I explained the history of the antipodean portals, the ancient sites they seemed to be centered on. I described the communities on Lewis, Newgrange, and then August and Bellcamp. Perhaps it was just bad luck this portal had been activated but didn't go anywhere inhabited? I reasoned. *But why reactivate it at all?*

"Well, that makes a little more sense," Will said. "We suspected he was just mad. But Ross wasn't here. Then six months later, he was. Clothes in tatters, and he had been somewhere. We just had no idea where."

Glancing to my left, I could see that Freyja was questioning a child, a small boy of perhaps five. Kindly, but firmly. He was scared. That was visible. But his mother's arms around his waist, kneeling beside him, kept him from running.

"Did you hear them speak?" Freyja was asking.

The little boy nodded. "Shouting. They shout at Auntie Alize. I didn't like it."

"I know. It isn't nice when people shout. But I need to ask. Did they speak English?"

The little boy looked confused at this. His mother smiled at Freyja.

"He was born here," she explained, "so he has ne'er heard another language spoken. Some Gaelic, some

English. But we all speak both, so he disne ken any different."

The mother looked into the boy's eyes, "Did ye ken the words they were using, Robbie?"

The boy nodded. He whispered something in her ear.

The mother looked back at Freyja. "He knew some words, so it seems likely it was English or Gaelic. What do you think that means?"

Freyja looked at the sky and then over at me. "I think it means we head for the Shetlands rather than the Faroes. If they were from the Faroe Islands, then likely they would have spoken Faroese or perhaps Danish. If he understood them, then it is more likely they were native English or Gaelic speakers."

"Okay," I drawled. "But you and I are native English speakers, and we aren't from around here. Many of the people on August spoke a language other than English too."

Freyja paused a moment. "That is true. But if they came here second, they are headed north at least. What other information have we got to go on?"

She looked back at the mother. "Can he remember anything else? Something they said. What they wore? What the boat looked like? How many of them were there?"

The mother sat and explained patiently to the little boy how important this was. The men had taken Auntie Lize, and we needed to find her.

Robbie stiffened his shoulders and said, "There were lots of them. They all had beards but all different colors. I heard one of them say Rob. That's my name," he announced proudly.

"Yes, it is Robbie," Freyja said patiently. "And it is a lovely name. You know lots of words. Did you hear any other words?"

Robbie nodded. "They said ay-lann."

Freyja glanced at me, and I shook my head in negation. Even with my limited Gaelic, mostly learned from Mum's colorful swearing, I knew this word from our travels. Eilean. Meaning island. This told us nothing.

"Anything else, Robbie?" I asked. "Anything at all."

He thought for a moment and said, "Mousey brock. My friend Brock has a mouse. I thought maybe they had one too."

His mother frowned slightly. "Mousey brock? Are you sure, Robbie? Why would they say, mousey brock?"

The little boy stuck his lower lip out in defense. "I *did* hear it," and promptly clammed up. It was evident that we were done here. His mother was trying to placate him, but he was determined to be taken seriously and refused to engage anymore.

Freyja stood and watched me, her head tilted slightly to one side. Damn. My glass face must betray my conflicted thoughts. *Think, dammit.* My brain wouldn't work. I was exhausted from days with no sleep. *Mousey? Brock? Mouse-ey Brock?* The name had an odd ring to it.

Then the lights came on. Stooping to look Robbie in the eye, I asked as gently as I could manage, so I didn't scare him, "You don't think it was Mousa Broch they said?"

He looked at me and nodded. I exhaled, not realizing I had been holding my breath.

"I know where they are going," I announced stiffly.

CHAPTER 34

BACK ON THE *SELKIE*, along with our new shipmates, I explained, "Lae loved the old broch near Carloway. She spent hours researching them and telling me about their history. She was desperate to see more. There are quite a few still in existence, around 500, I think, nearly all in the far north of Scotland. I am a little ashamed to admit that I only half-listened, but I heard enough. There are two very well preserved brochs on the Shetlands. One named Clickimin Broch near the capital, Lerwick. The second is on a small island off the Shetlands called Mousa. I put the two words together, Mousa Broch. Mousey Brock."

Freyja nodded and smiled grimly. "It is definitely the best information we have so far." She nodded at Jakob, and he gunned the engine, making the water spray up over the sides.

"Don't forget not to let it get in your face," she called to the newcomers. "It isn't safe. Best not risk it."

They rushed away from the edge but looked back at their domed community, now rapidly disappearing in the distance—the greens and colors shining like a beacon in a dark world.

"What else do you know about this broch?" Freyja asked.

I shrugged. "To be honest, not much. I *think* this was the one that was the best preserved. Maybe the island it is on was uninhabited? But if it is the one I remember her talking about, it was the tallest and most intact of all the remaining brochs."

"That makes sense," said Freyja, thinking. "Island, large solid stone construction. Perfect place for a community."

A few hours later, we sailed past Fair Isle, once a lovely green fertile island, now abandoned, dark and dead. I shivered as we passed it. Generations of farmers had lived here, died here. Now no one would live here again. The white crofts were still visible in the mid-afternoon sun, the orange light reflecting from their once luminous rendered walls.

After Fair Isle, we navigated to the east coast of Shetland's main island, where Mousa was, not far from the principal town of Lerwick.

"What will we do when we get there?" I asked Freyja quietly when she passed me on her way back to the wheel. "It isn't like we can just walk up and say, 'Hey, hear you may have accidentally kidnapped some of our people. Can we have them back, please?'"

"It is under control," was all she would say in a tone that made it clear not to ask.

I grabbed her arm. "Really, Frey, I need to know. My wife is with them, and she is pregnant. I need to know. *How* are you planning to get them back?"

Exhaling loudly as she did when she was exasperated, she spoke directly into my ear, "We have weapons. It will be okay."

My eyes sprung wide. "Seriously? You are planning to go in there like a Sunday afternoon movie shoot-'em-up?"

Freyja's look of derision was one I had seen many times and had never forgotten. "Hardly. But it helps when you have three people who know how to use them."

"Three?"

"Our new police friend, Gerry, also knows how to handle a weapon. He was with an armed response unit in London. Luca and Jakob are old hands, ex-military. Both have completed several international deployments."

"Wow." I had to admit, I was impressed. Being Australian and growing up with tight gun control laws, I didn't even know anyone who owned a weapon.

Freyja tilted her head to the side. "You didn't think I would get them back, did you?"

I admitted, "I thought it might not be as easy as you seemed to think. Let's just get them, shall we, then we can argue the merits of weapons?"

Freyja smiled and headed back to the watch.

Three hours later, it was dark, the daylight hours shorter here at this time of year. A conversation held quietly on the deck, and we agreed with Luca's proposal that dawn was the safest time to strike. With unfamiliar terrain, we needed to see where we were going. If we hit quickly and early, combined with the potential element of surprise, we might be successful. Waiting made me uneasy. Goodness knows what they were subjecting Lae and Isla to while we messed around and waited.

No one wanted to sleep, so we spent the time trying to circumnavigate the island from a distance, getting a feel for it, searching for a suitable landing place and identifying any likely settlements. We spotted the broch from a long way off, a solid cylindrical structure over ten meters tall. I gasped when I realized what I was looking at.

"What is it?" Freyja hissed in my ear.

"Look." I pointed. "It is green. But there is no dome."

Everyone peered to look, challenging in the darkness. It was true. Despite the mainland of the Shetland Islands being dead and brown, this tiny island was alive with color. Located on a low flat peninsula on the west coast of the tiny island, we also saw a moderate-sized fishing trawler tied up near some sheds and old stone cottages. In the darkness, it was impossible to tell if they were occupied.

"That looks like what Angus described," I overheard Freyja tell Luca, gesturing toward the moored boat. He nodded grimly.

We crept slowly and quietly past. It was the most likely place for the residents to be located. They wouldn't be leaving their only vessel unprotected, especially if they had captives. The island itself was small, only two-and-a-half kilometers long and only one and a half wide. With the wild wind, we were reasonably sure they couldn't hear us, the motor only making a low put-put sound as we made our third complete circuit of the island. It was on this circuit when I noticed it. Being dark and unable to use the flashlight, we relied on the night sky to help us see. The moon had moved out from behind a cloud for a moment, and I saw it. The islands were almost cut in half by an inlet. It was almost two islands, but not quite. I grabbed Freyja and pointed it out.

"Could we get in closer?" I quietly asked. "Could it be a good place to pull in?"

She nodded, edged the *Selkie* closer, and moored it against the rickety old jetty.

Leaving Nate to guard the vessel, the rest of us crept through the rough bracken and heather toward the broch on the hillside above. Faintly lit by moonlight, below we could just make out a small settlement of ten roughly built houses in the flat area around the broch. Mainly stone, salvaged from old cottages and farmhouses, they had more modern tin roofs—basic square structures with a single window and door. None of them looked secured, so there was no way to tell which house held the prisoners. We would have to hit them all in the morning. But how? There were seven of us, but ten houses plus the nearby broch. I wasn't even sure they could count on me, useless as I felt.

We backed a distance away to confer and generate a plan. Luca and Jakob took charge. We would creep in quietly at dawn before anyone was awake. Grab the first person who came out and get him to tell us the rest.

It sounded so simple, and it was, in theory. The reality was a bloody mess.

As the sun tinted the horizon, we heard noises inside one cottage. What sounded like a wooden chair being dragged across a stone floor. As the door opened,

Luca and Jakob grabbed the man as he staggered out of his home, obviously in need of a piss. But before they could reach him and shut him up, he shouted, raising three more. Soon there was a riot going on, punches and kicks being thrown all over the place.

Gerry calmly held his gun to the sky and fired. The boom of the explosion plus the reverberation among the stone houses was enough to make us all freeze and look. Gerry calmly pointed his gun at the nearest man and asked politely in his thick Welsh accent, "Would you tell us, if you please, where our womenfolk are?"

The man, clearly terrified, pointed toward the broch. Freyja, armed herself, I noted, backed toward the broch, flanked by Luca. The single guard, a handgun pointed at his head, rapidly relinquished his post. Checking for an ambush, she went inside, Luca remaining on guard. Freyja came back to the doorway. "They are here!" she shouted.

Things happened rather quickly after that. The raiders, who were unarmed, were rounded up and held in place by Gerry, who seemed to be rather enjoying himself. Luca and the two other men from Orkney checked the houses. Freyja and Jakob released the women, untying them one at a time as they came out, blinking like owls from the probing bright sun after being kept in the dark.

Standing guard over two of the prisoners, I watched them coming out, dirty and terrified. I watched them, praying that they hadn't been hurt. I saw Isla and lifted my hand to get her attention. She rushed toward me and fell into my arms. I winced as the impact against my stomach made me realize how much pain I was in.

"It's okay now," I crooned as she cried, and I stroked her filthy hair. "I am here. You are safe."

I was watching over her head for Laetitia. They were all out now. Where was Lae?

My body stiffened, and Isla felt it. "I'm so sorry, Cam," she sobbed.

"Sorry? I don't understand," I yammered. "They took her too. Where is she? *Where is she*?"

"She... she ... she didn't make it," Isla managed between sobs.

"Didn't make it? What does that mean?"

Isla fell at my feet, crying and sobbing. I grabbed the arm of one of the other women. One I didn't know. One that must have been from Shetland. I scared her. I could see the terror in her eyes.

"Where is Laetitia? Where is my wife?"

She looked blankly at me. "They... they..."

I was out of control by now. Freyja was at my side, trying to calm me. But the rage had taken hold, and nothing was going to stop me. I grabbed the raider closest to me by the hair and slammed him against a tree. I had a good foot on him and at least twenty kilograms. I was by far the bigger man, and we both knew it.

"*Where is my wife?*" I bellowed in his face.

He cowered and shook. I helped him along, slamming his body repeatedly into the tree. Jakob went to intervene, but out of the corner of my eye, I saw Freyja shake her head.

Finally, one of the older men sitting in the group piped up. "Let him be. He wasn't even there. Your fecking woman wouldn't stop her fecking crying, so we shut her up. Made the others learn their place right enough."

Dropping the bloody pulp of the man I had hammered into the tree, I rounded on the speaker. "*How ... did ... you ... shut her up?*" I boomed, barely recognizing my voice.

I heard the voice, clear and thin. It was a faint female voice. It came from behind me. It was the last thing I remembered before the world went dark.

"He cut her throat and threw her overboard."

CHAPTER 35

AS I SLOWLY BECAME aware of my surroundings, I could feel the ground moving beneath me. Consciousness overtook the last remnants of sleep, and I realized I was in the sunlit cabin of the *Selkie*. The ship was moving. I could feel the roll of the waves. Straining my ears, I could hear the women on deck talking. *Such a pretty sound*, I thought as I rolled over and was violently sick over the lino floor next to the bed.

Dazzling orange-red flames engulfed me, raging hot air blowing past me, and my body ignited. When I woke again, this time sweating profusely, I was too weak to move away from the flames, the last remnant of dreams still vividly real. The sheets were soaked through, and I was dripping in a feverish sweat. I thought maybe I was dying, but I didn't care. Kicking the sheets off, I lay there, the grips of fever taking me. *Am I hallucinating*? I thought. Maybe it was all a dream. But when the wracking chills gripped my body and shook me until my teeth rattled, I knew this was no dream. Wrapped in the remaining blankets, I shuddered, curled into the fetal position.

Hearing the door open sometime later, I had no physical capacity to look up.

"Ugh!" I heard, followed by three quick, purposeful strides, and Freyja was by my side, her hand on my forehead and a worried expression on her face. Cracking my eyes open to look at her, I promptly closed them again, the light piercing my brain like razor-sharp needles.

"You are sick!" she exclaimed. "You are burning up."

"No. Shit. Sherlock," I croaked before succumbing to another wave of wracking chills.

The sound was muffled, but I could still hear. She was calling out to the others, banging and rattling as they searched cupboards, under sinks, tore through bags. Searching for something.

"Fuck, fuck, *fuuucckk*!!!" I heard her bellow from the next room.

The chills had loosened their grip on me. I lay in bed, panting.

"Water," I gasped. "Water," I tried again, and Freyja finally heard me. She rushed to the kitchen and brought me a bottle of unopened water. Sealed. Fresh. I drank thirstily, feeling guilty for using up our precious resources.

She saw my look and said, "It's okay. We have plenty."

Finishing the bottle, she handed me another. I took one sip and watched abstractedly as she sat it on the bedside table. The waves of heat overtook the chills and ravaged my body like an inferno.

In the summer that I turned eighteen, armed with a new driver's license, I had been driving home from the bush block on a Sunday afternoon where Dad had been spending his leave. A bushfire had sprung up out of nowhere and was lapping at the side of the road. The car temperature built up quickly as I drove, unable to turn back but scared to move forward. Sitting still would have been suicide. I planted my foot and drove as fast as I dared, irrationally scared that I would be booked for speeding. Looking back now, I grimaced at my stupidity, back when I thought being fined for speeding was the worst thing that could happen. I was a fool.

The heat overtook me, and I lay back in the bed with no energy to move. Sweltering, it was like being back in that fire. Hazy. Unable to focus. The heat dissipated as I was falling. Down, down, gently being sucked away. Freyja had a cool, wet cloth on my forehead, but I could barely feel it. She was speaking to me, but I couldn't quite make out the words. She was so far away; I was drifting... I was out of my body now, floating above it. Looking down, I could see my body sprawled across the bed, Freyja moving erratically. Wrinkling my nose at the strange scene below, I felt strangely at peace. There was no pain, no heat, no cold. No sensation other than feeling free, floating, light, and soft. Closing my eyes, I relinquished my body to the light.

In the next moment, I was back in my body as I felt Freyja slam down on my chest with all her force. "*No!*" she yelled at me. "I am *not* losing you now!"

Gasping from being pounded in the chest, I sat upright, partly in shock, partly in agony, as I felt my ribs crack under her weight. My movement stopped her from coming down on me a third time. She threw her arms around me.

"*I am not letting you die!*" I heard her roar. "I forbid it, *do you hear me!*" She was angry. Furious.

Why is she angry? I wondered through my fevered haze.

The fever and chills took me in turns, wreaking havoc on my body until I had nothing left. Freyja tried to bring me food, water, but I couldn't keep it down. My body was wasting away, and truthfully, I didn't care. Over hours I saw Lae sobbing, begging me to help her. I reached out for her, calling her name. Visions of places and people swam in and out of my head, fogged up as it was. Sam's eyes wide open in the blood-spattered bathtub, Hugh's eyes closed in the crisp white hotel bed, Freyja's in terror as she was sucked into the portal. My mother's face, in pain, as she died, infected from the virus—all of them calling my name, begging for help. I saw Lae's face at the end, the look of shock as someone inflicted pain on her. My poor baby, never to be born. *It is so fucking unfair.* I slammed my arm down on the bedside table and felt the pain reverberate up my arm.

Freyja saw what I was doing and stopped me. She grabbed my hands, and I winced. In my fevered state, I held them up, noticing them bloody and bruised. I looked at them, surprised. They didn't look like my hands. These were swollen. There were scrapes, cuts, and large bruises all over them. I turned them over, slowly, inspecting them, puzzled, and turned them back. Freyja was watching my face intently.

"You don't remember, do you?" she finally asked, astonished.

"Remember what?"

"What you did."

"What … I … did?" Now I was perplexed. "What did I do?" I finally asked, baffled.

"You … went ballistic. You let out a howl that made every hair on my body stand on end. It was a scream of such *agony* that I can't even describe it. I have heard nothing like that before, and I hope I never do again. You threw your head back and roared, Cam. Then it was like you were possessed. I have never seen you like that. Never." She shook her head.

"What… what did I do?" I was almost too scared to ask.

"You started punching the man you were holding into a bloody pulp. Then the next, and the next. They tried to defend themselves alright, but you couldn't be stopped. You were insane with rage. So … we … let you," she finished, stilted, like a device running out of power.

"Did I kill them?" I asked softly, so softly that I wasn't sure I had said it out loud.

"No. You can rest easy. You took no life."

My head flopped back on the pillow, my face screwed up, straining to remember.

"I remember nothing," I whispered. "I heard someone say Laetitia was dead. That was all I remember. The next thing I know, I am here."

"Let me fill in the blanks for you then," she said, seeing that I genuinely was struggling. "Maybe it will come back then."

"Yes, they killed Laetitia. She was crying, refusing to submit. They had a spare as they put it, so they killed her."

"She was pregnant!" I whispered.

"They didn't know that. She was wearing a large sweater and a cloak when she was taken. They just thought she was chubby."

Despite my sorrow, I snorted at that. Waif-like Lae, chubby. That was ludicrous.

"Oh, Lae," I cried. "Why, *why* didn't you do what they told you?"

Finally, I asked, "Are they alright? The others who were taken."

"They are. But it was a close thing. Their vessel had arrived the previous night. That morning would have been too late. Ten men and ten women. One spare. They felt they could do without Laetitia. They had taken eleven in total from both of the communities, you see."

"Spare!" I sniffed with ferocity. *Spare*! She was never a spare. Although she probably felt it, that day, her birthday. Freyja recently returned and reunited with Di. She had left our house that day angry at me. For that, I would never forgive myself.

"They are ... unharmed?" I finally managed to say.

"Physically—yes. The men had planned to line them up and choose one each, so none were touched. There was a bit of groping, but they weren't raped. Yet. Emotionally—they may recover. In time. The sooner we can get them home, the better."

"Why? Why did they take them? Who were they?"

"I can answer that. After you ... bloodied them up a bit, they were quite talkative."

"But who were they? And why no women?"

"They were a group of Irish fishermen, originally from Belfast. A rough crew of single men, hard drinkers. Once the news broke, rather than sit around and wait to die like everyone else, they took matters into their own hands and set sail for the Arctic, the northernmost place they could still catch fish. They knew the area from fishing, and assumed that if the pandemic was spreading southward, then the farther north they went, the greater the chance of survival."

"Reasonable assumption," I admitted after a sip of water, still exhausted from the fever. "So, what happened?"

"They lived reasonably well for a time. Then the fish stocks dried up, and they drifted farther south. They started by raiding coastal towns, looking for food, fuel, and fresh water. Several were suffering from scurvy, their teeth falling out, and all of them malnourished. They discovered the Shetland community by accident just over two years ago. They were accepted, at first. But I gather they weren't popular and were eventually expelled. They took their fishing trawler and found the island. They continued to send out small parties raiding the mainland for food and building supplies, but after a year, they were desperate for... ahem... they lacked female companionship. Knowing that the Shetland community would find them on Mousa and having heard from the locals on the Shetlands that there were likely other communities, they went looking. For wives."

"They were selkies," I slurred, the fever making me feel weak and exhausted.

"Huh?"

Slowly, struggling to form words, I told her the tale of the selkies. My mother had told Sorcha and me the story many times over the years.

"Selkies were malicious, shape-shifting seal-men. They could change from seals to handsome human men. When in human form, they had to remove their sealskins. It was only when they were in their skins that they could return to seal form and their lairs under the sea. If their sealskin was lost or stolen, the selkie was doomed to remain in human form until it could be recovered. The selkie-men desired human females. A selkie-man in his human form was said to be very attractive with almost magical seductive powers over mortal women. According to my mother's stories, they had no qualms about casting off their sealskins and heading inland to seek women to kidnap and become their wives. Once taken down into their watery lair, the women couldn't escape and often pined away for their human life."

Freyja nodded, understanding what I meant. "They weren't handsome," she whispered. "They were just men. Brutal, repugnant men."

"What happened … to them?" I closed my eyes, hoping that they weren't here on the *Selkie*. I didn't think I could take that.

"It is probably best that you don't know," she responded quietly but firmly. "I have taken care of it. But it has nothing to do with you. You have nothing to be guilty about."

"Please tell me they aren't … here?"

"No. They are not. I would never let those women see us treating those monsters well. Not after what they did."

"Are they … gone?"

"Yes."

Silence filled the space as I tried to fill the void in my memory.

After a while, I asked, "What happened to me? How did I end up here?"

"You raged and screamed and hit anything and anyone in your way until you could barely stand. I have never seen anyone lose their shit quite like that. You started staggering, and finally, you fell. We carried you back here. It wasn't until you got sick that I realized you had burst your appendix wound badly. I have re-stitched it, not as neat a job as a doctor, but none of my patients ever complained. I cleaned it but not fast enough. You have a nasty internal infection, and of all things, we didn't bring a medical kit in our haste. I am afraid I have nothing for you—either for the fever or the infection."

I slowly sipped some water and lay back in the bed, exhausted. *How can I be exhausted? I have done nothing all day.*

"How long have I been like this?" I asked, looking around the tiny room. Light was peeping in from the small round window covered with a blind. It looked like a bomb had gone off in here. The double bed I lay in was placed in the center of the room. A small bedside table on either side. But everywhere, there were empty water bottles, sheets, pillows on the floor, blankets. My clothing, stained with blood I noted abstractedly, had been thrown over the back of the single chair in the corner facing me. The tiny bathroom I could see through the half-open sliding door looked little better with towels on the floor, packets strewn over the benchtops.

"Three days," she replied. "We are nearly home. We left the Orkneys about six hours ago. They were most grateful. We towed the fishing boat from Mousa and gave it to them, so it took us a little longer. It was the Orcadians who gave us paracetamol and penicillin. Like us, they have very little medicine left, but when they saw their women returned, they were happy to give us whatever they had. I gave you some, and it seems to be working. Time for your second dose now."

Obligingly, I swallowed the tablets she held out to me and let her jab my arm, realizing that I didn't recall taking the first dose. I remembered nothing at all from the time I saw the women come out of the broch, Lae not among them.

The *Selkie* docked as close to Garynahine as possible and sent out a party on foot. They returned a few hours later with a makeshift stretcher carried by some men, taking turns. The women were gone too. Most had walked the few kilometers themselves, desperate to get home. Fraser was not among those who escorted me. Home with Isla, I assumed, the overwhelming mix of emotions consuming me. Blissfully happy that Isla, the wife of one of my closest friends, was home, safe with her children, combined with the utter despair that my wife was gone. Joy for him, yet jealousy, rage, and resentment at the same time. The overarching question pricking at me was, how would I tell Louis?

After another surgery and a few days in the clinic, I was carried home, gently transplanted to my own bed. The one I had shared with Laetitia. Sorcha, Di, Sam, and Louis all came to visit. Louis threw himself on me. "Dadda, Dadda!" he chanted. "Where Mumma?"

Sorcha, seeing the look of horror on my face, came over and took him. She knew, everyone knew, but didn't feel it her place to tell Louis.

"Dadda sick, Louis. Auntie Sorcha and Auntie Dee-Dee take care of you for a bit longer. You love playing with Sam, don't you?"

Auntie Sorcha. I had never heard her use those words. It had a lovely ring to it. The role of the doting aunt suited her. I tried to smile at her but just couldn't summon the muscles. Di looked terrible, in the throes of grief, but equally worried about me. She had seen me in the aftermath of losing Freyja. She knew the dark tunnel ahead of me, the pit that I barely made it out of last time.

Once, as a child, I heard my mother speaking to a grieving friend. She quoted something. I couldn't recall the words exactly, but it was something like, "Grief is love, all the love you want to give, but can't. Grief is love with nowhere to go."

I pondered this as I lay looking at the ceiling above my bed. *Is that true? Is this love I feel and have no outlet for? I can never love Laetitia in the same way again. She is gone, dead, and our unborn child with her. But I have an outlet—Louis. Will that make the grieving different this time—I am not alone? I am not to blame for what happened. Even though I wasn't responsible for Freyja's disappearance, the fact was I had been blamed, and I felt guilty. Maybe it was guilt, rather than the grief, that overtook me on August, that led me to the dark place. Led me... here.*

I rolled over, facing the far wall, and closed my eyes so they wouldn't see the tears welling up in my eyes. *How can I lose two wives in the space of three years?* I knew from Freyja that we had been only a day behind the raiders, our boat being larger, faster, and more capable. If only we had set off sooner. Not lingered on the Orkneys. Maybe then she would still be alive.

"Let's go, sweetheart," I heard Di tell Louis from across the room. "Daddy tired. We will come back later."

"Okay."

Like raindrops, his little footsteps pattered out of the room. Footsteps Lae would never hear again. Never hear his sweet childish voice. She would never see him learn to climb, ride a horse, write his name. Watch him fall in love, get married, have children of his own. My heart wrung with pain, the pain of loss. Yet I still had part of her—him. This little man who looked so much like her—her dark hair and beautiful caramel golden eyes. Her soft, gentle expression. I would always have a part of her, forever. I had *him*. Making a silent vow to Lae, I fell asleep.

CHAPTER 36

FILTERED SUNLIGHT WOKE ME, and not wanting to be treated like an invalid, I tried to get up before anyone arrived. Fraser found me in the kitchen, cursing my stitches as I couldn't move easily from the table to the outside toilets.

"Hang on, man."

I heard him clattering around outside and then nothing. Sitting in the chair, I waited an eternity with a very full and uncomfortable bladder, waiting for him to return.

When he returned, he was brandishing a stick, roughly a meter long and fairly recently cut from a tree.

"Sorry I didn't have time to sand it back for you. I will finish it later."

Grateful for the stick, which even had a slight curve at the top—Fraser had evidently been looking for something in this precise shape—I hobbled out to the latrines.

Upon my return, I found Fraser making coffee and toast.

"It's fine. You don't need to..."

"I do." Turning to face me, he spoke softly, "You brought me back my heart. Restored my family. I will forever be in your debt."

Nodding, I tried hard to hold back the emotions threatening to flood me.

"I'm so sorry, man, about Laetitia."

I nodded, acknowledging the sentiment but unable to speak.

"We loved her too."

Fraser sat opposite me in his usual chair. As we ate breakfast, it occurred to me that it was not an uncomfortable silence. We sat in that space when two friends are there for each other but don't need words for communication. The emotion is shared, but it need not be verbalized. He understood.

"That day, she was taken, her birthday. I never got to tell her I loved her," I whispered, so low Fraser didn't look up right away.

"She knew. She told me once that it was worth all the loneliness of her childhood to hit the jackpot and meet you. She loved you so very much."

"And I ... her."

Silence descended upon us once again as we slowly finished breakfast. After some time spent chewing, Fraser spoke with more emotion than I had ever heard in his voice.

"I will say this only once as I know you likely don't want to hear it. But Cam, thank you. Thank you for saving Isla. For me and the bairns. I know it came at great personal cost, and we will always be here to support you. Your friendship means more to me than I can possibly put into words, and I am no artist. All I can say is thank you. Truly. My family is whole. I am whole because of you."

Standing up, Fraser clapped me on the shoulder and left.

Staring at the void created by his departure, I sat and looked at Lae's chair. Loose strands of her long chestnut hair stuck to it. She used to laugh that it was like tumbleweed, dropped everywhere, and stuck to everything. Now I would never see that hair again. I vowed not to remove it, so Louis could have the one tiny piece of her, still here, in our home.

Using the stick Fraser had provided, I limped into the greenhouses, only to find that Di didn't need me and waved me off, scolding me and telling me to go back to bed. Bed. Our bed was the last place I wanted to be. Unsure where to go, I staggered slowly, painfully, up the hillside that overlooked the village. Jam was at my feet but prudently kept well clear of the stick. A steep climb that usually I could do in minutes was laborious and left me panting and sweating. The fever had depleted me as much as the physical injury. I was still weakened but determined not to sit at home, surrounded by our life, and feel sorry for myself. This time I had closure. Unlike August, I knew what had happened, despite not seeing it myself.

"I miss you," I spoke aloud to the trees, the grass, and the singing birds. "I will never forget you. I will tell Louis everything about you. Your kindness, your generosity. How you changed me from a broken man to a whole one, just by loving me."

Perhaps my loss is someone else's gain, I thought. Not that I believed in heaven, but if I did, I would like to think of Lae sitting up in heaven with her mother, reconciled at last. Perhaps meeting her grandparents, aunts, uncles, cousins. Maybe she was needed more somewhere else. No. I couldn't believe it. She was taken from me by the actions of a beast, a monster. Taken too soon and taken viciously. I hoped she had not suffered, that it had been quick. Hopefully, she had drowned. That would be fast and painless. I closed my eyes and saw her long dark brown hair fanned out as she sank like a stone to the bottom of the ocean, her almond-shaped eyes open in shock. A precious pearl returned to the depths.

For hours I sat there, replaying memories of Laetitia. The good and the bad. How we had met, the days we spent together, the night under the aurora. The argument we had on her birthday over the pendant. *What I wouldn't do to change that last day.* But that was the irony, wasn't it? You didn't know it would be the last time you would see someone. I didn't doubt that she knew I loved her, but it broke my heart to think of her on that boat, scared, and knowing that the last words we said to each other were in anger.

"I'm so sorry, my love," I whispered. "I am so very sorry."

Jam, who had been off hunting for some time, clambered up into my lap, butted her head under my chin, and purred into my ear. Impossible to ignore her considerable presence, I scratched her ears and under her chin. Purring with contentment, she kneaded my belly with her claws. It was a distraction from the emotional turmoil to focus on the physical. The feelings of anger, loss, abandonment, and utter desolation. But as I worked through each of these feelings, a single sense floated to the surface. Responsibility. Louis. I was his only parent now. Despite the community approach to raising children here, he was mine, and I was his.

I promise I will raise him to be like you, was my silent prayer in farewell. With this goal firmly in mind, I started back down the steep, windy trail through the bracken and heather, back home.

Louis and I set a routine over the next few weeks. Rising early and taking a walk. With Louis still in nappies, it was slow going, but we loved this quiet time together, outside with few people around. We could smell Juliette's delicious bread and often picked up a loaf on our way home for breakfast. Louis asked about his mother, and I told him as simply as possible what happened. Wicked men had taken her. Daddy had gone after her. But she had died and wouldn't be coming home. Daddy still loved him and would always be here for him. He asked few questions, his language skills not quite being up to the task. But he accepted it with sadness and hugged me tightly.

I moved Louis from his cot to a trundle bed in our room, and most mornings, I awoke to find myself hanging off the edge of the bed, and Louis firmly snuggled into my back. Unable to roll back into bed without squashing him, I would get out of bed and walk around the foot to the other side, the cold side. I didn't mind sleeping with him. I was unbearably lonely, especially at night. With limited electricity here in the darker months, Lae and I had often lain in bed in the evening and talked about our day, our childhood, and our life experiences. Our hopes and dreams for our children. With no TV or radio, we had each other. Sometimes we read, sharing a single light, but mostly we talked. Just happy to be together. Having a small person to cuddle made me feel less alone and prevented me from descending into the abyss of despair into which I had plummeted when I believed Freyja dead.

Louis came to work with me, and no one seemed to mind the constant distractions. It wasn't like we were paid by the hour or had deadlines to meet. Gardening could be done piecemeal, pulling weeds, harvesting crops, pruning branches. It could all be done around Louis, and soon he was part of the furniture in the greenhouses, garden beds, and fields. He was always with me, never out of my sight. But no one objected. Di and Fraser often gave him little treats or jobs to do.

I wondered what would happen when he needed to go to school. How would I cope with being away from him? Sanjita, the assistant teacher to Lae, had stepped into the role permanently now. The school was one of the few places I actively avoided, the joyous sounds of children singing or counting reminded me too much of her, and the sharp stabbing pain in my heart each time I walked past the school was excruciating. I couldn't bear to enter that place that she had built and had been her passion and joy.

Nights were the loneliest of times. Night after night, I lay awake and listened to the wind outside the dome, buffeting the shell. Hearing the rain hit the shell, muffled, like being under an umbrella, I played over and over in my mind her last moments, the terror she must have felt. I wished that she had not antagonized the men, that she had stayed safe, like Isla. But she hadn't known we would come after her, that we would even know where they had gone. That we were *so close*—yet so far. Far too late.

Several weeks after our return, the community held a memorial for Laetitia. Out of respect, they waited until I and the rest of the abducted women felt up to attending. Lae had been loved by all. She always had a kind word for everyone, always offering to help. She was a truly unique soul.

The children made paper butterflies and a book of drawings, each with their favorite memory of her. She would have treasured it. Thanking them sincerely, I held it throughout the speeches, friends recalling funny anecdotes, stories that reflected her kindness and compassion. I had been asked to choose a memorial for the village. After much thought, I planned a small memorial garden in the town square in conjunction with the families of the three men who had passed. It was appropriate that I chose a climbing red rose as the dedication to Laetitia. Rose, her name. Red, the color of love. A climbing specimen, as she had taught me always to travel onward and upward. There was nothing standard about Lae. She would have loved that her memorial was living, not a stone or a plaque, planted to grow over an arch, a timber seat underneath. All would take care of Lae's rose. I knew that without question.

The three men killed by the raiders were each memorialized with a tree, carefully chosen by each man's family: an olive tree symbolizing peace, friendship, and knowledge; an oak tree representing strength and courage; and the third family chose an apple tree for health and happiness. Planned carefully to allow for expansion over time, the memorial garden would see other plants added, in memory of those we lost.

Much to everyone's surprise, Angus survived, although according to Sorcha, it had been precarious for a while. After the raiders left him lying on the beach, he managed to climb the cliff and stagger toward the nearest road.

"How he climbed that cliff with his guts spilling onto his legs, I will never know," Sorcha told me one evening when I asked about his progress. "The only time I have seen worse slash wounds was in Port Moresby."

So, they had intended to kill then, I thought. I needed to hear that. It was almost proof that he hadn't been a coward and just let them take Laetitia.

A week after I returned to Lewis, Angus was moved from the medical facility to convalesce in his own home. Freyja was staying with him, Sorcha making twice-daily visits to check on his progress. Conflicted emotions surged when I thought of Angus. Without his knowledge, we would never have even known that they had traveled north. Without that, we would never have found the Orkney community and located them so quickly. But part of me was resentful that he didn't try harder. Logically, I knew it wasn't his fault she was taken. But reason and emotion are two very different things. I knew I should visit him, to say thank you, but to do so seemed so final. It meant saying goodbye to Laetitia, and I wasn't ready to do that.

CHAPTER 37

FRASER RUBBED HIS EYES as he opened the door to me so early in the morning.

"Is something wrong? Are the girls alright? Louis?"

Feeling guilty, I mumbled an apology. I had been roaming around the village in the pitch darkness for hours, waiting for a suitable time to knock. I needed to speak with Isla urgently. The doubt was eating me up inside. The nightmares plagued me, day and night, to the point where I couldn't function anymore.

As Fraser became more alert and the rising sun cast light into my face, he saw my dull eyes with dark rings from lack of sleep, the sunken cheekbones from being unable to eat, the sickly pallor to my skin. Sorcha had told me days ago that I looked like a zombie. Seeing Fraser's expression as he looked me over more carefully, I realized this description was undoubtedly accurate.

"I need to speak with Isla," I pleaded. "I know it is early, but I didn't want the girls to hear. But I need to, please."

Fraser nodded and motioned me inside. He gestured me toward the living room, and I sat awkwardly on an armchair. After the arrival of Kari, Isla and Fraser now had an extended house with three bedrooms and larger living space. Looking around, I could see toys, unfinished knitting, the odd jacket or scarf left lying on the back of the chair. A hand-knitted blanket made of squares sewn together lay across the back of my chair. Feeling the sharp bite of the night air, I pulled it around my shoulders. Laetitia and I had owned a similar one, but I could not look at it. Just the sight of it reminded me of her, the blanket on her lap, knitting or sewing early in our marriage and wrapping it around Louis in the latter part. A single tear escaped my eye as I remembered the domestic bliss I had once enjoyed but would never have again.

Isla appeared at the door, a robe hurriedly thrown over her tartan flannel pajamas. She was barefoot, and the floor was cold. Her hair was disheveled from sleep.

"Tea?" Fraser asked, looking at her rather than me.

Isla nodded but hadn't taken her eyes off me. *I must look a right mess*, I thought, only mildly embarrassed.

Isla waited until Fraser had closed the door and looked at me expectantly.

All night I had been roaming, edging closer and closer to their house, with a single question on my mind.

"I think Laetitia might still be alive!" I blurted without warning. "I keep seeing her, in my dreams, but when I am awake too. She is on an island, stranded. She is cold and alone and starving. But she and the baby are *alive*. I keep seeing them. So, I am wondering, what if she survived and managed to swim to safety? What if she gave birth and is waiting for us to save her?

What if I am wasting time? So, I need to know. *Where* did it happen? Can you tell me where she went overboard? Do you know where it was? She could swim. Not well, I don't think. But she could swim. I think maybe she could have made it to the shore and..."

"She didn't." Isla was gentle but firm, cutting off my rambling as the speed of my speech grew faster and faster. I was panicked, distraught. We were sitting here wasting time while she was out there, waiting for me.

I stopped and looked at her, pleadingly. "Are you positive? There is a chance. There is always a chance. She could..."

"She *isn't*." Isla was firmer this time, speaking over my rabbiting. I stopped and looked at her, trying hard not to crumple.

"I saw it happen." Isla's voice was clear but quiet. "She was next to me. I saw her. Cam, I'm so sorry, but there is no chance."

"But..." I protested.

"I think he needs to hear it, Isles. All of it. For closure. Yours as well."

We both looked up to see Fraser in the doorway, balancing a tray holding a steaming teapot, three cups, and a small milk jug.

Isla looked at him for confirmation and nodded. A minuscule movement of her head. But we both saw it.

Fraser sat beside Isla on the couch opposite me. He poured me a cup and handed it to me. I sat cradling it while he finished serving himself and Isla.

It was Fraser who spoke first. "I know this is hard for you, both of you." He looked at Isla, then at me. "But I think both of you need this, for closure. Isla, you need to let this go. You couldn't have saved her, no matter what you had done. You were tied and desperately outnumbered. I know you blame yourself for not doing anything, but it was not your fault." Fraser turned to me. "And you, my friend, you need to hear this. Just once. Ask any questions you like. Then we shall never speak of it again. Isla needs to put this behind her."

Fraser looked at us both for confirmation. I nodded slowly, a little uncertain what I was agreeing to. Isla had gone white under her tanned skin but also agreed.

Holding the cup carefully in the palm of one of my enormous hands, I waited, almost too scared to breathe, as Isla steeled herself.

"They took most of us from the beach, you know that, one at a time. Lae was one of the first. They already had her and Mairi when they grabbed me. I had seen the boat and walked down to the beach to see if it was someone from Ireland coming with a message. As the ship came in, the men grabbed me from behind. They had a group of four men on land. I hadn't seen them or heard them. I was so fixated on the boat in front of me and the roaring waves, I didn't hear a thing. One minute I was waving to the craft; the next, everything went black. I woke vomiting on the deck of the boat, my arms tied behind me. It wasn't rope, it was softer, but I still couldn't move. I could taste the isoflurane they had used to knock me out. I recognized the smell from the vet hospital where I did my student placements back in Aberdeen. I dry retched for a while, and they all ignored me. When I had finished vomiting, I was gagged and pushed down into the cabin, where I saw Lae and the others. They grabbed two more after me, Orla, then Lucie. We could hear them yelling but couldn't do anything to stop it.

"I could hear them talking on the deck. They said that was enough. They would be seen and then wouldn't get away. I heard one man say that five was a good haul. We were scared, huddled together in the cabin. Wet, freezing, still feeling nauseous and trying not to choke from the gag. We couldn't speak. After a while, it was obvious from the speed of the boat we were in open water and moving at a faster pace. We were going somewhere. Then they moved us back up onto the deck. When they thought there was no chance of being seen, I guess. Lae was crying, and the men shouted at her to shut up. She tried. She really did. But she was so distressed, she curled up into a ball in the cabin. Eventually, they dragged her up onto the deck by her hair. The leader, Jason, his name was, kept bellowing at her to stand up, but she wouldn't. She was protecting the baby. But he told her to stand up, and she didn't. He told her to do what she was told, or he would make her and hit her hard across the face. When she fell, I held her close, and eventually, she cried herself to sleep.

We all must have nodded off because when we woke, it was dark. We were thrown against one side. Still tied, we could at least stand to piss. They wouldn't untie us, so we had to wet ourselves. We were given a small sip of water now and again, although most of it spilled down our fronts. The horrible, smelly, leering one named Ethan thought it was hilarious to watch us licking every drop, and he would make a great show of wiping the water from our breasts."

"Did they..." I interrupted, not sure I wanted to know.

"No. They didn't really harm us. They were rough, reeking of foul body odor, unwashed bodies, and stale beer. They were aggressive and mean. We were groped quite a lot. Nasty sexual stuff. Hands up our tops and down our pants. But not … harmed. They had intended to find each of them a bride, so they were waiting for when we reached their home to choose one each and to… to… finish the job," she managed.

I nodded, gesturing that she was to continue. Fraser was still holding her hand. She looked up at him for confirmation. He gave it. An infinitesimal nod.

"We were pushed back down into the cabin, still bound and gagged when the next women were taken from Orkney. The men had spotted that community when they sailed south, but apparently, at the time, there had been other people near the coast, so they opted to keep moving, as they knew they would be outnumbered. They had binoculars, so they could see the beach better than we could see them. They took another six women. The last two were together, so it was an accident that they ended up with eleven. They had only planned to take ten. Ten men, so they needed ten women.

"Once we hit open water again, they had us all up on deck, mainly as we needed to wee. We were all sitting against the outer wall of the boat, near the bulkhead. Lae was crying, curled up in a ball. They were struggling to have a conversation over her. I tried to get over to her, really I did. They were trying to work out what to do with the extra, as they called it. A servant? A spare in case one died? One wanted to kill me as I am half Indian. Another wanted to kill an Egyptian lady from Orkney as they didn't want black babies. This went on for a while. The leader, Jason, finally grabbed Lae by the hair and pulled her upright. He bellowed in her face, 'Will you just shut the fuck up!' As he pulled her hair, he must have grabbed the back of her gag because it moved. She screamed in his face, completely terrified. She was hysterical by this stage. He lost it, pulled the knife from his belt, and...." Isla stopped, tears rolling down her face.

"I can't..." she cried, burying her face into Fraser's chest.

"You need to," Fraser urged gently, his arm around her shoulder. "Just once."

Sobbing, Isla looked up at me. "He cut her throat," she said between tears. "It happened so fast that we didn't even see it coming. We were all seated, our hands still tied behind our backs. She screamed in his face, then almost like a reflex, he slashed her throat. She dropped like a stone. She hit the deck right in front of me. I saw the wound, Cam. There is no way. He used force."

"What... what happened to her?"

"He ordered the men to throw her overboard. It was as they picked her up and her cloak fell back that he realized she was pregnant. She was so tiny, and they didn't realize. He was cursing when he saw her belly. Clearly, they wanted the child. But it was too late. We all saw her Cam, lying there, motionless. It was quick, I promise. They threw her overboard, but she was already dead. They didn't even slow down."

Isla dissolved into tears and was enveloped into Fraser's chest. I sat there, frozen, now able to see precisely what had happened. She was gone. Unlike Freyja, unlike all of my dreams, Laetitia wasn't coming back.

"I keep seeing her," I whispered. "In my dreams. She is calling for me. She needs me. I thought she was lost. I thought I needed to find her." I was cold, numb. No feeling, no emotion. Just dead.

"I'm so, so sorry, Cam," Isla kept sobbing. "I am so sorry."

"It wasn't your fault," Fraser was soothing her. "You couldn't have saved her. There was nothing you could do."

I knew I should reassure her, too. But I was broken, paralyzed by the image of my beautiful Laetitia, scarlet red blood flowing down her long white neck.

We were interrupted by Niamh standing in the doorway.

"Mummy?" she asked hesitantly, sensing that something was wrong.

Fraser bounced up and over to her. "Morning! Let's get you off to the cludgie and make some breakfast, shall we? Mummy just needs to talk to Cam for a wee moment."

It was time to go. I had invaded their home for too long.

Standing, Isla looked up at me, her eyes pleading for forgiveness.

I dropped into the seat vacated by Fraser and held my arms out to her. We didn't need words. She knew I didn't blame her, and I knew she was an innocent victim in all of this.

"Was it quick?" I whispered in her hair as I held her.

"It was," she mumbled, almost incomprehensibly. "I promise."

I pulled back and looked her in the eyes. "I am so glad that you are safe and at home with your family. Truly."

"Thank you, Cam. For coming after us. For rescuing me. For … everything."

I stood and left without saying goodbye to Fraser. How could I look at him? He had his wife. His children had their mother. I had lost mine. Louis was mother-less. I wasn't resentful, but I was jealous. I had lost one wife. Now I had lost another.

Freyja avoided me for the first few weeks, knowing I couldn't let her in on my grief. For someone as prac-tical as Freyja, she at least understood I needed to be alone. To grieve. Soon she started coming past the greenhouse, stopping for a few minutes to chat, to tell me about Angus's progress, some unimportant piece of news.

Seven weeks dragged by. The baby would have been nearly due. Louis asked about Lae less as we put one foot in front of the other, breathed in and out, and tried to keep living. Just surviving was an effort. Some moments it felt like years I had been alone. Other moments I would turn to tell her something, show her something, and then felt the physical pain as I remembered. She was gone. The moments spread slightly with time. There were longer periods between bouts of grief. *Maybe time does heal*? I thought. But never completely. Like a broken plate, you could glue it back together, but it was never the same. It would never look the same, be as strong. It could still func-tion as a plate, but it would never be the same plate it once was.

CHAPTER 38

"I NEED TO TALK to you."

Looking up from the tomato plants I was staking, I saw Freyja looking... what was that ... worried?

"Give me a minute." I finished tying up the last three plants in the garden bed and stood up, massaging my sore lower back, arching back slightly to stretch.

"What's up?"

"Not here," she said haltingly. "Can we talk ... in private?"

Seeing Louis asleep on the chair in the corner, I went to ask Fraser to keep an eye on him. "I won't be long," I promised.

Freyja led me up the path behind the village, up the hill where I had gone the first day back. The first day of being here as a widower. Stupid word. Widower.

We walked in silence, me more slowly as despite the newer stitches coming out, I wasn't as strong as I had been a few months ago. Freyja waited for me as I neared the top, pacing, clearly agitated. I sat on the rocky outcrop that overlooked the village and waited. She would tell me in her own time.

"Do you recall the second night on the boat when you had the terrible fever? Before we got to Orkney?"

I considered and shook my head. "No, I have tried and tried to remember. But I recall nothing from the time I heard Laetitia had been killed to when the fever broke. Did I say something? Did I offend you?"

"No, nothing like that. You were crying and calling out—for her. I came to you. To look after you, comfort you maybe."

Unsure where this was going, I offered a tentative, "Thank you. That was kind."

"You were so lost. I thought we would lose you, too. We lost you at one point. I restarted your heart."

I nodded again. She had told me this part before. Was she looking for thanks? The look on her face... I couldn't interpret it. Facial expressions were never my strong suit.

"It was dark, the early hours of the morning. You had been calling for her, screaming. You were thrashing around. I was scared you would open the wound on your stomach. You kept calling and calling her name like she was lost in the night. I don't know if you were awake or just fevered. You were shuddering with the chills from your fever. I tried to calm you, hold you still, and comfort you and, well, you... you thought I was her. You kissed me. I tried to stop you, really I did. But you kept going, and well ... I was lonely too."

"I'm sorry. I didn't know."

Freyja put her hand up to stop me. "There's more. I kissed you back. Things got out of hand, and ... we made love."

My horrified gasp was audible even to my ears. "We *what*?"

Freyja was babbling now in a way I had never seen her do. She was so self-assured, so possessed. Never had I seen her flustered like this.

"You thought I was her. You were so gentle with me and called me kitten. You really don't remember any of this?"

"No," I replied stiffly. "I really don't. Why are you telling me now?"

"I am pregnant," she replied stiffly.

I laughed. I couldn't say why. It just happened—an instinctive response.

Freyja rounded on me. "This isn't funny! I'm not joking. I am pregnant, and you are the father!"

Unable to process this, all I could say was, "Are you *sure*?"

"Am I sure I am pregnant, or sure the baby is yours? Yes, on both counts," she replied hotly.

"Hey, you don't get to drop this bombshell on me and get cranky. You have had weeks to prepare for this. I didn't even know we were *together*. To find out you are pregnant, and I am to be a father..."

To be a father. The magnitude of that sentence struck me like a blow to the stomach. I already was a father, to Louis. To the baby Lae had been carrying. Now... now, *this*?

"There was a time when this would have made you very happy," she whispered as I stood to leave. "Can you find a way to feel even a little happiness?"

Numbness overtook me. My feet kicked against rocks, and branches cut open my arms as I fought my way, blindly, through the rocky landscape. I didn't care. I could feel the throbbing in my stomach and felt the blood trickle down from the fresh gash in my arm. It meant nothing. It was all pointless.

No matter what path I chose from here, I would be judged. Tricked, betrayed, manipulated, but also accountable, liable, responsible. All of these words could apply to this situation, yet none of them adequately summed up the complexity of it. Within a few days of my wife and child dying, I had impregnated another. She who had also been my wife. *It is like a crappy movie,* I thought sardonically. Only it wasn't. It was my life. And I couldn't escape it by leaving the cinema.

The joke is on me, I realized grimly. One night, a night I didn't even remember no less, had brought about a baby when Freyja and I had tried so desperately to have our own family. It wasn't fair. I had lost my wife and child, yet now I had a replacement? Was this a gift—or a punishment? What would people think? While I hadn't had a hand in Laetitia's death—there had been enough witnesses—but in the court of public opinion, I hadn't waited around before moving on. What would people think? If I acknowledged the baby, then I was a heartless, unfaithful bastard. But if I didn't, then I was an irresponsible prick who didn't take responsibility for his actions. Fundamentally, I lost. There was no way out of this. Either I was unfaithful, or I was an asshole. Maybe I was anyway. And to go back to my first wife? People would assume that I had been cheating on Lae all along. Why spoil an incredible story with the truth? It made great gossip. It would ruin Lae's reputation, making it sound like I had run back to my first wife at the first opportunity. And how could I share the truth without making Freyja sound like a whore who had taken advantage of me? If anyone believed it, and likely they wouldn't. It was a fairly unlikely tale. Losing your wife to raiders, rescuing the others, spiking a dangerously high fever, sleeping with your first wife with no memory of it, and fathering a child all in the space of three days. It was a reasonably impressive catalog of events.

Jam rubbed round my feet. Likely the only creature here who wouldn't judge me. Scratching her ears, I wondered what on earth to do. Leave? Stay? Where would I go? Not back to August, that was for sure. Newgrange maybe? Or the Orkneys, or even go looking for the community on the Shetlands. Bellcamp, where I was sure Callie and Tadhg would welcome me? But how did I run from this? A child. A child of my blood. He or she would be mine just as much as Louis was. A child that Freyja and I had once desperately wanted.

Some hours later, I woke, the sun's last rays tinting the trees and dappling the grass with gold. A gentle hand was on my shoulder, shaking me softly.

"Lae?" I came to myself to realize it wasn't Lae, but Diana, looking worried.

"Are you okay?" The worry was also in her voice as she looked me over.

I must have looked a right mess, torn clothes, dirty face, unbrushed hair. I looked down at my arms and saw the cuts from the brambles, the dried blood.

I shook it off. "I... I am fine," I tried to say with some conviction, but it wasn't convincing even to my own ears. Di knew me well enough to know this wasn't true but was too kind to say so.

"You have been missing all day. Fraser sent me looking. You left..."

"*Louis!*" we chorused in unison. In the light of the news, shocking as it was, I had completely forgotten about him. I scrambled to my feet, but Di returned the hand to my shoulder.

"It's okay. Isla has him. He is fed and getting ready for bed. I think he quite enjoys being with the girls, having siblings." As soon as the words had passed her lips, she realized what she had said. Her tanned face blushed pink. "I'm so sorry, Cam. I didn't mean..."

"It's okay," I said gruffly. "I know you didn't. I know what you meant. He would have loved a sibling, social creature that he is."

He may soon get his wish, I thought sadly.

Di was looking down at me. Her expression was one of curiosity. Dammit. My emotions must be on my face. Freyja had always told me that anything I felt was on my face, plain to read.

"Can I talk to you, Di?" I asked a little hesitantly.

"Of course. I am always here for you."

"No, I mean, I need to tell you something. I will tell Sorcha but not yet. You are my oldest friend, and I know you understand me. I hope you won't judge."

Di looked surprised but soon softened. "Of course. And no, I won't tell Sorcha. That is yours to do."

I told her—all of it. Losing Lae and the baby, the heartbreak. The fever, allegedly sleeping with Freyja but not even knowing.

"But she knew things, things I had called Lae, in private. It must be true. Here I am, an asshole, a cheat, and if I don't honor her, a man who abandons the woman he knocked up to boot."

Diana exhaled slowly. "Well, that is a pretty pickle you are in." She paused, thinking. "So, let's work this through logically. Assuming Freyja is pregnant, can we be certain it is yours?"

I shrugged helplessly. "I have no idea. I don't remember that night at all. I wanted to die. I was fevered and..."

"Okay. What are the chances it isn't your child?"

Actively considering this for a moment, I shook my head. "No. Freyja is not a liar. If it was Angus's, or anyone else's, why wouldn't she just say so? No one would care. Why foist a child on *me*? It looks badly upon her. Sleeping with a bereaved man. No. I am fairly sure she is telling the truth."

Di nodded, reluctantly agreeing. She had the benefit of knowing Freyja as long as I had. Freyja could be blunt, but she was honest, and there was absolutely no deception in her. If she said she was pregnant, and it was mine, then it was true.

"Alright, so what now? I guess the question is, what do *you* want, Cam?"

In all my ramblings about what others thought, I hadn't taken the time to think about what I wanted.

"Honestly, Di, what I want is to rewind the clock and have Lae back. To never let her go out to the croft that day. But I guess that is impossible," I muttered miserably.

Di looked at me kindly. "Sadly, that is beyond our control. I guess what I am asking is, what do you feel for Freyja and the child? You loved her deeply ... once. I know you did. I saw that with my own eyes every day we lived on August."

I looked into Di's gorgeous dark brown eyes, so filled with kindness, but a different brown to Laetitia's.

"I always will love her," I confessed. "But then there was Lae. Had I never come through the portal, yes. I would have stayed with Freyja and made a life. Likely a happy one. But things are different now, you see."

Di nodded. I suspected she didn't see but was too kind to say so.

"So, what do I do?"

Di shrugged. "I don't have answers, Cam, but know that I will always support you. I won't judge, and for what it is worth, neither will your sister. She loves you. You are all she has left."

I objected, but Di interrupted. "Would you judge *her* in a similar situation?"

That stopped me. "No…" I said after a moment's thought. "I would support her, no matter what. She is … family."

"What makes you think she would feel any differently about you?"

I hadn't thought about it like that but nodded. Suddenly, it felt like an enormous weight had been lifted from my shoulders. I felt lighter. No matter what the future brought, this time, I had people on my side, and that made all the difference.

CHAPTER 39

DI HAD BEEN RIGHT. While shocked and initially outraged at Freyja, Sorcha was supportive of me and my plight. After much discussion and emphasis on my part that I would actively be involved in the raising of any child of mine, we agreed the problem was what others thought, and the judgment that would inevitably follow.

"And what you don't want," she said forcefully, "is for that to affect Louis."

"Or Sam or the two of you," I responded woefully.

"*That* is none of your concern," Sorcha directed. "You worry about yourself. I will take care of my wife and family."

"Do we leave then?" suggested Di somewhat forlornly, her voice and face illustrating that this wasn't what she wanted. She and Sorcha had been accepted here. They, too, were part of the community, valued and loved. Di had slotted in with the agricultural team just as I had, bringing her specialties. Helping people with their home gardens, visiting people out on the crofts, Diana was liked by all.

Sorcha, in her medical capacity, had been welcomed warmly. She was knowledgeable, forthright, and a born doctor. She was respected and valued, often called in the middle of the night to assist a woman giving birth. Di and Sorcha were jointly working on the algae bioreactors in their limited spare time with great success so far. Most importantly, they were *happy*. How could I take them away from this? Sam was content here, attending Lae's school. Bringing them here had been overwhelmingly positive for them. But would I ruin it all now for the sake of one stupid night that I didn't even remember?

Keeping it from Fraser was the hardest. He would have done anything for me, but I couldn't share this. He had known Lae longer than I. She had been his friend first. Working alongside him day after day was difficult. Not that I didn't want to talk to him, I so desperately did. Fraser was a great friend, but I couldn't guarantee how he and Isla would react. Initially, Fraser tried to engage me in conversation but slowly stopped, suspecting that I was grieving, which was the truth. Yet, I was feeling so much more. Conflicted and torn. Frankly, my life was a hot mess. Again.

Under the guise of caring for me, Sorcha, Sam, and Di moved back in with us. Louis and I moved to the smaller bedroom I had slept in during my first six months on Lewis, leaving the larger room for them. Jam, still my shadow, adapted, now sleeping in our new room. I was happy to no longer be in Lae's room with the memories it held. But this was a tiny house, and it was rapidly becoming apparent it was too small for all of us. One night after the boys had gone to bed, Sorcha, Di, and I sat in the lounge room talking.

Sorcha, always blunt, announced, "We should start looking for a larger house."

"We could extend this one," Di said animatedly. "You know, build another room."

"There really isn't space," I countered. We had Fraser and Isla on one side. They had already extended into the space between the cottages with their three children. The other side was Hamish, Morwenna, and their family. They would need to extend themselves at some point, leaving us no room.

"So, we move," Di said.

"You know," Sorcha said thoughtfully, "this could solve a few problems."

"Like what?"

"What if we took on one of the crofts?"

I looked at her with interest. "I think I know where you are going with this."

"I don't," said Di. "What are you thinking?"

"I think we could all move to one of the crofts and take Freyja with us," Sorcha replied quietly. "She could have the baby without prying eyes. Cam has space to grieve and recover in private, and it is a great excuse, isn't it? Cam needs some quiet time, away from the village. You and he can start a small farm, growing enough food for us. Freyja is a vet, so she can raise livestock. I may have to travel back and forth to the village for medical treatment, but that is not so bad, especially if Mike lets me keep one of the horses."

"That..." Di said thoughtfully and stopped. "That is a great idea. The kids can run around and play together. But we can't stop people from visiting. How do we explain the new baby?"

It was Freyja who came up with the answer to that. Two weeks after Di and Sorcha had returned to my home, Di invited her for dinner. She accepted, cautiously, evidently scared that she would be poisoned midway between the main meal and dessert.

"I like it," she said slowly, when told of crofting. "But won't people talk about Cam and me? We are four adults living together. Two of you, at least, are a couple."

"They can talk," said Sorcha. "But with the distance, no one will know. If we stay in the village, everyone will know within a day."

"I know," Freyja said, her face dropping. "I have considered that myself. I even thought of returning to August on the next solstice."

"Seriously?" I asked. I had been quiet until this point, unsure of how to speak to my now pregnant ex-wife. "You are terrified of the portal. Not to mention the fact that you will be very pregnant by the solstice."

"I am scared of the portal," Freyja admitted. "But I am more scared of what gossip will do to you. What if... no. Let me get an answer and get back to you."

"What?" I asked.

"No, leave it with me."

Three nights later, we met again, and Freyja outlined her plan. Angus, who was by now fully recovered from being brutally slashed by the raiders and ready to resume his travels, would admit to fathering a child with Freyja. Then he would leave.

"People hate him anyway," Freyja admitted. "He said he was happy to do it. He is sad to lose me as a member of the crew but happy to do this for me. He knows people will believe the worst in him anyway, and he wasn't planning to stick around."

"That is exceedingly kind of him," I admitted. It was. I wasn't sure how I felt about people thinking that Angus fathered Freyja's baby. It was my child, and I intended to be a father to this child, whether I was in a relationship with its mother or not.

"Does he want the baby to have his name?"

"I don't see why," Freyja snapped.

"I guess…" but I didn't, really.

"Besides, people here don't even use surnames, do they? We just don't give him or her one."

"What is Angus's surname?" I asked out of curiosity.

"MacLeod. There were a lot of them here. Ancient ties to Harris, he says. Regardless, this baby will be a Jorgensen."

"That is an amazing act of kindness," Sorcha admitted, moving the conversation on. She had butted heads with Angus on a few occasions, and it was no secret that she didn't like him, despite saving his life and providing his medical care. Angus was ten years older than her, but she towered over him and found him shifty and untrustworthy. Sorcha was so similar to Freyja. Both had the same direct, forthright manner. I wondered, *If they had met under different circumstances, would they have been friends? Or are they too alike?*

Sorcha and Freyja kept a distinct emotional distance. Sorcha had grown to like Lae, consider her family. She had been ripped away, and this woman had excessively pressured her brother and his child. She was in no mind to be kind, although she was tolerant. Di was torn. She had loved Freyja like a sister on

August, but she too had grown very close to Laetitia. And her loyalties were to Sorcha now, which made her allegiance clear.

Between work commitments, it took us some weeks to find a suitable site. We knew we would need to start with something existing, an old house or barn in a protected location. The children couldn't sleep outside, nor in a tent, not with winter imminent. Not that it snowed here anymore, but it was bitterly cold. We just didn't have time to build something entirely from scratch. Eventually, we would need a site big enough for at least two houses, plus land for barns and other outbuildings, animals, gardens, and greenhouses.

Although sadness filled me that I was not building this home with Laetitia, I was glad to be away from prying eyes and sympathetic looks. The moments when I thought of her, went to tell her something, became fewer, and the space between them longer. After a few weeks, people had just not known what to say to me, and it was awkward for us both, people wanting to ask how I was, genuinely concerned, but conscious that it was all that I was asked.

We found a cleared site at the foot of a long green valley near Achmore, where my grandmother had lived, that house now demolished. Loch Acha Mor would provide us with a reliable water source. Originally a large barn rather than a house, the building had ample open space with a stone floor. The roof was gone, but the stone walls were largely intact. With a new roof, some doors, and windows, it would do as a home for this winter, and in spring, we could use this as the barn and build new homes. Two, perhaps three. One for Sorcha, Di, and Sam. One for Louis and me. Whether Freyja built her own home remained uncertain, so we needed to plan for at least three homes.

My wounds now healed, I repaired the barn with gusto. I enjoyed planning what I would use for the timber frames and trusses, making wooden shingles for the roof, and lining the inside walls with wool insulation and then timber lining boards.

Di let slip to Fraser and a few others that I wasn't coping with the loss of my wife, and that she and Sorcha were taking me away, away from the memories. Not so far, just half an hour on horseback or bike. But far enough.

Away from the gossip, I thought sadly but knew she was right. People would understand why I had moved, and my sister and friend with me. It was an excellent cover. Freyja, it was decided, wouldn't move with us immediately. She would wait until Angus had left and when her pregnancy was obvious. Angus had agreed to stick around for a few more weeks to enable this, so they could both move out of his house together.

A week after we announced our impending move, I arrived at the building site after finishing my greenhouse duties to find the team of builders well at work. Three men were on the roof. They had finished the roof trusses and were tying in the roof battens to hold the shingles in place. Another small group was building internal wall trusses, something we hadn't planned. I stood there, amazed.

Leo looked down from his place on the roof, saw me watching, and called, "Well, come and give us a hand then."

Humbled by this sudden burst of community spirit, I went to help: cutting, sawing, fetching, lifting.

The following month was the busiest of my life. Being busy was a great salve to my wounded soul. I was so busy working on the project, with so many people around working on our home, I fell asleep each night exhausted. Idle moments were rare, and I found that my moments of melancholy were lessening. Within months, we had a fully fitted home, four bedrooms, a living room, a small outdoor bathroom with a pit toilet, a shower with a water tank, and a recycled water system. Solar panels and a biogas unit supplemented with two algae bioreactors. We were entirely self-sufficient, which would be fabulous come winter. No worrying about children in a cold and drafty barn. We now had a fully insulated and furnished home, thanks to the generosity of our community.

When I opened the small outdoor room that was to serve as a pantry and root cellar, I gasped with surprise. It was lined, floor to ceiling, with jars and bottles, sacks and crates containing fruit, vegetables, nuts, and grains. An old meat locker held milk, butter, cheese, and eggs. There was enough food to last the five of us through the winter, I calculated, wondering when Freyja would come. Would there be enough food for six?

"Like it?" A familiar voice interrupted my thoughts. Fraser stood there, beaming.

"How did you do all of this without me seeing?"

"I have my ways. A little thank you."

"You need to stop saying that," I said, a little gruffly, overcome with the generosity. "I would always have done it."

"I know. But I mean it. Really. Although I am sad that we won't be neighbors anymore."

"I am, too," I said honestly. "But I..."

"Cam, I get it. Really. Isla is sick to the back teeth of people asking her if she is alright. She can't walk the five steps to the bloody loo each morning without at least two people stopping her. I can't imagine what it is like for you."

"They care. I get that."

"Aye. They do. But they are bloody nosy."

I smiled. He understood. It wasn't personal.

"This," I waved my hand around the filled pantry in an effort to change the subject, "is fabulous. Thank you so very much."

"Well, you can thank us by having us for dinner when you are settled."

"I will," I promised and meant it.

CHAPTER 40

WITH THE HOUSE COMPLETED far earlier than we had expected, Di and I had time to get some garden beds dug before the long dark days of winter, stock the greenhouses, and plant some fruit trees from the reserves in Garynahine. I had forgotten how much I enjoyed spending time with her, although I felt a little awkward when she talked about Sorcha. It was strange to think of my best friend and my sister partnered in a romantic sense. I wanted to confide in Di but was scared she would tell my sister. I loved Sorcha, but as a sister. I had never told her my hopes and fears and didn't want to share how I felt now.

Little by little, Di chipped away at my facade. Day by day, our relationship strengthened, and soon we were as close as we had been those few short years ago.

"How do you feel about Freyja joining us?" Di asked cautiously. This was delicate ground, and she knew it.

"Honestly, I don't know. I feel like I am betraying Lae and Louis, yet I feel responsible for her. She is my wife, and this is my child, too. I didn't leave her, divorce her. I will always care for Freyja, but could

I love her in that way again? I don't know. I feel so bloody *conflicted*. I don't know what I feel."

"It is okay to feel that way," Di said. "I can't imagine the absolute rollercoaster of emotions you have been through in the past three months."

"Three months. Is that all?"

The long cold dark months of winter, with few daylight hours, were filled with chatter and laughter. Di and I worked the greenhouses in the few daylight hours available, providing enough fresh fruit and vegetables to supplement the pantry. The sun rose mid-morning and set by mid-afternoon, meaning that we had long hours inside together, reading alone or to the children, playing cards, talking, preparing, and eating meals we wouldn't have time for in warmer months. Their learning also took place in the late afternoons when we had time to sit with them, help them learn to read and write. Jam often helped by walking on their books or darting a paw at their hands while handwriting, making them both laugh. Sam had never seen a cat before Jam and was obsessed with her. She was remarkably tolerant of him. Sorcha, initially wary of a Scottish Wildcat, was soon smitten, and so Jam spent most of her day being fed treats, curled up on a bed, or being carried around.

Surreptitiously, I watched Di and Sorcha together, blissfully happy. They finished each other's sentences, stealing a kiss or a hug while snuggled up together on the couch, reading or knitting.

"I never thought I would see you knit!" I teased Sorcha. "Mum tried to teach you a million times, but you would never try."

"I regret that," Sorcha admitted. "I refused *because* she wanted it. I was just being difficult. I didn't see the point—then. I could go to a shop and buy anything. I never knew…"

"None of us did," Di said soothingly. "And your mother wouldn't have minded. She probably just wanted to spend time with you. Tell me about your mother."

"She looked just like Sorcha," I chipped in, "and was equally willful and difficult."

"I do not look like her!" Sorcha rebutted, avoiding the behavioral traits I noted. So, she was a little self-aware then.

"When was the last time you looked in a mirror?"

Sorcha looked up at me, surprised. Mirrors were one thing in short supply here. No one had thought to bring many with them upon settlement, and we hadn't mastered the art of making them. Unable to heat the reflective material to a suitable temperature with a biogas unit to coat glass, we couldn't light fires or build a furnace under the dome for risk of damaging the fabric. The few mirrors that were here were precious, and we didn't have one. Wondering if it was too late to collect the small mirror Lae had in our bedroom, I quickly dismissed that idea. Hamish's family had already extended their house into our former home to accommodate his expanding brood. I couldn't very well go in and demand something personal. Here we dressed and brushed our hair in the usual fashion, but it had been several months since I had seen my reflection. It made sense that Sorcha, who had never been vain about her appearance, had not worried about her own.

"It is true," I went on, "you look more and more like Mum each day. Especially now that you plait your hair like that."

Sorcha's hand rose subconsciously to her hair, and a sweet smile crossed her face.

"You are taller, but her face, her mannerisms. They are all in you," I finished.

Di stood and reached for the boxes of photographs, cherishingly stored on a shelf in the living room. She handed me the box.

I fossicked through and came up with one, taken not long before the virus struck. It depicted us all having dinner at a restaurant; I didn't recall where. Our family was sitting on either side of a long table, filled with plates of food and glasses of beer and wine, laughing and happy. Other family members were there: our uncle and aunt, their two children, partners, and babies. Sorcha was alone, I noted. This must have been after Sam died, but before I left. Sorcha was at the end, a little hazy and out of focus. A smile was plastered on her face, but it didn't reach her eyes. A camera smile, fake, but only those who knew her could tell.

"Here." I passed the photo to Di, who gasped. The last time she had seen these photos was on the yacht in Melbourne, a lifetime ago. The night before, we had met the others—a time when the relationship was new. After that, we had been at sea, learning from Tadhg, traveling from Newgrange back here, setting up homes, meeting people, and getting on with life.

"I thought it was *you*!" she breathed. "Cam is right. You look so much like her. And you," she turned to me, glancing back down at the photo. "You are the spitting image of your father. There is no mistaking they are your parents."

"Show us yours," Sorcha invited, doing her best to include Di. *I have never seen Sorcha so ... gracious,* I thought, more than a little surprised.

Di didn't have as many photos as Sorcha and I had. Like me, she had only been permitted one bag to take initially, so those photos were all she had left.

"Did Kendra have any?" I asked in a low voice, not wanting to distress her. Di didn't mention Kendra much.

"A few," she admitted. "She made copies for me. They are here ... somewhere."

Sorcha and I looked at each other over Di's bent head, searching her box of photos. Di came up with a handful of pictures and snuggled in next to Sorcha, passing them one at a time as she described the scene, the people. Sorcha was handing them to me. Chinese New Year celebrations, birthdays, family holidays. Different people but still a family.

CHAPTER 41

ON MY WAY BACK from checking the greenhouse in Garynahine, I saw Freyja working alone in the fields, checking on a flock of sweet black and white sheep. I stopped my bike, the one given to me by the Newgrange residents, and lay it against the nearby fence. I waited until she saw me and came over to the fence.

"When are you coming to stay?" I asked as neutrally as I could. I still wasn't sure how I felt about all of this.

"Are you sure you want me?" she asked apprehensively.

"You are having a baby. You need to be with someone to assist. We can help you, feed you, and be there to support you. Besides, it is my child, isn't it?"

"It is. It is just…"

"Just what."

"Cam, I need to tell you something. Something else."

Recognizing this as a serious conversation, I sat down on the grass and waited for her to climb the fence and join me. After the "it is your baby" conversation several months ago, this really couldn't be any worse. But it was always easier to take unexpected news sitting down.

Waiting until Freyja was settled, I asked, "Well, what is it then?" seeing that she was struggling.

"It is all my fault!" she wailed, entirely unexpectedly.

"What is? The pregnancy?"

"Well, that too, but no. I meant Laetitia's death. It is all my fault!"

"How can that be your fault? You didn't kill her."

"No, not exactly, but I am to blame."

Unable to decipher this, I said, "Frey, I have absolutely no idea what you are talking about. Did you take her and murder her?"

"Of course not. But they saw *me*. After you had passed out that day at Mousa, we questioned them some more. To make sure there weren't any more of them, another ship somewhere. That was when they told us. They had seen the yacht with Angus, the guys, and me. But it was *me* they saw from a distance. We didn't see them, but then again, we weren't looking. It was a few weeks before the raid. They were sheltered in a cove. They had binoculars and saw us go past. I was on the deck, they said, my hair blowing in the wind. That was when they knew for certain that there were other communities out there and women in those communities. Until then, they had only known about the one in the Shetlands, the one they were thrown out of. They couldn't attack that town. They were known. So, they followed us at a distance. But it was me they saw, who led them here. If they hadn't seen me, then Laetitia might still be alive!"

My mouth fell open, unsure of what to say. It wasn't her fault. She didn't know who they were, hadn't even seen them. She could never have known what would happen. It truly wasn't her fault. But she, and the others, had inadvertently led them here. And it was that error that had indirectly led to Lae's death.

"I need some space."

Getting up, I turned, watching her look up at me miserably from the grass.

"I don't hate you, Frey, and I don't blame you. Truly. It is just... it is a lot to take in. The baby, now this. I just need some time."

She nodded, not understanding, but accepting it anyway.

That afternoon I spoke with Di about it while thinning seedlings in the greenhouse. "It wasn't her fault. I know that. She couldn't have known they saw the *Selkie*, that they saw her. Not just her. Saw all of them. Even if she did, she had no way of knowing that they followed them and scoped out our community. She had no way of knowing what they intended to do. So why do I feel anger toward her?"

Di paused and looked up from the carrot seedlings. "You hold her responsible because you no longer have Laetitia," she said calmly. "You said you argued the day Lae was taken, didn't you?"

Watching me nod sadly, she continued. "And that fight was in part about Freyja returning?"

"It was. I thought it was about the necklace, but it took me some time to realize that we would have fought about Freyja at some point. The necklace was just the catalyst."

"Well, there you have it. You are angry at Freyja because she, in part, is responsible. She had no control. I'm not saying that, and there is no blame. But she is responsible. Freyja returned, and Laetitia was jealous. I may also have added to that. My friendship with Lae was new. I liked her and enjoyed spending time with her. But then Freyja came. I hadn't seen her in so long, and it all came flooding back, the memories, the wonderful times we shared. Naturally, Lae felt excluded, a little jealous. But the fight you had that last day *was* about Freyja and the lack of closure Laetitia felt. Then when Lae died, Freyja lived. Now Freyja is pregnant, and you learn it was because she and the crew of the *Selkie* were seen that this place was found. You hold her responsible. But *blame* is something entirely different from *responsible,* Cam. You need to be careful not to *blame* her. Blame implies fault, and this is not her fault."

"When did you learn to be so wise?"

Di just fluttered her eyelids and returned to the carrots.

CHAPTER 42

FREYJA'S ARRIVAL IN HER fifth month of pregnancy at the end of February hadn't been without controversy, but the community just accepted it, considering us all as wounded souls. This was supported by what Sorcha told me when she came back from her medical rounds. People asked about me frequently, but with kindness and concern, she said, not with the intent of malicious gossip. After the initial uproar that Freyja was pregnant, Angus had left, and she was moving to be with us had been thoroughly discussed and digested, they had handled that piece of news well. Angus had prepped his vessel, rounded up his crew, and departed before anything was said. Nothing had been mentioned about her going or staying. She had simply stayed. Freyja had said nothing, but within weeks after he left, she stopped wearing the loose jackets that in the colder months hid her small firm rounded tummy, but as the days grew longer and the weather warmer, she ditched the jacket, and her pregnancy was on full display. It was clear from a mile away that she was pregnant, tall and slender as she was with a washboard stomach. She said nothing but went on with her daily veterinary duties before she started packing her things and moved out to the croft with us. It was a clever tactic, I realized. Angus had left, so people didn't know if she had hidden the pregnancy from him, he had left her because she was pregnant, or whether they had jointly agreed to it. The timing of his departure left the impression that it was Angus's baby without actually saying so. This enabled me, in time, to admit the baby was mine. Or not. I was remarkably grateful for this choice.

For the first time, I was grateful to Angus. I had always thought him a self-centered twat, but this act had been genuinely decent. I mentioned this to Freyja one morning, and she shrugged.

"He said people hated him anyway, so he may as well be hated for one more thing."

"But really, he didn't have to do it. It was decent of him."

"He wanted to. He said he wouldn't be here anyway, and he didn't want me ... shamed." Freyja's reddened with embarrassment. "He did it for me, not you."

"Maybe. But not saying anything helps me too."

Freyja moved into the house with the girls and me. Sam and Louis now shared a room. Sorcha and Di took the second room, and I moved into the smallest room, leaving the other large bedroom for Freyja. It had room for Louis's old cot beside the bed, something she would need soon enough.

As the weather warmed, we started planning new homes, one at a time. Di and Sorcha identified a site, and as the days grew longer, we each found time in the day to chip in a little. By April, it was finished, and Sorcha, Di, and Sam moved into their own home.

Freyja and I, as her pregnancy progressed, stayed together in the bigger house. I could be there to assist and support her and the new child, with Di and Sorcha only a holler away.

CHAPTER 43

"**WHAT SHOULD WE NAME** her?" Freyja looked up at me. It had been a long, arduous labor. Freyja was doing the hard work, assisted by Sorcha, me holding Freyja's hand, supporting her, encouraging her. Just like I had with Laetitia. But this time, it had ended in a cesarean, the baby in distress and Sorcha needing to deliver her quickly. I had never been so grateful for my sister's skill and focus. Several times she checked in on me too, not just Freyja. Di had been watching Sam and Louis, now sleeping, hopefully. Sorcha cleaned up and left, leaving the three of us to get acquainted.

"We?" I said, a little surprised. "It wasn't like I thought I would get a say in the matter."

"We," Freyja replied firmly. "I fully understand that this situation isn't ideal. But you have supported me, and I know you will always be here for her. You are her father, both biologically and in how you will raise her. It is only right that you get a say in her name. Can I ask what names were you considering for your baby?"

I cringed. *My baby. My baby with Laetitia.* Trying to cover my discomfort, I answered truthfully. "Well, we had considered naming her after my mother. But my mother's name was a difficult Scots one, Cairstine. I'm not sure it is appropriate under these circumstances. What was your mother's name?"

"Claira," Freyja responded but shook her head. "No. I won't do that. Do you...?" She paused.

"Go on."

"Do you want to name her after Laetitia?"

I thought about that for a moment. "No. I mean, I do, but I don't think it would be right. Not fair to you, I mean. Also, it would be complicated to explain."

Freyja nodded in agreement. "True. It might be a little hard to explain why the baby I allegedly had with Angus was named after your wife."

"What was Lae's mother's name?"

"Jasmine. But no. Lae wouldn't have done that. The relationship wasn't close."

After a moment's pause, she asked, "What was Lae's full name?"

"Laetitia Katherine Rose."

"How do you feel," Freyja asked slowly, "if we named our baby Katrin Rose? Katrin is a Norwegian form of Katherine, which..."

"Was your sister's name?" I asked gently.

"You remembered," Frey whispered.

"How could I forget?"

Katrin Rose joined our family. Freyja took to motherhood in a way I never thought possible. I found myself watching her, smiling, as she held little Katrin in her arms, holding her tiny hand in her own, completely besotted with her. We all were. Even Sorcha, who had been rather cold toward Freyja since her arrival here. Sorcha, Di, Sam, and even Louis spent hours watching baby Katrin asleep in her cot, her tiny little fingers curled into a little ball. Her arrival healed us all in more ways than I could count. Although she could never replace the two lives I had lost, in her, I could focus on new life and the miracle of watching her learn and grow day by day. I focused less on what I had lost and more on what was here in front of me.

"Can I ask you something?" Di asked me while gardening. "But I need you to look at me while I ask it. I need to see your face."

Sitting up, I looked at her. She had a serious, determined look on her face. It was most unlike Di.

"You can ask me anything. Should I be scared?"

"Scared … no. But it is important. Vitally important. And I need to stress that it is okay to say no. Really. I need you to take the time to consider this. It is a huge ask, and…"

"Stop waffling and out with it."

"Sorcha and I would like to have another child."

"Cool! Hang on…" The logistics of that particular scenario played out in my mind.

"Ahhh… how?"

"Well, that is where you come in," Di said a little sheepishly. "Sorcha has a child, and I desperately want one. Since we have been so close to Katrin, I feel like I *need* this. Sorcha and I have talked and talked about this. But we need a father." She took a deep breath and let the next words out in a rush. "We want the baby to be as close genetically to Sorcha and me as possible. And you and Sorcha are brother and sister… and…"

"And you would like me to father a child with you, so you and Sorcha can have a child together?" I assumed, talking over her last words as she rambled.

"Yes." Di looked at me, relief etched into her face. "We know you would need some time to think about it."

"I do. I do want to think about it. That is a fairly enormous commitment. Not to mention…" I lowered my voice, "you are my best friend and my sister's wife! Won't that be a little…"

"Oh, *no*!" Di squealed. "Not like that. Sorcha is a doctor. She can do the important part in a slightly more scientific way. We don't need to… to…" She started giggling madly, and soon I was joining her, her laughter was so infectious. Soon we were sitting side by side in the dirt, roaring with laughter at my relief, misunderstanding, and her nervousness about asking me.

When we had calmed down sufficiently to speak, I said, "Yes. I will help you."

Di sobered up and looked at me. "Are you sure?"

"Are *you* sure? I'm not exactly perfect."

"You are to me!" Di threw her arms around me. "Thank you. This means the world to me. To have a child of our own is… is… everything!"

Sorcha came into sight as we were holding each other on the ground. She stood at the end of the vegetable patch we were planting, surveying us carefully.

"What's going on here?" she asked, in perfect imitation of our mother.

"He said yes!" Di flew to Sorcha and embraced her. Sorcha pulled back and looked at me. "Really? You are okay with this?"

"Why not?"

"You don't … mind?"

"Well, I guess we need to work out the logistics of it all. But in theory, no, I don't mind. Why would I mind giving my sister and my best friend the best gift imaginable? A gift within my power to give. And it isn't like you will take him or her away ... will you?" A thought crossed my mind. "You will stay here, won't you?"

"Absolutely. We can even tell them when they are old enough. How you loved us enough to make a baby with us both."

"I do, you know."

"What?"

"Love you both."

CHAPTER 44

CARRYING A WOODEN CRATE holding our soon-to-be planted seed potatoes, I misjudged the distance navigating the corner of our house and whacked my protruding elbow onto the stone edge. Inhaling sharply as the pain radiated up my arm, I burst out, "*Fuck!*"

"Dadda?" A puzzled little voice rose, making me look down past the crate blocking my view. Louis was sitting on the timber garden bed edge, playing with some sticks in a muddy puddle, staring up at me in astonishment.

"You okay, Dadda?"

"I am," I said, wincing, rubbing my elbow. "I hit my funny bone, and it hurt."

Louis screwed up his serious little face, so much like Laetitia's. "Why you no laugh?"

"Huh?"

"You said it funny."

Dropping to one knee, I tried to explain. "Hitting your arm like that is called your funny bone. But it isn't funny, you see. I don't think it is even a bone."

"What is?" Sorcha asked as she came out of her home, and I breathed a sigh of relief.

"There you go—ask Auntie Sorcha. She is a doctor. She will know."

"Daddy hit his funny bone. But he said it not funny and it not bone."

"Well, Daddy is right," she explained. "It isn't a bone at all. Inside the elbow is a special nerve called the ulnar nerve. It runs down to your fingers right here." She picked up Louis's hand and pointed to his fourth and fifth fingers. "When you hurt it, it makes those fingers feel all funny. That is why it is called a funny bone."

Louis shrugged. He was still confused, but having been given an explanation, he was not prepared to ask any more questions.

That evening after dinner, I glanced over at Freyja, watching her covertly as she smiled down at the sleeping child in her arms. I was trying to assess how I really felt about cohabiting with her. She had changed from the Freyja I had known. Katrin mellowed her in a way I never thought possible. She was softer somehow; she had lost the sharp edges. Not that she wasn't always stunningly beautiful, but now she smiled more, and it softened her features, making her even more attractive. Parenting also relaxed her personality; she was no longer as blunt as she used to be.

Katrin lay asleep in her arms. Our daughter. My secret child. At four months old, she strongly resembled Freyja in her blonde-haired, green-eyed appearance. For this, I was eminently grateful. The last thing I wanted was a mini-me. Louis was curled up on the couch beside me, nodding off but trying hard to stay awake. Louis looked like a hybrid of Lae and me. Her delicate features and gentle light brown eyes, but his chestnut hair was more ginger than hers, more cinnamon, inherited from my mother. Despite my dark hair and blue eyes inherited from Dad, red streaks showed through, especially in my beard. Louis looked just like his mother with wet hair, but in the sunlight, he looked more like me, ginger highlights glinting in the sun. We all sat in comfortable silence, the picture of domestic bliss.

Freyja calmly stood and took the few steps to place Katrin in her cot. Katrin was sitting now, and it wouldn't be long before she was furniture surfing, pulling herself to standing, and using furniture to get herself around the room. Then, watch out world! A mischievous streak in her eye belied her angelic appearance. The soft halo of blonde curls cascaded down her face, framing her large, alert green eyes and dark eyelashes. But the eyes alone gave away the rebellious and determined streak within. It wouldn't be long, and we would be battling with little Miss Katrin.

Louis, alerted by the movement in the room, stirred from his stupor.

"Mama, me too." He held his arms up to Freyja to pick him up, and she obligingly scooped him up to take him to his bed in my room. My heart shattered into a million pieces.

Like an automaton, I kissed him good night and told him I loved him as Freyja held him out to me.

"Love you too, Dadda," he droned. Freyja looked down at me quizzically, sensing the change in my mood but said nothing. Laughing, she swept little Louis off to his bed, telling him he was nearly too big to be carried.

Escaping, I bolted into the night, barely pausing to close the door softly behind me. Laetitia had been right then. She had known all along. Her greatest fear had come true. I had left her for Freyja, and now another woman was raising her child, our child. *Oh God, what have I done?* Here I was, living with my first wife, with Louis and Katrin. Happy, I realized with a shock. *I am happy.*

The relationship with Freyja was one of friendship and convenience. It wasn't a romantic one, I told myself. But we raised our children as a couple. We worked together, lived together, laughed together. We may not sleep together, but in every other way, we were … *a family.* Devastation consumed me. How could I have betrayed Laetitia's memory so quickly? How could I have done this to her? She had been gone barely a year, and without realizing it, I had moved on. Not physically, perhaps, but emotionally. I had moved on with another woman. And that woman was my first wife. The woman Lae had always feared, constantly fretted that I would leave her for. And now I had. I had abandoned the memory of my love and moved on without even realizing it.

"You fucking cheating asshole!" I kicked the side of the barn and winced as the pain shot up my leg. But the pain felt real, so I did it again.

The light illuminating the doorway revealed the shadowy figure of Freyja walking outside. She always had the senses of a cat, able to see in the dark. Making a beeline toward me, she stood for a moment.

"Are you sick?" The puzzlement in her voice was unmistakable.

Unable to speak, I just hung my head so she couldn't see my face, my glass face, the one that she could always read and know exactly what I was feeling. How could she when *I* didn't even know what I was feeling? Conflicted, torn, and utterly devastated. *Oh God, Laetitia, I am so, so very sorry.*

Freyja lifted my chin to look into her eyes. She stood for a moment, reading me, analyzing me as only she could.

"He called me mama," she whispered.

I blinked. I didn't want to have this conversation. Not here. Not now. Not with her.

"You feel you have betrayed her."

"I do," I confessed aloud. "I really do."

"Is it Katrin?"

I pondered this for a moment. "No. Not really. I mean, that is part of it, I guess."

I sat down on the bench near the vegetable garden. Close enough to the house to hear the children if one of them cried out, but far enough away that Sorcha and Di shouldn't hear us. I could see the lights glowing around the frame of their windows and door, so they were still up.

"What is it then?"

I paused before answering. "I'm not sure I can explain this, especially to you. But I feel like I have betrayed her. Laetitia, I mean."

"Because … you are happy?" Freyja guessed, a hint of apprehension in her voice, like she was almost too scared of learning the answer.

"Oh, God." I dropped my head into my hands. *I am happy. Here. With her. With our children.* "I am a complete and utter asshat."

"No, you aren't."

"How would you know!" Anxiety made me speak more harshly than I intended, but Freyja blinked once and resumed her calm countenance.

"No. You are not," she said firmly. "I am in a position to know."

Stubbornness kicked in, and I refused to continue the conversation. It was childish, I knew, but I didn't want to have this conversation here, now, with her.

Freyja, recognizing the futility, stood up and said quietly, "You have done nothing to betray your memory of her. Your love for her. What you have done is continue to be a genuine, decent, and kind father to both of your children."

She walked toward the house, closing the door firmly behind her.

Hours passed as I mentally berated myself for getting myself into this situation. I woke to a small voice, "Dadda?" and a light touch on my chest. Jerking awake, I saw Louis looking at me, his face full of concern. Realizing that I must look a right mess after sleeping here, I rushed to reassure him.

"I'm fine, darling. Dadda came to check on the vegetables, and I must have fallen asleep! Silly me."

Louis wrinkled his little nose, so like Lae's, and looked at me suspiciously but said nothing. Picking him up, I sat him on my knee and cuddled him close.

"You look so much like your mother," I told him. "She loved you so very much."

"I... I forget..." His little face fell, and big fat tears rolled down his cheeks. "Dadda, I can't remember what she looks like."

Scooping him against my chest, I fought as hard as I could to not cry along with him. It was true. As the days went by, the sharpness of her image grew slightly less distinct. I could still conjure up her sweet face, her voice, and relive memories of the precious moments we spent together. But it was slightly fuzzier around the edges as days went by. Sometimes I would see someone or hear something, and it would remind me of her for no reason at all. I knew I would never forget the idea of her, the memories. But it was harder to pull the images to mind, even if I closed my eyes and concentrated as hard as I could.

"Louis," I said to get his attention, and he pulled his sobbing face from my chest and looked up at me. His face was so much like hers.

"Dadda?" Something in the tone of my voice had alerted him that something wasn't right.

"Louis, I need to ask you something."

"Okay," he sniffed.

"How would you feel if you stayed with Auntie Frey for a little while?"

Louis wrinkled his nose, perplexed.

How did I explain this to a child? That I needed time to grieve, to mourn. Needed time to close that chapter of my life and begin anew. My mind was still churning, much like the vortex that brought me here. But this time, it was internal, eating me from the inside out.

"Louis, Daddy is still sad about losing Mummy," I said. "Sometimes, when grown-ups are sad, it helps if they are alone for a little while."

Louis nodded sagely. Then a look of panic crossed his tear-streaked face. "Dadda, do you not love *me* anymore?"

A look of equal panic must have crossed mine as he threw himself into me again.

"No! No! Never that. My darling, I will love you always and forever. Just like I will love Mummy always and forever. I just need... I just need some time, darling, some time to..."

"Forget?" he asked.

"No. I will never forget your mother. She was very special, one of a kind. I don't know how to describe it. I just need some time. I need to go away. But I promise you. I will come back for you. I will always be here for you. If you don't want me to go, I won't. I will stay with you. But if you think you would be happy staying with Freyja and Katrin just for a little while, then I might think about going ... exploring."

This was the right word. As a two-year-old boy, Louis loved to explore. His little face lit from within like a moonbeam. "Can I come exploring too?"

"Not this time, darling," I whispered, watching his face fall. "It might be dangerous, but if I find some wonderful places to visit, then I might take you next time."

"Are you going to look for Mummy?" Louis asked in such a sad voice that I could barely stand it.

That is precisely what I was planning to do. Seek answers, seek closure. Resolve my past, so I could move on and have a future. With my recovery and then Freyja's pregnancy, I hadn't had time to process it all, move past this liminal space and start the next chapter. But how do you tell a two-year-old that?

"No, my darling." Scooping him up in my arms and looking into his face, I remembered the vow I had made to Laetitia that I would always place Louis first. *Am I abandoning him again?* No, I realized. I needed this closure to become a whole man again. To offer my son a world of possibility, I needed to be the best person I could be.

"Louis," I said, struggling to find the right words. "A wise person once told me that emotions are very important. Do you know what emotions are?"

"Like being happy or sad?"

"Exactly. But when you are a grown-up, you get more emotions. Big ones, like resentment, anxiety, and guilt."

Louis nodded wisely.

"Well, this person told me that emotions can teach you things. If you are sad, that means that you care. Does that make sense?"

Louis dropped his head to one side and said, "I was sad when Mummy died."

"That means you cared about Mummy."

Louis took some time to think about that and nodded wisely.

"Some grown-ups, like Daddy, have anxiety. That is a grown-up emotion, and you don't need to worry about it."

Louis tried the word on his tongue, "Ank-zy-ty."

Smiling, I nodded. "Exactly. Well, what anxiety means is that a person can't move forward. They get stuck. It is like when we ride our bikes, and there is a big rock in the road. We need to find a way around the rock. We can't go over it or through it."

"Like the Bear Hunt book?"

"Exactly like the Bear Hunt book. Daddy has this problem, and I need to find a way around it. To do that, I need to go away for a little while. Do you understand?"

Louis nodded, fighting back the tears. Trying to be brave. The sight of him broke my heart. Was that how Lae had felt, bound and gagged, being taken away from her family?

Nausea rose in my stomach at the thought, and I smiled at Louis.

"You are such a big boy now. Can you take care of Freyja, Jam, and little Kat while I am gone?"

Wrapping him in my arms, I felt him nod.

CHAPTER 45

"ARE YOU SURE?" SORCHA'S hands were on my shoulders, holding me at arm's length, questioning my sanity.

"I am. Certain."

"When will you go?" Di asked, evidently worried about me heading off into the wilderness alone. Again.

"Tomorrow. I will leave early, before dawn, so I don't wake Louis. He knows I am going, but if I physically see him... well, I might not get up the courage to go. And I need to. To sort things out in my head."

"And Freyja? What does she think?"

"I haven't told her yet. I wanted to tell you first."

"What do you think she will say?"

Shrugging, I gestured I didn't know, but it also wasn't a considering factor. I needed to do this. Of that, I was positive.

The rising sun illuminated my face as I rode over the crest of the hill. Bringing my bike to a stop near the crossroads that led to Garynahine in one direction and out to Stornoway in the other, I gazed back over the waking village. I knew I would be back soon. This wasn't goodbye, not this time. As I watched people exit their houses to go about their day, it was unmistakable. My life, my children, and my future were here, filled with possibility.

BOOK CLUB QUESTIONS

1. The Space Between, a liminal space, is a space between major events of your life. What lessons have you learned in the space between the major chapters of your life?

2. Before he returns to Lewis and Laetitia, Cam spends a night in a cave. What was the importance of this?

3. Loyalty is one of Cam's personal attributes. Would you leave your partner and young child to find a family member who may be alive?

4. In The Space Between, we learn that there are more communities. Why do you think the scientists kept this secret?

5. When they are searching for vehicles and resources in Melbourne, Daniella gets angry at Cam for stealing, despite there being no one left. Is she right? Is it still theft if the person has died? Where do you draw the boundary?

6. Why did Diana choose to go to Lewis? Would you leave your family to follow the possibility of love?

7. When Sorcha and Cam travel to Kiewa, they find their parents' settlement. Was this closure necessary? Why?

8. The last time Cam sees Laetitia, they argue, which tortures him. Could he have done anything differently?

9. When the men come and kidnap the five women on Lewis, Freyja gives the order to kill the kidnappers. Was she right to do so? Does this scene change your opinion of her?

10. When Fraser asks Isla to tell Cam her story for closure, his as well as hers, why is this an important step for their healing process?

11. Cam is conflicted when Freyja tells him that the kidnappers saw her, and that is why they came up with the plan to take women. Was this a reasonable reaction?

12. Why does Cam feel the need to leave Lewis at the end of the book? Do we sometimes need to leave a place where we are comfortable to find closure?

AUTHOR BIO

T.S. SIMONS IS AN Australian author of Scottish heritage. Living in the alpine region of Australia, she believes in the values of sustainability and community in a world where we place greater value on possessions than people. The Antipodes series addresses the question—if we gave young people the opportunity to start over, would we replicate the mistakes of the past?

She holds Bachelor and Master's degrees from Monash University and enjoys strong coffee, traveling, mythology, and snow skiing, while attempting to live as sustainably as possible. She is owned by two rather bossy standard schnauzers and two rescue cats who co-manage her household.

The Antipodes series includes Project Hemisphere, The Space Between, Infinity, Circle of Protection, and Sessrúmnir. She is now working on a related series, The Latitude Series.

More books from 4 Horsemen Publications

Fantasy, SciFi, & Paranormal Romance

Beau Lake
The Beast Beside Me
The Beast Within Me
Taming the Beast: Novella
The Beast After Me
Charming the Beast: Novella
The Beast Like Me
An Eye for Emeralds
Swimming in Sapphires
Pining for Pearls

D. Lambert
To Walk into the Sands
Rydan
Celebrant
Northlander
Esparan
King
Traitor
His Last Name

Danielle Orsino
Locked Out of Heaven
Thine Eyes of Mercy
From the Ashes
Kingdom Come

J.M. Paquette
Klauden's Ring
Solyn's Body
The Inbetween
Hannah's Heart
Call Me Forth
Invite Me In
Keep Me Close

www.ingramcontent.com/pod-product-compliance
Lightning Source LLC
Chambersburg PA
CBHW020519110726
47899CB00004B/1170